Th
Boy in th

By

Robbie Byrne

*To Paul.
Always be creative.
Love Dad xxx*

© Robbie Byrne, 2022.

Dedication: to my family and friends.

Other works:

Mulligan's Pennies
Night-Swimming
Mulligan's USA
Smile
Mulligan's Return
The Biggest Butterfly in the Whole Wide World

(Find all books on Amazon.com and Amazon Kindle)

Prelude

We all live or exist in our own self-created prison. My own personal cage surrounds and engulfs me like a heavy winter coat.

My cell does not have barred windows or stone walls, or pungent smells; there are no men weeping in the night. This self-created cell is my comfort zone, the four walls that trap me inside my own fear – inside the invisible cube; inside the box.

The walls of this box are soaked with good and bad memories, with new and lost lovers, wives, friends, glued to the sides of my box like aged, dampened yellowing wallpaper ready to peel and slip to the floor.

Little by little, piece by piece the walls of my box grow thicker, making it extremely difficult to escape its confined clutches and live in a happier world. At a young age I begin to realize that there is something else to this world than the narrow-minded view of my family, my community, my religion.

I've come to believe that we are all creators. We can create what we feel, what we experience, what we are. We exist and we think, and it's the thinking that creates our world, creates our surroundings; connects us all. I believe, no, I *know* we alone are the creators of our troubles, and also the creators of our bliss.

I have realized that not only I, but everyone and everything are leading up to something – connecting to something or someone - the world, not unlike me, is a work in progress.

*

Part One
(Autumn 1962)

Chapter 1

Saffron felt guilty. She felt bad. She had jilted her boyfriend, dated his best friend and now John was dead. Guilty as charged. *He trusted you, Saffron,* her inner voice nagged at her. *John O'Malley was gentle and kind, he liked you, he loved you, he took you shopping, bought you nice things and you, yes you, Saffron, betrayed him.*

She pushed her head into the pillow. *You went behind his back, Saffron. You wrote a letter to Joshua telling him you loved him, but you betrayed John.*

She was evil, wretched - a two-timing snake.

Saffron walked over to her bedroom window. Long gray drapes hung each side with sheer white panels in the center. Against a far wall was her dresser complete with mirror, a gift from her father. In a corner and spreading along the wall was a wall-to-wall wardrobe adorned with many dresses and skirts and blouses. Her room was painted in a peachy color not dissimilar to her own hair. She was comfortable. Her father was a bank manager in town, her mother stayed at home. They had a nice house in a nice area. She couldn't complain, not when she was still alive and John O'Malley was dead. She had no *right* to complain. But she had the right to feel sorry for her actions.

Looking out the window she could see the quarry in the far distance. The sloping path that led up to the ranch; the clay-hole, the pool, the *death* pool.

You wrote a letter to Joshua, didn't you, Saffron. A letter opening your heart to him, and yet you were still dating John. Don't you feel guilty? Don't you feel ashamed of yourself? Didn't you think you were creating a future that led to John going to the pool? That led him to fight with Joshua? Don't you think that by your actions you brought into being situations that could only lead to danger? That by your actions you made him swim away from you in disgust and become trapped in those cables beneath the water?

Stop it. Stop it. Stop it! Saffron slapped her head in an effort to stop her guilty thoughts from condemning her, torturing her, driving her crazy.

She slumped onto her bed and wept into the pillow. How could she now face Joshua? Can their relationship go on, can it flourish with that act of betrayal hanging over her like mistletoe at Christmas, waiting for the moment when Joshua will mention it, or condemn her for her actions?

She felt bad. She felt terrible.

But she hadn't seen Joshua for a week. She missed him. She *had* to see him. Her stomach suddenly fluttered with butterfly wings as she thought of him. She craved to hug him, hold him and kiss him. She wanted to be close to him, touch and squeeze him. She wanted to make *love* to him.

Saffron wiped her cheeks with a tissue, turned her head on the pillow, closed her eyes and slept.

*

Chapter 2

My name is Joshua. I sit here in a pew in St Patrick's Catholic Church surrounded by worshippers, some with heads bowed, some holding rosary beads in their frail hands, passing one bead from hand to finger as they recite the rosary prayer. My mother and Mrs. Feely, our neighbor, sit each side of me and are doing the same with their rosaries.

Father O'Brien stands high in his pulpit and flips through the bible looking for something appropriate, no doubt, for today's sermon. Rays of hazy sunlight beam through the stain-glassed windows. Etched into the glass are the elongated images of Jesus, Mary, Joseph, and the apostles. The windows brighten the area on and around Father O'Brien, as if God's intention is to highlight him and make him stand out among the crowd.

Dust motes fill the stuffy air. Summer is here and we've had six weeks of fairly good weather which is unusual for England. I miss the rain; at least it keeps the dust down.

Framed paintings of the Stations of the Cross' and images of Christ and his apostles adorn the walls; they look solemn. If the early painters had drawn smiles on those faces, would they have been tortured and murdered for it? God forbid that a worshiper should actually *smile* in church. Surely it wasn't all doom and gloom in ancient times? Why does everyone need to be so serious, look so gloomy? Is it a part of their service to God that they have to be sad, a prerequisite for worshipping a deity? To me, they're all missing the point: to *love* is to feel alive, because when you love you *are* happy and can't help but smile.

I gaze at the figure on the crucifix hanging behind the altar as Father O' Brien mumbles his sermon to his obedient flock. Every time he utters the words, Jesus Christ, a chorus of 'Amen's' echo around the church with the congregation making the sign of the cross in unison like holy automations. Every time I hear the word 'Amen' I replace it in my mind with the word, 'A-Baa' as in a lamb bleating and begging for its mother to arrive and feed it and guide it through its early life.

I feel sorry for the man nailed to the cross, his face contorted, his eyes closed and a halo of thorns piercing his skull. Even at my age I can't understand how people could be so cruel and do that kind of thing to another human being.

And what a grotesque figure to have hanging in a place of worship, a center for love and contentment, a hub for aiding and helping others in life. What an example to the world: a house of God that shows an ancient image of a man tortured, humiliated and murdered on a cross made of wood.

I look around at all these lost souls, trapped in their own tiny religious boxes. *I don't have to believe in a God. I don't have to believe in Jesus Christ as being the Son of God. I don't have to believe that I am or will be condemned to an eternal hell for not believing in this restricted dogma. I have, like everyone else, free will.*

Satan only exists in the minds of lunatics. Men do evil simply because they *are* evil, they were born evil; it's in their nature, it's in their genes. A concept so simple that even a seven year old child, like myself, can understand it.

Father O'Brien seems to relish the light shining on him through the stain-glass windows, as if he feels *he's* the chosen one, picked out from all God's representatives on earth to deliver this sermon today. His smile is as bright as the sun.

I'd often see him jogging past my house in his sky-blue tracksuit and white sneakers, a black cap pressed down on his head with the initials *JC* written across the front. He'd stop and do some stretches, then cross the bridge opposite and sprint up a hill toward the iron ore quarry in the far distance.

He doesn't drink nor smoke which is unusual for the priests I've heard about from my father. I doubt if he even partook in a gulp of altar wine before mass, not like Father Sweeny from St Brendan's Church a couple of miles away; he almost fell off the pulpit one Sunday morning.

Father O'Brien, thirty-five years old and handsome in a kind of pugilist way. I like him.

"Praise be to God," says Father O'Brien and, before the congregation say amen, the church doors fly open and a male voice shouts, "Father O'Brien. My da says God is full of shite!"

Everyone turns around, including myself and, rushing up the center aisle is Paddy Patterson, hair akimbo, arms flaying in the air and as naked as the day he was born.

"Jesus, Mary and Joseph," shrieks my mother and blesses herself three times. "Is there anyone sane in this town?"

"Holy Mary, mother of God," Mrs. Feely shrieks in unison.

The congregation is in turmoil, some blessing themselves, others bowing their heads, men trying to stand but being pulled back by their wives.

"This is the house of God," bellows Father O'Brien. "How dare you cause trouble in His place of worship."

Paddy runs up to the altar, his ass cheeks flapping from side to side; he bends over and spreads his cheeks wide. Mrs. Feely faints and slumps onto the pew. Mother, for once is speechless (she blesses herself again - three times). Paddy grabs the altar cloth and yanks it to the ground spilling silver goblets and bibles to the floor.

"I feel sorry for Mrs. Patterson," says Mrs. Watson from across the aisle. "Herself having to put up with the likes of him."

"He reminds me of my husband's brother, Jack," says mother.

"Running naked in church?" mumbles Mrs. Feely and pokes her head above the pew.

"No. Fecking mad!"

Meanwhile Father O'Brien and the two altar boys chase Paddy around the altar. They're joined by a couple of men (who manage to free themselves from their wives' clutches) and dive onto poor, mad Paddy Patterson and drag him to the floor.

"I hate you I hate you I hate you all!" Paddy screams as Father O'Brien covers his nakedness with the altar cloth.

"Now now, Paddy," says Father O'Brien, "your mother won't be very pleased with your behavior today, now will she?

"No." he says in a low voice. "But she's full of shite, too."

Paddy, now trussed up like a Christmas turkey just delivered from the grocery store was born with mental issues, or lack of them. He must be about twenty-something now and on occasion takes it into his head to visit our church. His mother is at her wits end with the man, but she refuses to have him committed to an asylum ("Lucky he doesn't live in Ireland," my da had said a while back, "over there they lock you away for the least thing.") I find out later what my father had meant.

Paddy screams at the top of his voice, "I am the angel of death and this here is Satan."

Mother blesses herself (even Father O'Brien blesses himself three times), Mrs. Feely faints (as usual) and the rest of the congregation blesses themselves repeatedly

"Where is Satan?" my mother barked at him.

"In hell, yer fecking ejit," pipes in someone from the back.

"Go and shite," said mother.

"He's here," said Paddy. "Can't you see him?" He places his arm around his imaginary friend. "Satan likes me, but he *hates* all of you."

Mrs. Feely's mouth drops open; she quickly joins the congregation in blessing themselves just in case, I imagine, they think Satan *is* standing there beside Paddy and they're shaking hands like two old friends meeting for the first time in years.

"All I can see is a fecking ejit," says mother. "Get out of this church," mother continues, "and take your fecking friend with yer!"

"Go home, Paddy," says someone.

"Yer ma will be looking for you," says another.

"Father O'Brien," a voice from the side of the church bellows, "will yer hurry up and do the fecking communion. I've got a pint waiting for me down at the pub."

One of the parishioners, a big, burly red-haired man walks up the center aisle, picks up Paddy as easy as lifting a young child and strides back toward the entrance. .

"His father has the patience of a saint," mutters mother.

"Has he gone, yet?" says Mrs. Feely and sits upright in the pew.

"Has *who* gone?" says Mother.

"Satan and his friend."

Father O'Brien wipes the sweat from his brow and before he can mutter a word to the congregation, the unbelievable happens. He clutches his chest; his smile disappears and is replaced by a grimace. He groans, almost yelps, then falls down the steps of his pulpit and rolls to a stop in front of my feet, his right hand clutching his crucifix.

*

*

Poor Father O'Brien, the congregation said afterwards. It must have been the shock of seeing Paddy Patterson naked, or having Satan inside his church that gave him the heart attack. Called back home to God, others said, but at least he died doing what he loved. Ran himself into the ground, literally, some smart Alec piped in. And there was me trying to escape from my box and Father O'Brien ends up in one.

I'll miss Father O'Brien - he had the most beautiful smile.

*

"Time to get ready for church," my ma says as she barges into my bedroom and pulls the blanket off the bed. I gape at my mother who is gaping down at the protuberance poking out of my pajama botSeans. My left hand is holding my erection.

"Jesus, Mary and Joseph," mother yelps and blesses herself three times. "You should be ashamed of yerself. There's poor Father O'Brien not two minutes in the grave and you're playing with yourself. Wait 'till Father Luke hears about this."

I don't quite understand what Father Luke (our new priest) has to do with me lying in bed with an erection, I mean don't priests get erections from time to time, or do they see themselves so perfect in God's eyes that they'd never admit it?

Ma turns and rushes out of the room slamming the door behind her, and leaves me lying in bed still holding my erection which very quickly droops and slithers down into my cupped hand like a tiny snake in deep shock and taking cover from predators.

My ma must think I'm the Devil's spawn, but I think if I'm having erections then my friends must be too, and everyone, including Father Luke must also get an erection (admit it or not). I'm curious, I suppose, like the proverbial cat.

Earlier that week, during R.E. (Religious Education) at St Patrick's school, my teacher, Mrs. Harrison talked about priests being the servants of God. Paddy Boyle who sat next to the window (he was always looking out over the fields and daydreaming) looked over at Mrs. Harrison and asked her if priests lived with their mothers 'cause there was always some old lady dropping in and out of Father Luke's house.

"Oh," replied Mrs. Harrison, excitedly, "That'll be the cleaning lady. She calls in three times a week."

Mrs. Harrison is a very good teacher, not that I know much about good or bad teaching, but she is old and is always smiling and caring and saying kind words to us. She says she always attends church every Sunday and Bible Studies on a Wednesday night. She squeezes my shoulder if I draw something nice and tells me I'm doing very well. I wish she was my mother, although I feel ashamed afterwards for having had such thoughts.

But I felt sorry for her that day when the whole class began to bombard her with questions about Father Luke. It was as if she was standing in front of a firing squad and being shot at in all directions at once. I imagined those bullets bouncing off her and ricocheting around the room.

"Put your hand up if you wish to speak," Mrs. Harrison said and could hardly be heard above the cacophony of squeaky, excited voices.

"Yes, Betty, what's your question?"

"Does Father Luke have a girlfriend?"

"Erm, well," stuttered Mrs. Harrison. "Priests, when they become priests, take a blessed vow of erm ... celibacy."

The class fell silent.

"You see ..." she continued, "Priests are celibate."

"Is that a disease?" piped in Steven, sitting at the back of the class.

"Erm ... well, no. It's a vow they have to ..."

"What's celibacy?" asked Betty.

"It means …" said Mrs. Harrison, her cheeks now blushing, "that when a priest gives himself completely to God he has to remain a single man. He can't marry a woman."

"Can he buy her flowers?"

"No," Betty, he can't.

"What about holding hands?"

"Certainly not."

"Can he kiss her?"

I think Betty was a cat in a past life because she is so curious about *everything*. Mind you, I must have been a cat, too.

"No. Betty. Now give someone else a chance to ask a question. Peter. What's your question?" Mrs. Harrison was stumped; she'd have to dodge Betty's questions like a batter dodging baseballs.

"Marie O'Sullivan goes round his house and she's not a cleaning lady," Peter said innocently.

"Oh, she does his books some days," said Mrs. Harrison quick as a button popping off a fat man's shirt.

"I saw Father Luke giving Marie O'Sullivan a bunch of flowers," said Betty, a wry look on her face.

"I … I …" muttered Mrs. Harrison, "that was the Passover."

"I saw him hold her hand," continued Betty, attempting in some childish devious way to stab Mrs. Harrison through the heart with some subconscious, imaginary dagger.

"My da says that's his bit of fluff on the side," piped in Liam from the front of the class.

"His … his … *what?*" Mrs. Harrison looked around the room as if searching for words that hung in the air she could grab hold of and use without embarrassing herself and inadvertently getting Father Luke into trouble.

"And " said Betty, coming in for the kill now and raising her voice so everyone in the class could hear her (and probably the whole school), her imaginary dagger now aimed directly at her teacher's heart. "I saw him *kiss* Marie O'Sullivan. I think she's his girlfriend."

The dagger flew invisibly through the thick air and thrust straight through Mrs. Harrison's deeply religious heart.

She opened her mouth to say something, closed it again and began to gasp for air like a fish out of water.

"My da says priests are full of shite," said Steven from the back of the class.

Her old teacher's legs couldn't hold her up any longer and she slumped back onto her chair.

"Steven," she managed to say between gasping breaths. "Please don't ... don't use that ... gutter language in school. Say you're ... sorry."

"I'm sorry, Mrs. Harrison."

"Now ... stand in the corner ... 'till playtime."

Steven meandered over to the corner and stood facing the wall. He knew the drill having been sent there four times that week already.

"Is there ... anyone ... *anyone* ... who has a *sensible* ... question?"

I raised my hand and, before I could open my mouth to ask Mrs. Harrison if Father Luke gets an erection, the bell rang for morning break.

Steven abandoned his punishment corner and rushed out of the room faster than a meteor shooting towards earth.

Mrs. Harrison looked relieved as her class full of curious and mischievous young heathens stumbled over each other to get through the door and outside to the playground.

So now, this early Sunday morning I have to attend church. That's the house rule. That's my mother's one and only rule. I jump out of bed, get washed and dressed and have the sticky up bits of my hair flattened by my mother's hand (she spits on it), and am shuffled off to church like a sheep put out to graze, except in this case the sheep are in the church and not the field.

*

Chapter 3

"Joshua, your sausages are burning themselves to death," my mother yells up at me. I didn't know sausages lived, let alone able to burn themselves to death. I'm lying in bed staring at the old oak wardrobe sitting in a corner in my bedroom. I see faces in the wood, weird, dark shapes that look like faces, though I know it's the texture of the wood that creates this illusion. Still, one of them is smiling at me, another is grimacing. Good and evil side by side. Maybe that's the way of the world.

"I'm coming, ma," I yell back. I slip into my jeans and tee-shirt and take the stairs three at a time. I grasp the banisters each side of the stairwell and almost fly down the stairs.

"It's on the table. Want some tea?" She pronounces it *tae*.

"Yes, ma."

"What's the magic word?" She glares at me.

"Please," I say and lower my gaze

"Doesn't matter how rich or poor you are good manners makes the man."

"Yes, ma."

"Give me the boy for the first seven years and I'll give you the man."

"Aye, ma."

"Live each day as if it's your last 'cause one day it will be."

"Ma?"

"Yes, son."

"Can I go play football with John?"

"No. You're going to church."

"But, ma, this might be my last day!"

"More the better then," she says and washes a dish. "If it's your last day then you'll die in the Lord's house. Thanks be to God."

I don't know what to say. Is she thanking God for me dying in his house, or is she a secret fortune teller predicting my premature demise?

And then I experience a queasy, nauseas feeling in the pit of my stomach that rises slowly up through my chest. I feel suddenly sad. A tear trickles down my cheek.

"What's up with you," says mother sternly.

"I hate going to church."

She blesses herself three times with her left hand (though using the left hand to bless oneself is regarded as the sign of the Devil in our church, but ma is left-handed). "May God Himself forgive you for your blasphemy."

With that said she walks over and slaps me across the face. "There. Now you have something to bawl about."

I push back my chair, it falls to the floor, and crying, run upstairs, storm into my bedroom and slam the door behind me.

"If you don't go to church God Himself will judge you and condemn you to an eternity in Hell!" She shouts up the stairs.

At least God wouldn't slap my face for no reason at all. I lower my head onto the pillow and cry myself to sleep.

*

Chapter 4
(Winter 1962)

    I lie in bed with three blankets tucked up to my neck. My body is shivering, my lips quivering. Boy, it's like living in a freezer in this house, though we don't have a freezer, let alone a fridge. Mrs. Feeley owns a fridge and my da thinks she won the football pools and hasn't told anyone. Come to think of it, no one really needs a fridge in this country, maybe during the short summer months, but we have a recessed pantry that remains cool during the summer. One rare hot day I opened the pantry door and there was da sitting beneath the shelves of tinned peas and beans sipping on his beer and smoking a woodbine cigarette. I could just about make out his face through the smoke. "Go and find yer own pantry," he says. "We've only got one, da," I reply. "Exactly," he says, takes a sip of his beer and closes the door.

    The pantry also serves another important purpose. Da hides in there when mother is having one of her raving episodes (most days of the week. Da is lucky, he only hears her at weekends). He allowed me to sit with him inside the pantry (another box) after church one Sunday as mother ranted and raved about something or other that both of us couldn't understand.

    "Don't ever make the mistake I did son," my father whispered to me in the dark pantry, "and get yerself married. If you want true freedom and joy, for God's sakes, stay single."

    The windows upstairs and down are covered with thick ice, on both sides of the glass. Ma says we can't afford to put the heating on during the day, only at night, and it's me who has to chop wood, collect coal, clean out the grate and start the fire every morning. During the week I rise at dawn and search through the snow out in the back yard for the pile of coal, then chop the wood, light the fire, then set off to do my paper round, return and then get ready for school. I never learned much at school because I slept through most of the lessons.

    Meanwhile ma is still in bed asleep. She sure needs a lot of sleep.

*

*

A gypsy knocks on the front door. I can see her through the gap in the living room lace curtains. She looks about fifty, dressed in a black, ankle length skirt and a big, scruffy and stained black coat. A large basket is cupped in her arms.

I open the door.

"Agh, young man," she says in an Irish brogue, though her accent is a little bit thicker than the Dublin accent I'm used to. "Would ye be a-wanting some wee trinkets and the like."

"I'll get me ma," I say, not knowing what to really say to a strange woman dressed all in black. She has a rounded face with a big chin, hairy, dark eyebrows and eyes blacker than onyx. She scares me a little, though ma told me that we descend from gypsies who travelled over from Romania to Ireland a few hundred years back. Maybe this gypsy is related to me?

Before I turn to fetch mother, the gypsy grabs my left hand and stares at my palm. "Agh. I see a wee bit o' sadness in yer soul. There's a passion there that will burst out not long from now, a talent or two, oh, musical, yes, ye will be very musical, I see ..."

"Who's left the fecking door open," says ma as she approaches. "It's fecking cold enough without ye leaving the ... oh, hello Rose. It's yerself."

Who else would it be, I thought. The Irish have some great and comical ways about them. I'm proud to be Irish; I wouldn't want it any other way.

"It surely is meself - as fresh as dew on a sweet morning rose," Rose says and beams a smile showing a mouthful of emptiness except for two nicotine stained crooked lower teeth. "I was just reading yer man's fortune. He's going to be a great musician."

"Oh, is that right. Well I hope he remembers his poor old ma when he's rich and famous."

"He'll look after you, for sure, missus."

"Will ye be after coming in for a nice cup of tae, now, so."

"Oh, that'll be grand, missus. Me old feet are wearing out."

Rose calls at our house twice a month and ma always invites her in for a cup of 'tae' before having a look-see in her basket of homemade clothes pegs and cheap trinkets and small statues of Christ and the Virgin Mary holding her Only Begotten Son.

"Ye can have ten girlfriends, son," mother would say, "but ye can only have one mother. Isn't that right, Rose."

"As sure as I'm sitting here, missus. Right it is."

Sometimes, out of the blue, ma would stand behind me in the dining room while I was eating my cereal (sometimes she'd make thick porridge that you'd need a pneumatic drill instead of a spoon to cut through it), and place her hand on my shoulder. After a few seconds, she'd squeeze my shoulder then walk back to the kitchen sink.

Was she remembering good times in Ireland? Her father and mother (still alive and living in Dublin), or just showing her care and love for me by way of a gentle gesture and a soft touch?

Her touch, whenever it occurs (rarely) is more important to me than receiving a vast inheritance from a lost relative (maybe a gypsy from Romania), that sweet, fleeting moment of connection between mother and son. I think she never was shown very much love from her mother so to be able to break through her insecurity (the Irish tend to keep their emotions locked up tightly in their hearts), to raze those walls of stubbornness, of an upbringing where love was just a word, is a miracle in itself, even if it was only for a few moments. I am proud of my mother. At least she (without probably knowing what she is doing) is clawing at the sides of her box, pushing at the lid to try to escape, to break free from the ridiculous restraining bonds of a religious and Irish upbringing.

At least she is attempting to break free. I have yet to find the strength, the courage to escape from my constrained box. She is far stronger and far better than I will ever be. I'm weak, although as I said, like the world – I'm a work in progress.

I leave them in the living room, chatting and laughing together like old friends, and make my way up to my bedroom, my sanctuary, my den, my dream room, my personal box.

Ma, though strict and with a strong slapping hand can be very friendly and loving, but in her own Irish way.

I suppose growing up in poverty-stricken Dublin during the 30's, 40's and 50's took its toll on the family. Not much caring or loving went on in my parents' family back then, according to my father. Everyone was too busy trying to put food on the table to care about soothing and kissing a scraped knee, or tucking kids into bed and telling them bedtime stories.

"Up the wooden hill to bedfordshire, and don't be turning the light on," is the usual loving, end of the day recital before bedtime. And, "Don't be sleeping in Seanorrow, Joshua, ye need to get the old fire going," instead of soothing words like, "I love you, son. Goodnight." Words I craved to hear from my mother which would've given me the chance to reply, "I love you, too, ma."

But if a magical and loving touch on my shoulder is all I receive, then the richer I am for it.

Yes. I am extremely proud of my mother and I love her unconditionally.

*

Chapter 5

Mother is reading one of Mrs. Feeley's books at the dining room table and dips her spoon occasionally into a bowl of Kellogg's cornflakes. A cigarette smolders in the ashtray. Once my mother starts reading something, nothing gets washed or dried and cooking is out of the question.

"Ma?"

"What."

"Why are priests celibate?" I ask, proud to have learnt a new word from Mrs. Harrison and even prouder that I can pronounce it.

Ma looks over the top of her book at me as if I have suddenly grown six-foot tentacles out of my head.

"Ask yer father," she says, and resumes reading her romance novel called *The Passion of Saffron*. I like it that Mrs. Feeley brings in books sometimes for me ma to read, though up to now she's only looked at the covers. *The Passion of Saffron* is where I found the word, 'erection,' and what it meant.

"Ask yer father what?" says da as he walks into the kitchen and pours himself a cup of *tae* from the pot on the stove.

"Why are priests celibate, da?" I ask and turn round to face him.

"'Cause they're all full of shite," he says, picks up a plate and sits himself down beside me. No church for him this week, though he's never attended church since his baptism - his mother had dropped him on his head as a baby, or so mother says.

It's Saturday morning. Father is home and on his plate is a pile of sausages, black and white puddings (dried pigs' blood and oats) greasy fried eggs, bacon, beans, and toast.

"Oh, listen to the pot calling the kettle black," says ma.

"Feck off," says me da. "They're all hypocrites. Anyway, the boy's only curious."

"Curiosity killed the cat," replies ma.

"Da says Uncle Chris killed the cat," I pipe in, and mother glares at him as if he had just turned into a cat himself. Anyway, I wonder what a cat has to do with celibacy, but it makes me think about Betty's questions in class.

"Ma?"

"What, son?"

"Has Father Luke got a girlfriend?"

Mother almost chokes on her cornflakes. Her dentures take a short trip to the edge of her mouth then slide back into position. She quickly picks up her cigarette and drags on it deeply.

"Father Luke would be condemned to Hell for eternity," mother says, coughs and blows smoke in my face. "And his tart, too. Hell's damnation. Both of 'em!"

"Well at least he won't be lonely," I reply and father almost falls off his chair with laughter. I laugh along with him as ma scowls at us.

"Betty at school said she saw Father Luke kissing Marie O' Sullivan."

"Jesus Christ!" Da spits out half the sausage he has in his mouth and chokes on the other half. He takes a big sip of tae to wash down his half-bitten sausage.

"Holy mother of God," says ma. "The Devil himself must be whispering such evilness into yer head. Priests are God's pure people and *they* don't even think about such disgusting things. And if you want to know anything about *that* kind of filthy behavior, then you'll have to ask yer father – not that you'll get much out of him on that subject."

"Joshua, me boy," says father ignoring mother, "Pour me out a cup of that lovely tae, will yer."

My father works away all week on a construction site up in Manchester. He's a hard worker and brings home a good week's wages. Saturday mornings he gets up, cooks his own breakfast then goes back to bed for a few hours in readiness for that night's binge drinking down the Irish club with his friends. He seems to enjoy working away from home, "Gets me away from that old bitch for a week," he told me one time.

God (if He exists) only knows how my father and mother got married, or *why* they remain married because they're always at each other's throats.

Father is as tall as he is wide. He's as tough as old boots and well used to shoveling and concreting all day in the rain and snow. He has a big bunch of black hair on his head, dark, bushy eyebrows, brown shiny Irish eyes and six teeth in his mouth. I know because one night he asked me to count them for him. One of these days he'll get some dentures, but, as he says, there's plenty of time for false teeth. Look at *herself* and her falsies, every time she opens her gob the fecking things fall out.

"Joshua," father says, "can ye ask *herself* what's for tae."

Tae – tea means a cup of tea, of course, but to the Irish (and Northern English folk) tea also means 'dinner' though we eat 'dinner' at 'lunch time' and tea 'dinner' in the evening. Me da says the word 'lunch' is only used by rich posh folk and royalty and not by us commoners. We sometimes call tea, 'char' which, according to Mrs. Feely (she's so clever) comes from the Chinese meaning of the word, or close to it, 'tcha.'

"Can ye tell *himself*," pipes in me ma, "he'll have to make his own tae 'cause I'm too busy."

"Da," says I, "You'll have to make your own tae 'cause …"

"I heard her," says me da. "Tell *herself* to go and shite."

"Ma," says I, "Da says to go and …"

"I heard him," she says, "Tell *himself* to go and feck himself."

"Da," says I, "Ma says for you to go and …"

"I'm not deaf, son" says himself. I place a mug of hot tea (tae) on the table in front of him. He takes a sip. "Grand, son," he says. "Ye make a fine cup of tae. Better than *herself*."

"Go and shite," me ma says, pushes her glasses up from the tip of her nose, wriggles her mouth to adjust her false teeth and continues reading.

"Anything in that book teach you how to cook?"

"Feck off," ma says, now more engrossed in her book (maybe she's found the erection word, or even worse, the *sex* word).

Me da shakes his head, picks up his cup of 'tae' and goes into the living room. I follow him.

"Da. Can I ask you a question?"

"For feck sakes," he bellows, "can't a man get some peace around here." He turns on the TV. "I got this telly for herself and all she does is read fecking books."

"Mrs. Feely brought them round," I say, inwardly hoping, (maybe praying) that me da would attempt to read one of them. I've never seen him hold a book let alone read one.

I know he reads the rag newspapers with the big-titty women on page 3 (I take a secret peek myself now and again), but nothing that would inspire or improve his mind. The only other book in this house is the Holy Bible, and that's taken the place of the missing wooden leg from the Welsh dresser in the corner.

"Da?"

"For feck sakes, what?"

"Does Father Luke get an erection?"

*

Father loves his roses. He spends most of Sunday out in the back garden tending to his 'little babies' as he calls them. It's his time of peace, his small area of paradise, his Eden, his salvation, his escape from concreting and jack-hammering and excavators and tractors and trucks and noise. His escape from the house, from my mother and her constant nagging, her groaning, her negativity. Nothing is good enough for my mother. Everything and everyone has some kind of fault in them. Nothing pleases her unless it makes her laugh, like the time we went to an amusement arcade in Wicklow and she almost laughed herself to death at a dummy clown banging its head against a glass window.

I feel sorry for my father having to endure the anxieties, the stress, and negativity of another person. Why should someone who is miserable, spread it to another person, therefore making someone else unhappy?

So father clips and waters and feeds his rose bushes. I look down at him from my bedroom window. He's standing beside one of the bushes with a clipper in his hand and staring into thin air. He stands this way for many minutes. I've seen him do this before. I often wonder if he's thinking about himself, his family, his wife, his life up to now. Is he dreaming of a better life, or wondering how in hell did he end up in this one?

His best rose bush, the one with the biggest reds is just outside the kitchen door. Sometimes I open the door and smell the beautiful scent. My mother despises roses and especially this one, and not because she is allergic to plants, but, I suspect, she hates them simply because my father loves them.

I get dressed and think back to the time, not so long ago, when I ran away from home (got so tired of being called a demon – though I suppose mother had good reason to call me such – I almost burnt the house down with Christmas candles one time) anyway, I thought I'd teach her a lesson, see if she'd miss her little Catholic boy for a night. I spent the night in a block of flats (Apartments).

I collected all the door mats (some had the word 'Welcome' woven into them) from each flat and covered myself to keep warm. It was mid-winter. In the morning, freezing and shivering with cold a welcomed bottle of milk was put in front of my face by a pleasant old delivery milkman. He smiled and shook his head as if he was used to kids sleeping beneath door mats in mid-winter and it was a normal part of a milkman's round to donate a bottle of cow-juice to a wandering waif. I then decided that a homeless life wasn't for me and rushed home. I was hungry.

I walked into the kitchen and mother stood glaring at me with her big Irish greenish-brown eyes; she dragged deeply on her cigarette and then stubbed it out in the overflowing ashtray. "I was worried sick and up all night fretting about you," she said and lit up another cigarette. I wondered if the smoke actually kept her alive. If for some crazy reason she was forced to inhale normal oxygen it'd kill her, for sure.

She hugged me around the shoulders and kissed me on the top of my head, then said, "Now get up to bed and wait 'till yer father gets home."

Trust me to run away on a Thursday night and *himself* coming home on a Friday. If I'd have escaped on a Monday, ma would have forgotten all about it by Friday evening.

So before I climbed the wooden hill to bed I sneaked into the living room and grabbed the big thick bible from beneath the dresser and replaced it with five of Mrs. Feeley's gifted books. I went to my room. Later, I heard my father come home, mumbling down in the kitchen and his heavy footfalls on the stairs. I shoved the thick bible down the back of my pants, jumped into bed and pulled the blankets up to my chin.

And there was *himself* now building up a hard sweat, swinging his leather belt through the air like a cowboy with a whip steering a herd of cattle, to land on my buttocks in a vain attempt to rid me of a Devil which didn't exist, in my mind, anyway.

After every third or fourth stroke I'd whimper a little and then give out a louder whimper and then start to cry – and then he stopped, put his belt back on (his trousers had fallen down around his thighs) and said. "There. That should send the wee bastard back to hell."

And besides my parents thinking me nuts, maybe the doctors, the social workers, my teachers will conclude that yes, young master Joshua has fallen out of his tree, a slate has slid off his roof, he's a sandwich short of a picnic and all the other worn out clichés regarding anyone's state of mind and, in my case (as, no doubt with many other cases) they'll promptly sign the dotted line of the documents that would have me committed to a pleasant little holiday of three months incarcerated inside a madhouse.

Suffice it to say (another cliché) I keep my mouth shut.

*

Chapter 6

Father Luke has clumps of graying hair poking out each side of his balding pate and looks as if he has just got out of bed, threw his cassock on and scrambled his way to the pulpit – with no time for a wee sip of wine in the vestry.

Ma and I sit in the front pew as always, she says she wants to be nearer to God. She must live in a double-protected box so restrictive that she can hardly move.

"Today I would like to read from … " says Father Luke; he coughs a few times and tries to clear his airway to either remove or swallow the hoarse frog in his throat. Too much altar wine last night, I assume. "I'd like to read from the gospel of Thomas, taken from The Gnostic Gospels, which we talked about last Sunday. Remember his writings were discovered in an earthenware jar in Egypt in 1945. Thomas said: *'If you bring forth what is within you, what you bring forth will save you. If you do not bring forth what is within you, what you do not bring forth will destroy you.'* I'll leave you with that and hopefully it'll make you think about yourselves and how we can make our world a little better."

I quickly glance around the church; the congregation is transfixed, mesmerized, mouths hang half-open, some folks shake their heads, either in disbelief or confusion, probably both. I imagine them thinking how could a man of the cloth, a Catholic, an Irish Catholic to boot, read something not taken from the Lord's bible. Blasphemous. And where is our usual fare of Jesus and God and hell damnation? Narrow, restricted boxes, each box containing a narrower mind. I wonder why I think this way. I wonder why I can't buckle down and go with the flow of everyday dogma, of being brainwashed by the church, by parents, by teachers, politicians, my peers? Seven years old and wise beyond my years. But Mozart was four when he began playing minuets on the clavier, five when he started composing small musical works, and eight years of age when he composed Symphony No 1 in E flat major.

"So how was church?" my father asks as ma and I enter the house.

"Father Luke is as mad as a loon," says ma. "Crazier than your brother Jack, bless his soul."

"Agh, he'll be a fine man in that case," says father and laughs.

My uncle Jack lives in a mental asylum in Dublin.

"I'll pray for Father Luke so he can stay on the righteous path," says ma and saunters into the kitchen, no doubt to make a strong cup of good tae.

Da is sitting on the couch surrounded by a few Guinness bottles and is barely visible through the thick, cigarette smoke surrounding him. It reminds me of one of my favorite movies, Great Expectations by Charles Dickens, and the scene where the convict first encounters young Pip and emerges from the thick marshy fog.

Da pokes his head through the cloud, coughs a few times and says, "Jesus, these fecking things are gonna kill me one day." No, I think my da'll live to at least ninety, still drinking his stout and sitting up in bed surrounded by marshy, foggy cigarette smoke.

"Why don't you pack them in," I ask anyway, waiting for a glob of spittle to come flying out of the cloud but he just looks at me and smiles. "Poverty. Work. No money growing up. No fecking money now to write home about. Then married. Got a kid. So I have a few pints and a smoke. Poor's man's luxuries."

I wonder if I will smoke when I grow up. I hope not.

"There was this old French woman …" da continues and coughs up a load of phlegm, clears his throat and spits it into the blazing, coal fire. The glob strikes the center of the small inferno and a burst of flame shoots up the chimney accompanied by a loud sizzling sound. What *is* he drinking? Peel paint off walls, I bet. "…anyway, this woman lived in a house paid for by her landlord. He agreed for her to live there rent free until she died and she agreed to do all the repairs, paint and modernize the place."

"Like you do, da?"

"Well, yer, kind of. So anyway, the landlord reckoned she would die in her late sixties because she was a heavy smoker, and he'd then have a decorated and modernized house to sell. But the landlord died first."

"Wow. She was lucky."

"Even luckier than that, son. She lived to be 114 and still lived in the same rent free house. She stopped smoking at 110 because she went blind and couldn't find the fecking ashtray!"

Da goes into a fit of laughter. I feel good that he's happy, even for a short time.

Ma walks in with a cup of tae in one hand and a small plate of custard creams in the other. "What's up with himself," she says. I relate da's story word for word to her.

She bursts out laughing and almost spills the tea and biscuits over me and da; she sits down in her armchair beside the fire and slaps her hands on her knees and throws her head back and roars with laughter.

Even the flames in the fire seem shocked and shoot up through the chimney, either to escape the merriment in the living room or flee from the madness of Irish folk. Probably both.

And once my mother starts laughing, it's a sight to behold, listen to and enjoy. I dare anyone not to join in when hearing her. Her hysterical laughter is contagious. If only the world could tap into her laughter for a split second the world would be a far better place because of it.

I remember living in Dublin and myself, himself, herself, and even Mrs. Feeley (minus Mr. Feely, he was killed in action fighting in the British Army in France during World War Two) went to a county fair down in Bray, Wicklow.

We were in an amusement arcade and in a corner was a big glass box with a clown dummy inside dressed as a sailor. If you inserted a coin in the slot the clown came alive (figuratively speaking) and erupted into spasms of hysterical laughter.

Ma spotted the clown and, well, she joined in laughing and laughing and laughing and everyone in the building stopped what they were doing and crowded around her.

Da sneaked outside for a cigarette, not wanting, no doubt, to be associated with that crazy hysterical woman indoors.

The clown stopped laughing and someone shouted, "Put another coin in quick. This is better than playing bingo."

Mother dipped into her purse, laughing still, almost crying with laughter, found a coin and, with shaking hands put it in the slot. The clown jumped to life and moved from side to side and back to front while roaring its dummy head off.

And every few seconds or so the dummy smacked against the front of the glass and mother roared again.

Then Mrs. Feely joined in. They held onto each other like excited kids as the clown banged its head against the glass and laughed like a crazed hyena.

Mother and Mrs. Feely howled and banged and crashed their heads against each other, ceased laughing for a split second and then they were off again.

She was laughing still on the open carriage train chuffing up and over Sugarloaf Mountain, much to the amusement of our fellow travelers. At the top of the mountain I sniffed the sweet sea-scented air of Bray. In the distance I saw Dublin port and the city, gazing out across the Irish sea and was sure I could see a little of England in the far distance. I told ma about the view and she just laughed the more.

And now here she is again, the incredible laughing Irish woman, sitting in her favorite armchair and attempting to light a cigarette.

Da half-smiles and I can see he's trying to force himself not to laugh. Ma stops and takes a few deep breaths. Good. She's got it out of her system. Then for some reason which even I can't understand I open my mouth and say, "Reminds me of that clown down in Bray."

She is off again thundering like something between a crazy lion, an orangutan and a laughing clown but much louder and longer. I thought maybe if she keeps this up she'll suffer a heart attack, maybe die laughing. Now isn't that a great way to leave the world.

"Excuse me, young man," the mourner at her funeral would say, "but how exactly did your mother die."

"Laughed herself to death," I'd say and receive some strange looks in return.

And then da joins the menagerie. A living room full of roaring lions, screaming orangutans, snorting pigs, even whistling birds because every time mother takes a breath, albeit a small one, the air whistles through her mouth, especially when she isn't wearing her dentures.

Suddenly Mrs. Feely runs in through the front door, no doubt expecting us all to be lying bloodied on the floor after being invaded and ripped apart by most of the animals she could recall at that moment.

"Blessed Jesus andGod almighty" she says, "I thought ye were all being fecking eaten alive!"

And then *she* joins in the merriment. This continues for about another thirty minutes, with a break for a smoke and a cup of tae and custard creams, of course, and then it's back into the breach once more, my friends.

I suddenly think of what Father Luke had quoted earlier: "If you bring forth what is within you, what you bring forth will save you."

I guess we are all saved this day.

*

Chapter 7

It's July and a scorching hot day. Unusual weather this year. Hottest summer for a long time. Not a drop of rain in two months. The air is thick and humid.

I knock on John's front door. A wooden plate hangs on the wall to the side of the door, it reads, *The Devil is not welcome in this Blessed House of God.*

The door squeaks open and I gaze up at a giant.

"Can John come out to play," I manage to ask Mrs. O'Malley.

"And who in God's name are you."

"I'm his new best friend. Joshua."

Mrs. O'Malley is twelve foot tall at least, or so it seems to me.

Thick, red curly hair all bunched up at the top and sticking out at the sides as if she's just got out of bed, massive gray-colored eyes, hands like shovels, big bulging titties that sag down to below her stomach. Her fingernails are long and yellowish, the same color as her teeth. She has a pointed nose with a big brown wart on the tip. She looks like a giant witch. I don't know whether to flee or stand my ground against this monster. Gritting my teeth I decide to take a chance and hope she had already eaten her breakfast and didn't like the taste of little boys.

She points to the sign on the wall. "I heard about you, yer little devil. Asking about erections. You're a bad influence on my John. Erections, indeed."

"But I ..."

"Ye'll not be giving *my* John an erection, that's for sure." She slams the door in my face.

I feel relieved that she hadn't decided to eat me, shrug my shoulders and walk to the back alley.

"Josh," I hear a voice coming from the other side of the garden fence. "It's me. I'll meet you up at the ranch."

"What's up with your ma?" I ask and try to peek between the slats in the fence.

"Oh, don't worry about that big old bitch. See yer soon."

I feel better now and less rejected than I did a few moments ago. Yes. John's right. His mother is an old bitch. An old giant witch bitch.

I giggle as I get to the end of the back alley and turn left up the steep hill. I could find my way to the ranch blindfolded (John and I call it the ranch but it's a quarry). I walk along beside a minor road with terraced houses on each side, take a right turn up an incline, climb over the wooden gate of St Patrick's school, across the playground, (had a few fist fights in this playground) over the football fields, through a hole in the school fence (the secret passageway to our ranch), over a main road, up another steep hill and onto a gravel path which meanders up a sandy hill and into the quarry.

I stand at the top and look down into a big pool of rainwater. These pools are called clay-holes. I turn and gaze over most of the west side of Corby town.

Down at the poolside (our private swimming pool on our private ranch) I strip bullock-naked, stretch my arms above my head, take a deep breath and dive into the water.

"Jesus, Mary, Joseph and all the angels in heaven. It's fecking freezing!" I imagine this is what it feels like if some idiot (that would be me) dived into the Alaskan sea.

I look into the depths of the pool as I swim towards the far side. Just visible about ten feet under the water is long, thick rusted steel cables all tangled up and twisted that dangle down into the deep clay-hole (some cables are thinner in width and are closer to the surface as you get nearer to the sides of the clay-hole). The sight scares me, so I swim faster to the other side, get out and lie on the hard mud.

I have quick flashes of my father and I down at the community swimming pool and him trying to teach me how to swim. The main reason why my da, and many other da's in Corby at that time decided to teach their kids to swim was that the year before, a five year old boy (I knew him from school) fell into one of the clay-holes and was caught on the cables beneath the water. He drowned.

The community was up in arms over the death of the boy and Corby Steel Corporation were blamed for the kid's death by way of dumping all their old and used cables, thick and thin gauges into the clay-holes.

Everyone knew their kids played and swam in these clay-holes but it was part of growing up. They couldn't watch their children seven days a week especially when they're out playing.

We got warnings about the holes but we didn't take much notice of what adults said.

Anyway, I was six years old when da took me to the swimming pool. I liked the water, although I must have swallowed half the pool in an attempt to stay afloat. My father's method of teaching someone how to swim was simple: throw them in.

So there's me gasping for air, paddling like someone having an epileptic fit and da laughing his head off poolside.

"Keep paddling, boy," he yelled at me. "Don't let the water beat you."

Beat me, I'm fecking drowning! It's a miracle, said my mother that evening. God gave you a helping hand. He saved your life. I think by floating on my back and paddling a little with my hands saved my life. I had no intention of letting the water beat me and drag me to the botSean. Da pulled me out. Of course it was only three foot of water but to me it seemed like an ocean. "There ye are," said me da. "You'll make a fine swimmer," then he patted me on the back, picked me up with his strong arms – and threw me back into the pool.

And now I can swim like a dolphin.

The Iron Ore quarry is massive. Our outdoor swimming pool is just one of many manmade pools spread around the quarry where massive holes appear after the ore is extracted and rainwater settles in.

Corby steelworks is one of the biggest producers of steel in the world and the crane or dragline that can be seen anywhere you stand in Corby, is the biggest extractor of iron ore in Europe.

I can see it now about a mile away dipping and rising and collecting ore with its massive shovel.

The ore is loaded onto rail wagons and taken straight to the blast furnaces for processing. Corby town is built around the steelworks and employs the majority of folks from the town and surrounding areas.

The sun heats my body and I'm enjoying just lying here naked. I hear birds chirping in the distance. A slight breeze massages my body. It makes me feel good all over.

"So *that's* what an erection looks like," John says as he approaches.

I cup my privates with my hands. I don't know what to say. Nothing to say, I suppose. What *can* I say.

"That's okay, Josh," he says and sits beside me. "I get them all the time."

He strips naked and dives into the pool. What a great friend, I think. Takes me for what I am. No taunting, no hang-ups, just says it as he sees it. Innocence. Honestly. Two traits that could be used as a foundation to build a better world.

I dive in after John and we swim to the center of the pool, and then float on our backs.

"Why do people say the sun is hot?" John asks quizzically.

"Stupid, eh," I reply. "It wouldn't be cold."

We laugh.

"My ma put her hand into a bag of ice and said it was freezing cold."

We laugh again.

"Or, when me da meets his mate he says, 'is that yourself? And his mate says, ' No, it's me brother.' Meself is at home with the flu.'"

And between laughing and giggling we shoot off a list of obvious things people say without thinking.

"Or," says I, "me ma sometimes says, 'that coal is black.'"

"Or, says John, "Bless me father for I have sinned? Yer wouldn't be in the confession box, otherwise, would yer?"

"Or," says I, "You're drinking again, me ma says to himself sitting on the couch drinking beer."

We both feel tired and swim to the side, get out and lie naked in the sun.

"Or," I continue, "We were in me uncle's car once and mother was giving directions. 'Turn right there,' she said. So me uncle turns right and ends up in a cow field. 'I said turn *right* there, not turn right here.' Ma was pointing left and saying turn right, she should have said, over *there*, turn left."

"Or," says John, 'This fish tastes fishy.' Me ma says that all the time."

"Your ma doesn't like me," I say.

"'Naa," says John. "She just doesn't like erections."

"My ma says a servant of God can't get one of those."

"Your ma's as mad as mine," says John. And then, "Here, last one in the water is a twat!"

*

Chapter 8

"I told you not to swim in them clayholes," mother barks at me.

"Who said I was up there?"

"A little birdie told me."

Birdie or no birdie my mother knows everything that goes on in our neighborhood, and if she didn't then it wouldn't be long before she did.

"Birdies can't talk," I say.

She glares at me, frowns and puts her left hand on her hip. "The birds see me hanging out the washing, so they sit on me shoulder and whisper things into me ear."

My mouth falls open. I almost believe her. What a great imagination she has. I do know (John told me so) that his aunt lives near the main road below the quarry so she must have spotted us coming down the hill soaked to the skin.

And, although I'm not completely sure, his aunt most probably did some hand signals with two bath towels (working-class morse code) and transmitted information to John's mother who in turn transmitted information to Mrs. Feely (her house is at the botSean of the hill leading up to the quarry) and from there the silent message is brought next door to my mother's. That's why as soon as I step inside our front door I'm confronted with my misdeeds and there is no way to lie my way out of it.

No boy (or girl) can fart or piss behind a tree without our neighborhood fully knowing about it. The beginnings, I think of something that may well catch on, neighborhood watch, or something.

"We didn't swim, ma. We only sat on the bank," I say, again foolishly, with my hair soaking wet and tiny pieces of green algae stuck on top of both ears.

"Aye," she says with a glint in her eye. "I believe yer. Now go get that green stuff off yer ears and come down for yer tae."

It's like standing in front of your mother with chocolate smudged around your mouth and saying, "What chocolate."

I rush upstairs three at a time and run the bath. I always fill it up to the dark-colored tide marks circling the tub so when the water is above these marks it looks like a clean bath. My mother isn't the best cleaner or scrubber of baths or sinks in the world, but I suppose you get used to the grime, though it's usually me who scrubs the bath after I use it.

"Don't ye be forgetting to scrub the bath after ye've used it," she shouts up the stairs. "Ye's are all dirty shites as far as I'm concerned. I haven't got time to be scrubbing up after you and yer father."

This confuses me because she doesn't work and has plenty of time to wash and clean, but maybe her days are filled with supping tae with Mrs. Feely and when she returns home, she reads those romance novels until it's time to cook the evening meal.

I sit at the dining room table all clean and scrubbed, the algae now swishing its way along underground pipes. There is a vinyl covered dresser set against the far wall emblazoned with framed black and white photographs of my grandparents, mother's wedding day (her and father are not smiling on their big day) and smaller photographs of me sitting on my granddad's knee.

In another photo taken when we visited Dublin not so long ago, I'm kneeling beside my grandfather and mother and father stand behind them. What I notice about this photo is that my grandparents are holding hands. It's obvious they are in love. Sometimes, in the kitchen I watch as mother holds that framed photo in her hands and clasps it to her chest. I'm sure I heard her give out a tiny moan before placing the picture back on the dresser. She loves her parents, I guess and misses them every day. Especially her father.

Dinner (tae) is served and I dig into the Dublin Coddle (potatoes, sausages, pieces of bacon, lentils, turnips, carrots and onions all chopped up and cooked in water until boiled and eaten with slices of bread and lashings of butter to fill a boy's and a man's stomach until breakfast the next day. A hearty Irish meal that will, I imagine, become a delicacy one day.

Once a month we splash out on steak. Thin frying steak to be exact. And mother will cook the living daylights out of the meat until it resembles, both in sight and taste, the leather sole of a shoe. You can't cut it with a knife, though that is difficult in itself because all our knives (the whole six of them) are blunt. I have to pick the thing up with my fingers and gnaw at it like a wild dog to bite off a piece, then spend ten minutes chewing it to be able to swallow the piece without choking to death. But still, I'm not complaining, there are people in the world who'd murder folks just to smell a frying steak, let alone eat one.

Stomach full, I swish down my lemonade and, without saying anything sneak out of the house and head across the road to the playing fields. A football (soccer) match is about to start and I see John standing on the sideline holding a red football shirt.

"Hurry up, Josh," he says, "game's about to start."

I take off my jersey (a woolen open-necked thing that my mother thinks is in high fashion and everyone else thinks a girl should be wearing) then slip on the football top. We run onto the field and the game begins.

The other team (from Hazelwood school two miles down the road – we haven't decided as yet on a name for our team) kick off and the center forward runs up and kicks the ball as hard as he can and it hits me right between the legs. I scream and the Hazelwood captain laughs.

The bastard.

All I can think of now is how to get my own back on that bastard who kicked the ball in my bollocks (testicles), and will I be affected for the rest of my life with pain and maybe testicular cancer. The bastard's name is Michael Sheridan, one of them posh kids who live on the rich side of town. He must either be brave or an idiot to play football in our area. The rest of the players are chasing the ball while I'm kneeling on the ground clutching my balls.

"To you, Josh," shouts John sliding the ball over to me. I jump up, still grasping my balls, receive the ball and run toward the opposite goal. I could easily boot the thing into the back of the net from this distance but stop suddenly - my balls are on fire. The ball is taken up by a Hazelwood defender, booted high up field and catches our goalkeeper off guard (he's picking his nose) and the ball flies over his head and into the back of the net.

"Fucking hell, Josh," says John. "What the fuck is up with you!"

I shrug my shoulders and grab my balls again. John shakes his head and runs back to the center line for kickoff.

I grit my teeth and try to think of other things besides the pain in my groin and imagine myself running up to the goal, dribbling (a series of short kicks and taps on the ball) around midfield players and defenders and kicking the ball so hard it slams into the goalkeeper and shoots him backwards through the goal netting. Then the ball lands two feet in front of me and my dream comes through with the exception of the goalkeeper being slammed through the net because I dummy kick the ball and he dives in the opposite direction.

Score: 1-1. Cheers hit the air and I get pats on the back and a slap on the ass (don't know who that is, pervert) then it's back to the center kickoff and on with the game.

John is red in the face now from dribbling and running with the ball from the center line all the way down the right wing; he kicks it high in my direction across the goal-line.

Everyone jumps in the air in an attempt to head the ball away or shoot it over for a corner, but I jump at the last second and am about to head the ball into the back of the net (a goal for sure) when Michael Sheridan (the testicle kicker) grabs me around the waist and tackles me to the ground.

I get up and punch the bastard square on the nose, then kick him between the legs. He goes down, moaning and groaning as the referee (a lad called Jock, from Bonnie Scotland) runs up to me and shoves a red card in my face (it's a red piece of cloth he'd swiped from his mother's sewing basket) and a red card means being sent off the field for the rest of the game.

"Ye canny go aroon kicking folks in the bollocks!" he screams at me. "Off," he yells, waving the red cloth in my face. Before I can open my mouth John runs up and goes eyeball to eyeball with Jock.

"That bastard kicked the ball in Josh's bollocks, and now he's pulled him down. That would've been a goal."

"He just kicked him in the bollocks," yells Jock.

"Well, that makes us even." I pipe in.

"Rules are rules," says the ref.

"If you send Josh off I'll kick you so hard in the bollocks you won't be able to piss for a year!"

Jock thinks about this for a moment then looks down at Michael writhing in agony on the grass. "Foul," he says and changes his red cloth for a yellow one. "One more foul like that and *you'll* be sent off."

I put out my hand and offer to help Michael up off the grass. He shrugs it away, manages to stand, stares me in the eye and says, "I'm gonna kill you, yer Irish bastard."

"You and whose army," I say and stick my chest out, clench my fists in readiness for a brawl.

"I'll get you back one day, don't you worry," he says.

"Ye'll have to catch me first," I say and run back towards the center line.

"Don't take any notice of that snob," says John. "He's a wanker."

"A lot of them around today," I say as the ref blows his whistle for the second half kick-off. I slip the ball to John who boots it over to Andy on the right wing who in turn gallops up the right side like a racehorse, while we dash down the center of the field, jumping over midfield players trying to kick us in the shins, kneecaps, stamping on our toes (we didn't even have the fecking ball) and defenders grabbing our shirts and trying to wrestle us to the ground. God knows where the ref is; he's supposed to *referee* the game.

Amid shouts and screams from our players to receive the ball Andy kicks it high across the goal and the keeper punches it out right into the path of my left foot. I dribble the ball around and in-between three defenders as they kick and shove and slide around me trying to get the ball (and get me, too) and, as a bonus, kick the shit out of my shins, but I jump and dummy and give the ball a good old thump with my left foot and it goes whizzing into the back of the net like a Bobby Charlton super kick.

Our team go nuts and I get pats on the back and a kiss on the cheek from John (that's fine, we're good friends) and then another slap on the ass (I turn round quickly and there's Jock the ref standing there. He winks at me. Bloody hell, I think to myself.

Anyway, I support Manchester United and had gone with my school (and John) to see them play live at Old Trafford in Manchester.

It was fantastic watching Bobby Charlton, Seanmy Smith, and especially George Best displaying their amazing skills. George Best is from Belfast and never did play for England, if he did, then he would have been known worldwide and got even more famous than Pele.

Best was unbelievable. He'd get the ball on the half-way line and dribble, *dribble* his way around six or seven players, jumping over their legs and then dribbling through the defense and around the goalkeeper then walk the ball into the back of the net, pick it up and hand it to the open-mouthed goalkeeper. In my opinion he was one of the best footballers in the universe.

As soon as we get home from Manchester it's on with the football strip and boots and over to the playing field where our team will be warming up and waiting for us to join them for a game. Images of Best always run through my mind as I tackle and dribble and score goals.

Score: 2-2. Hazlewood have just scored. Michael, the bastard, still limping a bit, heads the ball into the net. Our goalkeeper needs a good kick in the bollocks for letting in two goals, the first one he was picking his nose and the second goal he was busy scratching his fecking ass.

Kick-off at center, ball is passed to me, I glance downfield and spot the goal and the keeper bouncing around on two feet, probably emulating his own first division goalkeeper idol when I know, I just *know* I'm going to score a goal from the center line, sixty-five yards, or one hundred and ninety five feet.

I have a killer left foot, I'm also left-handed, and I can see clearer out of my left eye than my right. I sleep on my left side, chew food on the left side of my mouth, so I'm a complete leftie, as they say.

I kick the ball and it soars high and fast through the air, confuses the goalkeeper, who has come out of his box (risky coming out of your box when you're not ready for it) and the ball swoops down behind him, doesn't touch the ground and slides into the back of the net like a basketball going through a hoop.

You can probably hear the cheers for miles around. John's mother will be waving her bath towels frantically to and fro to signal Mrs. Feely, who in turn would inform my mother that something's afoot. I bet when I go home mother will tell me the final score. Anyway, John and the rest of the team do their patting on my back (no slap on the ass this time) and they lift me up on their shoulders and carry me back to the center line: A happy and ecstatic bunch of young lads finding great pleasure in a simple game of football.

The whistle blows for the goal and before we can kick off again, the ref blows his whistle for the end of the match. Score: 3-2 to our team. Walking off the field I notice Michael Sheridan glaring and growling in my direction.

Today I'm a hero having scored a hat-trick and the last goal equal to any professional player. It's fun playing football. For a couple of hours a week we create our own kind of magic.

*

That night I dream of kissing a blue-eyed girl. I see a gypsy and she says to me, "Hello, my name is Rose." A policeman pops into my dream and he is cock-eyed. Suddenly I'm riding on a bus and the conductor is singing in an Irish accent, "Oh Danny Boy, the pipes the pipes are call-ha-ling." And then I'm standing outside a gypsy caravan and turn and see a man playing a set of Uilleann pipes around a camp fire. Beside him sits a woman with two children perched on her knee, she is swaying to the music. Into view comes a square box, and then hundreds of wooden and metal boxes appear and suddenly disappear.

I see a village by the sea. Cliffs. The sky is almost black. A storm approaches. Massive waves lift from the sea and gush through the narrow alleys and lanes of the village, smashing gates and fences and cottages as if they were matchsticks. I hear a woman scream. I hear children scream.

I wake up screaming.

*

Chapter 9

"Seven is a magical age," I tell myself. I'm reading an article from a magazine. "God rested on the seventh day. There are seven days in a week. Seven means completeness or divine perfection. The number seven is used in the bible more than seven hundred times. There are seven colors of the rainbow. There are seven notes to the diatonic tone. The British 50 pence piece is seven-sided."

I place the magazine on the kitchen table. Mother had bought it the day before in an attempt to improve my mind. Most of the material is about the bible. Maybe she thinks because I dislike religion that this is a better and more enjoyable method of learning. Maybe I'm not so keen on biblical readings but I'm certainly good at reading and writing.

Funny, I can't remember being taught how to read or write. Sure, the infant teacher did scribble letters and the like on the chalkboard, but I can only remember picking up a pencil and writing simple words. Maybe it's a gift I have. Other kids in my class struggle with spelling and writing but I don't see what all the fuss is about. Teacher pats me on the head and tells me 'well, that's good, did your parents write that out for you last night?'

Even though I'm holding the pencil and actually writing the words in front of her nose, she still doesn't believe a child can write this way. She concentrates on the kids who are struggling to write rather than the kids who can write. If I became a teacher I'd do things differently.

Easter is around the corner and mother is busy shopping and buying chocolate eggs and sweets for Easter Sunday. I'm sitting on the couch watching Star Trek on TV and wishing I could experience the same adventures as the crew of the Starship Enterprise. The coal fire is burning brightly today. I'm becoming an expert on lighting coal fires.

"Church on Sunday, Joshua," says my mother. "It's Easter Sunday. The day Our Lord rose from the dead and went home to heaven."

"So why did He die?"

"He died for the sins of mankind. To save us."

"To save us from what?"

"Why do you have to ask so many questions. Why can't you just accept things the way they are?"

She leaves the room, her slippers flip-flopping along the linoleum floor and slams the living room door behind her. "You better turn up for church on Sunday, Joshua," she yells from the kitchen.

I guess I'm going to church on Sunday. Lately I've managed to escape being confined in that stuffy, humid building and feigned an upset stomach or a toothache or something, though I have to be careful about my teeth because mother wouldn't think twice about dragging me up to the dentist to have them pulled out so I'd have *no* excuse to miss church.

Mother must have been outside and talking to Mrs. Feely over the garden hedge because about ten minutes after mother had slammed the living room door Mrs. Feely knocks on the front door. Mother lets her in and she sits beside me. "Maybe you can talk some sense into him, Mrs. Feely," says mother and leaves the room, this time closing the door quietly.

"Now, Joshua," says Mrs. Feely and holds my hand. "What's all this nonsense about not wanting to go to church."

"I don't like it there."

"Well, that's beside the point. You have to attend church, just like every other Catholic has to attend church to give praise to the Lord."

"But why," I say and raise my voice. "I'm happy as I am."

"It's not about being happy, Joshua. It's about faith. Do you believe in God?"

"Well, not really," I say adamantly.

Mrs. Feely gasps and blesses herself three times. "Jesus, Mary and Joseph. Everyone believes in God. If you don't believe in Him you'll spend all eternity roasting in hell."

"I don't believe in hell, either."

She blesses herself another few times and gasps and clutches her chest. "Do … do you believe in Jesus Christ Our Savior? Say you do, oh please say you do."

"Not really."

"What do you mean, not really. You either do or you don't."

"I think the whole thing is a fairy tale."

"Holy Mary Mother of God. Forgive this child."

"It's like Star Trek. They whizz around space and land on different planets and I wish I could do the same. I imagine being there with them and sharing their adventures. But I know that will never happen. It's only a story."

"So you think the bible and all the saints and God and Jesus and all the holy things that have happened are all fairy tales?"

"Yes."

Mrs. Feely, speechless, leaves the room. I hear mumblings in the kitchen and then the side entrance door opening and closing. My mother remains in the kitchen and doesn't bother me for the rest of the day.

Can't blame her really. Imagine having a heathen living under your roof? Imagine giving *birth* to a heathen that lives under your roof? Maybe she knows I'm a lost cause and that maybe she feels sorry for her only child and the only child probably in England who will one day spend eternity in God's trashy playground called hell.

I do of course believe in God, or rather my God is in the shape of nothing that can be seen or touched. My God is everywhere. My God is in the couch I'm sitting on, in the curtains, the walls, the floors, the flowers, plants, sky, moon, oceans, the air I breathe, aSeans, molecules, protons, neutrons, light, heat, the body I have, the thoughts I have, the food I eat.

My God is everywhere and by definition, being everywhere at once means that it is universal and so the universe, every universe, every aSean and molecule is in the universe and so is in me and everyone and everything else. Jesus was a man, tortured and killed because he claimed to be God.

Walk through Corby town any day and you'll come across some idiot standing under the town clock preaching and screeching that he is Jesus or God and wants to change the world. God is the universe and the universe is God. I wanted to tell mother and Mrs. Feely this but they'd only think I'd gone nuts. If I lived in Ireland and spouted all this then I'd be confined to a mental asylum, like so many other 'free' thinkers.

I read another article in the magazine that talked about freedom of speech and how in reality such a concept didn't exist. And the more I think about it, the more I realize that the writer is correct. There is only freedom of speech if it falls within the limits of a government, a religion, a set of ethics set down by Christians. As the writer states, 'You can say what you wish as long as it doesn't condemn or degrade others." So if you can say what you wish and it's called 'free speech,' then how can a person be condemned for saying it even if you insult someone.

But my alternative way of thinking about the world and God doesn't make me very popular with parents, priests, teachers at school, the Irish, English, Scottish or Americans. And do I care? No. As in the beautiful and eloquent straightforward words of my father. "They can all go and take a flying fuck!"

See. Freedom of speech.
    Amen.

*

Chapter 10
(School)

At age 5 I hated school. At age 7 I hated school. And now at age eleven I hate it even more. Ever since that first day at St Brendan's infant school I hated it. Certain teachers like Mrs. Harrison and Miss Johnson made the hours in the classroom bearable. I remember vividly the very first day at school. It was a beautiful sunny September day and I was standing by the window waving goodbye to my mother. I was terrified. Almost five years old and on my own for the first time.

I experienced a crunched-up nausea feeling in my stomach that day. Separation anxiety I guess, but later in the morning as Miss Johnson was reading a book to the class, I raised my hand and asked if I could go to the toilet.

"It'll be break-time in a few minutes, Joshua," she said without looking up from 'Nursery Rhymes for Infants,' "can't you wait?"

I guess not because I stood abruptly and clutched my stomach, knelt on the floor and shit myself. The kids in the class were disgusted and shuffled over against the far wall.

"Told yer I needed to go," I said and shuffled to the store room at the end of the classroom. Shit streamed down both my legs with each embarrassing step. I made it to the room and shut the door after me. I didn't know what to do, so I took my shorts off and wiped myself as best as I could.

Miss Johnson came in holding a large towel (It was yellow with big pink elephants sprawled on it) and wrapped it around my shoulders. She held her nose between her thumb and index finger. I stank. Probably put her off having children of her own. She reached to a top shelf and produced a pair of blue shorts that most probably belonged to some other poor, embarrassed infant.

"Take these," she said, squeezing her nose tighter, "Go to the toilet and clean yourself then change into these."

"Okay, Miss Johnson," I said, never wanting to return to her class, or this school, or any school again for the rest of my life.

"The children are out playing so you should be fine walking along the corridor." She turned quickly and rushed out of the storeroom. I heard the clip- clop of her high heels as she galloped down the corridor, retching and, most likely, searching for the nearest toilet.

I cleaned myself as best I could in the toilet cubicle, careful to keep quiet when some boys came in to use the urinal, then sneaked along the corridor in my clean (a bit too tight) blue shorts, sneaked out the school glass doors and ran across the playground toward the school gate. Laugher and giggling followed me like mad ghosts as I climbed the wooden gate and galloped (faster than Mrs. Johnson, I bet) between the terraced houses, past my friend John's house (he was a bit older than I and was attending Our Lady's School on the other side of town) and down the hill toward my home. I hoped mother was up town doing the shopping otherwise she'd slap me for dirtying myself.

Near the botSean of the road my stomach churned again and I shit myself once more. What was *in* that Dublin Coddle? Or was it mother's greasy cooking or some bug because I had diarrhea for three days afterwards. It was as if my shit had a mind all of its own. It just slopped out anywhere and everywhere. Had to spend most of the day and night sitting on the toilet pot, much to the angst of my ma and da.

Anyway, mother didn't open the front door to my knocking so she must have been out. I climbed up the back entrance wall like a chimpanzee, got on the roof and squeezed myself through a small gap in the toilet window. Great timing, too, because just as I landed on the floor my stomach churned once again.

After an hour of sitting on the pot (I think I had fallen asleep) I quickly cleaned myself up in the bathroom and changed into some shorts and a tee-shirt.

My original shorts were beyond saving and Miss Johnson must have thrown them in the trash. My tee-shirt tail was covered with shit so I slid that in among the dirty laundry in the basket hoping my mother wouldn't smell nor notice them (she never did, luckily for me, the cigarette odor took care of that).

School kids tried to tease me every day in the playground but I wasn't standing for any of it. I kicked and punched and head-butted anyone who called me 'shitty arse' or 'shit in pant's boy) and so began my life of fisticuffs and strife. At home the arguments between mother and father reached higher levels every week and I carried on the family tradition with my fists at school. Pretty soon word got around that there was a tough nut up at St Brendan's Infants school, and most days after school there was always some kid from another school waiting outside the gates for me to walk through and then the kicking and punching and head-butting would be on.

It was kind of fun for a while, then, after it started to get painful and boring, I just stopped fighting and let one kid kick me a few times on the ground and that was it, Joshua Hanley was no longer the best fighter in school. After that no one bothered me and Miss Johnson seemed to like me even more because I had decided to give up fighting and her class was the better for it.

St Patrick's school was next and that was where I met Mrs. Harrison, the mother I wished I had, (much later I realized what an idiot I was for thinking such nonsense, because she could have been a grouchy old bitch at home, worse than my mother).

St Brendan's Catholic infant's school was from age 5 to 7. St Patrick's Catholic junior school from age 7 to 11. Kids took an 11-plus exam and those who passed went on to Grammar school and were usually the intelligent kids with potential for college and university. The rest attended Our Lady's Catholic senior school. At age 13 we'd attend Pope John XXIII up to school leaving age at either 15 or 16. Some of these kids managed to fight their way out of the poverty box and win a place in university. Most were born into wealth, or at least middle-class, and if not, then their parents were open-minded and had creative skills of some kind.

I wished that, maybe in a different life, I would be born into an educated family and carry on their tradition of attending a university.

Such is the stuff of dreams.

*

Chapter 11
(Christmas – 1969)

Christmas has arrived and all is well with the world according to the songs on the radio and programs on TV. Santa is coming down the chimney tonight after I go to bed and fall asleep.

"But ma," I say, "I stopped believing in Father Christmas a long time ago."

"You did? Who told you there's no Father Christmas?" My mother says as she stands by the kitchen door, one hand on her left hip.

"I never told you Father Christmas didn't exist?"

"You did, ma."

"It was probably yer father."

Poor da, he gets the blame for everything. When he'd finish work on a Friday night and travel down from Manchester, he'd stand outside the side-entrance to our house and throw in his cap. If the cap was thrown out again then it wasn't safe to enter, so he'd nip down the Irish Club for a few pints. It was some kind of silent code between them, I suppose, but all codes could be cracked and even manipulated, especially by an eleven year old boy, namely myself. Sometimes if I'd done something wrong and I got the usual, 'wait 'till yer father gets home,' from mother, then I'd wait inside the door and when the cap came swinging in, I'd pick it up and throw it back out through the door. This worked for a whole week until my mother asked father had he any intention of leaving her because he never came home until very late Friday nights and drunk into the bargain.

When father found out about my shenanigans he just shook his head and laughed. "There's no use beating the shite out of you, son," he said, "'cause when you're older, you'll only beat the shite out of me." Made sense to me at the time.

We have a big Christmas tree with all the baubles and clumps of cotton wool to represent snow. Mrs. Feely, feeling lonely without Mr. Feely, had brought in a few gifts and gauzy fairies to hang on the tree.

An old tradition of our family was to place lighted candles in the windows upstairs to help guide Father Christmas to our house. Though by now I had given up believing in fairy-tales (there was more than enough fairy tales in the world including the religious one) and I was allocated the task of candle-bearer.

"Nip upstairs and light some candles, Joshua, will you," says mother. I raised my eyes skyward but found some candles (half used from last year) and a box of matches in the kitchen drawer and go upstairs to complete my Christmas task. Five minutes later I come rushing down the stairs and into the living room where father and mother and Mrs. Feely are watching Coronation Street on TV.

"The fecking curtains are on fire," I yell at them. For a few moments no one takes any notice. "Dad! The house is on fire!"

He runs upstairs followed by mother and Mrs. Feely (Out of breath and clutching her chest - I think she is about to have a heart attack) and flings open the bedroom door (I had shut the door to prevent a draft of air getting in – seen it on TV) and air rushes in, but a big gust of air only makes things worse. The curtains are completely engulfed in flames and then the fire spreads across the ceiling.

"Jesus, Mary and fecking Joseph," screams mother. "The devil himself did this. That boy is a demon, I tell yer. A *demon*."

"Phone the Fire Brigade," father shouts above the roar of the flames.

"We haven't got a phone," says mother. "You're too stingy to buy one."

"I'll phone from my house," Mrs. Feely yelps, spins on her heels clutching her chest still and disappears downstairs.

Meanwhile yours truly - standing behind my parents - slowly creeps backwards and into the toilet. I lock myself in and hear muffled sounds and shouts and screams from beyond the toilet door - I intend to stay put in relative safety for at least the rest of my life.

Luckily for us (lucky for me) the fire brigade (fire service) is stationed only half a mile down the main road. I try to pee but nothing comes out. Sweat forms on my brow, my body feels weak, my stomach churns, my intestines cramp up; I quickly pull my pants down and sit on the pot. What have I done? It's bad enough getting up to my various shenanigans outside the home and being called the 'devil' by mother (and after this probably everyone else) but burning down your parents' home seems a little too much – even for a demon.

In the distance I hear the familiar sound of the fire engines, not a loud siren and horn hooting, but the quiet almost pleasant sound of bells ringing. They stop outside our house and I take a peek out of the toilet window. Firemen and hoses running into the living room (Mrs. Feely stands near the front door still clutching her chest, but this time she has her hand over her mouth.

Footsteps on the stairs, the sounds of gushing water and mother shouting, "Where is that little shite. As God is my witness I'm going to send him back down to where he came from, back to hell and his Uncle Nick."

Uncle Nick being the devil himself, of course. My mother, I should say, despite being brainwashed by all the religious hype and fairy tales of angels and God and the like, is creative in ways of condemnation, especially if it concerns her son, Joshua *the demon* Hanley.

"Where is that little bastard," I hear my father shout; the door knob twists a few times. I'm done for now, for sure.

"Come out of there, Joshua," he screams at the door. "Yer grounded. Ye'll stay in this house for the next month."

"What about school?" I ask and hope he'll tell me to fuck school, grounded means grounded. No such luck. "Ye miss school and there'll be no pocket money for a year."

"And no playing with yer friend, John, either. Do yer hear," mother adds. "No playing football or doing yer shenanigans at the clay-hole."

"Yes, ma," I say. Being grounded I can easily bear, but not being able to see John really hit me in the solar plexus.

At least I was safe in this toilet – for now. My tiny box, this haven for wayward boys, my comfort zone, so to speak. Suppose we all find some kind of safety when we hide or retreat into our own imagined boxes. One day I will break free, rip my box to pieces and enjoy the beauty of the world.

So I'm sitting here on the pot with my thoughts when suddenly a head pokes through the small top window. "Come on, lad," says the fireman in a deep but friendly voice. "Let's get you out of there."

He reaches down to me with a shovel-like hand and picks me up off the pot and squeezes me through the window, hands me to another fireman and am placed on the ground.

"Stay here," he says, and runs into the house carrying a hose.

I have no intention of waiting to see if the fire is extinguished or, worse scenario, burnt to the ground, so I high-tail it along the main road toward Exeter Estate to spend the wintry night in an apartment block under the stone stairs, wrapped tightly in 'Welcome mats' (another box of sorts).

This is the first time I run away from home. The second time I volunteer to join the British Army.

*

(Confession)

Saturday morning, dad is sleeping in. He usually stays in bed most of Saturday and then visits the Irish club for a binge session. Sunday he sleeps to mid-day and spends the rest of the day with his roses in the garden. During the week he shovels concrete, erects wooden shuttering to hold the concrete and performs many other skills related to the construction industry. He's a hard worker and I admire him.

Being grounded for setting fire to the bedroom isn't that bad. There's no way I could be grounded, not with the toilet window to sneak out through and back in again. "I'm proud of you," my mother had said after two weeks of being confined to the house. "Proud that ye have stayed indoors all this time."

School summer holidays certainly help with my escape plans. Mostly John and I hang out and go swimming. But it's nice for mother to compliment me, rare as it is.

The fire had destroyed their bedroom ceiling, the window frames (the glass also shattered) the two wardrobes (mother inherited them from Mrs. Feely, who inherited them from her great aunt), the double bed, all the linen, the carpet and floorboards, plus my mother's antique dressing table. What the fire didn't destroy the firemen saturated. Even the wallpaper had to be replaced. And all because my mother wanted to light the way for Father *Fecking* Christmas.

Father did most of the repairs. He had to work overtime Saturdays and Sundays for a month to pay for it. It was after this disaster that my parents invested in home damage insurance. A friend of his from the Irish club helped out with re-plastering the walls, while dad wallpapered and laid a new carpet.

In a way I think mother was pleased to now have a newly decorated and furnished bedroom; she'd been asking my father to redecorate for years. She should have thanked me.

"I don't get much joy from that shite between the sheets," she told me, "So a new bedroom makes up for it."

Each to their own I say.

Saturday is also time to obey my mother and visit Father Luke down at St Partick's church. Confession day. "Get all those sins off yer chest," my mother had said earlier that week. "Don't forget to mention about you playing tents in bed, running away from home *and* swimming naked in the clay-hole. Oh, and don't forget to mention you almost burned the house down and murdered your father, meself and Mrs. Feely into the bargain. He should give you a few Hail Mary's and an Our Father or two for that lot and a whole line of the Stations of the Cross. *And* for almost giving Mrs. Feely a fecking heart attack."

My mother is funny (a bit weird) but comical at times. It's the way she explains things and how she says things that make me smile, sometimes makes me laugh. And then she'd ask me (in a serious tone, which made me laugh the more) why the feck I was laughing at her. I tell her she makes me laugh and then I tell her a joke and off she goes with that hysterical Banshee shrieking and laughs the house down for twenty minutes or so.

I'm not so keen on going to confession. The experience scares the shite out of me. I'm frightened of kneeling in a darkened room, the black box, the *Holy Box* that always sends shivers up my spine. Every time I kneel down in there I imagine the floor opening up and being swallowed whole and fall down screaming into the burning pits of hell. (My ma would probably be happy with that scenario.)

Last time I went to confession I carried so many sins I thought I'd need a haversack to get them to church. Father O'Brien had listened to my wrong-doings, though most of what I'd done didn't seem like sins to me. And now he's dead and they say he's gone to heaven to confess his own sins to his God.

So for support I call on John. He's a protestant and, like his parents is not too keen on Catholic teachings.

"I'd look a right twat if I got caught going in there," John says in a whispered voice outside his front door.

"Ah, come on, John," I almost plead, "No one will know"

So, reluctantly he joins me in walking the mile down to the church.

"My dad says most of that Catholic religious stuff is rubbish."

"Your dad's clever."

"All fairy tales to brainwash the masses. You don't believe in that crap, do you?"

"Never have."

"Then why you going to confession?"

"'Cause me mother told me to and she'll ask Father Luke if I went."

"My dad says the Catholic Church banned people from reading the bible at one time. That guy who translated the bible into English was killed by the church. And there's a lot of things in the bible that tell the opposite of what the church preaches."

"Wow," says I in awe, "Your dad's really clever."

"He reads a lot. Fancy an ice-cream?"

We nip into the corner shop near my house and John treats me to a '99, me being deprived of pocket money and all. We lick our ices as we meander down Gainsborough road toward the church. I can see the steeple in the distance.

"My da says if you turn your back on the church, everyone will turn their back on you."

"Twats," we say in unison.

We walk up to the front door and John stops. "I can't go in there. It's scary."

"Just sit with me, eh? You don't have to confess anything."

I walk in (John holds onto the back of my shirt) and dip my fingers in the Holy water cup on the wall and bless myself. We sit on a pew behind three old biddies (ladies) and I wait my turn. I reckon their box is bigger because there are three of them.

The last old woman steps out of the box and it's my turn. I glance at John (he looks skyward) and I go into the box and close the door behind me.

It smells of old damp wood in here and smoky. Either Father Luke is having a sly smoke or he's got a candle burning behind his wired cage window. Probably smoking.

I go through the usual diatribe. "Bless me father for I have sinned. It's been a long time since my last confession."

"How long, son?" Father Luke seems to slur his words; maybe he's been drinking the altar wine.

"Er, I don't know, father."

"So you'll have a lot of sins piled up in that case, son?"

"A haversack full of 'em."

"Tell me your sins, son, and I'm sure the Lord will forgive you."

"Well, I erm, my mother calls it playing tents and, erm, she reckons I was doing something wrong."

"And do you play tents a lot?"

"Only when it's warm," I say sarcastically. "And the grass has been cut."

"You know, the good Lord provides us all with a home to live in. Why sleep outside when you could be tucked up in a warm bed."

"Huh?"

"This tent, son," says Father Luke in a serious tone. "Did you fail to get it up properly, fail to erect it correctly, or did you light a candle inside and set fire to it. I remember hearing of a young parishioner who did exactly the same."

What the feck is this ejit on about, I think.

"Say five Hail-Mary's and …"

"I never set fire to no tent, father. It was the house I nearly burnt down. And we ain't even got a tent. I was playing tents in *bed.*"

He clears his throat. "Oh. I see."

"I set my mother's bedroom on fire with a candle."

"And you did this because?"

"Well, me ma likes to make Christmas special though she says she doesn't believe in Santa Claus and told me it was all a fairy tale, but I think she believes in Santa 'cause I overheard her and Mrs. Feely talking about the time my mother put a mince pie or two on the mantelpiece over the fire and made sure the fire grate was brushed clean and neat for himself slipping down the chimney and so I *know* she does believe in Father Christmas (I take a deep breath). And she wants to make Christmas time special 'cause most of the year is depressing and we've not got much money and last year I got half an orange for me Christmas and the other half for me birthday, 'cause me birthday, see, is three days after Santa calls around and I think she wanted to make up for the lack of presents and borrowed a candle from Mrs. Feely, like she did last year and asked me to go light it on the upstairs window ledge, (I take another deep breath) so Father Christmas could see our house and maybe fly down the chimney and drop off a few gifts."

"Your mother believes in Santa Claus? No one has ever seen him."

"You believe in God, don't you, and no one's ever seen Him, either."

"I .. erm … well, so you set your bedroom on fire."

"Not on purpose. I lit a candle and put it on the window ledge but it wouldn't stand up and fell over and touched the side of the curtain. The curtain caught fire and I pulled it down thinking I could stamp on it but it touched the bedspread and that caught fire, then I pulled the bedspread away and it set fire to the carpet which set fire to the wardrobe which set fire to the ceiling. I ran downstairs and told me da."

"Did he reprimand you?"

"Huh?"

"Rebuke you?"

"Eh?"

"Did he tell you off?"

"Oh, yer, then a fireman pulled me out the toilet window."

"Erm ... Okay. Say ten Our Father's and another six Hail Mary's and God me with you, son."

"And there's more."

"I think that's enough for one day, son."

"But mother said I have to get it all off my chest."

"I've got to get ready for afternoon mass, son."

"This won't take long. Me and John, he's my best friend, oh, and he's a protestant and doesn't like Catholics at all, plus he's scared of this church. Anyway, we went swimming up in the clay-hole where we're not supposed to go, and I swam naked and sunbathed naked and John came by and I had an erection and he shrugs his shoulders and dives into the pool. Mother says it's wrong to think bad thoughts and get all excited and I'm confused 'cause how else are babies made?"

"No use asking me about babies, son. I'm a priest, remember."

"Do you get erections?"

"Jesus, Mary and Joseph," Father Luke says and almost chokes on his words. He clears his throat. "Say three sessions of the Stations of the Cross, twenty-two Hail-Mary's and three dozen Our Fathers." He blesses himself, his hands shaking. He drops his bible, bends down to retrieve it and bangs his head on the shelf. I feel sorry for Father Luke.

And then he rushes out of the confessional box like a champagne cork out of a bottle and slams the door behind him. His black cassock gets caught near the botSean of the door and I hear a ripping sound as Father Luke's footsteps echo and then become fainter and recede. I'm still kneeling and gaping at the grill. I go out to get John and he's not there. I find him outside sitting on a wall.

"All done," he says.

"Yer. I guess. Father Luke needs to get ready for mass."

"My dad says that confession is all a load of old bollocks."

"I asked him if he gets erections like everyone else."

"What'd he say," says John and jumps down from the wall. We walk out of the church yard.

"He ran out of the box."

"Figures. Hey. Let's go swimming."

"Last one in's a twat."

"You're on!"

We run along Gainsborough road as happy and cheerful as two larks singing in the morning. No worries, no stress, no religion, only childhood dreams and excitement. Slowly, gradually I sense I'm sorting things out in my mind and piece by piece discovering truths about life, nature, religion and God.

Slowly and gradually I'm undoing the strong linked chains of suppression that surround me and trap me inside the brainwashed box, the ignorant box, the lack of seeking happiness box. Slowly and gradually I'm realizing how to think on my own, to have my own views on how I want to live my life. I think myself extremely lucky to be able to see the world from a different viewpoint. I sense I am heading towards the truth.

And the *truth* shall set me free …

*

It's a beautiful day. At least 90 degrees. Rare for England, but some years we have a heat wave and take full advantage of it, at least the kids do. The older folks stay indoors sipping hot tea and cold drinks.

After the confession fiasco John and I make our way up to the quarry, our ranch. What a brilliant day for a swim in our own massive swimming pool not too far from our homes. The only other swimming pools we had ever seen were those in Hollywood movies, a universe or two away from the way normal poor folk live or exist. This clay-hole is our pool, our Hollywood, our luxurious way of living.

We dive in (last one in is a twat) and swim like excited dolphins to the other side. Beneath me I see those thick, tangled steel cables and wonder when someone is going to clear them out. But, as in the usual way with City councils, nothing ever gets done unless the community protests and the City worries about their name being dragged through the newspapers. It's the same everywhere, in every country, or so John's dad had said. Nothing changes in that department.

We relish the hot sun on our bodies. Our swimming trunks, when wet, weigh almost more than we do. The sides of the pool are piled high with earth and rock dug from the ground by the big excavator. I hear the whirring engine sound of the crane in the far distance.

"How long's your dad been a priest," I ask.

"He's a reverend, not a priest," says John. I think he sounds a little insulted.

"What's the difference, then?"

"Well, they can marry and have kids for one. Priests are celibate."

"Father Luke is okay," I say.

"All the others are twats."

We laugh, but deep down I sometimes wish my father was a reverend, and then he wouldn't have to shovel concrete all day.

"What you gonna do when you grow up, Josh?"

"Become a priest," I say.

We laugh as only young boys can: An innocent merriment that will lose its joy as we reach adulthood.

We doze for a while under the boiling sun. There's not a cloud in the sky. The whirring of the crane engine ceases. Two birds do a figure of eight high in the sky then soar away. Now silence except for the odd chirp from a passing bird. A slight breeze sweeps over me; it feels like a feather is tickling my body. Tiny ripples of light shimmer across the still water. *This* is paradise. *This* is my heaven.

I glance at John, the only friend that truly understands me, my soul mate, my guide, my best friend. He stands on the edge of the pool and glances back at me; I recognize something strange in his eyes, something innocent yet wise, maybe his soul, an old soul trying to warn me about something. He turns to the pool, stretches out his arms above his head and dives into the water.

It truly *is* a beautiful day.

*

"Kick 'im in the head," screams some kid standing above me. I'm on the ground in a grassy knoll not far from Our Lady's school. I had been fighting with some idiot during the afternoon break in the playground and a teacher had broken us up. God only knows why we were fighting, maybe he snarled at me, or I stuck my tongue out at him, didn't take much in this town to get battered around the head. And that's what the twat was doing now. I try to get up onto my knees but he keeps punching me in the face. Blood gushes out of my nose but I don't give up, I try to stand.

"Stay down, yer ejit," says the kid punching me, some Irish tough guy from Exeter estate. "Feck off," I yell at him.

As if this isn't enough some other tough guy decides to get in on the action and kicks me in the ribs. I go down again. This doesn't seem fair to me. I wait for another punch or kick when suddenly I hear a familiar voice.

"Leave him alone," shouts John at the two ejits.

"And what'll ye do," one of the ejits says.

Next instant I hear a couple of quick punches and yelps and look beside me to see the Exeter boys writhing on the ground. I feel a hand over mine and suddenly I'm pulled up off the grass.

"You okay, Josh?"

"Where'd you come from?"

"School bus broke down so we all had to walk home."

He hands me his handkerchief. "Come on. Let's get away from these twats."

John is stronger than I and now at least 6 inches taller. He's got broader shoulders and a thicker neck. He saved me. He protected me. Now that's what I call a true friend.

We walk in silence along Corporation street, down Forest Gate road and through the park at the botSean and up the hill to the town center. Not much of a center, blink and you're through it, but we only live about a mile from the town clock.

"Coming swimming Saturday," John says.

"Wouldn't miss it for anything."

"Are you alright. No dizziness or anything?"

"No. I'll be fine." I clear my throat. "John. Thanks."

He smiles and we head for home.

*

Chapter 12

Susan Bletchley is a pupil at Kingswood school a couple of miles away from our house. She is non-catholic. A 'heathen' as my mother would say, mind you, to her anyone who isn't a Catholic by birth is doomed to either purgatory, limbo or hell itself, no matter how good they are.

Anyway, I meet Susan while I'm down at the brook trying to catch newts and put them in a jam jar. John is on holiday with his parents at Butlins holiday camp somewhere up north. She comes up to me.

"What's your name, then?"

"Joshua."

"I'm Susan. What you doing?"

"Catching newts," I say.

"Can I join in?" She says in a squeaky, high-pitched voice.

"Alright," I say and hand her my jam jar. "Just pick 'em up with your hand and plonk 'em in the jar."

She dips her hand in the brook water, catches a newt and places it in the jar.

"What we do now?" she asks.

"Pour 'em back in the brook," I say and tip over the jar. The newts plop out and swim downstream, probably relieved at not having to spend the rest of their lives cooped up with each other in a glass container full of mucky water.

"You put them back?"

"Can't tie a leash on 'em and take 'em for a walk now can I?"

Susan giggles and I smile. I think she likes me.

"You're funny. I like you. Wanna fuck?"

I open my mouth to say something, but nothing comes out except expired air. Did she just say, "Wanna fuck?" She says it as if she's asking for a cup of tea and a plate of custard fecking creams.

With my mouth still hanging down to my chest she repeats the question. "A fuck. You know. Sex."

"I ... well, see I ..." I manage to stutter.

"You've never done it before, have you?" She giggles again. "You're a *virgin*."

"You mean like the *Holy Virgin?*"

"Don't know her. Does she go to Kingswood school?"

"She *is* Our Lady," I say incredulously. I assumed everyone knew about Our Lady. Obviously not.

"You're a virgin," she sings. "Virgin, virgin."

"I'm not one of them," I bark defensively.

"Have you had sex with a girl?"

"Well, erm … no."

"Then you're a virgin," she says and giggles. I wish she'd stop giggling.

"It's okay," she says in a soft, kind of motherly voice. "I'll be gentle with you."

I've never had sex before, though I've had sex education lessons at school which consisted of a red-faced Mrs. Gibson holding up an opened condom, showing us how to stretch it over a phallus-like piece of smooth wood created by Mr. Grant, our woodwork teacher, then explaining about sexually transmitted diseases and the need to wear a condom when having sexual relations with the opposite sex. In class all the boys looked over at the girls and all the girls quickly looked out the window, their faces turning redder by the second.

Susan takes my hand and walks me a few yards to a small bridge. She kneels down and unzips my shorts, takes my penis out, puts her red-lipstick-covered lips over my penis and begins to lick and suck, her head pushing forwards and backwards. I just stand here (my mouth open still) and don't know what to do until I begin to feel sexually aroused.

She turns around, bends over, pulls her flowery dress up around her buttocks, slides her pink knickers down and points a finger at a bunch of hair between her legs. "Fuck me in the vagina like you really mean it," she says.

I've never seen a vagina before, let alone a hairy one. I knew babies came out of them but I've never seen one so close up and it kind of scared me at first. It doesn't look very pretty to me, but I suppose they're not really for looking at.

So I slip my erection inside her (it's all kind of juicy, wet and slippery in there) and auSeanatically, naturally, fuck her like I really mean it. It is good. It is more than good. This is the first time I've experienced this and it feels wonderful, amazing. I overheard my father say to one of his friends down the Irish Club one day that, "You spend a few hours coming out of one and the rest of your fecking life trying to get back in!"

"Don't come," she says. "Stay still and let me wriggle."

I stand perfectly still (like a soldier standing to attention, though I *am* standing to attention in more ways than one) and still don't really understand why she wants to wriggle while I'm inside her but I soon find out why when she moves back and forth on my penis and starts to moan and groan and then yells.

"Shut up," I say, "Me mother'll fecking hear you."

The brook is only about twenty feet across the road from our house and mother's got ears like a cat on heat. She can hear anything. Her groaning and yelling echoes under the bridge and, if my mother hears Susan yell in ecstasy she'll no doubt come running across the road to investigate and see her son standing half-naked with a heathen stuck on the end of his prick, though she'd probably call her a tart (All girls not formally introduced to my mother are called tarts).
She slips off me and stands, pulls up her knickers. "You live across the street, don't you?"

"Well, yer, but me ma's making the tae."

"Making the what?"

"Tae, erm … tea, or dinner," I say. Susan must be English.

"You're Irish, then?"

"Yer. Is that a problem?"

"Irish boys turn me on," she says and licks her index finger and imitates sucking a lollipop, I think (I may be wrong).

"I could say you're from Our Lady's school and we're working on homework together."

"Sounds like a plan to me," she says and giggles, wipes her index finger on her dress, grabs my hand (I forget about the jam jars) and walks with me out from under the bridge, across the road, up the garden path, past the rose bushes and through the side entrance to my house.

"Ma," I say as we meet her in the kitchen. She is cooking a Dublin Coddle and it smells delicious. "This is Susan from school. She's helping me with my homework."

Mother gives her the quick once over. Usually mothers know immediately (maybe they can smell them) what a girl is like just by one quick glance. It must have been one of her off days today, either that or she's got a cold, because she nods her approval of Susan.

"That's nice," mother says, "But tell me, Josh. Since when have you ever had homework?"

"Just this week, ma. We gotta study prehistoric animals."

"You better study yer father in that case," she says and laughs. I think for a moment she's going to embarrass me in front of Susan with her long enduring Irish laugh, but we're spared the hysterical hyena laugh this time.

"Coddle smells nice, ma," I say as I lead Susan upstairs. She pinches my botSean as we climb.

"Thank you son," she says. "Yer tae won't be long."

I don't think *I'll* be long either as we rush into the bedroom. By the time I have my shorts off and thrown to the floor, Susan is stark naked, lying on my bed and has her legs spread open and pointed to the ceiling.

Susan Bletchley literally sucks me in and blows me out in bubbles, as the saying goes. Of course later on I find out she liked variety in her boys, and one day while up the woods Susan decides to fuck most of the boys in the football team (soccer) that happens to be playing near the woods that evening. I have her first, then she keeps saying, 'Who's next,' and I think, well, feck this, I'm done.

I exit the woods (leaving Susan the nymphomaniac with the football team) and walk home taking a short cut over the football fields. I see two little dogs chasing each other around the goal posts.

The white mutt has a leg missing and is doing a good job chasing the black mutt who doesn't have a leg missing.

I stoop and pet them. I wonder how I can sneak these two into my house. My father doesn't like dogs, or doesn't like spending his hard earned money on feeding them, so I could hide them in the shed at the top of our garden. Mother won't mind, I'm sure.

So I pick up the one-legged dog, little cute-looking mutt and name him Clyde and the black mutt I call Bonnie, after the infamous American bank robbers. I walk around the side of the house, sneak through the side gate and put the dogs in the shed. Later, after tea, I sneak a blanket and some food out of the house and sit with them in the shed in the company of cobwebs, spiders, daddy-long legs, (lanky spiders) beetles, centipedes and ants.

Mother thinks I'm up at John's house (I didn't tell her he's on holiday, it would only get her started on why *himself* never takes us on any type of holiday whatsoever) so I stay with the dogs 'till late, pass by my mother on the way to bed (she's snoozing in the living room) then bring them a little food first thing in the morning before I light the coal fire and begin my paper round.

Bonnie and Clyde are brilliant dogs. They sleep in the shed while I'm at school, wait patiently for me to come home and sneak them some food and water. (I tell mother about the dogs. She's on my side, anything to get back at *himself*). Mother, bless her, even nips down to the corner shop – in her pink, frayed slippers – to buy a tin of dog food. I think she feels sorry for Clyde and his missing leg. Maybe she knew a dog one time with only three legs? After feeding I tie two pieces of thin rope around their necks (makeshift leashes) and take them out for a walk. Of course father won't be home from Manchester until Friday night, so I have a few days of freedom with the dogs.

John came home from Butlins on Wednesday, so I decide to show him my new friends.

"Cute little things, ain't they?" John rubs their backs.

"This one I called Clyde and the other one is Bonnie."

"Bonnie and Clyde," says John. "Just like the film. What happened to his leg?"

"Who knows," I say and wish I did know.

"What's your da say about it?"

"He doesn't know yet. I'm hiding them in the shed."

"Your da's going to go apeshit when he finds out."

"Let's take them swimming," John says excitedly.

"Can he swim with only three legs."

"Probably swim round in circles." We laugh and together head over to the quarry. Today it is hot.

We reach the clay-hole and dive in. Bonnie and Clyde stand on the bank and look curiously at us. "Come on," I say. "Get yourselves in here. It's great." I whistle at them.

Clyde jumps in first, sinks below the surface then emerges panting and doggie-paddling like crazy. John's correct. Clyde can't swim in a straight line and keeps going round in circles. Still, he seems to be having fun.

At Our Lady's school we had a 'drama' class one afternoon that entailed the pupils acting out the roles of Bonnie and Clyde. Didn't make much sense to me all the stretching and rolling on the floor and knees up to the chest while Miss Young (wearing a tracksuit) spread her legs in the air and crossed them over numerous times. What that had to do with Bonnie and Clyde I'll never know nor understand. Still, it gave us something to pass the time until the bell went for home-time (sweetest sound of my life).

We dry ourselves and are drenched again when the dogs decide to vigorously shake their bodies. Walking back to the house is pleasant enough but it's far too hot. Must be eighty-five in the shade, usually folks won't leave their houses if the temperature rises above eighty. It gets very humid here, too. Sticky and yucky.

John pats the dogs and waves goodbye to me as I stroll down the hill toward my house, Bonnie and Clyde either side of me, walking slowly (Clyde hobbling slowly) but they seem content and happy. I'm content and happy with my two new friends, my companions. These dogs I sense love me and I in turn love them. I feel, in a way, free of any stress, of the constraints of religion, of my mother's nagging, my father's indifference. These tiny dogs make me feel kind of wanted; they accept me for what I am and don't expect anything in return. I sometimes wish people were more like dogs and give unconditional love.

I reach the side entrance of my house. Bonnie and Clyde whimper. Clyde barks once. I look behind me and see my father walking up the garden path, a look of rage on his sun-burnt face. He must've left work early.

He walks in and sees me with the two dogs. "No dogs allowed in my house," he barks at me and grabs Bonnie. "You can keep the cripple, this one has to go."

Father storms back out the door carrying Bonnie. Clyde whimpers.

I stroke little Clyde and hug him into my chest, swaying a little with him as you would a baby. "I'm sorry, little Clyde. I'm sorry."

*

(One Boy and his Dog)

Dogs don't reason, they react. Birds fly, fish swim, dogs need to walk. I learn all this in Mrs. Gibson's class. It helps me understand Clyde. Give them discipline. They look to the leader of a pack for guidance and security. An owner is the leader of the pack. Don't confuse excitement in a dog for satisfaction. Dogs need to walk for their mental and physical wellbeing. I try to remember all this.

Clyde and I are getting on like roast potatoes and gravy. We walk as often as is possible, usually after school, then back home for 'tae' and back out again to roam the warm summer nights.

I stroll through the woods at the back of my house with Clyde on a leash. He seems to be managing walking on three legs, but I know not to walk too far. I pass the spot where Susan dropped her knickers for the soccer team. I smile, shake my head and walk on. I often wonder what had happened to Bonnie.

Oak trees stand tall either side of the path with elms and firs further back. Lush grass grows between the trees with a little sprinkling of daisies and buttercups in-between.

And then I spot a small black dog under an elm tree twenty feet or so from the path. It's Bonnie. I run over followed by Clyde and kneel down to inspect the whimpering dog.

"Hey, Bonnie, ssshhh, now. You'll be fine."

Bonnie barely lifts its head; she licks my palm. Clyde hobbles up and licks her face, excited to see his sister.

"Let's get you sorted out, eh," I lift her in my arms. "There's a nice cozy shed waiting for you at home."

I hide Bonnie in the shed. Mother comes out and takes a look at the dog and almost bursts into tears. "The poor wee thing," she says. "Curse that father of yours. No heart, I say. He's got no heart at all."

She cares for the dog while I attend school. Every day I rush back home to be with Bonnie and Clyde.

Mother feeds and keeps the dogs warm. She even gives them a bath in a small tub and disinfects Bonnie's scrapes and sores.

I watch as she sits beside Bonnie and for hours strokes his neck and the back of his head. Every day she does this until after the sixth day, Bonnie stands and wags its tail and jumps up onto Mother's lap.

I'm surprised at my mother. She holds back her affection, care and love for me yet lets it overwhelm her and shows it all to Bonnie, a dog.

Such is the human soul, I guess.

*

Chapter 13

I don't like Our Lady's school. Hate all the teachers except Mr. & Mrs. Gibson. He is an English teacher, a laid back, ex-hippie kind of guy who smokes cigarettes in class (great example to his pupils) but he's a good teacher nonetheless.

"What do you want to be when you grow up," he asks me in class one day.

"A man," I reply.

"Ah, a comedian in our midst."

"Rogers. What about you?"

"I wanna join the circus."

"You're already in the circus," pipes in someone from the rear. Usually the bullies sit in the back row.

"You all have to look forward," says Mr. Gibson. "Study and learn as much as you can. Education is the key to the future. I mean, who really wants to work for the council collecting trash?"

"My dad does," says Peter in the front row.

"And you want to follow in his footsteps?"

"He gets good money, smells a little bit, but he says he's happy. At least he's got a job." Peter shoots a glance at Liam across from him. Liam's dad is unemployed and most people consider him unemployable seeing that he's a fully blown alcoholic. Liam stares straight ahead.

"Now, now, we'll have no condemnation in my class."

"Sir," Susan, a tiny blonde girl asks. "What's condemnation?"

"Something that mists up your windows," someone in the back row says.

"Class is full of comedians," says Mr. Gibson. "It's where you put someone down or accuse someone of something."

"Sir," asks Seamus, a boy far too big for his age with muscles to match.

"What great piece of wisdom will we gather today from your lips," says Mr. Gibson, lighting up another cigarette and putting his feet up on his desk (another great example to the sponge-like minds of youth).

"My dad says the only thing he learned to do at school was fight."

"That isn't quite …"

"And the school he went to in Glasgow was real tough."

"I think times have changed since your father's day, Seamus, don't you think?"

"The teachers had to carry knifes to protect themselves."

Everyone laughs and a red-faced Mr. Gibson sits upright and changes his tone. "Open your books at chapter 29. 'How to construct and write a correct sentence."

We always have a bit of fun with him at the start of the lesson but I suspect it's because he needs to smoke before the teaching really begins. Still I like him with his long beard and short nose, thick lips and bald patch at the top of his head. I suppose I really like him because he's married to the music teacher, and that lesson is immediately after this one.

Music and I seem to have fallen for each other. And it's more the traditional type of sounds I prefer like Irish traditional and World music. I can't be doing with all this noisy rock and roll stuff, except of course, the Beatles.

I look forward to the two lessons we have with Mrs. Gibson every week. I think, out of everything, it's her who, by just being her, gives me the inspiration to attend Our Lady's school. Mrs. Harrison had given me the inspiration to attend St Patrick's school.

Anyway, she's pretty and has long, mousy-colored hair, green eyes and high cheekbones. Her lips are a healthy pink and full. She has a full and shapely botSean. I sometimes scribble her features in my exercise book as she plays the piano.

When Mrs. Gibson crouches down to pick up her pen from the floor, lust rushes through my veins. I feel a little ashamed gazing over at her knees and thighs and, when she almost slips to the floor and grabs the side of her piano, and thereby displaying the tops of her thighs and pink knickers, I almost faint with pleasure.

I look around the class and all the boys are sitting at their desks with open mouths. One boy even has saliva dripping down his chin. I don't think Mrs. Gibson means to show off her underwear but we are all the better for it.

The following day she plays an Irish air on the piano for our entertainment and, most probably is carried away by the beauty and passion of the tune because she closes her eyes and sways slowly from side to side.

We can see straight under the piano and her mini-skirt (all the fashion) had crept up to the tops of her thighs and there is that sight again, but this time she's wearing white knickers with thin black lacing around the edge (at least we know she changes her underwear every day).

Suddenly, twelve pencils drop to the floor and twelve heads (the girls in the class giggle, some shake their heads, a couple put their hands over their eyes and one girl stares along with the boys) duck beneath the tables to get a better view of Mrs. Gibson's beautiful legs and white, black-laced knickers.

It makes our day. School is the most boring experience of my life and, talking to my friends in the playground we all agree that the only thing we look forward to at school is Mrs. Gibson and the excitement of not only noticing her underwear, but what kind of underwear she wears each time we take her class.

"I counted about twenty different colors of knickers," says Seamus, his eyes gleaming with young lust.

"That means she owns twenty pairs of knickers," I reply.

"How can you be so sure," asks Tiny Tim who is taller than all of us.

"Lookit here," says Seamus and shoves a notebook in Tiny Tim's face.

"Every lesson I write what color her knickers are. And after a month she starts to wear the knickers again from last month."

Tiny Susan, chewing gum, passes by. "You lot are perverts. "Disgusting perverts."

"What color knickers you got on today, Sue," says Seamus, brazen as ever.

"Wouldn't *you* like to know," she replies and struts away, her ass now wiggling more than usual.

"Probably can't afford any," says Tiny Tim, the king of sarcasm.

"Fuck you," says Susan and gives him the birdie.

"Suck my dick," says Tiny Tim.

"I would if I could find it," says Susan and wiggles her little finger at him. "I heard there's a maggot dangling between your legs. And they don't call you Tiny Tim because of your height."

Tiny Tim opens his mouth to say something but nothing reaches the air but a gasp.

We all glance at him and he shrugs his shoulders. "What do girls know about it, anyway."

In the music class there is a penny whistle in the key of D that folks think originated from Ireland but in fact it's an English instrument and had been played on the old ships a-sailing around the world when Britain ruled everyone and everything that either walked, crawled, breathed or tried to breathe.

Mrs. Gibson plays a little tune on it and, although she can play the piano better she is quite good bad on the whistle. I soon perfect the breathing and tonguing techniques needed to control the air flow of the whistle and start my very first tune, *The Minstrel Boy*, an Irish song.

Mrs. Gibson gives me encouragement and inspires me to learn more tunes on the whistle. I hate school but I love music. The freedom of music. The beauty of the soul of music. Music will save my soul.

I'm allowed to take the penny whistle home for Easter. We have a week off from school. I sit in the shed with the dogs (when da is down the Irish club) and play them what I know. Bonnie and Clyde seem to like my playing because they howl along with me.

The next day, Saturday, while my father is again at the Irish Club drinking his brains out, I decide to take the dogs for a walk uptown.

"Ah, bless his wee soul," says an old woman standing under the town hall clock. She stoops and strokes little Clyde's fur. "What happened to the poor mite's leg?"

"I don't know," I say. "I found him like this."

"It's God's will, for sure," she says and blesses herself. "Ye were meant to find him and care for him."

I half-smile having heard this kind of tripe a million times from my mother every time some incident happens (or doesn't happen.) It was always 'God's will,' always some unseen deity who saves someone from a car wreck, from a storm at sea, from a bullet missing them by inches, or someone who dies in a car wreck (it's God's will, I tell yer). The human race will believe in anything to justify its existence, to fill in its deep feeling of insecurity, to fulfill the ridiculous religious dogma of having to live a difficult and miserable life on earth in order to be saved and receive their just or unjust reward in some imagined haven they call paradise.

"And who is this?" says the old woman.

"That's his sister, Bonnie."

"And she *is* Bonnie, too," she says in a high-pitched voice as if talking to a baby. "A Bonnie wee lass and all."

The town center is packed with shoppers and mothers dragging screaming kids around by the arms in and out of grocery stores and clothes shops and Woolworths. I like Woolworths because every day walking home from Our Lady's school I'd pass through the town center and into Woolworths and buy two pennies worth of broken biscuits which are the leftovers or crumbled pieces they can't sell. Anyway, I'd get my big bag and munch on them all the way home, as happy as a dog in a butcher's shop.

Today I'm going to a pet store to buy some dog food. The dogs have been eating mother's greasy bacon, sausage and egg-breakfasts the past week and are getting fat. "It'll make his other legs stronger," she said after placing a plate of her morning special in front of Clyde.

"Ma," I had replied. "He'll get too fat to walk anywhere, legs or no legs."

I walk into the pet store and smell the stench of hamsters and rabbits. Lined along the wall is glass tanks filled with all kinds of tropical lizards and snakes and frogs and little hairy crawly things.

I pass a green and yellow parrot sitting on its wooden perch. "What you want. What you want," it squawks at me. I approach it and whisper near its ear, "*Fuck off.*"

The parrot frowns at me as I go up to the assistant and ask if there is any good dog food, especially for Clyde because he is missing a leg.

The assistant, a balding man of fifty or so, grimaces and says, "He still has three other legs."

"He did have four," I say.

"And now he has three. Great school you went to."

He shakes his head. "Here," says the assistant, taking a bag of food from a shelf behind him. "Feed him this once, and only once a day." He then hands me a couple of tins of 'Chappie' with a color image of a smiling and healthy Labrador on the front of the can. "There's good minerals in this one. That'll be one and six, please."

I take out a load of my saved-up pennies and place them on the counter. The assistant counts them, penny by penny, looking at them closely as if I'd just made them that morning in the hot forge in my back garden.

Our currency can be confusing. 'One and six' is 1s 6p, or one shilling and six pennies. There is twelve pennies in a shilling and twenty shillings in a pound. There is the farthing, which is a ¼ penny, a ha'penny, (half penny) three pence or (thruppenny bit) pronounced 'thrupence.' Sixpence (a silver coin also called a 'tanner'), 1 florin (a medieval silver English coin) which equals 2 shillings; a half crown equals 2 shillings and 6 pennies. 1 Crown equals 5 shillings; 1 Pound equals 20 shillings (240 pennies) and 1 sovereign is a gold coin valued at 1 pound.

I like the slang names for our money. Penny is a 'copper.' A shilling is a 'Bob.' A guinea is called a 'yellow boy,' and is a coin made of gold from the Guinea coast of Africa and is worth 21 shillings, which is a pound and 1 shilling. 5 pounds is a 'fiver,' (in Cockney slang it's 'Lady Godiva'). 10 pounds is a 'tenner.' 20 pounds is a 'pony.' 50 pounds is 'half a ton.' 100 pounds is a 'ton.' 500 pounds is a 'monkey,' and 1000 pounds is a 'grand.'

"You're a penny short," says the grumpy assistant.

I search deep in my pockets and, in a tiny corner in my left pocket (I keep my pennies in the left pocket because the right side has a big hole in it. Mother says I use that hole to play with myself when I'm bored.) I find a single penny and hand it to the reincarnated soul of Ebenezer Scrooge.

"Thank you," he says begrudgingly, as if I should present him with a crown instead of a penny for his unique salesmanship and knowledge of canines.

"Come on, Clyde, let's go feed you."

I'm more than happy to be leaving this store with all these reptiles and snakes glaring at me as I walk. I open the door, look at the parrot and give him the birdie.

"*Fuck off*," squawks the parrot. I rush out the door dragging poor little Clyde and Bonnie behind me and swear I'll never step foot in that place again.

*

Clyde loves the dog food. I'm lying on the couch watching an episode of 'Star Trek.' Captain Kirk yet again fights another strange looking alien and beats him. I wish I could be transported to another world, another existence where I could journey around space and meet strange looking aliens and fight and beat them. Or even travel back in time to see how my ancestors used to live. "Yer head is always in the clouds," my mother would say on occasion. I wish.

Clyde finishes his meal, licks his lips and jumps up onto my chest. His breath is foul so I push his head away and he turns around and lies on my torso. Bonnie is eating her food in the shed just in case my father walks in.

I stroke his coat and he gives out a little happy whimper. I lie here and watch the USS Enterprise zap into warp drive and zoom away through space.

Bonnie runs into the living room and jumps up on me. The dogs start licking each other and seem excited to be back together again. Mother must have let Bonnie out of the shed. "Have her back in the shed before yer father comes home otherwise ye'll have to use yon bible again to cover yer arse."

How does she know about me using the bible as protection for my buttocks? Maybe she spotted the heavy book missing from the botSean of the dresser? I've come to the conclusion that not only do mothers' know best, but they damn near know *everything*.

"Don't forget," says mother, now standing in the doorway and drying her hands on a dishcloth, "dentist at four." She looks at the dogs scrambling around the living room floor, pulling a sock between their snarled lips. She smiles and shakes her head. "You taking me, ma?" Her smile suddenly vanishes.

"Well, who else is here to take yer. Yer father wouldn't bother his arse. Wouldn't even take meself when I needed me teeth taken out. The bastard."

I pick Bonnie up and take her back to the shed just in case my da arrives back from the Irish club early.

Mother, Clyde and I walk to the bus stop and pass John's house on the way. "Can you take care of Clyde for a while," I ask John who is doing nothing in particular except watching TV. " I have to go to the dentist."

"We can watch Star-trek together," he says and takes the leash (still a piece of twangy old string (didn't have enough pennies to buy a proper leash at the pet shop). "He'll be safe with me, Josh."

"Thanks," I say and glance through the front door and into the living room. I spot a pair of crossed legs on a couch facing the TV. Nice legs, too, and she's wearing a thigh-high skirt.

John follows my gaze. "Oh, that's me new girlfriend. Wanna meet her?"

"Na, we need to get to the dentists."

"Wisdom teeth?"

"Yer," I say and smile at him. He smiles back.

"Have fun."

Not my idea of fun going to the dentist, but John means well. I'm lucky to have such a great friend, even if he has found a girlfriend.

Dentist is an Irishman from Limerick. Hi. Sit there. Heard the joke about the guy goes to the dentist (not this one) and the dentist checks him out and says, well, young man, your teeth are perfect, but your gums have to come out." He laughs and I try to but can't with his pliers in my mouth.

After he pulls my two botSean wisdom teeth out, he says, "Some ice cream and rest is best.

We get off the bus and walk home. I'm feeling a little wheezy after being gassed half to death at the dentist. Mother waits outside John's house as I knock on his door. There's no answer; Probably still out walking little Clyde. I shrug my shoulders and walk with mother to our house. We walk into the kitchen and see my father sitting at the dining room table with little Bonnie in his arms.

*

Mother and John stand each side of me; father stands above the grave with a shovel in his hand. Clyde is wrapped in a few black plastic bags. I kneel down and pick him up, then slowly lower him into the grave. Father dug the hole in the center of his rose bushes, saying that when I look at the roses and see that they've grown and blossomed so well, it's due to Clyde. I think that was a nice thing to say, something he had to say - his kind of eulogy.

Mother quietly weeps and John lowers his head.

"Goodbye Clyde," I say and can't say anything else. I don't want the others to see me cry, I'll do my grieving in bed later.

Father steps into the kitchen and brings out little Bonnie is his arms. He hands the dog to me and starts to fill the grave. I guess I'm allowed to keep Bonnie now that Clyde has gone from my life.

"He'll find his missing leg in heaven," mother says and weeps some more. For once I have to agree with her, not that I believe in heaven, but for Clyde's sake, I want there to be a doggy heaven so he *can* find his missing leg.

"It's God's will," says mother and goes inside.

*

I don't blame John for Clyde's death, far from it. I tell him not to blame himself; Just one of those things that can't be predicted. Dogs get hit by cars all the time. He takes it bad, though. He stops calling round for me to go swimming and when I call on him, he is never there, gone out with his new girlfriend, according to his giant witch of a mother.

Deeds can't be undone, words can't be unsaid. A marred friendship can never be the same.

*

I spend more time out of school than in school. It isn't anyone's fault, no one forces me to stay away, no one advises me to experience other things rather than turn up for school lessons five days a week. No. I make the decision to become a truant, if that's the right word. As I said earlier I hated school. I think I was born that way - maybe it's got something to do with my heritage and having gypsy genes on my father's side. Always the itchy feet; always wanting to try new things; always wanting to move, to travel.

I meet Sam O'Neil in Pope John's school (Our Lady's school now a memory, thank God). He has just turned fifteen like myself and is a happy soul and a bit of a gypsy, too. We have something in common, we both hate school. His father is Irish and hails from Donegal, hence his big mop of dark curly hair.

*

Chapter 14

We decide to save money (steal it from wherever) and walk to the town center and catch the 292 or 295 bus to Kettering, the next town about seven miles west of Corby. To raise cash for our adventures I'd sneak into my da's bedroom on a Saturday night (he'd be blind drunk from bingeing down the Irish club) and quietly go through his pockets, take out a few coins and a pound note or two and sneak back out. I wasn't worried if mother caught me because one night, not too long ago, I went to the toilet and happened to look at the open door of my mother's room, and there she was going through his pockets. I doubt whether she was looking for love letters or condoms but rather stealing the money he kept back from her.

Anyway, this fine sunny summer day Sam and I reach the town center bus terminal, excited and wearing mischievous smiles on our faces ready for today's adventure, whatever that may be.

"I still think we should have gone for a jog," says Sam. Sam is a lot fitter than I will ever be. He loves to run, especially in the rain. The more it rains the faster he runs and the longer he runs.

"You should've been born a fish," I say.

"You not fancy it. We could run on Saturday."

"How do you know it'll rain on Saturday?"

"It rains every day, Josh."

"I'd rather play football."

"Ah, suit yourself, then."

We are still in school uniform (we hadn't as yet worked out how to pack our normal clothes and where to change) and board the 292 bus to Kettering. We like this particular bus because the conductor is an Irishman and a bit of a comic. He makes our trips enjoyable. It seems as if he hasn't got a care in the world. He sings while he goes around the bus, upstairs and downstairs (smokers upstairs) and always makes us laugh.

I hear singing coming up the stairs. "Oh Danny boy, the pipes the pipes are cal-hor-ling, from glen to glen and down the mountainside … Ah, the gypsy boys are back. How are yer, boys. Isn't it a fine day for a bus ride, now?"

"Hi, Paddy," I say, "how they hanging?"

"Oh now ye'll have to be asking the wife about that, Josh. She'll know for sure." We laugh.

"Two returns to Kettering is it, lads?"

I hand over 1s 6p and he rolls a little handle on his ticket machine strapped around his neck. "There ye go. Keep them tickets safe."

"Thanks, Paddy," I say.

"Where is it today, lads? The Museum of Modern art; The reference section of the main library; Or the World War Two memorial park?"

"Na," says Sam. "Wicksteed Park."

"Ah. Fish and chips, ice-cream and bumper cars?"

"It's great there," says Sam.

"I used to hitch it from school in Ireland," says Paddy. "Mind you I had good reason to hitch it. Most of us kids did back then. See, the place was run by nuns and let me tell yer, boys, those nuns were perverted, cruel and mean bitches. I hated the place. No school for me, I said, time to fly the coop and travel."

The bus stops and some girls get on and climb the stairs. "Tickets please. Have yer money ready and if you haven't got any, God bless you, 'cause you'll need to get off my bus. Tickets please."

Paddy sways his way to the back seats where two girls sit giggling at each other.

"Two returns to Kettering please," says one of the girls with a high-pitched voice.

"Now what would two little lovelies like yerselves be doing going to Kettering during school time?"

"It's ... erm ... half term," says the other girl calmly.

"Thought it was half term last week?" says Paddy.

"That was the Catholics. We're Protestants. Different, see."

"And what's your name and telephone number," says Paddy, "so I can phone up your mother and tell her what you're up to?"

"Ain't got a telephone."

"Only joking," says Paddy and laughs. "What happens on the 292 bus stays on the 292 bus."

"Huh?"

"Her name's Madge," says her good-looking friend.

"What's in a name, "says Paddy. "A rose by any other name would smell just as sweet."

"Yer wha?" squeaks Madge.

"That's a little Shakespeare for you," says Paddy. "A great Irish poet."

"Does he live in Corby?"

Sam and I laugh out loud. "Shakespeare is from Scotland," says Sam.

"Really," I say. "My ma says he's from Dublin."

"There you are," says Paddy. "I was right."

"Actually," says the pretty girl, "Shakespeare was born in Stafford-upon-Avon, in the county of Warwickshire. He's an Englishman."

Silence except for the rumbling of the bus along the main road.

"I bet his mother was Irish," says Paddy. He clears his throat. "Listen girls," he attempts to speak with an educated English accent. "Education is very important. I used to love school, never missed a day in fifteen years. Our teachers were highly educated and also very friendly and guided us through our studies. I never played truant at all. Not once, do yer hear. Not *once*."

Sam and I look at each other and frown.

"Then why you a bus conductor then?" says Madge. "Why ain't you a doctor or somit?"

Paddy switches back to his Irish accent and says with a little sadness in his voice, "Me old mother died a week after me father and two weeks after both me grandparents immigrated to Australia. I was adopted by a poor English family."

"Oh," the girls say simultaneously."

"He should be on TV," I say.

"Not to worry," he chirps. "I'm as happy as a dog in shite."

He turns around to us and winks; then sways off toward the staircase and downstairs to collect fares from his other passengers. He sings, "Oh, the monkey and the kitten were playing in the grass and the monkey stuck his finger up the fecking kitten's arse!"

The girls roar with laughter and Sam and I join in.

"What a nut job," says Sam.

No one really knows the full history of Paddy McCauley, whether he attended a nun's school in Ireland, why and how he became a bus conductor, or if he had a wife and family, no one knew, but most importantly, the man has the ability (it's a personnel skill, for sure) to turn a sad situation into a merry one and make everyone he speaks to go home with a smile on their face. *It's the giving that makes you what you are* and, in Paddy's case, he gives everything to make people laugh and smile.

We reach the edge of town and leave the housing estates behind us. I see a small dragline crane in the distance above the hilly mounds of the quarries. I quickly think of John and our blissful days swimming in those clay-holes during hot summer days. Our personal ranch. Maybe we will one day become good friends again.

Sam and I slink down in our seats as the bus passes Pope John School and drives up a hill toward the main road to Kettering. I sneak a look out of the bus window and see my classroom just beyond the school yard. Through the class window I see Mrs. Gibson holding something in her hand and obviously showing it to her class (probably a sex education class for the third year students). Each school starts off its student classification at the age they start that school so senior school begins at Our Lady's and ends at Pope John's and starts at age eleven which is the first year seniors, Pope John's school starts at aged thirteen which is third year students, and if you leave school at age fifteen you are a fifth year student. If you choose to stay on at school you are a sixth year student or belong to the sixth form. These are the brainiest kids and usually go on to college until aged eighteen and then the main universities for four years or so and get all the best paid jobs and, as my father often said, "They end up as rich as royalty with not a penny's worth of common sense among any of 'em."

So it's kept simple – senior third year is thirteen years of age and so on.

The bus chugs up the hill and passes Kingswood school (I quickly think of Susan Bletchley), down the other side and reaches the main road, turns right and heads toward Kettering. The two girls sit behind us.

"Where you two going, then," asks Madge with the squeaky high-pitched voice.

"Wicksteed Park," I say.

"Can we come, too," says the pleasant sounding one.

I turn round. She has greenish-blue eyes and hair the color of peaches. "It should be fun," I say and blush.

She stands and asks Sam if they can swap seats. Sam obliges, though reluctantly.

I hear a familiar voice from the botSean deck. "Oh, the monkey and the kitten were playing bag-and-tell and the monkey told the kitten to go to fecking hell."

If mother was here she'd be laughing her head off already.

"He's so funny," says the quiet-spoken girl.

"What's your name?" I ask and sit upright.

"Saffron," she says and smiles. "And yours?"

"Joshua," I say. I like this girl. I like her very much.

"You got a girlfriend?"

"Erm ... No."

"Do you want a girlfriend?"

"I ... erm ... I don't know." And I don't know because I've never had a girlfriend before, not a proper girlfriend that takes her time and doesn't give me a blow job under a bridge just after meeting her and drops her knickers to her knees five minutes later.

"You don't know or you don't want a girlfriend?"

She's persistent, for sure, this one.

"Yes. Will you be my girlfriend?"

"No."

"Oh," I feel deflated.

"I've got a boyfriend," Saffron says and quickly kisses me on the lips. "Though maybe not for long."

Paddy walks up the center aisle. "You three are a right pair if ever I saw one."

"Huh," says Sam.

"It's a joke," says Paddy. Listen. " Seamus goes to the doctor and the doctor says, 'I can't diagnose your trouble, Seamus. It must be the drink.' 'Oh, that's alright doctor, I'll come back Seanorrow when you're sober.'"

"And there's more. Listen. Paddy comes out of the dentist after getting all his teeth pulled. 'Never again, he says.'"

"Ah, Paddy," says Sam. "Will yer stop, I'm about to pee me pants."

"One more. 'What's wrong with Murphy, says Liam. 'I don't know. Yesterday he swallowed a spoon and he hasn't stirred since.'"

To think we've got another five miles of this to put up with.

"Mickey goes to the doctors and says …"

*

Wicksteed Park is a haven for truant kids. I don't understand why the truant-catchers haven't realized this and thrown nets around our squirming bodies, dump us onto open-backed trucks and carted us back to school like sheep being herded to market.

Still, it's fun in the park with its soccer fields and flower beds and benches and bandstands and brass music, fare rides and bumper cars and swing parks and ice-cream parlors and food stalls and amusement arcades. Today is extra special because there is a travelling fair in town.

"I want to go on the waltzer ," says Madge.

Sam obliges, dips into his pocket and pays the attendant. Off they go as Saffron and I stand back and watch them spin round in the waltzer. A fair attendant who looks like a typical gypsy with long black hair, an ear-ring in each ear and chewing gum stands behind the waltzer and travels with it as it circles and turns and then grabs hold of the metal top and spins it faster. I've been on one of them and it's amazing.

"Fancy the Ferris wheel," Saffron says.

"It's very high."

"Chicken?" She taunts.

We get on the Ferris wheel seat (made for two) and begin to ascend, stopping every few seconds to allow other people to get on down below. And then off we go. Up high and I see the bus station in the distance and the tops of terraced houses and the park itself. I see Sam and squeaky Madge being swung around almost at the speed of light in their waltzer. Sam is laughing, his companion is screaming.

We stop at the top of the ride, something has obviously stopped the wheel from turning; maybe someone hasn't got the correct change. Saffron, without as much as a 'how do you do,' kisses me on the mouth. I close my eyes and relish her sweet breath.

I could never approach a girl at school and ask her for a date. And now I play truant and don't ask a girl for a date and a girl kisses me.

*

Chapter 15

I call on John. He ceased being my friend because of Clyde's death, but I hold no grudge against him. Maybe he feels guilty? But I have to make up with him, I feel sad not being with him and swimming in the quarry.

I knock on his front door a few times. The door opens and standing there is John, a big smile on his face. "Josh. How you bin?"

"Great. Fancy a trip down town?"

"Is the Pope a Catholic?" (akin to 'Do bears shit in the woods.')

"What about your girlfriend?"

"She can come, too," says John, turns and walks into the living room. He emerges holding his girlfriend's hand. My mouth drops open and my heart almost stops.

"Saffron, this is Joshua."

John looks happy and excited as we walk along Gainsborough road toward the turn-off to town. He holds Saffron's hand and they laugh and giggle about something. I walk behind them.

"Hey, Josh," says John turning around. "Why you behind us?"

"Three's a crowd, yer know."

"Not at all," he says and hugs me around the shoulders. "Come on. You're part of the team."

I feel happier now that I'm included in their company, though I do feel a negativity emanating from Saffron. Maybe she feels ashamed because of the kiss she'd given me on the Ferris wheel, or another kiss on the bus ride back to Corby. After getting off the bus at the station she didn't say goodbye; she just walked away without a word. Maybe she was ashamed of what she had done behind John's back. Or maybe kissing and hugging me in a town seven miles from Corby, somehow made it okay to be unfaithful to John, and when she returned to her home town, the rules of fidelity came back into play. Obviously John doesn't know what had happened between us – he would have said something about it by now.

We reach the town center, a main pedestrian walkway down the center with various stores each side. You can hold your breath walking through the town center and still have plenty of air left in your lungs by the time you reach the end.

"Anyone for ice-cream," John says. "My treat."

"99 for me," I say.

"Same here," says Saffron.

There is an awkward few moments between us when John enters the ice-cream parlor. A silence that fills the air with expectation; there is a palpable sexual tension, like an invisible magnet forcing us together. Our wrists touch, a sensation like a tiny electrical shock tingles up my arm. She looks at me, stares into my eyes. I see now the spark in her greenish-blue eyes. I like her. I want her. God, I think I love her. She kisses me softly on the lips, squeezes my hand and walks over to the parlor window just as John alights with three ice-creams.

"Three 99's," he says and hands out the ices.

We saunter through the town center on this pleasant sunny day. Not a drop of rain anywhere, which is a miracle in this country. The town clock strikes two. It's a weird looking clock with a circular background festooned with stars and planets that spin continuously.

"Top of the morning to yer," I say as Paddy, the singing-comedic bus conductor approaches. He's holding a child's hand and walking beside him is a red-haired woman.

"And the rest of the afternoon to yerself," says Paddy and smiles.

"Nice day for a murder," I say.

"Oh, it's a grand day for a murder," replies Paddy. The Irish and their humor are closely related. We create all kinds of stupid and meaningless things to say to each other; it's our way to break the ice upon meeting someone, or to help make someone feel better or cheer them up by having them either laugh or frown at our jokes and sayings. But Irish folks don't take themselves seriously and most of the time take the 'Mickey' (take the piss, extract the urine, wind someone up) out of themselves and others.

We had a humanities lesson at school about what not to say to Irish folks if on holiday in Ireland, though my father told me most of it anyway. The teacher told us that there are certain things a tourist should *not* say (and they do). Don't speak in a phony Irish accent. Don't mention Leprechauns and pots of gold. Irish people *don't* eat corned beef and cabbage - restaurants have it on their menus for tourists. Don't compare food or drink to your own country. Do buy a round of drinks if there is some locals in the pub (usually each person buys a round of drinks for friends and family), don't talk about politics. Irish folks are democrats and liberals. Do *not*, I repeat, do *not* order those American drinks called 'An Irish Car Bomb' or a 'Black & Tan,' you'll most likely be thrown out of the pub – by the locals. Don't say you are one hundred percent Irish. Don't say 'Top of the morning to you,' that's all Hollywood nonsense (except if the Irish themselves say it and that's usually to taunt tourists who think it normal to greet someone like that). Don't compare Ireland to your own country.

Irish people are friendly and, if you drive a car over there, it's polite to wave at other drivers in their cars especially in the countryside.

Now I look at Paddy and know before he says it what he is about to say. "How are you two love-birds getting on?"

He said it *and* in front of John. *And* he's looking at Saffron and I.

I stare, *glare* at Paddy in the hope he comprehends my fear at this moment. He glances at Saffron and then John. I think he gets my meaning.

"Oh, John, this is Paddy. He's the conductor on the 292 bus," I say in a feeble effort to change the subject.

John smiles and nods. "Heard you're a bit of a comic?"

"Ah, yer know, gotta keep the troops happy. This is my wife, Mary and this little one is Mary."

We smile and nod and I start to walk away. I have to get out of this situation as quickly as possible. "Must go - as the Russians say."

We give a little wave and stroll back through town. John doesn't mention anything about those awkward few moments and I hope he didn't understand what Paddy had said.

"I need a piss," says John and runs into the brick-built lavatory beside the market place.

"That was close," says Saffron and leans back against the wall.

"You're telling me," I say. I feel her hand grasp my left buttock. I quickly reach my hand behind her and grope her right buttock. We can't seem to keep our hands off each other. She hands me a piece of paper. "Read it later," she says. I slip it into my pocket. We stand apart until John alights from the toilet and together we take the short walk home – in silence.

*

John must suspect something is going on between Saffron and I. You'd have to be blind *not* to know something is amiss. Maybe he chooses to ignore the signs. Maybe he wants rid of her and hopes I'll take her on as my girlfriend. All he has to do is ask me and I'll be there quicker than a squirrel running up a tree.

It's Saturday evening. I'm sitting on my bed with Saffron's piece of paper in my hand. Mother is downstairs watching Coronation Street with Mrs. Feely and father is getting drunk down the Irish club with his pals.

I read aloud. "Joshua. I like you a lot. I also like John but something's missing between us. There's no spark. No connection. I don't have the same feelings for him that I have for you. Please don't tell John, it will break his heart.'"

Well, there it is. I feel all fluttery and excited but I also feel terrible going behind my best friend's back and, well, stealing his girlfriend. I don't know what to do or think. I can't get Saffron out of my mind. I climb into bed, cover myself with a sheet and feel excited as I imagine Saffron lying naked beside me.

*

I knock on Mrs. Feely's front door.

"Hello, Josh," says Mrs. Feely. "What can I do for you."

"Have you got one o' them dictionaries?"

"Well, yes, I think I have one somewhere. Come in. Oh. Take your shoes off, first."

I take my trainers (old sneakers) off (that's all I ever wear) and leave them by the doorstep. I wonder why Mrs. Feely never takes her shoes off when she visits our house? I walk into the lounge and suddenly realize why she doesn't want any dirty old sneakers dragging dirt into her home. The carpet is pure white and my feet sink deeply into it. The wallpaper is a maroon color and hasn't got any ripped pieces like ours, or any rising damp in the corners. In a corner is a highly polished China cabinet (no bible supporting the cabinet) and a long, antique dresser with a big TV on top.

Mrs. Feely bends down and finds a dictionary in one of the dresser drawers.

"What word are you looking for?" she asks, and licks her index finger in readiness to flip a page.

"Saffron," I say.

"Why, that's a spice. Now, let me see." She flips through some pages, stops at a particular page and runs her finger down it. "Here we are. 'Saffron is a spice derived from the flower of the Crocus Sativus. It's the most expensive spice in the world. It's been used for centuries as a seasoning and coloring agent in food. Ancient civilizations also used Saffron for medical purposes. It can help with depression, asthma, insomnia, arteriosclerosis,' - hardened arteries, dear – 'and cancer.' There yer go. Now you know about Saffron."

"Wow." I'm impressed. Saffron is hot stuff, in more ways than one.

"Maybe someday you'll put some in your cooking."

She hands me the dictionary. "Take this, Joshua. It may help you at school."

"Really?"

"Oh, I've got a few hanging around the house. My husband used to read a lot, you see."

I thank her and grab my shoes by the doorstep and run back into my house. I like Mrs. Feely. She has a beautiful soul.

*

Chapter 16

Today it's raining dogs, cats, mice and every other kind of animal and insect as I run outside and collect some fire wood. On the way back indoors I shovel a couple of scoops of coal from the bunker and go back into the kitchen before I'm swept away by the torrential rain.

I pile the wood on the floor beside the open oven door and turn the cooker on. I place a pile of last week's newspapers near the wood so both can dry out. And as the materials for lighting the fire heat up, I sit beside the oven and warm myself.

It's 5:30am and this is my normal everyday routine. After I light the coal fire in the living room, I face the lashing rain and swirling wind and walk uptown to do a paper round before returning home to get ready for school. No wonder I keep falling asleep in class. As well as hating school, I hate making that fire, hate doing the paper round, hate feeling tired all the time, hate being called the coalman by other kids. Sometimes I forget to wash beneath my fingernails where soot and coal dust gather.

And this particular week I have to prepare my own breakfast (though that's nearly always a bowl of cornflakes or porridge) because my father is at work up in Manchester and my mother had caught the ferry over to Dublin.

My grandfather is seriously ill and mother dropped everything, got the bus to Kettering, the train to Liverpool and the ferry across the Irish Sea.

"Ye'll be fine here, Josh," she says. "Just light the fire to keep the damp down and no hitching it from school, do yer hear?"

"Yes, ma," I reply, not looking forward to being on my own all week.

"And Mrs. Feely is going to cook you a few meals and drop in now and again to see how you're doing. And besides, you've got wee Bonnie to keep you company."

My mother, nee Doyle, often mentions her mother when cleaning house or baking a cake or making porridge, all the recipes she learnt from watching her mother slave over a hot stove in their cramped kitchen in a cottage in Dublin. Poverty in Dublin at that time was horrific. My father became head of the household at age twelve when my grandfather died of polio. He told me once (he rarely talked about his youth) that his family was so poor they couldn't afford to buy him a pair of shoes. He and his friends would follow the horse-drawn coal-cart around the neighborhood and steal lumps of coal from the back of the cart. His family, five sisters and three brothers plus his mother were always hungry, but at least father made sure they were warm. Later, he'd return and shovel the horseshit into bags and take it home to help grow roses. I guess that's why he likes roses so much.

Mother's father worked at Guinness' so at least there was food on the table every day. Her mother would feel sorry for my father and his family and on occasion take a bag of food around to their house. She did this for years. And maybe that's why my mother sometimes bundles together a bag of tinned food and loaves of bread and delivers them to one or two poor families up on Exeter Estate.

"She used to sit me on her knee and sing little songs to me," said mother not so long ago. "When I was upset she'd take my hand and stroke it softly, like this." Mother takes my hand and caresses it with her rough skin, even so, it makes me feel good, feel wanted, feel loved. I can only imagine how pleasant and soothing it must have felt to a young girl sitting on her loving mother's knee.

"And father would sit beside us and hold my mother's hand. He'd read a story to us both. He'd work overtime at the brewery to make sure mother had extra money to buy food for your father's family."

Her eyes begin to water.

"And one day I went with my mother around to your father's house. I felt sorry for him having so much responsibility on his young shoulders. We became friends and, well, eventually got married, and had to move over here to find work. To leave my mother and father behind was the hardest and most saddening thing I ever did. I love them both more than life itself."

She arrives home a week later carrying a suitcase and a large brown package containing two tall ornamental Persian cats. I remember these scary cats when I lived at my grandmother's cottage. I was three years old then and those cats scared the life out of me with their long necks and big black eyes.

Mother and I sit at the dining room table sipping hot tea. Her eyes are red from crying. "I met my brothers at the house," she says. "They want me to move back to Dublin, but I told them I couldn't leave your father here by himself."

My parents have a weird kind of relationship. Can't quite figure it out, maybe they feel safe and secure being together and hating each other in various ways, rather than breaking out of their respective boxes and making new lives for themselves out there in the unknown. I think fear of change keeps them together, like many married folks, I reckon.

"They loved each other so much," mother continues. "My father bought her flowers once a week, Gerber daisies, her favorite. He'd sit and read his newspaper and she'd sit opposite him reading a book. I used to watch them sometimes as a child and notice that mother and father would stop what they were doing for a few moments and look over at each other. They'd smile and then go back to what they were doing."

I feel emotional, but swallow hard and try to hold back my feelings.

Mother wipes her eyes with a tissue. "I tried that once with your father and all he could say was, 'who you looking at?'

My father used to work the nightshift in Guinness' brewery and every morning mother would find him perched on the front doorstep, half drunk. She'd take him in and help put him to bed. Father hardly drank alcohol. It was the fumes from the brewery that made him drunk. I used to look out my window in the morning and see a whole line of men sitting on their doorsteps all along the street, all workers from the brewery. "

I've never heard my mother speak so much. And, for the first time, I'm seeing a more sensitive and emotional side to her. Did it take the death of her father for my mother to break that stone wall of hardness that surrounds her heart and break free from her box?

"Anyway, father had the cancer and he was laid up in bed. Poor mother cooked and washed for him, gave him the medication, read stories to him. My two brothers, Joe and Eddy, took me shopping to get me away from the stress of watching my father fade away each day. Joe bought me a nice wee cake and a cup of tea in the café above Woolworths. Your Uncle Joe is a fine man. Quiet, but he has a big heart. Eddy's okay, too, but he's a bit rough around the edges. Anyway, when we got back home, we called for mother to come see what we had bought for her. We thought she'd like a new dress because she'd cared for father full time for the past few months or so. We called for her but she didn't answer, so we went to father's room and …" She wipes away another tear. "And there they are, lying side by side, holding each other's hands, a tiny smile on their faces."

Mother blows her nose. My mouth is wide open, I can't hold back any longer; a tear trickles down my cheek. I picture the image in my head of my grandparents lying side by side in bed, holding hands, loving each other so much right up to the end and can't help myself, can't stop myself, can't prevent what's rising up inside me; I hug my mother and lower my head onto her shoulders and weep.

She grips my small hand with her strong, calloused fingers and softly caresses it: a mother hen protecting her baby chick. We weep together.

"He died while we were out shopping. Mother couldn't live without him. She would have been completely lost without him. They'd been married for seventy years. Her soul-mate. In all those years I only heard my mother raise her voice once against him and that was when he accidently smashed my grandmother's best dish."

I hug my mother tighter and rock back and forth as if *I* am the mother hen consoling and loving my baby chick.

She straightens up, sniffles, wipes her eyes, blows her nose and stands. I sit back down the other side of the dining table. She pours another two cups of tea and places one in front of me. In her hand is a silver and onyx crucifix attached to a silver chain.

"This belonged to your grandfather. He told me to give you this and to wear it with pride."

I carefully take the crucifix out of her palm and place it around my neck.

"'Let it guide you through life and love,'" he said.

I twist the cross between index finger and thumb and sudden images of my grandfather come to me. He has a thick mop of black hair on his head; a tall, broad-shouldered man with dark brown eyes and a caring and pleasing smile. Sitting beside him is my grandmother, a thin-faced woman with a high brow and thin lips, a cute dimple in her chin and sparkling, pale-blue eyes.

They are holding hands.

"That cross has been passed down through the years," says my mother. "My father told me this cross has been passed down to the first male born in each generation. My father wore it, and now he's handing it down to you. Father says it's very old and there's some kind of connection going way back to Romanian gypsies. And you should pass it on to your first born, if he is a boy, of course."

I'm amazed and feel proud to now be the owner of such a relic.

Mother opens a cupboard drawer and takes out the family album. She shows me a sepia photograph of my grandparents and it's the same image as the one in my head. Had I looked at that album before and memorized that photo? I don't think I've seen that album before. She finds another old, edge-torn sepia photograph of her grandparents. The man had his hands clasped over his knees, thick black hair on his head, long eyebrows and a high forehead. The woman next to him, my great-grandmother has her hair tied in a bob. She is the only one smiling but they are holding hands. I turn the photo over and it says, 'Philip and Megan Doyle. 1888.

Mother takes out an old sheet of paper. It has a sketch drawing of the cross. Underneath it says, 'Onyx cross. Property of Mr Paddy Doyle, husband of Iona Doyle, and father of Megan Doyle. To be passed on to the first male born of his generation. 1848.'

"There's a family secret, you see, or at least your grandfather thinks there is. He told me the cross will show the wearer certain things in life and, if two of the same crucifixes came together then something magical would happen."

"Magical," I say, thinking of what had just transpired when I had touched the cross. "Where's the other cross?"

"Now how would I know," says Mother, frowning. "Anyway, it's all a myth. A fairytale. Your grandfather liked to tell a good yarn. He was full of stories. Don't believe everything you hear."

Mother goes upstairs. I hear her blowing her nose in the toilet; I hear her footsteps cross the landing and the soft thud of her bedroom door closing.

She weeps.

*

Chapter 17

Boredom is the greatest killer of all. I fill the boring hours asking questions of my parents, trying to explore their minds, find out what makes them tick. I wile away time by filling in all the hours of the day by swimming, sleeping, school, home, making the fire, doing the paper-round – and trying to figure out a way to connect to Saffron. And there it is, there's the gist of my thoughts, my boredom - I want to date her, be excited by her, walk with her, hold her hand - make *love* to her.

I've just turned sixteen and ready to leave school next April, Easter break. Thank God.

I'm sitting on a step in the back garden and watching my father water his roses. Is *he* just filling in time, coloring in the boring moments of his life by relating to nature?

"Christy Brown, the famous Irish writer," says my father, "lived on the next street to us."

"The man who wrote 'My Left Foot'?" We read that book at school, or rather, the English teacher read it and we threw pencils at each other in class. But this is a rare occasion for me to be able to talk to my father (he's on holiday for a week from his job in Manchester), though he usually doesn't open up about any subject, especially family.

Maybe it's too difficult to talk about his past, but he does from time to time allow a little information to escape from the deep annals of his psyche.

He's watering his precious roses on this scorching hot and humid August day. The roses are big and healthy looking, red and pink and yellow. Earwigs just love them.

"Christy Brown wrote a few books," says father, "and they made a film out of 'My Left Foot.' He was disabled and we'd see him getting pushed in a wooden cart by his brothers down to the canal. A great place for swimming, place was swarming with kids." He chuckles to himself.

"What's so funny?"

"Oh, we'd take a bar of soap and have a bath. Some kids used to wash their socks and undies in the canal, then walk home soaking wet."

I watch as my father waters his small vegetable patch. His shoulders broad, his arms strong and muscular.

"What's wrong with Uncle Jack?" I say.

"Well, he's not all there, yer know, in the head. Me mother said she accidently dropped him on his head as a baby and he hasn't been the same since."

"Really?"

"Who knows. It's hard to tell fact from fiction with my family, or your mother's for that matter."

"He wanted my sweets," I say and remember it all too well. Before we moved to England, we dropped into my grandmother's house (my father's mother) for tea, (tae) and it was there that I first met Uncle Jack. He spotted a bag of sweets I was eating and chased me around the dining room table for twenty minutes trying to steal them.

"For Jesus' sake, will ye give the poor man a sweet!" barked my grandmother at me.

"But they're mine," I replied.

"Share and share alike now," she said.

So I stopped running and opened the bag of sweets and offered one to Uncle Jack. He cautiously came up to me, poked two fingers in the bag and took out a sweet, just the one. I thought he was going to steal the whole bag.

"Jack's in a mental home now," says father. I sense sadness in his voice. "Poor man never really had a chance. Still he seems happy there. Three meals a day, no bills to pay. Your mother thinks I should be in there with him." This time he laughs out loud.

"Mother used to visit him now and again. He's happy enough, I suppose. Mind you she had enough on her plate with my father gone. And then she died and Jack was on his own."

"What did granddad die of?"

"Polio. Stuck in a wheelchair for years."

"I wish I had met him."

"Oh, he was a good man, as far as I knew. Kept mostly to himself. In our house it was a case of being seen and not heard otherwise he'd give you a good slap around the chops."

"How did you meet ma?"

"What's this, twenty fecking questions," says father and drags himself and the water hose over to the other side of the garden.

"Just curious, that's all."

"Her mother used to bring food around to us. Took pity on us, I reckon. We weren't proud. Dublin was starving back then and my father had polio, so we had no choice really. Your mother tagged along and helped clean the place up a little. There were nine kids. If my father hadn't been confined to a wheelchair we would have had a football team."

We laugh and it's good to laugh. Occasionally a crack appears in the thick walls my parents have erected around themselves since childhood and a narrow streak of light shines through like a finger of sunshine peeking through a cloud. Lately, probably by my insistence and persistence in asking them questions about their past I've maybe sparked off some kind of healing process within them. And by releasing, piece by piece the trauma and hardship of their youth it might well benefit me as well. We can all try to escape confinement in our self created boxes.

I remember Paddy the bus conductor's words, 'You three are a right pair if ever I saw one." Doesn't make sense, but that's the point, nothing seems to make sense in this family. I sometimes wish I was born into a wealthy family, living in a big posh house with massive gardens and a swimming pool and attending the best schools. But, there again, I'd probably be more bored out of my mind than I am now.

"I'm off to bingo," says mother, poking her head out of the kitchen window. It's hotter than the inside of an erupting volcano and there's mother going out with her gray overcoat on and wearing a head scarf. "I'll be back about nine."

"Thank's for the warning," says father.

"Shag off," yelps mother.

"Feck off," barks father.

*

It's Sunday. I'm lying on top of my bed. Bonnie is asleep at my feet. Earlier I went to church (that Catholic mass is a sure way to catch up on lost sleep, so boring) and rush home to scan through Mrs. Feely's dictionary. I look for the word, 'Onyx.'

I read aloud, "'Onyx is a variety of the micro … crystalline quartz called chalcedony.' Wow, that's a mouthful. 'Chalcedony is an ancient port on the Sea of Marmara in Asia Minor. In Greek it means claw or fingernail. The Persians wore the stone around their neck when going into battle to give them courage. It's also a symbol of strength and helps to defend against negativity. Black is the absence of light and therefore can be used to create invisibility.' This stuff is good."

"Joshua," mother shouts up the stairs. "Come and look what the cat dragged in."

It must have been a big cat to drag Father Luke through the front door, but that's my mother's sense of humor – confusing. I wonder what Father Luke thought about himself being mauled by a cat, hypothetically.

I sit opposite him. Mother sits beside him, her arms crossed and with a stern look on her face.

"Father Luke says you were asleep during mass," says mother. "Is that so?"

"And snoring loudly, too," says Father Luke.

"Sorry if I woke everyone up," I say sarcastically. My mother told me once she should have given me the middle name of sarcastic. I like that. Joshua Sarcastic Hanley. Or Joshua Sarcasm Hanley. Sarcastic Josh. There yer go.

Mother blesses herself as Father Luke takes a deep breath.

"My parishioners do *not* sleep during my mass." Father Luke seems angry for reasons beyond my comprehension. I mean, what's the big deal. I fell asleep in church, isn't that the fault of the priest, or the way the mass is conducted. Blame the Catholic rituals rather than the parishioners.

"Do you not get enough sleep at night?"

"Well, father. I'm very tired by the time I get to bed."

"Out gallivanting up there in the quarry," says mother. "Swimming and cavorting around."

I don't understand where cavorting comes into it, and I don't think mother knows what that word actually means. "Maybe it's because I'm up early making the fire and doing a paper-round," I say.

"You don't do those things on Sunday," says mother.

"And that's why I should be sleeping in on Sunday," I say.

Mother blesses herself again. *She* sleeps in on Sunday morning, in fact when I return from church at noon she's *still* in her bed. This is an early lesson in hypocrisy. Don't do what I do, do what I say. I must look up other meanings of that word in Mrs. Feely's dictionary.

"Granted, you weren't the only boy sleeping through mass," says Father Luke. "But I've already visited them and gave them their penance. I want you to say five Hail Mary's and ten Our Father's. We'll have none of this sleeping lark in *my* church."

"Yes, Father," I say, and grin sarcastically.

Mother blesses herself again. If mother was paid one pound for each time she blesses herself we'd be millionaires – thrice over.

"Nothing to smile about, lad," says Father Luke.

I go down on my knees, put my hands together in prayer and begin mumbling the first Hail Mary.

"Do that upstairs," says mother. "I don't want yer dirtying me carpet."

I go upstairs and lie on my bed. Hail Mary's and Our Father's. Oh sure. Instead of saying that mumbo-jumbo I get out my dictionary and look up the word, hypocrisy. "'A situation in which someone pretends to believe something that they do not really believe, or that is the opposite of what they do or say at another time.'"

Mrs. Mary Hypocritical Hanley. That sounds about right. "'And tonight, folks, for your entertainment,'" says the MC at mother's bingo hall, "'may I introduce you all to Mr. Joshua Sarcastic Hanley, and his mother, Mrs. Mary Hypocritical Hanley.'" And we bow as the applause roars around the hall.

I shake my head in disbelief at the hypocrisy of my mother, the Catholic Church, the teachers at my school, my friends, even myself sometimes. Maybe the world needs hypocrisy to survive.

I hear Father Luke saying his goodbyes downstairs and the front door closing. I try to sleep but it's no good so I turn on the bedside light and begin to read one of Mrs. Feely's books. What interests me the most is a book on mental institutions during the 1950's and 1960's. Mrs. Feely had wondered why someone so young was so interested in mental health. I didn't tell her about my Uncle Jack and that he was a patient in a mental asylum.

All it took, apparently, to lock someone away was a family member to claim they were not sane and, insane in those days could mean they were guilty of such simple acts as masturbation, atheism, homosexuality, being lazy. By the end of the Second World War Ireland had more people in asylums or mental hospitals than anywhere in the world.

Uncle Jack had been committed in the late sixties to a mental hospital called Grangegorman, in the north of Dublin. A little earlier Jack would have had to sleep with 3 or 4 other patients in one bed. Some patients had to sleep huddled together on the floor to keep warm. A town called Ballinasloe had a population of 5,596, and 2,078 of them were patients in the asylum. By 1961, one in every 70 Irish people over the age of 24 was confined to a mental hospital.

I count myself very lucky living in England. If we had stayed in Ireland I'd probably have been locked up for sure for masturbation, questioning the church (certainly not for being lazy) and for running away from home. Uncle Jack would be chasing me around the asylum's dining table still trying, in his mind, to steal my bag of sweets.

I feel sorry for my Uncle Jack. I close my eyes and think of him with his little suitcase waiting outside my grandmother's house for the car to come and take him away. I imagine my grandmother weeping and hugging him. I imagine my dad and his siblings standing close by, not able to help or prevent this incarceration in any way, maybe blaming themselves for not doing enough to help their disabled brother.

I see him getting into the car and the car driving away and grandmother screaming after her son and running after the car as the rest of the family hold her and hug her and guide her back indoors. And Uncle Jack's face seen through the rear car window and a look of concern and confusion on his face as if he probably thinks this is just a little day trip everyone's arranged for him and he'll be home later for tea and supper and to be tucked up in his comfortable bed by his mother and sung to and kissed on the forehead and told to go to sleep because Seanorrow holds another one of God's glorious days.

I close my eyes and try to sleep.

*

(A Fond Kiss)

Today is beautiful; a light breeze caresses our skin as if urging us to continue our secret tryst. Saffron lies beneath me and her legs are wrapped around my torso as I slowly penetrate her. The world around me does not exist. There is no quarry, no sky, no sun, no breeze, no clay-hole, no thoughts, no John, just pleasure. I kiss her and her kiss is like a sweet melody to which lyrics have no place or meaning.

She moans, she grips my buttocks and heaves me deeper inside her. Together we release our pent up lust, our craving for each other in a few beautiful strokes. It is pure music.

We are silent. Not because we are spent and tired and amazed at how we had just discovered our connection to each other, but because just over the quarry hill John is swimming in the pool. We run together down the hill to the main road.

Betrayal: bitter yet sweet in its creation and its completion. Knowing or doing something behind a person's back, hurting them in unsaid and unseen ways, surely that's an evil act? And yes, I betray my best friend. I sneak like a slithering snake behind his back and kiss his girlfriend and touch her. I tell John we are going down to the ice-cream van on the road at the botSean of the quarry and would he like a '99 brought back. Sure, he said, that's good of you, my friend.

And we stop on the other side of the quarry hill and make love as he swims in the pool and then we rush down to the van.

Now, ice-creams in hand we arrive back at the pool and I give John his '99; he is basking in the afternoon sun.

"Thanks, mate," he says excitingly. I glance at Saffron and she looks away. She too, I think, is feeling guilty.

She sits beside John and squeezes his thigh. I sit on the other side of him and together we lick and savor our ice-creams.

I betrayed my best friend and so, by definition, that makes *me* evil. Evil or a cheat or a bastard or a cad or a backstabber or whatever name is suitable for a wretch like me.

Saffron had told me that she will soon break it off with John and date me. And when that time arrives, John will obviously know that Saffron and I had betrayed him and that our beautiful friendship will be over.

"Long time getting these ice-creams," he says with an edge to his voice.

"Big line of folks wanting ices," I say in a vain attempt to sound convincing.

"It's a hot day and all," says Saffron and looks across the pool.

We finish our ice-creams in silence.

"Okay," says John and stands up. "Last one in is a twat!"

*

Chapter 18

Rose the gypsy is correct in her prediction about me learning how to play music, bagpipe music to be exact. But it happens in a peculiar way.

"I know what we can do," says Sam as we walk through the town center on a cool summer's night.

"Find something to eat," I say.

"Well, yes, but there's no way I'm paying for it."

"Steal food?"

"Listen, my dad works for a bakery and he says they load up and store their cakes in vans overnight, and deliver them to the shops the next day."

"Lodell's bakery?"

"Not far from here," says Sam. "Come on, Josh. All we have to do is crawl under the back fence and nip into the vans and hey, cakes galore."

"I don't know," I say, nervously.

"Ah, come on, Josh. No one will know. It's easy-peezy."

So myself and Sam make our way through the town center, take a short cut through an alley under the town clock, over a car park and down a back lane behind a front row of shops. Near the botSean of the lane is a wire fence and beyond that are at least ten bakery vans.

"You first," I say. He crawls beneath the fence and I follow. We creep like raiding commandos towards the first van, stand up and open the door. "Enough cakes here to feed the town. We can sell them cheap and make ourselves some cash, Josh."

So we open one box and grab a cream cake and halve it and stuff it in our mouths and munch and enjoy and smile and laugh at our new money-making scheme (the first and last money-making scheme) and grab about ten boxes each and run down to the fence, crawl back under it dragging the boxes behind us, stand up and come face to face with a policeman.

"Enjoying a of exercise are we, lads," says the tall, broad-shouldered copper (policeman).

"Yes, erm, no," I stammer, "Erm, we found these boxes lying around and thought we'd tidy up a bit."

"Yes," says Sam. "I think it's terrible the way folks just throw their rubbish all over the place, so we thought we could clean the place up a bit, yer know, do our bit for the community."

"I see," says the copper, and frowns at us with thick long eyebrows. He reminds me of a bald eagle I saw on TV. He's also cock-eyed and I'm not too sure if he's looking at me or Sam.

"Well, why don't we take a visit to the station. We can help the community even more by keeping you young buggers off the streets."

With that we are frog-marched (what *does* that mean?) back through the center of town and into the cop-shop, (station) taken to a windowless room and told to sit at an empty desk. We wait and wait.

"I wish I had a cake to eat," says Sam.

"Shut up, yer ejit." You've got us in enough trouble as it is."

"My dad's gonna kill me," says Sam. "And my mother will suffocate me. And my brother will kick the shit out of me. And my sister will …"

"You think *you've* got it bad," I say. "My da will not only murder me, he'll wallop me with his leather belt and *that's* worse than death."

"But you've got the bible, remember," says Sam, "keeps your arse safe."

"I *did* have the bible 'till me da figured out why he was whipping the shit out of me and there wasn't a genuine tear in sight. He used it to light the fire."

"Wow, you *are* dead," says Sam.

"I wished he'd have given the bible to Mrs. Feely, I'm sure she likes reading that kind of thing. And someone went to all that trouble writing all those words down, too. Seems a waste."

The cock-eyed eagle-browed copper enters the room, sits down in front of us and takes out a pen from his inside pocket. He glares at Sam and stares at me, or it could be the other way around, I'm not sure.

"Now. You," he says.

"Me?" I say.

"No. Him," says the copper.

"Me?" says Sam.

"Am I *looking* at you?"

"I'm not sure," says Sam.

"Don't be cheeky," says the copper. "Now. What's your name?"

"Who me?" I say.

"No. Father frigging Christmas. Who do you think?"

"But you're looking at *him*," I say.

"Looking at whom?" says the copper.

"Sam," says I.

"So, your first name is Sam," says the copper. "What's your last name?"

"My name is Joshua," I say.

"But you just said your name is Sam."

"No. *He's* Sam, *I'm* Joshua."

"Okay. Let's keep this simple. Let's start again."

"What's *your* first and last name?"

"Who? Me or Joshua?"

"What's your problem, lad?" says the copper.

"Which one of us are you fucking *looking* at?

"Don't you dare use such language in this station, young man," says the cock-eyed, eagle looking eyebrow.

"You, boy, go stand over there out of the way."

Sam stands, scrapes his chair on the stone-tiled floor and walks over to the corner of the room.

"Face the corner," says the copper.

Sam turns and faces the corner like a naughty schoolboy.

"Now," says eagle face. "What is your first and last name?"

"Joshua Hanley," I say calmly.

"Good. And your middle name?"

"Sarcastic," I say without thinking and regret it.

"Listen, boy. You may think this is all a laugh, a game, but believe me, laddie, when I get through writing this report you two will definitely get a year's holiday in a nice little paradise called Juvenile Hall, otherwise known as hell on earth."

I am about to tell this cock-eyed, eagle-browed copper that I already live in hell and he should sample some of it by moving into our house.

"You," says the copper.

"Me?" says Sam, still facing the corner.

"Yes, you. Sit down."

Sam plonks himself down on the hard wooden chair.

"Now. What's your first and last name?"

"Sam.O'Neil."

"Middle name?

Sam is silent for a few moments.

"Middle name?"

"It's the same as that Irish show presenter on the Late Late show, I think it's called," says Sam, "have you heard of him?"

"Irish show … what are you talking about," says the copper. "All I'm asking for is your middle name."

"He's famous in Ireland," says Sam. "You must have heard of him, surely, his last name's Byrne."

"WHAT'S YOUR MIDDLE FUCKING NAME?" I hear footsteps in the hallway, maybe someone thinks we're being murdered in here.

"Josh. Promise me you won't laugh."

"I won't laugh," I say.

"My middle name is Gay," he says.

I laugh inwardly and the copper howls with laughter

The bastard.

*

So Sam's parents arrive to collect him. I watch as his father slaps him about the head and his mother weeps as they rush down the police station corridor. My parents have no car so I'm driven home in a Black Maria (Ma-Rye-A) and I feel like royalty.

It's Friday night so da will be back from work in Manchester and by now swigging pints of stout with his mates down the Irish club. Ma will be watching Coronation Street, I bet.

Eagle-brow delivers me to the front door. My mother opens the door and is wearing her curlers and pink nightgown and frayed slippers, her left big toe sticking out the front of her left slipper. Hanging on the wall behind her is the Virgin Mary with the words 'Bless all who enter this house' written in black ink below her Holy feet.

"Is there something wrong, officer," mother says and places her hand on her heart. "And why are you pulling my son's ear?"

"There's been an incident," he says.

"Is it me brothers? Have they been in an accident?" She blesses herself. "Or Mrs. Feely, has she gone and died on us?"

"No, mam," says the copper. "None of that sort. Is this your son?"

"What have yer done now, yer little shite. It's lucky yer father is down the club, that's for sure. Bringing the police to the door. God help us."

"Are you Mrs. Hanley?" says the copper.

"Who else is here, for feck sakes," says mother and places one hand on her hip.

"You *are* Mrs. Hanley?"

"Well I'm not the fecking Virgin Mary."

The copper clears his throat. "Your son was caught stealing cakes from Lodell's bakery."

"Jesus, Mary and Joseph," says mother and puts both hands over her heart.

"I'll need his father to call in at the station Seanorrow to sign some paperwork, Mrs. Hanley. "And he needs to bring Joshua, too."

"If he's still alive by then," says mother, and grabs my ear and pulls me inside. That woman has tremendous strength. "Thank you, officer."

The cockeyed, eagle-browed copper slightly nods his head and taps his helmet with two fingers, turns and walks down the garden steps leaving me to my mother's wrath and my father's leather belt.

*

Thank God for Guinness, that great Irish stout that has cooled the stomachs of many, stirred the hearts of lovers, fighters, rebels and filled many a bed in a maternity ward. Father was too drunk to deal with me when he arrived home from the Irish club, filled with booze, cigarettes, man-sweat and dirty jokes.

I am lucky (this time) because my father has a different strategy for dealing with those who steal cakes and run away from home. Not that I'm about to run away tonight, I've kind of grown out of the running away thing, gets a bit boring after doing it a few times. Besides, I'd most probably put the milkman out of business if I keep sleeping under door mats and accepting bottles of fresh milk in the morning.

Bonnie, my father and I head along Gainsborough road. I bought her a new red and blue leash and it's far better than that old string I was using. She must really like the leash because every time I arrive home from school (when I'm not hitching it somewhere in Kettering) Bonnie is waiting for me in the side entrance with the leash between her teeth.

Father is walking in front of me and I'm tagging behind and Bonnie is tagging behind me. I haven't a clue where he's taking me. Maybe he's going to dump me up in the woods like he did Bonnie that time. I feel a little apprehensive now, even scared. Will he dump me, his only son in those dark woods?

We cut across the football fields, through the swing park, walk along a path in the woods (Oh, there's where Susan Bletchley and the football team scored a few home runs), and emerge on Beanfield Avenue for a half mile then turn onto Greenhill Rise.

Father knocks on the front door of a nice little two-up-two-down abode (a green door) and a man of about forty-five answers.

"Ah, Liam," says the man. "It's yerself."

"Hello, Sean," says father. "I've brought Joshua."

"Let's have a look," says Sean and grips hold of my hands. "Good strong hands, average length fingers. Broad shoulders. Aye, I think you'll make a good piper. Come in. Liam, would you like to watch TV in there while I show the lad a practice chanter. And take the dog with you."

Sean opens the living room door and my father walks through. Just before he closes the door I notice something being shown on the TV. A white haired man is facing an audience and someone is saying, "Welcome to the Gay Byrne show."

So that's Gay Byrne.

"Follow me," says Sean as we walk into the kitchen and dining room area.

He opens a dresser drawer and takes out a long, wooden piece of wood with holes in it, places his fingers around the holes and begins to play something. I don't quite know what he's playing but it sounds pleasant enough.

So, there's me thinking and worrying that my father was taking me up to the police station or dumping me in the woods like Snow White, though I hardly think he'd go as far as trying to tear my heart out with a knife, but he takes me to this man called Sean who is obviously a bagpiper.

He hands me the piece of holed wood. "This is a practice chanter. Eight holes where your fingers press lightly against and a plastic reed inside that makes the sound.

Sean shows me what fingers to place on different holes and shows me the bagpipe music scale. By the time I leave I have learned the full scale of the Great Highland Bagpipe. He plays a few jigs and reels and I'm hooked. It's as if piping is in my blood going back many generations and just biding its time before circumstances arose that would lead or guide me (in this case my father guided me) to grow to love the traditional music of both Scotland and Ireland. I guess I was born to be a bagpiper.

We say our goodbyes and it's arranged for me to call at Sean's house (he has a shed attached to the side of his house which he uses as a practice room) twice a week for practice and to join the other members of his pipe band playing and learning new tunes.

"Now *that* should keep you out of trouble," says father as we walk home with Bonnie. I'm happy because now I have something else to strive for; something else to fill in those boring moments; something to share with Saffron; something to perfect.

I glance at my father and he is smiling.

*

Sean Flanagan is a great influence on me. In a weird and wonderful way he is the father I should have had, though saying this makes me feel guilty because my father has many good traits.

Sean is quiet spoken and humorous, modest, generous and immensely talented. He can listen to a broadcast of traditional music on the radio and scribble down the musical notes as quickly as the fiddler or piper is playing the tune. And he also plays the Irish or Uilleann pipes (Uilleann means 'elbow' because the pipes are driven by a bellows under the arm) and penny whistle and must know hundreds, maybe thousands of reels, jigs, marches and airs.

He is married to Katie, a pleasant woman but sterner and more disciplined than Sean, and maybe that's the right balance for them, his yin to her yang, as they say. I like Katie. Sometimes while we practice in the shed she'd arrive with a pot of tea and a plate of custard creams.

Tonight, we sit in the shed and I've already mastered the bagpipe scale and am now playing my first ever tune, the Irish song, 'The Minstrel Boy.' (I already learned it on the penny whistle with the help of Mrs. Gibson). My fingers feel stiff and I seem to be making a mess of the tune.

"Just relax," says Sean, "let your fingers flow and your brain do all the work."

So I relax, close my eyes and let my fingers flow and I manage to get through the tune. After a lot of practice that night and at home, I master that tune, and am very keen to learn another.

The next day, a Saturday, I play my practice chanter in the back garden and the neighbors stand at the fence and watch me. Bonnie, her tail wagging and tongue dangling out of her mouth is sitting on a step, her head cocked to one side as I play.

I can't wait to get on the big bagpipes and 'graduate' (as Sean says) onto the Uilleann pipes. Mother comes out and hangs out the laundry and bobs her head from side to side in tempo with the tune. When I finish the neighbors cheer and clap and I give a bow. Mother smiles and looks at the neighbors. I think she feels proud of me. Proud that someone in the family is learning an instrument which, for many years has been absent in our clan.

I do know that my grandmother on my father's side played bagpipes for a time when she was young, and my Uncle on my mother's side played the Uilleann pipes and was quite well known for his skill in Dublin back in the 40's and 50's.

I want to carry on the family tradition and be equal to or even a better performer than they were. This gives me the purpose, the drive to learn as much as I can about the Highland bagpipe and then *graduate* to the Irish pipes.

The Scots bagpipe (Highland bagpipe – big pipes) has only one pipe reed which only has one octave, whereas the penny whistle and Uilleann Pipes have two octaves, and at a squeeze, a third octave can be played in certain tunes.

Learning to play the bagpipes consumes a lot of my spare time. I think this is meant to be because the more I practice the less bored I am, the less trouble I get into and the less I see of John. We haven't 'officially' parted our ways, but we don't call on each other anymore. I wonder if Saffron has finished with him yet. She said she was going to tell him. Even if John now knows about us we don't have to argue or fight over the reasons of our friendship break-up. Fighting over it, to me, would be a waste of time and energy.

Bonnie barks a few times and I bow and give a big grin to my audience and then glance over to the side fence at the corner of the house and spot Saffron peeking through the wooden laths. I play the 'Minstrel Boy' again just in case she had missed my first performance, although I am really showing off. I like this attention, the audience listening to me and cheering and clapping afterwards, yes, this kind of thing can be additive – but I like it and it makes me more determined to hone my musical skills and practice as much as I can each day – and night.

I finish playing and the neighbors kind of half-heartedly applaud, well, they had heard this tune not a minute earlier and probably want me to perform a fast jig or reel, something different, at least. I make a pledge to myself that I will learn as many tunes as I can from now on.

The neighbors go indoors having been musically sated for today. Mother finishes hanging out her laundry and goes back inside whistling the 'Minstrel Boy.' She closes the kitchen door.

"Hey, Saffron," I say. She is wearing a black mini skirt, a tight white blouse that shows off her average but firm breasts. I swallow the lump in my throat.

I open the gate and let her in. "Wow," she says, "I didn't know you were into music?"

I answer by touching the back of her neck and slowly and tenderly pulling her toward me. I kiss her and our tongues meet and twirl and twist and dance to the silent music emanating from our young and pulsing hearts.

I think I am in love with this girl, I *know* I'm in love with this girl and the feeling is amazing.

"I finished with John," she says.

I feel her cheeks softly with both hands. "I love you, Saffron."

She kisses me and while our tongues dance again I wonder if she loves me? I mean all she has to do is say yes or no. Isn't that the way of things? I now feel like an ejit having told her I love her. Is it too early to reveal my emotions?

Why couldn't I have waited until another time, a better time, but will there be a better time? It is as it is. I love her and I've told her and now, after we finish kissing she's going to hold my cheeks in both hands and look deep into my eyes, and I'll see a sadness in hers and then she's going to tell me she doesn't love me, and it's sweet that I feel this way about her. That what we had was just a fling. For feck sakes, this is killing me. My heart is palpitating; I feel my face flushing and sweat rolls down the inside of my thighs. *Jesus* …

She stops kissing and pulls away and holds my cheeks in both her hands and looks into my eyes and there it is, there is the sadness and oh God, please don't say …

"I love *you*, Josh," she says in a soft voice. "Since the very first time I saw you on the bus, I knew."

I'm about to have a heart attack.

We kiss. And Bonnie barks.

"Excuse me," says mother standing behind us with both her hands on her hips. There is definitely a twinkle in her eye. "Would either of you two lovebirds like a cup of *tae* and a piece of cottage pie?"

*

Love is – well, no one really knows. Maybe true love *is* connection?

*

"I love you, Saffron," I say and kiss her on the lips again. Our tongues meet, our juices blend together. I feel just grand.

"Your mum's a good cook," says Saffron as she gets out of bed and begins to dress. Her young body is firm, smooth, beautiful; perfect. I watch as she slips into her panties, straps on her bra over her firm breasts and pulls her blouse over her head. She smiles at me. I smile back.

"Two things she can cook properly," I say. "Cottage pie and Dublin coddle. Her mother taught her."

"Do you think she knows what we've been doing up here?"

"I told her I was going to show you my chanter."

"You certainly did that!" says Saffron and laughs.

"The thing about a chanter is you need two hands to play it."

"You're a naughty boy, Joshua Hanley."

"Come back to bed. Let me prove it to you."

I watch as she looks in the mirror and brushes her hair.

"My mother does that, except she talks to herself, or talks to the mirror."

"Is that normal?"

"It is in my house."

I watch as she moves the brush from the top of her head and down the sides of her shoulders.

"Saffron?"

"Yes, Joshua."

"Well, you know that I like bagpipe music?"

"Yes, and you're going to be good at it, too."

"I was thinking, erm, there's this band called the Scots Guards. Brilliant pipe band and I want to audition for the band."

"Oh, so you're leaving me, now?"

"We can write and see each other when I get leave."

She sits beside me on the bed and grasps my hand. "Joshua. If that's your dream, then follow it."

"It'll be exciting," I say and touch her cheek.

"My brother Bill is in the army."

"How long's he been in?"

"Oh, four years or so. He loves it. Hardly ever comes home, 'course I don't blame him with my parents bickering all the time."

"I'll always come home to visit you," I say and squeeze her hand.

"Come on," she says. "Let's go for a swim."

Bonnie appears from beneath the bed and licks my feet.

"She's been there all this time?" says Saffron.

"I guess she likes to watch." Bonnie jumps up onto my stomach.

"Jealous, are we?" I ruffle her black coat.

"Come on, lover boy. Let's go swimming. Bring your other lover, too."

"Ha-ha- ha." I throw on a pair of shorts, a tee-shirt and some pumps (old sneakers) and we sneak out the side entrance. Mother is taking a nap in the living room; the heat-wave this summer makes her tired most of the time.

"Stay here, Bonnie," I tell the dog. "We'll be back soon."

I shut the side entrance door and hold Saffron's hand. We walk across the main road and over the small bridge (an image of Susan Bletchley suddenly comes to mind of her down on her knees and blowing me under this bridge), up a small hill, turn left and up another hill. We part hands and walk faster when we pass John's house, then turn a corner and rejoin hands.

We walk past St Patrick's School and through the bottom gate and cross the main road and up another steep hill and then along a graveled path and into the quarry.

The water in the clay-hole looks cool and inviting and in no time at all, we are both naked and dive into the pool.

"Mind those cables, Saffron," I say. "They'll cut you to pieces."

We swim to the other side and lie naked on the bank. It's a pleasant feeling swimming naked and lying on the bank afterwards. It makes me feel kind of free, for an hour or so, anyway. It just seems natural to be naked together with the one you love. We are young so there's no hang-ups about lumps and bumps, fat and cellulite, hair or no hair, just two lovers lying naked beneath the hot summer sun.

"Enjoying yourselves, eh," says John as he approaches us from behind. I quickly stand and face him.

He looks me up and down. "Well Saffron," he says and sneers. "Guess you like 'em big."

Before I can say a word he dives at me and we splash into the shallow section near the bank.

"Stop it," Saffron screams. "Please John. Don't do this."

I'm under the water being pummeled left right and center. John is bigger and stronger than I am. I hit out with both my fists and one hits his stomach. He bends over in pain and I push up out of the water and have enough time to take a deep breath just as John swings his fist at me and hits me on the jaw. I slip beneath the water, dazed, my mind foggy. Boy, this guy can punch. How the fuck can I get out of this, or even beat him. Muhammad Ali, my boxing hero, would have pinned himself up against the ropes of the ring and had his opponent wear himself out throwing hard punches at him. But Ali isn't fighting in water.

I try to surface but John is holding my head down. I faintly hear Saffron screaming up on the bank. Well, this is it, I reckon. My journey on this earth is now ended at the grand old age of sixteen, with the love of my life screaming for my assailant to leave me alone. And in those few moments as my lungs begin to hurt, I wonder what it's like to die? Maybe it's not as terrible as folks make out, though they've not died and returned to tell us about it.

I see the raging anger on John's face through the water and he's crazed, his eyes are on fire, he is a demon, a devil, a monster all rolled into one in these few moments of madness.

My vision is blurred. Soon I will open my mouth and take a breath and water will rush in and I'll suffocate and then that will be it. The end of Joshua Hanley. I feel sad for my mother, she'll be heartbroken, as too will my father, though he won't show it so much, and Saffron and the times we haven't yet lived nor enjoyed, she will be sad and grieve and at the funeral Sean Flanagan will play the 'Flowers of the Forest' lament on his bagpipes and all will weep and wail and they'll lower my coffin into the ground and wail some more and prayers will be said and folks will attend the wake and get blind drunk and people will say, 'Oh, wasn't he a grand lad,' 'do anything for anybody, that lad.' I gave him a dictionary one day,' Mrs. Feely would say, 'such a clever and talented lad. Did you know he was learning how to play the bagpipes? And 'He would have made a very good piper," Sean Flanagan would say.

And then John lets go of my head; I surface and he spits at me and swims away. Maybe Saffron's screams had gotten to him? Maybe he realized that in a few moments if he didn't let go of me, then he'd be spending the rest of his life behind bars.

Whatever he thought worked well for me. I gasp and suck in air and almost vomit. Saffron jumps in beside me and helps me to the bank.

Bonnie appears on the top of the hill then runs down the embankment toward us. "Who let her out, for God sakes."

John swims to the far side of the pool. His strong arms swing over his head as he does the overhand stroke. One second he is on top of the water and a split second later he is gone.

"He's gone under," I say to Saffron, who is not really listening but busy drying me with a towel. Three seconds, four, five, six, something is wrong.

I dive into the pool leaving Saffron holding the towel and most probably a look of shock on her face and swim towards where I had last seen John go under the surface. Bonnie, on the other side of the pool, dives into the water and swims towards me. "Go back, Bonnie," I shout at her. "Get out of the water!"

I go under and see John; his head is only a foot or so beneath the surface. His right leg is caught in a gap in the thick cables; he's trying to pull his leg free with his arms; bubbles rise from his mouth.

I almost open my mouth to call out his name but realize that is a waste of time. I swim down to his leg and try to pull the two cables apart but the way they are crossed over each other there is only a small gap in the middle. Blood is gushing from a wound on his lower leg, the cable wires have dug into and under his skin.

I look into John's eyes and in them I see horror and sadness, and then his beautiful innocence and questioning look. And deep in his eyes I see a look of tragedy, senselessness and forgiveness.

I shake my head frantically. No. No. No you are *not* going to die, not today.

I quickly surface and take a deep breath and dive again and grab under his arms and pull and heave and twist and turn but his leg remains stuck in the cables.

Bonnie suddenly swims up to me. She dives down to John's trapped leg and grabs a part of his sneaker between her jaws. What is she *doing*. I swim around in front of John and he looks one last time into my eyes – and in those eyes I recognize how delicate life is, how precious life is, how easy it is to die. The life is being ripped from my best friend, John O'Malley. He grins slightly as the last of the air escapes from his lungs and rises to the surface as bubbles. I reach down to grab Bonnie but her jaws are stuck on John's sneaker. She is still. I look up at John and he floats and slightly sways from side to side, no life left in him on this beautiful hot summer's day.

I burst out of the water and gasp and scream at the top of my voice his name - again and again and again.

*

We bury Bonnie beside one of father's rose bushes. He says that next year's roses will be beautiful.

*

Chapter 19
(Funeral for a Best Friend)

Sean Flanagan plays the 'Flowers of the Forest' at the graveside. John's giant of a mother and father, half her size, weep huddled together at the foot of the grave. It seems the whole town has come out to pay their respects to another 'Clay-hole' victim.

As they lower John's coffin into the grave his mother wails and steps forward and almost falls on top of the coffin. Bystanders grab her just in time, but I think, at that moment, she would have preferred lying in a six foot pit with her only son.

Saffron and I stand in the front line with my parents, Mrs. Feely and Paddy the bus conductor. Sean ends his tune and lowers his head.

Saffron rests her head on my shoulder and weeps. I look to the sky and, with tears rolling down my cheeks, I nod and half-smile, hoping that maybe there *is* a place called heaven and that John and Bonnie reside there. I know he will care for her.

Hope springs eternal.

*

Chapter 20

My mother, in her wisdom (and Mrs. Feely's and my Aunt Liza's) decide to send me up to North Yorkshire for a respite away from death and funerals. She is concerned about my emotional well-being, or rather, Mrs. Feely suggests that I need a break (I overheard her while hiding on the stairway).

So Uncle Joe, Liza's husband drives down to Corby, stays overnight, then we drive North to his farm. I love it because the farthest I'd been lately was to Wicksteed Park. The drive is fine, turn left at Corby and hit the A1 and keep going north until we reach Northallerton. Uncle Joe is the silent type (his wife does all the talking) and his philosophy on life is simple. "See, it's like this Joshua. The Chinese and I believe that we only have a certain amount of words to speak in a lifetime, and when we use them up then we die. This is why I don't talk very much."

"But Aunt Liza never stops talking," I say, tongue in cheek.

"That's where the saying, 'she'll talk herself to death,' comes from."

Aunt Liza didn't come with Uncle Joe to pick me up but they did visit us last year and I had to hide in my bedroom with the pillow over my head when her and my mother got into it.

"You're a fecking snob," my mother had shouted at her. "Joe. You're my brother. Is she a snob or not?"

Uncle Joe, true to his Chinese philosophy didn't utter a word, but shrugged his shoulders and quickly disappeared down the Irish Club to join my father who had already had enough of the cat-fighting and was obviously enjoying a nice, cool, refreshing pint of Guinness. So Uncle Joe is glad of the break away from 'her indoors,' as Londoners often say.

The English countryside is very green. I hardly see any dry patches anywhere on our journey. Coming into Yorkshire we are surrounded by hills and then mountains, especially driving near the Lake District area. The land is beautiful.

We reach Uncle Joe's farm and fight our way through chickens and hens, a couple of snorting pigs and a horse, and go inside the farmhouse. A lovely, quaint-looking red-brick building with wisteria and azaleas' adorning the areas above the window sills, the doorway, halfway up the wall and around the side of the house. A far cry from our little terraced abode in Corby.

"Ah, it's our Joshua," says Aunt Liza. "Good journey?"

"It was alright," I say.

"Now. First things first. Rules of the house. Leave your dirty shoes outside. Make your bed when you get out of it. Clean your hands before dinner. No sneaking out down to Northallerton. And no …"

"Liza. Give the boy a break. He's family, not a lodger."

She glares at Uncle Joe, picks up a pot and bangs it on the stove top.

"Come on, son," says Joe. "I'll show you your room."

I take off my shoes and leave them at the bottom of the stairs. Maybe it isn't a good idea coming here after all, I think. I follow Uncle Joe up the narrow stairway and along a creaky wooden hallway to the room at the end.

"Here yer go," says Joe. "It's a nice wee room."

Uncle Joe pats me on the shoulder. "Remember. Only talk when it's important to talk. Your life may depend on it."

He closes the door and leaves me wondering whether he is talking about the Chinese philosophy or Aunt Liza, with my life depending on not getting on the wrong side of her.

The room is small but cozy. Small narrow cottage windows and white laced curtains. An oak wardrobe with the grain showing swirling images and faces just like the one in my room at home. There's a nice wooden cabinet with a lamp and off-white shade beside the bed. The bed is a little bigger than a single but not quite as big as a double. I lie down on the bed and it feels comfortable.

I feel sleepy and hold my crucifix in my left hand. My eyes are heavy and soon I'm halfway between sleep and wakefulness. I suddenly find myself walking along a minor road with a hillock running along one side. There is a bus depot on one side and a major road on top of the hillock. At the end of the minor road there is a bridge.

It's hot and humid.

I walk through a big gap in a fence and go under the bridge. On the side of the bridge is a home-made banner, and scribbled in big black letters is the words: 'Land of the Brave = Land of the Homeless.'

A woman is sitting on a wooden box surrounded by a tattered suitcase and old cardboard boxes.

"The police are coming tomorrow to clear out my home. I've nowhere else to go." I hear her but her lips are not moving.

She looks to be in her mid-sixties; she is petite with straw colored unkempt hair. She has three teeth missing from her lower jaw.

"What's your name," I say, although I don't hear myself saying anything, it's as if my subconscious is asking the question, or we are communicating on a different level.

"Hilda," she says and stands. "Living here is peaceful. People leave me alone. I'm not a drug addict or alcoholic, nor have I got any mental problems. See, my husband abandoned me four years ago and I have no family, so I ended up on the streets. What can I do?"

Before I can answer (and I don't know what to say, anyway) I find myself walking through long grass and the hot sun is beating down on my shoulders. I feel a brisk sea breeze come over me. I walk to the edge of a cliff and gaze down onto a beach and the sea beyond. A man, woman and two children sit on a blanket in the center of the beach; they are building sandcastles. A blonde-haired little girl and a dark-haired boy scoop up sand with their plastic buckets and pour it over the man's legs.

The little girl crawls away from the sandcastles and seems to be heading toward the sea waves but the man catches up with her, picks her up and swings her in the air. She laughs and screams with excitement as the boy runs up and is picked up by the man.

Suddenly I find myself standing outside a small terraced cottage in what looks like an old village. A sign comes to mind with the words, 'Port Isaac' written in bold lettering. Overhead I see dark, ominous clouds gathering for an upcoming storm.

The clouds get thicker and darker by the second. I hear doors shut and locks slide over and windows being shut and curtains drawn and lights coming on inside the line of cottages. A finger of lightning crosses the darkened skies and is followed by a tremendous roaring drum-roll of thunder – and then it pours with rain. I feel my clothes but they are dry. The rain is in my dream but not affecting me in any way.

And then the lightning flashes again and again in quick succession and the thunder turns into one long, continuous ear-shattering roar. The rain gets heavier and a wind rises and howls and rips a wooden bench out from beneath a cottage windowsill and hurls it into the air as if it's made of matchsticks. Garden gnomes and plant pots and garden chairs and tables lift off the ground and fly through the air to smash into cottage windows and doors and scrape along the narrow, winding lanes.

At the end of the lane I see a torrent of water rushing up towards me; the water takes detours left and right and down alleyways: A small tsunami roaring like an angry monster up the lane. It engulfs everything in its path and climbs into the air as if opening a wide, watery mouth and plunges down on top of me.

I awake abruptly. Beads of sweat run down my cheeks. A nightmare. Did it mean anything? I suddenly think of the family down on the beach and wonder if they had survived that storm, or what I had experienced of the storm in my dream?

"Joshua," Aunt Liza shouts up the stairs. "Your dinner's ready. Don't forget to wash your hands."

*

*

Dinner is amazing. I've never seen so much food. There is a big roasted turkey, plates of cabbage, broccoli, green beans, stuffing, peas, and gravy. At the far end of the table sits a big currant cake and a container of whipped cream.

A feast fit for a king.

"Bet you don't get fed like this at home, Joshua, " Aunt Liza says proudly.

Uncle Joe raises his left eyebrow.

"No," I say. "We can't afford to eat like this. But this is amazing."

"Hmmmm," says Uncle Joe.

After dinner (tea, or tae) I take a stroll outside and sniff the fresh air mixed with cow and pig mature. Still, it's nice to get away from Corby for a break. I climb a wooden fence and walk across a wide field. There are cows at the bottom of the field and Elm and Oak trees standing between the hedgerows.

The sun is out and feels hot on my shoulders and face. I cross another two fields and over another fence and walk down a lane toward the main road. At the junction a sign says, 'Northallerton. One mile.'

I step over a turnstile and into another field. The low hills seem to be everywhere and very green. England at its best. In the distance I can see the roof of a farmhouse but decide not to head in that direction. Instead I climb one of the hills and rest my back against a lone oak tree near the top.

I hear a rustling in the leaves above me, look up and see an upside down smiling face. "Hello," says the face. "My name is Peter."

The boy jumps down from the tree and stands, his hands on his hips, in front of me. "What's your name?" he says in a squeaky kind of voice as if his testicles had yet to drop.

"Joshua," I say and stand. We're the same height.

"Where do you live?"

"I'm staying with my Uncle Joe over there," I say and point toward his farm.

"He's a nice man. His wife's a bit of a bitch, though."

"That's my Aunt Liza. She's not so bad."

"If you say so." Peter holds out his hand. "Peter Forbes."

I shake his hand. It's frail, the skin too soft for a boy. He cringes as I squeeze his hand tighter. "Joshua Hanley."

"Wow," he says and stretches his fingers. "You're strong. I like strong."

Peter speaks in a posh accent, whether it's real or false I can't tell. He's most probably from an upper middle-class family, mummy is probably a lawyer with a big firm in town and daddy is a managing director for an industrial complex somewhere.

"I live not far from here," says Peter. "Would you like to see my home."

Nothing else to do. Besides, if any trouble went down then I can easily look after myself, and, if not, then I can certainly run fast enough away from trouble. "Yer. Why not."

I follow him over the turnstile, across a field, then turn left and over another field, this time filled with cows, chewing, farting and shitting. I smile to myself as the cows do their thing but Peter keeps a straight face, as if he's gotten used to it all.

"So where's mummy and daddy," I say sarcastically.

"Are you being sarcastic," says Peter, stops and turns to me.

"Yes," I say. "That's my middle name. Joshua Sarcastic Hanley."

"Is that *really* your middle name?"

"Are you *really* stupid?"

"Well, mummy said I was and even daddy confirmed it one day by slapping me on the head."

"Me and you, sorry, I mean *you and I* are going to get on like a house on fire," I say, hoping he knows what I mean.

"Like a house on … Oh, I see. You're funny."

The farmhouse is larger than my Uncle's and far more expensive looking. Not a piece of dirt or mud anywhere to be seen. Obviously this is not a working farm. There's a couple of brick outhouses attached to the main house and Peter tells me they are offices used by his parents when working at home. At the moment they are both in London on business and won't be back until Friday evening, three days from now.

"You stay here on your own," I say.

"There's lots of food. I just watch TV and films."

"Wonder what that would be like," I say. "You're lucky to have all this."

"Are you poor?" Peter asks. "My mum says there's a lot of poor people in our country."

"Well, not poor but certainly not rolling in pound notes."

We enter the kitchen (we keep our shoes on) and Peter takes two bottles of coke out of the fridge.

I take one of the cokes, unscrew the lid and guzzle down half the bottle in one go. "I'm learning bagpipes and the penny whistle," I say.

"I'm learning the piano and clarinet."

"Yer."

"Can you shoot an arrow?"

"What, a bow and arrow?"

"I kill rabbits."

"You *kill* rabbits?"

"Of course."

"No thanks."

"Can you milk a cow?"

"Does it involve killing rabbits?"

"You're funny," says Peter and takes a big gulp of his coke. "Are you hungry?" He opens the fridge door.

"Is the Pope a Catholic?"

"You mean, do bears shit in the woods."

"You've got a sense of humor after all."

Peter smiles and pulls out two half chicken legs and two bottles of coke. "Let's eat. I'm famished."

We sit at the kitchen table and devour the chickens, occasionally sipping our drinks.

"Have you got a boyfriend," says Peter.

I almost choke on my chicken leg. "A boyfriend?"

"You know, a boy that is your friend."

"Oh. Used to. John he was called. Dead now. Drowned."

"Oh, I'm sorry."

"Life goes on, eh?"

"Life goes on. I had a friend once, he died, too. Fell out of a bedroom window."

"Really?"

"In this house."

"Holyshit," I say.

"In my room."

"Visiting was he?"

"I slept in the guest room."

"Why didn't he sleep in the guest room, if he was the guest."

"Well, we kind of had a tiff, you see."

"I don't follow."

"We were sleeping in my room. Friends, you know, we hadn't seen each other for a long time – we attend different boarding schools, you see, and well, we wanted to share our exploits and such. He slept on the floor."

"Don't tell me, your parents were in London?"

"All that week."

"And that's when you fell out."

"I didn't fall out; I was tucked up in bed."

Fecking ejit. "No, not fall out of bed, fell out – had a tiff – with your friend."

"Oh. Yes. Sorry I thought you …"

"So why'd you fall out? Hey, this chicken is good."

"I told him I didn't love him anymore."

This time I do choke on what was left of my chicken leg and almost swallow the bone.

"Are you okay?"

I clear my throat and glare over at him, sitting there at the kitchen table, innocence painted all over his face.

"So that's why he was sleeping on the floor?"

"No. That's why I slept in the guest room. I broke his heart."

"Listen. I was only out walking and getting some air. I didn't think I'd end up in a farmhouse talking about broken hearts to a ... well ... a ..."

"A queer?"

"Your words."

"I prefer the term, gay."

"So why did he sleep on the floor?"

"He erm ... wasn't really sleeping?"

"He was reading Hamlet," I say.

"*You do suit your middle name,*" he says and giggles.

"He was whimpering. I think he was confused."

"You're right about that."

"He screamed at me then dived through the bedroom window."

"Holy shit." I scratch my head and wonder how in the hell did I get into this situation.

"Thanks for the food and drink," I say and spring to my feet. "I think I better get back to my Uncle's."

"Thank you for listening to me, Joshua. It's so lonely here all on my own."

"You're welcome," I say.

"You're such a sweet boy."

I stand and walk quickly out through the kitchen door, across the spotlessly clean cobble-stoned yard, over the turnstile and, as soon as my feet hit the ground I speed away over the fields faster than a hare being chased by blood hounds, and don't stop running until I reach my bedroom, dive on the bed and pull a pillow over my head. "Jesus Fecking Christ," I mumble under the pillow.

I decide not to tell Uncle Joe about Peter the gay boy from the next farm. And definitely will never tell Aunt Liza about him, first thing she'd do is use the situation as ammunition to start an argument with my mother. And she'd win because I *was* with a gay boy.

"You talked to a *queer* ," she would say. "A *queer*."

"Mum, they like to be called, gay." I'd reply.

"I don't care how happy he is, he's still a *queer*."

Of course this conversation will never happen but if it ever did, even in the distant future, mother would react in the same way.

I stay away from the farm house next door because, well, to tell the truth, I'm kind of scared. Scared of what Peter might have in mind in the way of asking me to sleep on *his* bedroom floor, or worse still, he might ask me to sleep in his *bed*. And keep the windows open. God forbid, if I was religious I'd be down on my knees right now and praying.

And then I start to get niggling thoughts like, *hey, Josh, me boy, maybe deep down you are really a queer, or gay*. I quickly and psychically shake these thoughts from my stupid head.

I force myself to sleep.

*

Time is now up. My great holiday in North Yorkshire over. Bags packed, I kiss Aunt Liza on the cheek and she hugs me. "You're welcome back here anytime, Joshua. You're so well behaved."

I blush and believe her anyway.

Uncle Joe and I drive away from the farmhouse. I look out the rear window and Aunt Liza is waving at me. I'm sure I see her wipe her eyes with a tissue - probably a bit of dust in the air.

We drive down the winding lane and turn left towards Northallerton.

"Did you enjoy your stay? Asks Uncle Joe.

"It was grand," I say.

I glance out the window and in the distance I spot Peter's farmhouse.

"That's a nice house up there."

"Oh, the Forbes' place," says Uncle Joe. "Terrible what happened up there. A tragedy."

"I heard. A young guy jumped out of a bedroom window."

"How'd you know that?" Uncle Joe looks at me curiously, his left eyebrow raised.

"I met Peter and he invited me into his house."

"Joshua," Uncle Joe stops the car and turns to me. "Peter Forbes jumped out of his bedroom window. Almost ten years ago to the day."

*

Chapter 21

I lie in bed (my own bed) back in Corby and am excited to be seeing Saffron in a couple of days. I missed her so much.

I can't tell her about meeting Peter Forbes. Or his ghost! I still can't believe what had happened. Is there another place, some kind of so-called paradise that actually exists? I'm feeling kind of scared at the moment but how did that happen? How could it happen? I better keep that event to myself. Tell no one, not even Saffron.

Was it the onyz cross that my grandfather had given to me via my mother. She said it was all mumbo-jumbo, but I was there, I met Peter at that tree, we did visit his house and ate chicken legs and bottles of coke. Jesus!

Uncle Joe promised not to tell anyone, not even Aunt Liza. " keep it to yerself," he had said. "No one will ever believe you, and you'd probably end up in a madhouse."

He didn't have to tell me twice. If this had happened in Dublin, and I had mentioned it to someone, *anyone,* I'd now be sitting in an ambulance and on my way to the lunatic asylum and mixed in with all the other folks who had seen ghosts. Of course I would get special treatment because I was actually *talking* to one.

"Holy mother of God," as my mother says. "And all the saints and angels in Heaven!"

*

Chapter 22

"Come on, Josh, says Sam, not even out of breath after jogging the past two miles. "You want to look fit for Saffron, don't you?"

"I'm not as fit as you, Sam," I say, or rather try to say between heavy breathing. .

It's Sam's idea to get me out and about, jogging around the park, the football fields, around the streets of Corby. He'd called on me earlier in the day and, to tell the truth, I was surprised to see him. After our 'cake adventure' and police interrogation, I thought his parents would ban him from seeing me for life.

"Come on. Let's sprint up this hill."

The guy is trying to kill me, for sure. We sprint, or should I say, Sam sprints and I run as fast as I can, which is not very fast. I suspect a tortoise could run faster than I. We reach the top of the hill which is paved and in a built up area of town. At the top of the hill is the town center.

Sam stops outside a newsagents and takes deep breaths. I catch up and double over, desperately out of breath, almost vomiting in fact, but I take deep inhalations and my head stops spinning.

"Water?" says Sam.

"Sure." He goes in the shop and comes out with two bottles of water. I guzzle mine down in one gulp.

"Careful, You don't want to get cramp."

"I don't want to die of thirst, either."

"Let's just do an easy jog on the way home," says Sam. "It's all running and gym work in the army, you know."

I'm sorry now that I had mentioned enlisting in the army. Sam wants to enlist, too.

"I'm going into the Scots Guards," I say.

"I fancy joining the Coldstream Guards."

"Better than this dump, that's for sure," I say.

"Ah, Corby's alright. Lot of other towns worse than this one, according to my dad."

"Ain't it funny, though," says I, "if you ask someone what's it like to live in a certain town, they say it's a shithole."

"My dad says he must have visited a thousand shitholes in his time because everyone he had asked about their town or city said it was a shithole."

We laugh as we jog back down the hill and onto Gainsborough road and along past the corner shops and red telephone box and into my garden. We sit on the concrete steps between two big fir trees my father had planted years before and inhale and exhale deeply and slowly.

"The recruitment guy said all the guards are trained down in Pirbright, in Surrey. I'm waiting for them to call me."

"Me, too. Hey, maybe we'll be going down the same day. We could travel down together. My dad can give us a lift to Kettering station."

"Sounds like a plan."

"I got offered a welding fabrication job at the steelworks," I say.

"My dad wants me to be a diesel fitter. But live here for the rest of my life. No thanks."

"I want to travel."

"Me, too. I think we've got gypsy blood in us, Josh."

"I *know* I've got gypsy blood in me," I say.

"Travel the world, eh, Josh, while all our mates are working day in, day out in the steelworks. Get married. Have kids. Drink down the club. Weekends go to Wicksteed Park, back to work, wife, kids. Not for me. Not yet anyway. Race you down the hill." Sam sprints away.

I sigh deeply and try to keep up.

"We're joining the British Army, Sam," I yell at him. " Not the fecking Olympic team."

*

PART TWO

Chapter 23

Saffron had slept through the night on top of her bed. She stretched and yawned. Today was Sunday. Of all days to feel depressed. The Lord's day, according to her mother, was a special day when all was good with the world. She was a regular at St Patrick's Catholic Church. Her husband was an atheist. Saffron didn't really know what she was, in religious terms. She just liked people and often helped them in little ways by opening a door for an old woman, or helping her mother around the house on wash days. Saffron was confused yet intrigued by her parents' views on worldly affairs, especially when it came to religion.

Her mother Linda, a staunch Catholic of Irish stock but born in Edinburgh got married to Chris soon after they met on Waverly train Station platform. Chris was born in Glasgow and was on a trip to Edinburgh castle where he had been stationed while serving with the Scots Guards back in the fifties.

They got talking and she told him she was leaving Scotland to work as a secretary in the newly built Corby Steelworks. "It's a new town and lots of people are looking for a new start, so why not down south," she had said.

Chris disliked living in the suburbs of Glasgow so remained on the train with Linda all the way to Kettering station. He found a job in the new steelworks as a foreman in the rolling mills. They've been together ever since.

"Mum," Saffron had said earlier.

"No. There isn't any more pocket money this week," replied Linda angrily.

"Why do you assume I want something every time I open my mouth?"

"Where is my scarf?" asked Linda, as she looked in drawer after drawer of her dresser.

"It's on the hanger by the front door," said Saffron, "Where you always leave it."

"Oh." Linda wrapped it around her curly, bushy head of brown hair. "My memory is getting worse by the day. Anyway, what'd yer want?"

"I need some money for makeup, mum. *Please.*"

"Do you see that tree out there," said Linda pointing to a single fir standing in the center of the back garden? Nip outside and pluck a few quid off the lower branch will you."

"Funny. You should be on TV."

Linda dipped into her purse and handed over two pounds. "Trying to look good for your new boyfriend?"

"Mum, sshhh. I told you that in confidence."

"Folks are gonna find out sooner or later. Anyway, what's wrong with Michael Sheridan. You like him, don't you."

"I like Josh."

"I'm not trying to interfere, Saffron, but you have to think about your future. Michael is from a well-to-do family. He's smart and his mother told me he wants to go to university. He could be a doctor or a bank manager. Surely that's better than getting serious with a pauper."

"Josh is not a pauper."

"Look where he lives, Saffron. What sort of a life could he possibly give you?"

"He's going to join the army."

"And what sort of a steady job is that, eh? Break your heart he will, especially if he gets shot or blown up or something."

"How can you say that?"

"Well, it's not a life for a wife, is it? And what sort of a job will he have when he gets out? Working in the steelworks?"

"I love him, mum."

"Love won't put bread on the table, dear."

Saffron stormed upstairs and, just before she closed her bedroom door, she heard her father clamoring down the stairs. She raised her eyes skyward and was glad she was meeting Joshua today. How dare her mother want her to date Michael Sheridan. He's a nerd.

Today she decided she was going to try to be happy. Today was a Sunday and, although she didn't attend church as often as her mother wished, she wondered if Joshua wanted to attend church with her. Perhaps they could say a prayer together – for John.

She took off her pajamas and stood naked in front of the full length wardrobe mirror. She knew she was pretty and hoped Joshua liked her firm breasts, tiny waist and long legs. She turned around and checked out her bottom. Firm and rounded. Images of Joshua's body flashed through her mind; she felt a stirring between her legs; she quickly slipped on her knickers and put on her jeans and purple blouse. Her hormones were on fire.

Her mother was going to attend the evening service, so there was no chance of her being seen at church. If her mother spotted her then she would end up having to commit her time to attending church *every* Sunday. No way.

Saffron's stomach turned as an image of Michael Sheridan flashed through her mind. One day at school he had stood behind her and squeezed her buttocks with both hands. She had turned and slapped him hard across the face; his spectacles fell to the ground. "Don't you ever do that again, you lanky four-eyed twat!"

Her stomach fluttered this time with butterfly wings as she thought of meeting Joshua. They hadn't seen each other for a whole week. She wanted to hug him, hold him and kiss him. She wanted to be close to him, touch him, *squeeze* him. She wanted to make *love* to him.

*

They held hands in the front row as Father Luke stood on his high pulpit. Joshua often wondered why they had to strain their necks to look up at a priest. Did the 'Servants of God' feel somehow superior to the rest of their flock by rising above everyone else? And why did he think like this? Why couldn't he accept everything at face value and let himself be brainwashed like the rest of the congregation? Why *was* he so different?

Saffron had her head bowed and her hands joined together in prayer.

"Who you praying to," said Joshua.

"I'm saying a prayer for Bonnie's soul," she whispered. "Just in case there is a Heaven."

How lucky he was. A beauty, if ever he saw one. And today church didn't seem so bad, so boring, not with his girl sitting beside him. He wanted her. His loins stirred. He craved to make love to her, though not at the clay-hole. After John's death the Town Council had decided (or were swayed by the angry protests through town) to fence the whole quarry off and fill all the pools in with soil. They intended to flatten the pool areas of the quarry and reinforce the fence that surrounded the big excavator plus employ security guards to keep everyone out. No more swimming. No more deaths – hopefully.

Joshua felt a deep loss over John's death, especially since he couldn't release his friend's trapped leg. But guilt itself served no purpose. Guilt just dug away inside a person, eating away his self-esteem, and only creating depression.

He had tried and failed to help his friend. His friend died. *He* was alive. What more was there to think about? They were the facts and the facts spoke the truth. And Bonnie had been so brave. *Dogs don't reason, they react,* said his inner voice. She tried to help him save John and had paid the ultimate price.

Joshua had noticed on the way into church that John's parents were sitting on pews halfway up the aisle. He glanced at them and was about to nod his head in greeting when they both bowed their heads as if in prayer.

Did they blame *him* for their son's death? They had never said anything to him about trying to save their son's life, not even a handshake or a manly pat on the back, and they had snubbed him at the funeral wake. What would they have done if he had ignored John's plight and had just left him under the water without attempting to save his life? Would they still have snubbed him, disliked him? Is it because their son died and he lived that they held some kind of grudge against him? He had tried his best, hadn't he?

Joshua felt guilty enough having not saved his friend without having to deal with his parents actually blaming *him*. For his sanity he had to try to either erase or put those guilty feelings away; in his mind he packed them up in a lead-covered box and placed the box in another container situated deep in his memory.

He used an imaginary key to lock that container and then wrapped chain after chain and massive locks around it until he was satisfied that the guilt was completely locked away and safe. He imagined the pool where John died and, standing on the bank, he threw the key as far as he could into the area where the tragedy had happened.

"Joshua," said Saffron and prodded him with her elbow. "Are you okay?"

"Oh. I'm fine," he said and sat upright. "I was miles away there."

"Today I'm going to read from Matthew 17:20 about the boy possessed by a demon. The disciples came to Jesus privately and asked. "Why couldn't we drive out the demon? And Jesus replied, 'Because you have so little faith. For truly I tell you, if you have faith the size of a mustard seed, you can say to this mountain, "Move from here to there," and it will move. Nothing will be impossible for you.'"

The words of Jesus fascinated Joshua. They made sense, not in any religious way but in everyday life. What if the Bible and all those teachings of Christ were meant to mean something else and not bowing and scraping and crawling in church and praying to a God somewhere up there in the heavens, but actually meant people could do *anything* if they set their minds to it, and believed wholeheartedly in whatever they set out to achieve? Now *that* made more sense to Joshua than all the baloney preached every day by priests and pastors, bishops and popes. With a little wisdom an intelligent person could easily understand the *real* truth in Jesus' teachings.

Think out of the box, Joshua, his inner voice said to him. *These sheep are what they are – sheep, they follow the easiest and quickest route to salvation, like the lost starving and thirsty lamb in the field who, out of insecurity and desperation clings onto the nearest group and follows them out of the field, along the country lane and down to the river. Remember Joshua. What you think about you bring about. Have faith and* your *world* will *change.*

"In the name of the father, the Son and the Holy Ghost," said Father Luke at the end of the mass. Everyone stood, genuflected, blessed themselves, even Joshua and Saffron followed suit, in case they were thought of as blasphemous, and they couldn't be condemned for *that* in their congregation. Joshua reckoned that if the congregation, the parish, anyone in fact, knew his views on religion he'd be ostracized, condemned and maybe even sent over to Dublin to be incarcerated in a mental asylum like his Uncle Jack. And if that were to happen, with all the sins he committed on a daily basis, then they'd surely lock him away for life.

"Stuffy and hot in there, today," said Saffron outside the church.

"No air conditioning," said Joshua. "I hate the humidity in this country. One day I'm going to live in America. They have air conditioners over there."

"Will you take me with you," said Saffron, pleadingly.

"We can live in a little flat, or apartment as they call it," said Joshua excitedly. "And get one with a swimming pool right outside the door. We can find work, come home at night, have our tea, and go swimming."

"Watch films, or movies."

"Lie on the couch together."

"Have some drinks."

"Kiss each other."

"Talk about our day."

"Make love."

They smile and walk hand in hand along Gainsborough Road toward Joshua's house. They are happy, content, and full of dreams and love for each other on this Our Lord's day, nineteen hundred and sixty nine.

*

"Rain, rain, fecking rain," said Mary sipping her tea.

"Ah, sure doesn't the grass need it all, now," said Mrs. Feely, lifting her teacup near her mouth and holding the handle with two fingers, her pinky finger sticking up in the air.

"Ah, now, look at her majesty sipping her tea," said Mary and laughed. Mrs. Feely was silent for a few moments and half-smiled.

"Ah, don't mind me," said Mary. "I'm only jealous I wasn't brought up in a posh house like yourself. Here, have a custard cream. Our Joshua loves these."

"Thank you. These *are* nice. Anyway, our house wasn't exactly posh, Mary."

"Yer had a toilet *indoors*, didn't you?"

"Aye, we did that."

"Then that's posh in my book. We had to piss in the drain in the back yard. And if yer needed a number two, we had to fill a bucket full of water, if there was any, mind, and then flush it down the toilet bowel in the shed."

"Ah, yer having me on, now, Mary. Even the good Lord himself used a toilet."

"Now who's having *me* on, Mrs. Feely. Don't yer know that Jesus didn't need to take a number two at all."

Mrs. Feely almost choked on her custard cream and quickly washed some of the biscuit down with a sip of tea.

"You've got a way with words, for sure," said Mrs. Feely. "You remind me of our Brendan, bless his soul." They both bless themselves. "He was always telling the jokes."

"I bet yer still miss him."

"Every day without fail, Mary." Mrs. Feely's eyes filled up.

"Wasn't it in the army he … " Mary pulled a tissue out of the end of her sleeve and gave it to Mrs. Feely.

"He was killed in France. Shot by the Germans."

"And you've never wanted to, you know, remarry?"

"Brendan was my sweetheart. We met at school in North Dublin. He never raised his voice to me. He used to bring me bunches of flowers and a wee box of chocolates, just because he loved me, he said. We were married five years before he was drafted into the British Army. The best five years of my life. Here yer are, Mary. You'll need this."

Mrs. Feely handed the tissue to Mary.

"Thanks," she said, sniffed and blew her nose. "What part of north Dublin did you live?"

"Ballyfermot, not far from Phoenix park."

"We lived near the park, too. Drummore Road, it was."

"I used to walk past there on me way back from the shops. You were probably one of the kids playing out on the path."

"We used to play hop, skip and jump along there."

"Aye, they were fine days. We were poor but happy," said Mrs. Feely.

"I've read those books you gave me," said Mary.

"I've got another one for you, 'Love on the Rocks.'"

"Himself hates it when I read."

"Doesn't he do a bit of reading himself?"

"He couldn't read the label on a whisky bottle. He can certainly drink what's fecking inside. And he always asks Joshua how to spell words when he's filling out his worksheets?"

"Shame. There's so much joy in reading."

"Anyway, he hates it that I'm educating meself."

"Just tell him what you usually say?"

"And what's that, Mrs. Feely?"

"Feck off."

*

Chapter 24

Joshua waited for what seemed a month outside Saffron's front gate.

"Won't be long," she had said. "Just need to change."

The area was middle-class suburbia, or at least posher (higher class) than where he was living in Gainsborough Road. Nice trimmed lawns and rose bushes in the front mixed in with petunias and Gerber daisies. There were no cracks in the pavements, no weeds anywhere to be seen. Even the lampposts were straight and actually had bulbs in them.

Folks were out in their driveways washing and waxing their new cars. No tiles missing from the roofs. In Joshua's neighborhood they usually had most of the roof tiles stolen.

Saffron alighted from her house *thank God* wearing a tight white blouse which complemented her firm bust, a black mini skirt and white ankle socks. The blouse had frilly bits around the collar. To Joshua she looked very sexy in a short skirt because of her long, slender legs and nicely shaped buttocks. He counted himself lucky to know this girl. As she walked towards him he felt a little stirring in his loins. *Oh boy*.

They sauntered hand in hand to the bus stop. The town bus would be here soon. Saffron searched in her bag and took out a packet of cigarettes, stuck one in her mouth and lit up.

"I didn't know you smoked," said Joshua. "Filthy habit."

"Don't you start," said Saffron and inhaled deeply, coughed and covered her mouth with her hand. "My mother nags me about it all the time."

"They'll kill you, you know."

"My grandfather smoked 'till he was ninety," said Saffron, and took another drag of her poison.

"It's still a bad habit."

"Helps with stress. Calms me down, you know. Sure you don't want one?"

"Go on, then. Why not."

She took a cigarette out of the packet and lit it for him, then handed it over. Joshua took a deep drag, pulled a face and coughed. "These taste like shite."

"Takes a bit to get used to."

He inhaled again and coughed. "God almighty."

"Poor Bonnie," said Saffron and took another drag.

"I miss her," said Joshua. "

"She'll be in Heaven with Clyde right now."

The town bus pulled up with Paddy McCauley swinging on the middle bar like a monkey up a tree. The buses were the old type, similar to the London buses with the entrance at the rear and open.

"Hey-up. Here's Pinky and Perky."

"Oh God. Anyone but him," said Saffron.

"Top of the morning to yer, Paddy," said Joshua and smiled.

"And the rest of the afternoon to yerself," Paddy said and ushered them onto the bus. "Bit of shopping today, is it?"

"I need a pair of jeans," said Joshua.

"Ye'll have to sit upstairs if yer smoking."

Saffron climbed the stairs followed by Joshua and, unbeknown to him Paddy stood at the foot of the stairs looking up Saffron's mini skirt.

The comedic bus conductor walked into the lower section of the bus and sang quietly to himself, "Such a pretty sight, I'll eat my snickers, to see such legs wearing tight black knickers, and wobbly cheeks that can't fight back, with nylon twisted up her sweet crack."

He giggled to himself, took a couple of fares and climbed the stairs to the top deck.

"Ah, now, me beauties," said Paddy. "That'll be two and six for the both of you."

Joshua handed over money and received two tickets in return.

"It was so sad about young John," said Paddy in a concerned voice that Joshua was wary of because Paddy was always fooling around and he wasn't sure whether Paddy had a serious side to him or not.

"I miss him," said Joshua

"Me, too," said Saffron.

It was quiet for a few moments as Saffron and Joshua gazed out the window as they drove past terraced houses and small parks, while Paddy stared down at Saffron's thighs. The bus trundled along the main road which led to Gainsborough Road and up Leighton Road and into the town center. The bus stopped and two ladies got on.

"Oh look, Josh," said Paddy. "There's your mother and Mrs. Feely just got on the bus. "Come on up, ladies," said Paddy. "Join the party."

Joshua quickly handed his lighted cigarette to Saffron, who in turn handed it to Paddy (who doesn't smoke) just as Mary and Mrs. Feely reached the top of the stairs.

"Welcome to my kingdom," said Paddy. "Only beautiful people are allowed up here. Joshua off you go."

"Feck off," hissed Joshua.

"I didn't know you smoked," said Mrs. Feely.

"Only upstairs," said Paddy and stubbed out the cigarette in an ashtray on the back of one of the seats. "Now where would you fine ladies like to sit?"

"On a seat, I imagine," said Mary. She rustled Joshua's hair. "Bit of shopping is it?"

"Hi-yer, ma. Yer. Saffron's going to buy me a new pair of jeans."

"Oh, that's nice," said Mary sitting down with Mrs. Feely behind Joshua and Saffron.

"That's the last time I let that husband of mine do the washing," said Mary. "Ruined the boy's jeans, he did. Imagine putting bleach in with the darks. Ejit."

"Ah, you're lucky you have a man to do it," said Mrs. Feely.

"He's useless that shite is. Last week he mixed the colors with the whites; put the dirty washing in the dryer and the clean and dried washing in the washer. I hung out last week's fecking laundry. I married an ejit!"

"I washed our bedroom windows once and fell through 'em," said Paddy.

"Was there no glass, then," said Mrs. Feely.

"Some ejit had opened the windows," replied Paddy and Mary laughed and roared and laughed and Joshua raised his eyebrows skyward and Saffron giggled and Paddy shook his head and Mrs. Feely giggled a little and covered her mouth with a wrinkled hand.

"That'll be ten bob for the two of you to the town center," said Paddy and stuck out his hand.

"It was only two and six yesterday," said Mary.

"You've aged since then."

Mary roared with laughter again. It reminded Joshua of the time in Wicklow in the amusement arcade.

"Have a free ride today," said Paddy, "on the house."

"Ah, bless yer, Paddy," said Mary and Mrs. Feely in tandem.

The bus stopped and a bunch of school kids jumped on and scrambled up the stairs dragging satchels and tote bags behind them. They took up most of the seats on the top deck.

"Keep it down, now, kids," said Paddy. "There's other people on the bus, you know."

"Piss off," came a female voice from the throng.

"Who said that," said Paddy.

"Fuck off back to Ireland," shouted a male voice.

"Right. I won't throw you all off the bus 'cause yer need to go to school." Paddy stood in the center aisle in the middle of the fourteen year old brats.

"Why don't you bunch of ejits shut up," said Mary and Mrs. Feely nodded her approval. "Whippersnappers, ye haven't shit yellow yet." Mary was referring to the waste products produced by a new born baby, which tended to be a yellowy color until baby started eating solids in which case the waste turned into a normal brown hue, and meant, in Irish terms, that you were immature and acting like a baby.

"It's okay, Mrs. Hanley," said Paddy. "I can handle this bunch of deviants on my own, but thank you all the same. So get your money out. A shilling each." He took their coins and rolled out strips of beige colored tickets from his machine.

"So how's it going at school," said Paddy to no one in particular.

"We hate school," said a girl near the back.

"Teachers' are crap," said a boy in the middle.

"All they're good for is belting you with the cane," said another.

"Well," said Paddy. "Without a proper education you won't be able to get a good job."

"And end up as a bus conductor," said some smart sprite near the front of the bus.

Joshua giggled and Saffron nudged him sharply in the ribs.

"Do you know," said Paddy without any qualms, "that I wished I had the opportunity to learn at school, stay at school and somehow go to college. I wanted to better myself."

"And graduate to bus inspector!" said another bright 'ejit' at the back of the bus. The throng of miscreants laughed aloud and even Mary joined in, though she hadn't quite got the gist of the conversation, nevertheless, laughter is laughter.

"I like your humor," said Paddy. "I think you should *all* be bus conductors.

"Ah, we're only kidding yer," someone said from the rear. "We like yer really."

A load of 'yays' rang up and down the top deck of the bus. Paddy beamed a smile. He could sell oil to the Arabs with his calm and humorous style.

"Joke," said a voice, followed by the whole bunch chanting, "Joke, joke, joke."

And not one to disappoint a young and eager audience Paddy went into his comedy routine. "Well, a guy goes to the doctor and the doctor asks, 'have you flu?' and the guy says, 'no, I came by bike.'"

There was a momentary pause before the throng burst into laughter. When that died down Mary was laughing still.

"Seamus and Paddy were riding on a bus and Paddy had a box on his lap. 'What's in the box,' said Seamus. 'Chickens,' said Paddy. 'And if you guess how many chickens I have in here you can have both of them.'

Mrs. Feely screamed with laughter this time, followed by the kids and lastly by Mary. Joshua and Saffron had turned around in their seats to watch the proceedings and only smiled at Paddy's jokes because they'd heard them a few times before.

"You're funny," said a voice from the front.

"Funny in the fecking head," said another which raised a few more laughs. Meanwhile Mary and Mrs. Feely were doing their Wicklow amusement arcade performance and laughing hysterically all the way through. Paddy had to raise his voice to be heard above their laughter.

"God grants Murphy two wishes. 'I'd like you to build a suspension bridge,' says Murphy, '350 miles long spanning from Dublin to Liverpool with reinforced concrete bases, suspended cables criss-crossing the bridge with a wind and sea protection shield sixty feet high on each side.'

God scratches his Holy head for a few moments and says, 'That's an enormous engineering feat and so technologically advanced that not even *I* could grant that wish. What's your second wish?' Murphy scratches his balding head and says, 'I'd like to know how a woman thinks?' And God says, 'So when do you want me to start the bridge.'"

The kids laugh, Joshua and Saffron laugh this time not having heard this joke before, and Mrs. Feely and Mary had now entered a stage of extreme hysteria. The bus pulled into the depot in the center of town. Before it stopped the crowd of kids left their seats and were running down the stairs and jumping onto the pavement like skydivers jumping out of an aeroplane.

"Steady now, kids," said Paddy. "Don't be falling under the bus."

Joshua took his mother's arm and guided her down the stairs, followed by Mrs. Feely and then Saffron.

"Did you know," said Paddy now walking behind Saffron, his eyes glaring at her buttocks. "That the Irish Navy is the only navy in the world that sails home for its dinner." The two ladies screamed with laughter and continued laughing and giggling all the way from the bus depot to the market place nearby. Shoppers and pedestrians gawked at them as they passed and probably surmised that they'd just either been let out of the local mental asylum or had alighted from Paddy McCauley's fun bus.

"Don't be spending all my money down the market, now, do you hear, Mrs. Hanley," came Paddy's distant voice.

"Oh, Jesus," gasped Mrs. Feely, clutching her chest and out of breath. "That man'll be the death of me."

"We'll see yer in the co-op café," said Joshua to his mother.

She waved her hand in agreement and walked arm in arm with Mrs. Feely among the market stalls.

"I wish my mother was like that," said Saffron.

"Oh, your mum's alright," replied Joshua.

"She's a bitch," said Saffron. "Right," she said and quickened her pace. "Let's go and buy you a nice pair of jeans."

*

"We've a new driver today," said Paddy as Joshua, Saffron, his mother and Mrs. Feely got on the bus for the journey home. "Green as peas," he continued, "but we all have to learn sometime."

"Can he drive in a straight line," said Mary.

"Only when he's not going around a corner," said Paddy and started rattling off tickets.

There were about seven passengers on the lower deck and eight on the top deck. Paddy was about to climb the stairs to the top deck when the same bunch of deviant school kids, now dressed in jeans and tee-shirts, charged toward the bus. Paddy stood at the entrance.

"There's no *way* you lot are getting on my bus," said Paddy.

"This ain't *your* bus," said a lanky, acne-puckered kid.

"We're going to the school disco," said another.

"What school?"

"Kingswood," they said in unison.

"Take the 291," said Paddy, "that'll drop you off right in front of the school. It's due here in about five minutes."

"But we like listening to your jokes," said a voice from the back.

"Ah, come on," said a girl no bigger than a hobbit, "My boyfriend's waiting for me."

"I like sitting upstairs," said a boy at the rear.

"Only 'cause you want to smoke my fags," said a kid next to him.

"Come on," the throng said in chorus. "Please, please."

Paddy pressed a bell and the bus slowly drove away.

"Nothing personnel, kids. Take the 291. Enjoy the dance."

The bus drove off, turning at the end of the depot and onto the main road, past the police station, the co-op on the corner and down a hill to a roundabout.

Roundabouts: a big circle with roads leading off to different locations. A motorist has to give way to other vehicles on his right and sometimes it can be hectic with cars jumping the line and speeding in front of other cars, some speed too much and bump up the curb and end up on the grass in the center of the roundabout. English roundabouts are as common as afternoon cakes and cups of tea.

The bus turned left at the roundabout instead of turning right and onto Gainsborough Road. The new driver had obviously taken the wrong direction which would have been okay under normal circumstances, but a half mile down this road was a low lying bridge that all drivers had been taught not to approach, except maybe this driver.

Paddy recognized the driver's mistake quickly and ran downstairs and up the aisle towards the driver's cab. Out of the front window he saw the bridge approaching fast. His eyes met those of the driver and, for a split second they both knew what was about to transpire.

He heard the screams from upstairs, then a tremendous banging, screeching and scraping noise. Glass splattered everywhere downstairs. He dived on the floor as did the other passengers on the lower deck. The driver sat motionless in his seat, a look of extreme horror and shock on his face.

The right side of the engine had smashed into the side stanchion of the bridge and steam billowed out. In an instant the engine caught fire and flames enveloped the bonnet of the front panels and window frame of the driver's cab.

"Get out of there," Paddy yelled at the driver, but the flames had engulfed the whole cab and all Paddy saw was the driver's left arm desperately attempting to clamor out of the cab. The door by the engine side had been smashed in and buckled; there was no escape that way. And the way these buses were constructed, the side door and the front and side windows were the only means of escape in an emergency but were all now covered in flames.

From the inside of the bus on the lower deck the driver was separated by metal frames and glass and had no means to climb out and lower himself onto the lower deck floor.

Paddy watched in horror as the driver burned to death.

The screaming continued upstairs. He climbed up and stood on the top stair and looked up at blue sky. The metal roof of the top deck had been completely ripped off and all that remained were metal stumps of the window frames bent and jagged like rotten teeth.

"Jesus, Mary and Joseph," said Paddy and blessed himself.

The screaming stopped. He slowly crept along the aisle looking into each seat cubicle for bodies, for anybody, hopefully alive. Saffron and Joshua were huddled together on the floor beside their seat.

"Make your way downstairs and off the bus," said Paddy.

They stared at him, not moving, in shock.

"Come on. Move," said Paddy, louder this time. "The bus is on fire!"

"Where's my ma," said Joshua, near to tears.

"She's up front. She's fine, I'm sure. Now downstairs with you."

Joshua and Saffron cautiously crept downstairs as Paddy crawled forward and looked in each seat cubicle. An elderly couple, the woman's head leaning on the man's shoulder seemed unharmed and Paddy guided them back to the stairs.

A young adult stood up in the next cubicle, nodded at Paddy, took his girlfriend by the hand and they made their way to the stairway.

"Mrs. Hanley," said Paddy with panic in his voice. He walked to the front of the bus where he was sure the two women had decided to sit. "Mary. Are you alright?"

"Mrs.Feely," Mary croaked. "Mrs. Feely she …"

Paddy reached the front seat and saw Mary on her knees and bending over Mrs. Feely. There was blood everywhere. "Oh sweet Jesus," said Paddy and fell to his knees. He wept, his shoulders rising and falling. "Not this. Not on my bus. Not on my bus."

Mrs. Feely's torso was stuck between the bottom front section of the bus and the seat cubicle - her head was missing.

*

Mrs. Feely was well liked by everyone that knew her, and probably those that didn't know her. It was a Catholic funeral which meant a mass in St Patrick's Church officiated by Father Luke. The church was packed.

It was a hot and humid day and most of the mourners had no choice but to take their suit jackets off and sit in shirt-sleeves, which, to some busy-bodies gave them the chance to take stock of whom, or whose wife had ironed or had not ironed their husbands' shirts that day.

Mrs. Feely's brother, Jimmy, the only surviving member of a family of six, sat with his head bowed on the front row with Joshua, his parents and Saffron next to him. Jimmy had travelled over from Ireland; he worked as a bank manager for the Bank of Ireland in Dublin. He had thick, brown hair like his late sister.

Paddy and other representatives from Corby Bus Corporation filled the second and third pews. Behind them sat the Mayor of Corby and some of his councilors.

Sean Flanagan led the procession up the long aisle of the church playing the "Minstrel Boy" on his bagpipes. He was dressed in a green and yellow kilt complete with a goat-skinned sporran, a black, silver-buttoned jacket, and a Tam'O Shanter bonnet.

Father Luke and his altar boys followed the piper towards the altar.

The coffin was carried feet first up the aisle, and, when all were settled, the sound of the bagpipes ceased and was replaced by sniffling and quiet weeping. Father Luke climbed his mighty perch and gave the eulogy.

Her brother Jimmy said later at the wake that he'd attended all his siblings' funerals, including his parents and that Margaret's send-off was by far the best.

"It was the bagpiper that gave it the edge," he had said.

*

Mary Hanley never quite got over the loss of her friend. She never called her by her first name, always Mrs. Feely, maybe because she was more like a mother to her than a friend. *If you hadn't dropped your purse on the floor, Mary,* said her inner voice, *then you'd also be six feet under.* She had been picking up her purse from under her seat when she heard the tremendous ripping and scraping and screaming.

"Thank you, God," she now said and blessed herself three times.

For years afterward she'd often find herself standing at the back garden fence and looking over at Mrs. Feely's back kitchen door, waiting expectantly to see her and come out and talk through the gaps in the fence. Something they had done for years, a kind of ritual between them. And they'd talk and complain and compare views on 'herself' over there at number twenty-three with her piles of gin and whiskey bottles outside the back door, or 'himself' two doors down prancing about his back garden wearing one of those disgusting 'G' strings that only strippers wear in those dirty clubs in London. And did yer hear what so and so said about the other so and so and on and on and on …

And Mrs. Feely would reply by way of slight exhalations of air and tiny twitches at the corner of her mouth and if it was a whopper, like the guy wearing a 'G' string in his back garden, well, 'God Almighty save us' she'd spout and puff and suck in air and blow a low whistle and clutch her chest and shake her head and scratch the back of her neck and bless herself and …

… Mary wiped her eyes for the umpteenth time and stirred the pot of Dublin Coddle atop the gas cooker. Mrs. Feely loved her broth and many times Mary handed her a wee dish of her stew through the gap in the fence.

She took a deep drag of her cigarette and inadvertently flicked the ash on the carpet. She rubbed the ash into the carpet with a frayed slipper. She laughed inwardly thinking of what her husband said most Friday nights when he returned from work, "When the carpet's full, can you please use the ashtray."

"He used to smoke worse than yourself," Mary said to herself out loud. "And then he just woke up one morning and decided not to smoke. How can anyone do that so easily?"

Mrs. Feely had often urged Mary to give up the dreaded fags, but it was to no avail. It was like asking a bear to stop hibernating. "But what about the health of your son," she had said.

"Oh, he'll be alright" said Mary. "At least he's not taking drugs."

Of course it hadn't dawned on Mary (it did on Mrs. Feely, but she remained quiet) that cigarettes and nicotine *are* drugs. "If they had been discovered nowadays," Mrs. Feely had said quite sternly (which was not normally like her) "they would be outlawed and tobacco company executives sent to jail."

Mary sauntered through to the foot of the stairs and shouted, "Joshua. Will yer leave that poor girl alone and come down and light the fire for yer poor old mother."

*

Chapter 25

"It's called a Goose set," said Sean Flanagan as he showed Joshua how to hold the sheepskin bag beneath his left arm. The 'Goose set' Joshua was told is a beginner's version of the full set of bagpipes. It consists of an air-tight bag made from either sheepskin or cow hide and has to be seasoned with a special mixture to maintain its air tightness. Attached to the neck of the bag by strong string is the practice chanter with a small plastic reed inside (and not like the big bagpipe chanter where the finger holes are much larger and has a cane reed inside) and drone stocks which are already tied to the three positions where the bigger drones will be attached at a later date. The stocks are corked off and the piper gets used to blowing the bag and playing the tunes he knows on the 'Goose set,' until such times as the piper is ready to play the Great Highland Bagpipe.

Blowing air into the bag wasn't a problem for Joshua and what helped was a one-way valve inside the blow-stick which prevented any air from escaping. It's the co-ordination that is tricky at first, blowing the bag up, pumping the left arm to maintain the air pressure and blowing again to fill the bag up and so on. At first it's difficult because Joshua was blowing when he should have been pumping, and pumping when he should have been blowing. It's a bit like rubbing the top of your head with your left hand and rubbing your stomach with your right hand but in different directions.

"If you think this is difficult," said Sean, "Wait 'till you graduate to the Uilleann pipes. With them you have to pump a bellows under your right arm and the air is pushed through a tube to a bag under your left arm, and then you have to regulate that air to fill three drones, a two-octave chanter and three regulators. Now *that* is true co-ordination and skill."

"Wow," said Joshua. "

"And then," said Sean excitedly, "then you have to play all the tunes. And some of the fast Irish reels have second octave notes followed by first octave notes played in a split second. And all while maintaining the required air pressure in the bag under your left arm."

Joshua was fascinated. A challenge. He was determined to perfect playing the Highland Bagpipe and couldn't wait to 'graduate' to the Uilleann pipes.

"Let me show you," said Sean and reached above his head to a wooden box on a shelf. He took the box down and got out a set of Uilleann pipes.

Joshua's eyes almost popped out of his head as he watched Sean strap the pipes around his waist, pump up the bellows and start to tune the drones to the pipe chanter. He began to play a slow air and it reminded Joshua of Mrs. Feely's funeral. After a time Sean played a jig, a hornpipe and then a fast reel and used his right wrist to tap brass keys along the regulators which gave the pipes a chord accompaniment.

Amazing, beautiful, Joshua thought and couldn't wait until the day he could play pipes like these. He also hoped he could play and perform as efficiently and as eloquently as Sean Flanagan.

Joshua almost skipped all the way home carrying his pipe box with the goose set tucked up neatly inside. He couldn't wait to get them out and play for Saffron and his mother.

And the next morning in the back garden with the neighbors watching, he marched up and down the cracked paving slabs playing the few tunes he knew on his practice set. To the left of the garden and about two hundred feet away was a big block of flats. An old couple sat on deckchairs on their balcony near the top floor and clapped and cheered every time Joshua finished playing. Joshua smiled, waved and took a bow as his mother hung out the washing on the line. She raised her eyes skyward and, not wanting to be thought of as aloof, also applauded.

He wished Saffron was there to watch him, but she wasn't due until that night.

Joshua couldn't have known that, in the future, he would be performing at funerals, and the most important service of all was when he performed at his mother's funeral.

*

Joshua got into the habit of rubbing his crucifix between his thumb and index finger. First thing upon waking he'd squeeze the cross, not only to ensure it had not fallen off during the night, but also searching for the magic that his grandfather had said was in the crucifix.

Whenever he thought of something, or wished for something, he'd rub the crucifix. And sometimes it worked. Sometimes before he slept he thought of something then rubbed the cross and, while asleep, had dreams similar to what he had thought about.

One time he wished that he'd be given a new bagpipe tune, his first jig, to learn later that night at practice. Near the end of the lesson, just as Joshua was thinking that he was a fool to think the cross can grant him a wish Sean Flanagan walked in from the kitchen and handed him a sheet of manuscript paper.

"Your first jig," he said. "The Irish Washerwoman."

Of course since that night he'd learnt that tune, played it over and over, so much so, that even his mother took to doing an Irish jig out in the back garden alongside the neighbors. Even the old couple on the balcony were swinging arm in arm around each other.

"You could make some money out of this," said Saffron when she called round that morning.

"I just love playing," said Josh. "Money would be a bonus."

But word soon spread (the sound of the bagpipes soon spread) that young Joshua was playing bagpipes and all the younger folks kept him in mind when their older folks were ready to pass on from this life to the next.

He was, by now able to play 'Amazing Grace,' 'Flowers of the Forest,' a couple of 4/4 marches, the Irish Washerwoman (his mother's favorite) and was considered ready by Sean to be able to perform at funerals. "Experience is everything," Sean had said while fitting him out for a piper's kilt and jacket. "But you have to start somewhere."

And his very first funeral, his very first *gig* was to perform at the graveside of Mr. O'Connell, a ninety-year old who had just been released from hospital, got home, had a strong tot of whisky and dropped dead in his chair while watching Coronation Street.

So, now, in his bedroom, Saffron sat on the bed and watched him getting dressed into his piper's gear.

"Wow," said Saffron. "You look smart."

"Well, thank you, Saffron. Kilt is a little too big for me, though."

"Let me help." She took the leather belt from around his trousers and wrapped it around his waist, tightened it and tucked the ends in at the back.

"There you go."

"Any good at doing ties?"

Saffron tied a windsor knot in his tie.

"Where you learn to do that?"

Saffron sighed. "My dad. He wears a tie every day at the bank."

"Lucky for me," said Joshua and walked to his mother's room to inspect himself in her full length mirror, the only other mirror was in the kitchen. Saffron followed him.

"Not bad," said Joshua, "Even if I say so myself."

"My handsome piper," said Saffron and kissed him on the lips. She groped him between the legs. "Hmmmmm. What's this? It's gruesome."

"It certainly has grew some. And will grow some more if you keep doing that." They giggled.

"I heard that Scotsmen don't wear anything under their kilts," said Saffron, salaciously.

"Lucky I'm Irish, then," said Joshua and held her tightly around the waist.

"You'll be late for the funeral," his ma shouted up the stairs. "Poor old Mr. O'Connell will be waiting for you down at the church."

"Mr. O'Connell is dead, ma," Joshua shouted back and rolled his eyes.

The funeral mass was long, the church hot and humid but old Mr. O'Connell had a great send off with lots of flowers and mourners and 'Flowers of the Forest' at the end performed by the new piper from Gainsborough Road.

Everyone seemed to be there except the Pope. Joshua played well, though it was only the Goose set he was playing, they were loud enough to make a great impression on the mourners and the family of the deceased. Joshua's very first gig. He was pleased and couldn't wait until the next one, though waiting for someone to die so he could perform seemed a touch morbid.

The Irish wake, as all Irish wakes go was brilliant. Drink, music, dancing, joking, kissing, shouting, screaming, fighting and sleeping – all went down well. Saffron didn't drink much but she had to almost carry Joshua home that night (he vomited a few times in the bushes on the way home) and she also had to carry his bagpipes under her other arm.

"Oh, look at the poor lamb," said Mrs. Reilly from number 206, standing at her front gate as Joshua and Saffron passed by. "Doesn't he take after his father, so."

"Only turned sixteen," said her neighbor, Mrs. Byrne from the other side of the wire fence. "Heaven help us when he's allowed in the pubs."

"Ah, don't be bothering him, now, Mrs. Byrne. "Sure didn't he play the pipes for old Mr. O'Connell. Gave him a grand old send off, so I hear."

Saffron smirked at the two old biddies and struggled along the road carrying the drunken piper (the name of a tune Joshua learned later on) and soon they reached his house.

"I'm ... okay, now, Saffron," slurred Joshua as he negotiated the steps leading up to the front door.

His mother opened the door, took one look at her son and blessed herself. "The devil is in him tonight, for sure," she said.

*

Hangover: Joshua's first. Never again, he thought. How many folks have said that in the morning after waking up with a thumping headache, a mouth as dry as a Californian desert and blurred vision? What the hell was he *drinking* last night?

A trip to the beach was what he needed. Saffron's father had agreed to drive them to the seaside town of Skegness over in Lincolnshire. Sixteen years old and he'd never been to the coast, never visited a beach, anywhere.

Today was the day to change that.

Joshua stretched his arms and legs and yawned. Boy, he could sleep for days. He was sure Saffron had kissed him goodnight after tucking him in last night and then got a taxi home. He hoped she was safe. Later he was going to apologize to her for being so drunk.

He filled the bath with hot water. God, he wished they had a shower like those American folks. Imagine being able to stand up and let the water flow over you. Best invention ever, though Joshua never stepped into a shower until he joined the British Army.

Washed, shaved (started shaving a few months back and since then the stubbiness on his chin got thicker and rougher every day), brushed and squeaky clean. Joshua got dressed and filled a small backpack with socks, underwear, tee-shirts and his new pair of jeans. He ran down the stairs three at a time and rushed out the side entrance.

"No porridge today?" his mother yelled after him. "You don't know what you're missing."

Joshua knew exactly what he was missing, as did his stomach, which gave him the incentive to run a little faster up the road toward Saffron's house.

The drive across country was pleasant. All those green fields and yellow rape seed fields amazed Joshua. He'd not been out of town in a long time, except for that trip up to North Yorkshire to visit Uncle Joe.

He wondered for a few moments about Peter, the gay ghost. Was he haunting that place, still? He shook the thoughts from his head.

Saffron's dad, Chris drove a dark blue Ford Cortina Mk 3, an improvement on the old Mk 2 he had driven for years with more leg room in the rear. Joshua sat in the back seat with Saffron in the passenger seat. He wanted to sit up front but the glaring look from Saffron's dad told him in no uncertain terms that he wouldn't tolerate any hanky-panky between him and his daughter on this trip. To Joshua, this seemed stupid, because her father wasn't staying with them only dropping them off at the hotel.

Still, they had to play the game, he supposed. Plenty of time for hanky-pankying later on. He hoped.

They drove along mostly narrow winding roads towards Skegness, getting stuck for miles behind caravans, slow trucks and farm tractors. It was virtually impossible to overtake these vehicles with all the sharp bends in the road. Eventually they drove through the City of Lincoln.

"Lincoln cathedral is up on that hill, there, can you see it? A city can't be called a city unless it has a cathedral," Chris commented and kept up a running commentary all the way through Lincoln and all the way up to Skegness.

When they reached the small hotel near the beach, Chris had to shake Joshua awake. He was hung-over still from the night before. Today he had the attention span of a gnat and, with Saffron's father droning on and on, he quite easily nodded off to sleep.

"Here we are," said Chris. "Your home for two days. I'll come and pick you up Sunday afternoon about three."

"Thanks, dad," said Saffron and kissed him on the cheek.

"Don't do anything I wouldn't do," said Chris and drove away.

"This'll be fun," said Joshua. "I've never been to the beach before."

Saffron kissed him fully on the lips and groped his bottom for good measure. "I've been dying to do that all day," she said.

"I've been dying to do something else all day," said Joshua, grabbed both their backpacks and led her into the hotel.

*

Skegness had great attractions like Fantasy Island, Nature-land, Skegness Pier, The Parrot Zoo (Joshua fancied visiting that place, maybe he'd find a talking parrot). There's also The Tower Cinema, The Lucky Strike and many small venues and restaurants where families can eat and have fun.

The hotel room was small but neat and tidy with white-laced windows and two single beds. They quickly pushed the two singles together to make a double. They were both sixteen now and the legal age for sex in Britain was sixteen, not that teenagers took any notice of such laws.

Joshua picked up a visitors brochure from the bedside table. ""A poor travelling showman called Billy Butlin came to Skegness in 1921. By 1929 he had built an amusement park on the south side of the pier, and by 1935 he had built the Butlins Holiday Camp between Skegness and Ingoldmells.' That's where John went on holiday with his folks."

Saffron came out from the bathroom in a long pink robe. "Is there a shower in there," Joshua said and began to get undressed.

"Don't be silly. This is England. We like to bathe."

"One day I'm going to live somewhere with lots of showers."

"Try America," said Saffron.

"I might just go there."

"As long as you take me," said Saffron and dropped her bathrobe to the floor.

*

The speeding cyclist passed them as they walked hand in hand along the beach front. Up ahead there was a loud crashing sound; lying beneath the bike was a young woman.

Joshua rushed over and lifted the bike from the woman. The young scruffy-looking cyclist was on his knees and holding his head.

"Are you okay," said Josh. He knelt down beside the woman. Saffron knelt beside him.

"I think so," said the woman.

"Ejit," said Joshua. He should be arrested for riding on the path."

The cyclist stood, grabbed his bike and, before anyone could say anything, sped away.

Joshua helped the woman to her feet. "Are you hurt?"

"Just my pride, I think."

Saffron handed the woman's handbag to her. "You'd think people would be more careful around tourists."

"Thank you."

"Come on, Josh," Saffron said suddenly. "Let's go hire a donkey."

"It was nice to meet you," said Joshua.

"Thank you for helping," said the woman.

They walked down the ramp and toward the donkey stall, followed by the woman. She followed them all the way down to the donkeys.

Saffron turned around. "Are you following us," she said sternly.

"Oh, sorry, no. My friends are over there riding donkeys. I was going to join them."

Saffron and Joshua jumped on a donkey and rode along the beach. The woman rode one, too, and joined her three female friends near the edge of the sea.

Joshua eventually ended up behind them (Saffron was twenty feet or so behind Joshua); he soon caught up to the woman and her friends, not because he wanted to, but he obviously was riding a faster donkey, if there was such a thing. He must have hired an ex Derby champion.

He noticed the woman had broad shoulders and her mousy blonde hair flowed over her shoulders and halfway down her back. She was pretty for sure. Her eyes, though he'd only looked into them for a split second were a blue-ish gray. She had a pert nose which perfectly matched her face, and firm breasts. He had noticed her pointed nipples through the thin pink blouse she wore. Something had stirred below. She was also smaller than Saffron.

"Hi again," said Joshua as he passed the woman. "Oh, my name's Joshua, by the way."

"As in the bible?" said the woman.

"I guess so. What's your name?"

"Annie," she said and beamed a smile.

*

They didn't care that they looked stupid riding donkeys on Skegness beach, especially since everyone else riding donkeys were much younger than them, except Annie.

"I feel like a right ass on this thing," said Joshua.

"I fancy an ice-cream," said Saffron jumping down from her ride.

"Two '99's coming up," said Joshua and fell off his donkey.

They were having fun. Sunshine, sand, ice-creams, lunch, dinner later, a few drinks sneaked into the hotel room, off to bed, make love, wake up with the sun blazing through the laced curtains. Paradise. All the simple treats that break up the mundane existence of everyday boring life, according to Joshua Hanley's philosophical outlook on his life to date. Sometimes, he thought, the things that are free like sunshine, fresh air, peace of mind, relaxation were worth more than living with the stress of keeping safe a million pound or dollar lifestyle.

Sitting there during those moments of bliss beneath the warm sun and watching the sea, licking ice-creams, holding the hand of the one he loved couldn't be topped by all the money in the universe.

For a few moments he felt guilty about ogling Annie. But why did he get that twinge, not only in his loins but also in the pit of his stomach? He shrugged his shoulders and just put it down to experience. After all, he'd never meet her again.

They gazed out over the sea.

"So," said Saffron, "did you like her?"

"Like who?"

"Oh, come on, Josh. I saw the way you looked at her."

"I was just being polite."

"Your eyes nearly popped out of your head gaping at her nipples."

"I wasn't gaping at …"

"It's alright, Josh. You're a man. That's what men do."

"Then why are you angry about it?"

"I'm not angry, just, well …"

"Ah, you're jealous," Joshua teased. "The green-eyed monster."

"I don't care," she said peeved, "you can date who you bloody like. See if I care!"

"Who said anything about dating her? Jesus, Saffron. You're my girl."

"Then why did you ask her name?"

"You heard me?"

"I may be stupid, Josh, but I'm not deaf."

"I was …"

"Don't tell me. You were only being polite."

Silence between them as they listened to the sounds of gulls squawking overhead, cars driving up and down the beach front main road and the happy yelping from children nearby.

Joshua squeezed Saffron's hand. She took it away. He gripped it again and this time said, "I love you."

She gazed into his eyes and he could see her soften a little. "I love you," said Saffron and added, "You make me so happy."

Joshua leaned over and kissed her cheek. "You make me feel *alive*."

*

Joshua slept again on the way home. He wasn't hung-over this time, just worn out from making love to Saffron at every opportunity that arose. Young love.

"These damn tractors are a nuisance," barked Chris as he pulled out onto the opposite lane to see if any oncoming traffic was coming his way. He quickly swerved back in as a semi-truck sped past.

"Dad," said Saffron, worried, "I'd rather get home later than not get home at all."

"It's alright for you, young woman," said Chris, "but I have a meeting first thing in the morning."

Chris tried again to overtake the tractor. The driver of the tractor turned to him and waved his right arm frantically, obviously attempting to warn him not to overtake. Too late.

A truck approached on the opposite side of the road and Chris had no option but to brake hard and try to slip back in behind the tractor, but in doing so, caused his car to swerve and the front of his car hit the rear of the tractor, spun out onto the opposite side of the road and was hit by the skidding truck.

The car spun and faced backwards then swerved and sped through a line of hedges before taking off into the air, spinning a few times and landing on its roof in the field.

*

Joshua was dreaming of lying peacefully on a beach when suddenly he heard a tremendous crashing sound, and scraping, and tires screeching, opened his eyes and saw the world upside down, now spinning and twisting and a loud thud and then darkness.

He opened his eyes and tried to fathom out where he was, what had happened and realized he was hanging upside down in the back of the car.

The seatbelt dug into his waist but he managed to free himself, get out of the car and run around to Saffron's side and yanked the door open.

"Saffron, Saffron," he said frantically, "Are you okay?"

The car burst into flames.

He reached in and undid her safety belt and dragged her out and away from the car. She was unconscious but breathing. The flames reached the rear of the car and he heard a 'whoosh' sound as the fire engulfed the passenger side.

Joshua placed Saffron on the grass and ran back to the driver's side door but, before he could open the door, another 'whoosh' went up and that side was engulfed in flames.

Frantically he ran back to Saffron. "I can't … your dad, Saffron … he's …" Grabbing her in his arms he rocked her back and forth and watched as the car exploded.

*

Chapter 26

A night-lamp shone a dim, gloomy streak of light across Saffron's right cheek. It was the only light in the hospital room. Saffron had been in a coma since the crash four weeks earlier, and Joshua had not left her side except to use the restroom and eat.

She had been transferred from Skegness Infirmary to Kettering General Hospital. Every day (maybe every two days if he stayed overnight at her bedside) Joshua rode the 291 bus from Corby to Kettering (Corby, as yet had not built a main hospital, though there was a maternity ward in the town).

Joshua, his head lowered onto her thigh reached up and gripped her cold hand. With his free hand he gripped and squeezed the crucifix around his neck.

"I need you to come back to me, Saffron," he quietly said. "We can travel to America, take the ferry over to Dublin, you'd love that city. Full of crazy people like me. Come back to me, Saffron. Please come back to me."

He rubbed the crucifix again hoping that whatever power lay within would help bring Saffron out of her coma.

Nothing happened.

*

The funeral of her father had come and gone. His wife Linda was devastated and even more saddened by Saffron's present condition. She visited occasionally (every night the first week) and got a lift to Kettering with her friend, Mavis.

Nothing happened as Joshua squeezed the crucifix again and mumbled to himself. "Please God, if there is a God; please bring Saffron out of this coma. I need her. I love her."

They say to be careful for what you wish because sometimes it may come true, and, in part his wish was granted.

He went home to shower and get a good night's sleep. During the night Saffron awoke from her coma – and couldn't remember anything.

*

Joshua arrived at the hospital the next day unaware that Saffron had come out of her coma. Linda was waiting for him outside her daughter's room.

"She awoke during the night," said Linda.

"That's great. Can I see her?"

Linda grabbed his arm. "I don't think that's wise."

"What do you mean? I need to see her."

"She's lost her memory. She thinks I'm one of the nurses. I even had to remind her that her name is Saffron."

"I need to go in there," said Joshua taking her hand from his arm.

"No, Joshua. You can't. She needs to recover."

"Seeing me will help, won't it?"

"I'm thinking of her future, Josh. What life will she have with you? No education. No chance of a professional job. I want her to own a house in a nice area, own a car and enjoy the good things in life. I want her to marry someone who is educated, who works as a professional. You won't be able to give her that."

Joshua looked from Linda, through the glass window to Saffron sitting up in bed, and back to Linda. "What are you saying?"

"Look. She doesn't remember me, so she won't remember you."

"Let me try. She'll know who I am."

"If she recognizes you, stay. If she doesn't, then leave. Couldn't be any fairer than that."

Joshua took a deep breath and walked into the room followed closely by Linda. He looked at Saffron and smiled. She returned the smile. Joshua's heart beat rapidly as he waited for her to say his name.

"Are you the new nurse?" Saffron said and smiled again. "That's two this morning already." She nodded at her mother.

Joshua stood for what seemed hours; his head began to spin. He felt nauseous. He turned and ran down the corridor and into the toilet – and vomited.

"He must be new," said Saffron.

"There's someone I want you to meet, Saffron. He's going to call in later."

"Oh. Who is it?"

"Someone you know, or knew before the accident. He was your boyfriend."

"Really," said Saffron, "I mean … I have a *boyfriend*?"

"Yes, Saffron. I'm your mother. And your boyfriend is Michael Sheridan."

Saffron smiled; she glanced through the open door and down the corridor and watched as Joshua stood staring back at her. He half-smiled at her, turned slowly and walked out of her life.

*

Chapter 27

Annie O'Connell swept the dust from her kitchen floor, filled up a bucket with water mixed with bleach and scrubbed the tiles. After this she cleaned the floor with a soft cloth wrapped around the end of a brush, sprayed some floor polish on the floor and brought it to a good shine.

Being a trainee nurse wasn't easy at the best of times and, working in the General was sometimes a bind with all the bed pans and smells and scrubbing and disinfectant and expectant mothers and illnesses, comas and death.

On her days off she liked to clean her flat, which wasn't really that difficult since it was only one hundred square feet. A small kitchen, hallway and restroom with single bedroom beside it. Not much, but it was *her* place, her tiny *palace,* somewhere to live peacefully, put her feet up, relax, chill out, walk around the flat naked without bothering anyone or anyone bothering her.

Annie liked the life of a single woman. She'd had one boyfriend a year earlier and that was fine, or the sex was fine. She never really loved him, or was in love with him. The only connection they had was sex, sex and more sex, which was okay with Annie, she was young, she had urges, she needed pleasure and she got it.

Her grandfather had died the year before. She loved his big, strong hands, and would often run her finger down the deep groves in his palm. Giant hands. Hands that had shoveled concrete in all weathers up and down the country's motorways.

Joshua, that guy she had met at Skegness beach reminded her of her grandfather in certain ways, his glistening, kind eyes, his broad shoulders and his smile. And wasn't it ironic that Joshua lived in Corby and had played his pipes at her grandfather's funeral. She never had a chance to thank him for his piping.

But she somehow felt connected to Joshua and couldn't understand the reason why. Who knew what attracted a person to another person? Was it some kind of hidden magic working somewhere deep inside a person? Did love emanate from the soul?

Joshua was special. He wasn't like her last boyfriend demanding sex and telling her that it was her duty, as a woman, to satisfy a man. No, with Joshua she felt that even if they never had sex, she would love him still.

"Idiot," she said to herself as she turned on the vacuum. "You don't even know each other. You haven't been on a date. And if you did, what would you do or say if he rejected you?"

She thought of not so long ago when she stood in the hospital room doorway and looked on as Joshua wept for his girlfriend lying on the bed in a coma. She had needed, wanted, craved to walk up behind him and squeeze his shoulder, kiss him on the back of the neck, turn him around to face her, kiss his beautiful lips. All her emotions spun around inside her soul, inside her heart craving to be set free to surround and engulf this man with her love.

She liked Kettering General hospital and one day wanted to become a ward sister. She was determined, enthusiastic, loving, caring, nurturing. 'Not a bad bone in that child's body,' her mother had said when she was six or seven years old.

Her father was always away at sea but a vicious drunk when at home. Annie witnessed her father's antics daily and wished daily that he'd pack his bags and return to the navy. As a child she composed a little ditty that she'd sing as her drunken father beat her mother over the head with an iron frying pan.

> "If wishes were fishes they'd fill up the sea
> But wishes ain't fishes as far as I see
> So pack up your bags and tally away
> And never return to sadden my day."

The kettle boiled and she poured the water into her mother's teapot, part of a set of China her mother had kept for years in their China cabinet back home. Her father dead these past four years and mother dead two years. Divorced years ago. Grandfather died this year. Everyone seemed to be dying. They say dying is a part of living, which Annie thought was stupid, how can you live when you're dead. Most probably it was meant to sound more like: dying is a part of life. Still, who was she to argue with those great poets and philosophers?

After tea she got dressed in a black skirt and top, pulled up her black tights, God, she was even wearing black underwear, and grabbed her umbrella on the way out of her flat. Rain. Rain. Rain. Always raining, mind you last year had been a scorcher of a summer. A rare occurence.

She drove a Morris Minor. It was a small, rounded type of car with small wheels and tires, but comfortable enough for Annie. She loved this car because it had belonged to her grandfather and had been passed down to her.

The Morris Minor was called the 'British Miracle' the little car that symbolized Britain's emergence from post-war poverty. Teachers, district nurses, midwives, grocers, doctors all had a Morris Minor. The shape of the car reminded Annie of a poached egg with windows. She couldn't remember the last time she had put petrol (gas) in the tank.

As she took the road through town toward the hospital, she felt around her neck for her crucifix. She loved her onyx cross with its white metal edges and was grateful her grandfather had given it to her before he died.

"I want to give you this," he said and handed her the crucifix. "It's been passed down through many generations of my family. In fact I shouldn't have it at all because it's the first girl born of each generation which should inhcrit it, but since there's been no girls born in my family, I've been keeping it for you. I was going to give it to your father to pass on to you, but well, a drunk would sell his very soul for a drink and I wouldn't want that."

Annie smiled at the memory; she missed her grandfather deeply.

Chapter 28

Joshua's thoughts meandered all over the place. One thought quickly ran into another and before long (just after waking) his mind was busy with scraps of dreams, images of Saffron and her big smile, quick flashes of them making love, her serene face when in her coma, her innocence when out of her coma. He saw himself standing in the corridor gaping at her beautiful smile.

It started as a whimper and rose into a groan as he fell to his knees beside his bed; he lowered his head onto the sheets. And then he wept. And then he wailed like the Banshees of old and almost reached a scream that sounded pitiful, horrific, frightening,

His mother rushed in and knelt beside him and took him in her arms. She hugged him and rocked him back and forth and comforted her paining and broken chick.

"Ma," sobbed Joshua. "I love her so much."

"I know, son. I know."

"She means everything to me, ma. What will I do, ma. What will I do?"

"God is good. He has another path for you to follow."

She stroked his hair. "You have to be strong, son," she said soothingly. "The only way to survive, son, is to be strong."

"As strong as you, ma?"

She looked skyward. "Yes, son. As strong as me."

He glanced at his mother's face and noticed a tear trickle down her cheek.

*

*

Heavy rain lashed against Joshua's face as he jogged through the woods. He tried to keep his breathing steady but he wasn't used to running like this. Not like Sam. Sam loved to run in the rain. He'd tried to get Joshua to jog along with him but he was more interested in playing football and later, learning the bagpipes. Joshua had found an easier way to exercise his lungs, rather than harming his knee and hip joints by jogging. And why he was running this day he didn't really know, nor understand. This morning he had got out of bed and dressed in a pair of his red football shorts, white socks and sneakers, pulled a white tee-shirt on and left the house.

His thoughts were muddled, his emotions all torn up and scattered around his head. "Why?" he kept saying to himself.

Joshua tried to put his thoughts into some kind of order but in a universe full of chaos, surely that was going to be an insurmountable task.

His breathing steadied a little as he jogged along the narrow track that wound its way through the woods. The rain gushed in little streams into gutters running along the track and trickled off leaves and twigs and branches above his head. A hare stood in the center of the track about twenty feet ahead and watched as Joshua approached, then sped off into the woods. He remembered once riding the bus to town one day and a hare rushed out into the middle of the road and was squashed under the bus tires. He closed his eyes and cringed and felt sorry for the hare, most probably out hunting food to take back to its young family: A sudden occurrence - one second crossing the road, a second later - dead.

Joshua came to the edge of the woods by a main road. He waited for a clear crossing then sped across the road, down an embankment and into a park area. In the center was a small lake. The rain made tiny holes on the surface as mallard ducks swam gracefully across the water.

He stood on the edge of the lake and took a few deep breaths to control his breathing. Images of his friend John sprang to mind and of him beneath the surface of the clay-hole, his foot caught in cables and struggling for life. And Saffron not knowing who he was, memory loss, *his* loss. She now existed in some kind of no man's land where he could never reach her.

He stepped into the water up to his knees. *Just walk into the lake and the water will touch your waist, then your chest, then your chin, and keep walking until the water covers your head and keep your mouth open and very soon you'll be dead and floating along with the ducks. Easy. So easy.*

The water came up to his chin and he instinctively took a deep breath. He walked on and the water covered his head; as he walked deeper into the water he gripped the crucifix; he closed his eyes and suddenly images sped through his mind.

Next door neighbors watching as he performed on his bagpipes in the back garden. His mother hugging him; his father clipping roses; John and himself swimming happily in the clay-hole; himself collecting coal and firewood and making the morning fire; running around town hauling a bag of newspapers for morning readers; Mrs. Feely handing him a dictionary; Father O'Brien with his beautiful friendly smile; John's coffin being carried down the center aisle of St Patrick's Church and Sean Flanagan leading and playing the 'Flowers of the Forest' lament; the burial at Rockingham Cemetery and bunches of flowers and relatives and friends gathering around as Father Luke said 'Ashes to ashes, dust to dust;' and the last image he had was of John desperately gasping for air before he drowned.

Now his own lungs were about to burst and he knew it would be so simple to just let go, just open his mouth and let the water gush in and in a few seconds or so his heart would stop beating and all his troubles and memories and anguish and grief and pain and life would end. Easy. Simple. Dead. All gone.

Joshua opened his eyes and saw blackness in front of him and a trickle of light shining through the water above his head. He tried to breathe but there was no air. His right foot wouldn't move. He struggled and punched the water around him in an attempt to walk backwards. And then he realized what was stopping him from going backwards or even forwards and certainly was preventing him from fighting his way toward the surface. His foot was jammed between two big rocks on the bottom of the lake.

He was dying. Just like John had died. And now he knew, yes, he now knew what John was feeling in those seconds leading up to his death, what he felt, his frustration, his pain, his fear, his heart pounding and thumping against his chest.

Was this what it felt like to feel so hopeless? To not be able to do a damn thing to save your own life. To know that his mother was, at this very second at home preparing Dublin Coddle for her son. To know that his father was working out in the rain in Manchester shoveling concrete to build a motorway. To know that his talent for playing an instrument will now be wasted. To know that he'll never experience future lovers or wives or children. To absolutely know that his life is almost over.

He couldn't save John from drowning, and now who was there to save him from the same fate. *What goes around comes around, Joshua,* said his inner voice.

The water rushed into his lungs. Easy. Simple. Dead. All gone. A splash. Water skirting around him. A hand, then a face, someone in a tracksuit; two hands grabbing his foot. The hands lift a big stone; his foot is free.

Joshua slipped into unconsciousness as he was pushed to the surface and dragged onto the embankment.

A couple passed by and stopped. "Call an ambulance," said the man in the tracksuit. One of them ran back down the winding lane to the restroom and cafeteria area.

Two strong hands pushed upwards on Joshua's upper back. Again and again the hands pushed and pressed and then water gushed out of Joshua's lungs. He was turned over and given mouth to mouth.

Joshua spluttered and coughed up a lungful of water. He opened his eyes and took a few seconds to focus. "Sam," he said.

Ambulance sirens wailed in the distance.

*

Joshua was checked out and released from the emergency room that evening. He told his parents he had been running along the winding lane beside the park lake and had slipped on some mud and rolled into the water. His foot got stuck between two rocks and it was lucky that Sam was out jogging. 'God be praised,' Joshua's mother had said, 'it was a miracle, I say. A miracle.'

He had told Sam the same tale and Sam had said he believed him.

"You saved my life, Sam," Joshua said after leaving the emergency room.

"Least I can do for an old pal," said Sam and smiled.

"I'll never forget it, Sam."

"Ah, you'd do the same for me," said Sam and never mentioned the fact he had spotted Joshua running along the lane and stopping, then walking slowly into the water.

"Hey," said Sam. "Did you get your sign up papers?"

"Not yet. What date you got?"

"September 14th," said Sam. "I'm excited."

*

That night in bed Joshua read the letter that had arrived in the post that day. His sign up papers. Report to Pirbright barracks, September 14th, 1970 – seven months from now. He hoped his depression would be lifted by that time.

Joshua gripped his crucifix and made a promise to himself that he would never, *ever* again attempt to take his own life, no matter what happened to him in the future.

He closed his eyes, slipped into sleep and dreamt of Saffron.

*

*

St Patrick's day arrived two weeks after the jogging incident. Irish folks (and those pretending to be Irish) marched through the Corby streets starting from the Irish Club, down the side road and onto the main road and then down Gainsborough road towards town, then cut back down Leighton Road, back onto Gainsborough and back towards the Irish Club for the usual eight to ten hour drinking binge.

The main reason why the Irish drink so much is simply because they can. Centuries of training and genetics have given the Irish a stomach made of lead and a liver made of steel.

Anyway, Joshua knew that Saint Patrick went to Ireland to convert the pagans to Christianity. He was born in 385 AD to Roman parents (in Scotland or Wales). At the age of 16 he was kidnapped by Irish raiders who sold him as a slave. He herded sheep in Ireland for several years and got to know the people. At age 22 he escaped to a monastery in England and spent 12 years finding God.

Patrick used the Shamrock to represent the mystery of the Holy Trinity: the Father, the Son, and the Holy Spirit. He never cast out all the snakes in Ireland because snakes didn't exist in that country, it being too cold for them to thrive.

Scholars believe the 'snakes' were the religious beliefs of pagans and their practices rather than snakes. The color originally associated with Saint Patrick was blue, not green - usage of the color green arrived later. The Harp is the symbol of Ireland and not the Shamrock. King Henry VIII used the harp on coins as early as 1534.

Joshua knew all this and sometimes told his Irish friends about the true facts but they never believed him, wanting to believe the fairy tale version rather than the truth. *Similar to religion, eh, Joshua,* his inner voice piped in.

He was fascinated when he found out that there are more Irish people in America than there is in Ireland. Between 1903 and 1970 St Patrick's day was declared a religious holiday in Ireland, meaning all pubs were shut on that day. That stupid law was overturned in 1970 and the pubs opened and the beer again flowed copiously.

Today, Joshua was in the front row of St Brendan's Pipe Band led by Pipe Major Sean Flanagan. Joshua had, over the past year 'graduated' from the 'Goose set' to the fully equipped bagpipe. He'd learnt a lot more tunes including jigs, reels and hornpipes and some competition sets. Playing bagpipes was fun, and kept him fit, too. Inhaling and blowing, marching and playing the tunes being equal to a workout in the gym, but a lot less strenuous.

A bagpiper's lungs are not bigger than normal lungs; they do however become stronger, firmer. Maybe the lungs clear themselves out every time a piper puffs and blows into the bag? He read once that fungus and yeast bacteria could build up inside a piper's bag and, if the inside of the bag is not disinfected from time to time, the piper can suffer a lung condition such as hypersensitivity pneumonitis, which is usually found in the dry dust of the droppings and feathers of pigeons. Also the blow stick should also be disinfected.

The band wore a uniform of dark blue jackets with yellow cuffs and collars, and Gordon Highlander kilts, brogues (or black shoes – I borrowed my father's), red and off-white checkered knee socks and white side-buttoned spats. Eight pipers, four side (snare) drummers, two tenor drummers and a bass drummer marched down Gainsborough Road towards Joshua's house.

His mother waved at Joshua as the band marched past playing the 'Minstrel Boy' and 'Kelly the boy from Killane' and Joshua felt a little embarrassed. He kept his eyes to the front as they passed his house.

Folks lined the streets waving little green flags; some folks wore tiny bunches of shamrock in their lapels. They applauded as the band passed.

The band sounded good, although classed as 4th grade out of a classification of 6 grades, there was room for improvement, which would take time, but the problem with keeping a young band intact was that most kids started work in the steel works, some went on to college, some joined the army and some found work in different towns or moved with their parents to seek a better life in other countries.

It was sunny this day of March 17th, 1971and the crowds lined the streets (Irish and English) to celebrate. Contrary to popular belief in America (and some other English speaking countries) the normal everyday Irish, English and Scots do like each other. Joshua had never experienced any animosity between either Irish, English or even Scots people, except in very small incidents that the media blew out of all proportion. Except of course, for the Northern Ireland troubles that started in 1969.

After about two miles and all the band sets played, the band turned into the car park of St Patrick's Irish Social Club. Sean Flanagan, sweat running down his cheeks, dismissed the band and we all rushed into the club and made for the bar.

So the drinking started. Hundreds of glasses of stout poured behind the bar and handed over the heads of the crowd to folks at the back. Joshua's parents supped their drinks at a table near the stage. And so began the ceilidh, (ceilidh means a social event where Irish or Scottish folks meet and enjoy music and singing, traditional dancing, and sometimes storytelling.) On stage was a band called, 'Paddy's Rovers' which comprised of an accordion player, a fiddler, a banjo and guitar player and the singer, who also played the 'spoons' (two normal metal spoons hit between hand and knee to produce sounds.)

Joshua was a little happier today with all the pipe tunes he had to remember and play, which certainly kept his mind from wandering and thinking about Saffron. He sat down next to his ma.

"How yer feeling, son," she said.

"Ah, yer know."

His mother glanced at her husband and raised her eyebrows. He picked up a pint of stout and handed it to Joshua. "There ye are, son. You deserve a good drink. In my books, you're now a man."

"Thanks, da," said Joshua and guzzled half the stout down in one go.

"Steady, son," said his da. "Drink it nice and steady and spread out yer drinking all night."

"He's right, Joshua," said his ma. "A man needs to get drunk slowly so he can enjoy it."

"Listen to yer ma, son. "She's knows best, so she does."
"And what's that supposed to mean?"
"Your brothers. Drunks, both of 'em."
"Oh, listen to the kettle calling the pot black."
"It's listen to the *pot* calling the kettle black."
"Feck off," said ma.
"Go and shite," said da.

Joshua shook his head and smiled. He took another sip of his Guinness, looked at his parents and said, "You two ejits are so funny." He began to laugh. After a few moments his parents joined in and then his mother went into her Wicklow Amusement Arcade laughing mode and soon outshone the ceilidh band with her hysterics.

Her laughter had everyone in the big hall of the Irish Club laughing and giggling. Even the band stopped playing and joined in. Joshua overheard the fiddler asking the banjo player what they were laughing about. "Fucked if I know," said the banjo player, "but who really cares."

"Do yer want another drink, ma?" Joshua asked.

And she laughed even more.

Even his da was laughing, though he took a quick break now and again to sip his Guinness.

Joshua shook his head in disbelief. What a family, he thought. How lucky he was to be a part of this clan. All the money in the world couldn't create this kind of camaraderie; this time of beauty. He considered himself a very lucky.

And then the laughing decreased and the drinking increased and continued and didn't end until all the Irishmen (and English, Welsh and Scots) and their wives and most of their sons and daughters were either full up on Guinness, whiskey, white wine (red wine was for the French back then) cider, shandy, lemonade or Coca-cola. Joshua couldn't remember how he got home, but that never worried him, simply because *no one* ever remembered how they got home after St Patrick's Day celebrations. But, to be sure, *everyone* certainly remembered the thumping hangovers the next morning.

*

Chapter 29

The crucifix had hung around Joshua's neck for three years now. It became a part of him. He never took it off for bathing or sleeping. There was no religious concept to him wearing the cross, and, in his mind, the only connection was of a man, true or false, that was persecuted by his own people, showed great endurance and love for those people and had, in the end, hope for them. *It holds powerful magic, Joshua,* said his inner voice, his deep subconscious, maybe even his soul. *Religious symbol or not, there is great magic in that cross. Remember this when you need it in the future. Because, Joshua, you* will *need it.*

Lying in bed and staring at the faces on his wardrobe, he gripped the cross, closed his eyes and tried to think of Saffron. Images of a woman appeared in his mind, but they were not of Saffron but that of Annie, the woman he'd met on the beach at Skegness. She's riding a donkey. Why does she appear to me, he wondered? He tried to meditate and counted slowly his inhalations and exhalations until he thought he was relaxed enough to squeeze the cross again.

He liked Annie. *You liked her from that very first moment you lifted that bicycle off her, from that split second of looking into her eyes. Remember, Joshua, you felt amazing.*

Joshua tried to suppress that niggling (nagging) inner voice of his, tried to subconsciously tear it to pieces with his hands and bury the bits deep in some darkened vault down there in the mysterious and dangerous dark parts of his mind.

"Go away," he said to the faces on the wardrobe, though he knew he was talking to his inner voice, or was he? Maybe he was slowly going insane? Maybe this was the precursor for building up and developing mental issues? Maybe he would end up in a mental asylum like his Uncle Jack? Maybe that was his destiny? Everything going along fine until his grandparents died together in the same bed. His best friend died, and he couldn't even save him. Then Mrs. Feely got decapitated on the 292 bus. And then Saffron goes into a coma, awakes and doesn't know who he is. Jesus. What next?

Questions, too many of them and not enough answers. Always an imbalance between asking and knowing and the knowing falling far behind the asking. Maybe that was the point of living – of *not* knowing everything. Knowing enough just to get by.

He gripped the crucifix and an image appeared of him lying on a bed, and Annie, her hair flowing over his face, on top of him, naked. They were making love.

"Joshua," his mother shouted up the stairs in a kind of high-pitched sing-a-long voice.

"Yes, ma?" That was all he needed right now, his mother wanting him to do something around the house. Though, to be fair, he'd not done much this past month. He'd finished with his paper round job, thank God, and, because it was now summer, the fire didn't need to be lit until the evening, though he doubted if the fire will ever be lit again since they just had a gas fire connected and a central heating system installed.

"There's someone at the door to see you."

"Is it Sam?"

"No. Someone called Annie."

*

Annie stood at the door and wondered why she was there. What right had she to call upon him without first phoning, or writing a letter, or communicating in some other way. But that wasn't the way Annie O' Connell worked. That wasn't the way she was brought up. Her grandfather had always taught her to be brave, to go out and seek what she wanted, never be shy to ask a question, and if you see something you want, then earn it, work for it, save up for it, chase it, like it, own it.

And that was what she was doing right now; going after something that had stirred her heart right from that first moment she had looked into his eyes on that beach at Skegness. She knew what she wanted and she would do anything to get it, even if it meant turning up on Joshua's doorstep to ask him out on a date.

Was she being too forward? Would he think she was some kind of a tramp, a money-grabber, a gold-digger, a tart? She didn't think so. Joshua had a good heart; she knew that much from the way he had talked to her and by his soft tone of voice. Besides, she felt connected to him somehow.

His mother seemed a nice lady, though she did give her the once over when she opened the front door, but that was probably normal when a stranger turned up uninvited on a person's doorstep.

*

Joshua opened the front door and there she was, Annie. She was dressed in a yellow and blue striped summer dress and white sneakers. Her mousy-colored hair flowed over her shoulders. She had a little rouge and mascara on and a touch of lipstick. Her eyes were an entrancing bluish-gray. Her teeth were straight and white. No nicotine stains whatsoever.

"Hello," said Joshua. His heart jumped a few beats.

"Hello," said Annie.

They gazed into each other's eyes for a few moments each waiting for the other to break the silence.

"Would you like to come in?"

"I feel as if I'm intruding. I was just passing on my way home from town and thought I'd ... well, see how you're managing."

"You heard about Saffron's memory loss?"

"I'm so sorry."

Joshua stepped outside and closed the door behind him. He glanced up at the front bedroom window and noticed his mother looking down at them.

"I need something from the shops," said Joshua. "Would you like to come with me?"

"Okay."

They walked the few hundred yards to the line of shops. A red telephone box stood on the corner. Across the road the local pub landlord was helping unload barrels of beer from a truck.

"How did you find out about Saffron?"

"Oh, her friend, well, my old school friend, wrote me a letter from America. Her family moved over there last year. Her mother is great friends with Saffron's mother."

"Madge Montgomery?"

"Yes. They live in a place called Bakersfield, somewhere near Los Angeles."

"Good for her," said Joshua. They sat on a low wall outside the newsagent's shop.

"How are you feeling," said Annie and, for some reason that she couldn't quite understand reached over and squeezed his hand.

Joshua took her hand and squeezed. "I'm glad you came, Annie. I really am."

*

Chapter 30

The newly bought tins of beans smashed through the lounge window and bounced on the tarmac road outside. Next, a large stewpot flew through the open window and landed a few feet from the beans.

"Stop it stop it," screamed Annie's mother and grabbed hold of her drunken husband's jacket. He turned quickly and slapped her across the face and sent her rolling into the side cupboard.

Another batch of tinned foods flew out the window. "I bought all this food, and I'll destroy all this food," screamed Annie's father as she cowered in a corner of the lounge.

"You're nothing but a drunken bastard," yelled her mother as her husband turned around, glared at her, then picked up a statue of the Virgin Mary from atop the welsh dresser.

"Not that. Please not the Virgin. That belonged to my grandmother."

"Well, she can have it back – in pieces." He threw the statue out the window.

"Do you think I spend months at sea to come home and get nagged to death. I might as well stay away."

"Don't do us any favors, you drunken bastard," yelled his wife. "You're good for nothing, do you hear. Not worth anything."

Her husband stormed into the kitchen and came back armed with an iron frying pan. He walked straight up to his wife and hit her on the side of the head and again on the top of the head. He lifted his arm to hit her again but Annie ran over and covered the top half of her mother's body with hers. "Don't daddy," she said. "Please don't hurt her anymore."

Annie's father stood for a long time staring down at the bloodied head of his wife. He turned and threw the frying pan out the window, picked up his suitcase and stormed out of the house, down the garden path and out through the wooden gate.

Annie ran into the kitchen, got a cloth, wet it and brought it back to her mother. She wiped away some of the blood on the side of her head. "It's okay, mum," cried Annie. "I'll look after you now."

Her father took the side road which led to the main road and down to the railway station. He was never seen again by Annie, his wife, or anyone else in Corby for that matter.

Six years later word got back to Annie that her father had died in a drunken brawl in some harbor in the Far East. His merchant seaman days were over. He never gave much to the family except strife and violence and left behind a terrible legacy of emotional turmoil and poverty.

Annie was six years old. At seven she helped her mother sew blankets and birthday dresses and communion and confirmation dresses for the congregation of St Patrick's Church. Every penny helped to buy food, clothe them and pay the bills.

She was a late developer mainly in height, but she was street clever and handy with her fists, too. Anyone that called her a 'midget' she'd fight and kick and punch and pull hair and always won her fights. It was obviously in her blood, or her father's blood. But she wasn't a bully. Sometimes she could be kind like the time a little girl lost her mummy in the supermarket and Annie cared for the child until the manager had located the mother.

Usually after school she'd sit on the floor in front of the TV (given as a gift from the church) and draw sketches of people's faces. She was good. Some day she wanted to become a real artist and paint in an attic overlooking a flowing river with thatched cottages on each side and the sun shining down and folks passing her cottage riding bicycles and she would invite her new neighbors in for tea and crumpets and they would discuss her drawings and her paintings and folks would be amazed at her talent and she'd find an agent down in London and they'd display her work in an art museum and people with money would buy her paintings and artwork and she'd be able to buy a bigger cottage with a bigger attic workshop and invite her mother to live with her down south and her mother would say yes and feel *so* happy.

"Annie," her mother shouted through from the kitchen. She suddenly bumped down to earth and out of her reverie. "Yes, mam?"

"What'd yer want for your tea, love?'

"Roast beef, roast potatoes, carrots, broccoli, parsnips, mashed potatoes, sprouts and gravy. And oh, vanilla ice-cream and cream cake for desert. *And* a big glass of lemonade and ice."

"Beans on toast and a glass of orange it is, then," said her mother.

*

Chapter 31

Whichever way Joshua looked at it he had to fulfill his dream of joining the British Army and performing with the band of the Scots Guards. He was driven - it was his *fate*.

"I understand your desire to travel," said Annie, upset that he chose to join the army, a dangerous occupation at the best and worst of times. "We can't change our genes."

"My gypsy genes, you mean," said Joshua and tenderly stroked her hand.

They got a lift from Sam's dad (sitting in silence most of the way to Kettering station) and now embraced each other on the platform. Sam had already said goodbye to his dad (his mother was too upset to go with them) and was already on the train. Joshua's father was at work. His mother had kissed him on the forehead at the front door that morning. 'Be careful and don't forget to write," she had said. "And, if you come into a little money, don't forget to send some to your old ma – for the bingo."

On the station platform Annie tried to keep her feelings locked inside her but failed miserably. "I won't see you again," she said and began to weep. "You'll meet some other girl and I'll soon be forgotten."

Joshua hugged her. "Let's just see, eh, Annie. We're both young and I'll be away for a long time, so you never know what's going to happen."

"Don't forget to write," said Annie, her eyes red and tears rolled down her cheeks.

He got on the train and leaned out the carriage window as the train pulled away. As she got smaller in the distance his heart began to palpitate and his face became sweaty and cold. Was he experiencing a heart attack? No. He was already missing Annie, craving her. And with that deep craving he clasped his crucifix, closed his eyes and wished that he and Annie would soon be together again, to love, to laugh, to enjoy life and live happily together for the rest of their lives.

Hope, he understood, springs eternal.

*

Chapter 32
(The British Army)

"Right," said Sergeant Wilson. "Line up in three ranks, suitcases by your right side. Get your papers out and wait in turn to enter the office."

Wilson; tall, broad-shouldered, muscular and about thirty years of age, stared icily along the front rank of young recruits.

"Any questions?"

"What time's the pub open," said some bright spark at the rear. Everyone laughed except the Sergeant.

"What's the birds like round here," said another spark, birds, of course meant 'women.'

The stone-faced Sergeant glared, his eyes bulged. He opened his mouth wide as if at any moment he'd roar and spew out dragon fire, reducing these raw, idiot recruits to ash before they had even started training. He closed his mouth and remained calm.

"When do we get to shoot a rifle," said someone standing behind Joshua.

"You may have noticed," said Wilson, "that I'm not replying to your stupid and petty questions. Would anyone like to tell me the reason *why* I'm not replying?"

"You don't know the answers."

"You see, it's quite simple," said Sergeant Wilson calmly. "Before you go into that office to officially sign up for Her Majesty's Service, you lot are still civilians and, by British law, unfortunately for me, I can't treat you like recruits, so you can say what you please. But, as soon as you come out of that office, *you are mine*. So, is there anyone else would like to ask a question?"

Complete silence except for the sound of chirping birds on the office rooftop. Joshua and Sam looked at each other and shrugged.

When everyone had 'officially' signed their lives away as cannon fodder for the British government, they were marched (by Sergeant Wilson) to the barracks. Joshua's stomach churned; for some unknown reason he actually felt homesick. To think he had spent the last six months or so wishing to get away from his home and now he felt homesick for the place.

Sergeant Wilson stormed into the dormitory and scared the shit out of everybody.

"This is the army," he barked. "There's no mammies here to wipe your tears or wipe your fucking arses. You're here as boys and, after two years you will become men. Age or clothes, poverty or wealth doesn't make the man.Get unpacked, undressed, I want you fuckers in the shower in ten minutes, no excuses. I don't care if your dick is fifteen inches long or two inches small, or you got man boobs or nipples the size of your tiny fucking brains. I don't give two shits if you have bollocks the size of melons or marbles, or if you're circumcised or normal. Do you hear me?"

"Yes, Sergeant," they replied in unison.

"Well, I must be deaf 'cause that response was pathetic. Do you fucking HEAR ME!"

"YES, SERGEANT!" This time they were so loud they frightened the birds off the roof.

"Good. Now get at it."

Joshua, Sam and maybe everyone in the dorm suddenly wondered what they had gotten themselves into. They were soon to find out in no uncertain terms.

*

The recruits settled in over the next few days, not knowing their arseholes from their elbows, as Sergeant Wilson said ninety-nine times a day.

The routine: 6.00am reveille. Shit. Shower. Shave. Into Fatigues (casual dark gray trousers and jackets), walk to breakfast hall. Quick smoke, back to barracks, make beds and fold all sheets and blankets into a square in top center of bed. Tidy locker and leave doors open for inspection; every item of soap, razor and shaving cream all lined up and perfectly in line with each other. Hand towels folded and creased in the proper manner and placed on locker shelves with a two inch gap each side. Boots and shoes laced up and tied and placed side by side at the bottom of the locker. Suitcase with name, rank and regiment stenciled in white on front and placed on top of locker with edge of suitcase perfectly aligned with the top line of the locker.

Floor swept, washed, dried and highly polished with wooden 'bumper' so shiny a person could see their own reflection in the linoleum. Another quick smoke then get dressed in heavy khaki waist length coat and trousers, highly polished boots and go outside for muster parade. Time: 7.00am.

"Today," said Sergeant Wilson, "We have rifle training in the classroom."

Joshua liked the feel of the Self Loading Rifle (SLR) that used 7.62mm bullets. He'd never handled a gun before and felt secure now that he had a gun although it was the property of the army, but felt it would come in handy if he was sent into battle, which was likely, him being in the army and all. His country was not a gun culture society, like America, where everyone seemed to want to own a gun. His father had told him once, "If you own a gun, sooner or later you're going to get shot." Those wise words didn't quite ring true when you were in the army and needed a gun. He hoped that because he had a gun that he wasn't going to be shot and quickly gripped his crucifix to help make him feel more secure; he smiled to himself in an effort to dispel such thoughts.

"Who you smiling at boy?" snapped Sergeant Wilson.
"No one, SERGEANT."
"Thinking of Susan's juicy twat back home, eh? Bet she's got her legs spread right now and fucking the whole football team down in Crutchville, Staffordshire."
"You *know* her?"
"What's your name, boy?"
"Joshua Hanley, SERGEANT."
"And you. What's your name?"
"Sam O'Neill, SERGEANT."
"Have *you* got a sweet, pretty girlfriend waiting for you at home?"
"No, SERGEANT."
"Are you a *queer*?"
"No, SERGEANT."
"Then why ain't you got a tart?"
"Had one once, SERGEANT."
"Oh. She dumped you and found someone with a bigger dick that could bring a smile to her face, eh, soldier. I bet since she left you she's had more cock than there is handrail around the Queen Mary."
"You do have an eloquent way with words."
"I have a way with *what*?"
"You have a way with words, SERGEANT."
"Get down and give me twenty!"
"Take the rifles apart," said Wilson as Sam did his push-ups. "Inspect them, clean them, oil them, put them back together and make sure your rifle works because one day you will need them."
"Okay, showoff, that's enough."
Sam jumped up and brushed his hands on his trousers.
"One of the things we teach here is cleanliness," said Sergeant Wilson and glared at Sam. "You don't clean your hands on your uniform. Get down and give me another twenty."

*

So the classroom training continued for months, interspersed with Gym work, weight training, boxing, march and shoots (a five mile run wearing and carrying full gear, rifle and ammunition) then a mile run over the assault course and onto the firing range. By the end of two years of this training, Joshua, Sam and most of the recruits (some had cracked up and were thrown out) were so fit they only needed three to four hours sleep a night and could probably stand in for the football team from Crutchville, Staffordshire, and fuck Susan with the juicy twat back home all night long.

Joshua wondered when he would be allowed to join the Pipes and Drums, but was told he'd have to complete two years soldier training before he even saw a set of bagpipes.

Guildford: A great town (not too far from Pirbright) for the young soldiers to drink themselves into oblivion. After many months of training it was time to let their hair down (or what was left of it).

Joshua and Sam liked to frequent two pubs, the Seven Stars and the Horse & Groom. Great pubs and nearly always filled with soldiers at the weekends. They'd visited the two pubs every weekend starting September to the weekend before October 5th. That weekend they were on exercise on Salisbury Plains.

It was October 5th, 1974 and the IRA (Irish Republican Army) had detonated a 6-pound gelignite bomb in the Horse & Groom pub at 8:30pm. It killed a civilian, two Scots Guards soldiers and two members of the Women's Royal Army Corps. Another 6-pound bomb was planted at the Seven Stars pub and detonated at 9:00pm. The patrons were evacuated after the first blast and therefore there were no serious casualties.

Joshua and Sam watched the tragedy unfold on TV in the mess hall in the training camp at Salisbury. Joshua gripped his crucifix as he sat on a couch and closed his eyes.

He heard a tremendous explosion, suddenly opened his eyes and found himself standing outside the Horse and Groom pub. Thick smoke gushed out of the smashed windows; revelers spewed out of the front and side doors of the pub. Flames licked the sides of the windows and doors and shot up through the roof. He heard sirens in the distance.

Joshua opened his eyes, still sitting on the couch.

"Josh," said Sam. "You alright?"

"Yer. I'm good."

"Shit. We'd have been drinking in that pub tonight."

Suddenly the mess door burst open and an officer shouted at everyone. "Full alert. We're going back to Pirbright. Tonight. Come on. MOVE!"

*

This was a depressing and frightening period in Joshua's life, maybe in most peoples' lives, with the IRA detonating bombs over there in Northern Ireland and lately, crossing the Irish Sea and planting their bombs in English Cities. In August, 1970 two Royal Ulster Police officers were killed by a booby trap bomb in Crossmaglen, South Armagh. November 16th, the IRA shot two alleged criminals in the Ballymurphy area of Belfast. March, 1971, the IRA kidnapped three off-duty Scots Soldiers in Belfast. They took them to a mountain road outside Belfast and shot them in the head. These men were the first off-duty British soldiers to be killed in the conflict.

During this time British people lived in fear that the trash container in the walkway in the center of a City center had a bomb hidden inside and would explode any minute. People lived in fear that any pub that soldiers frequented anywhere in England would explode and kill innocent people.

Folks lived in fear of sitting down in front of the TV at night and watching protestors in Northern Ireland throwing Molotov Cocktails at soldiers. They lived in fear when they saw paratroopers on TV open fire on innocent people in the chaos of battle. They lived in fear when they sat on a bus to travel anywhere thinking that a bomb was hidden somewhere on the vehicle. They lived in fear when taking a coach ride to a City in case the coach exploded. The least noise or car back-firing and they'd all dive to the ground.

*

Joshua and Sam arrived back in Pirbright barracks, still on high alert; they finished their basic training, cumulating in all platoons completing a six mile march with full kit and rifles, the assault course and firing range. That afternoon they did the passing out parade and most of the parents of the soldiers were present, except Joshua's and Sam's. But they were now ready for action. Joshua was a little sad that he couldn't join the Pipes and Drums of the Scots Guards just yet because the whole Battalion, including the band was presently doing a tour of Northern Ireland. Each piper was allocated to a different platoon and Joshua was to join Headquarter Company in Ballymurphy, Belfast. Sam was to be sent to G Company as an infantryman.

Being a bagpiper didn't bring any concessions, not in a civil war, or any war for that matter. The pipers were trained as soldiers like everyone else and were expected to fight for their country in the same way. Joshua lived in fear on mainland England, but his fear became more intense in Northern Ireland.

*

(Northern Ireland)

Ballymurphy is a staunch Catholic area. The Ballymurphy Massacre occurred between 9th and 11th of August, 1971. The 1st Battalion Parachute Regiment killed eleven civilians, which is also called the Belfast Bloody Sunday, which also refers to another massacre of civilians by the same battalion a few months afterward.

Joshua and Sam shipped over to Ballymurphy on January 1st, 1974. The estate resembled many towns in Northern England with long lines of terraced houses and alleyways running through them.

Peoples' accents were harsher and louder than the folks that lived in Southern Ireland and, to Joshua, they always had an angry undertone to their words.

He was stationed in a school just off Springfield road and half of the school became the platoon's headquarters and the other half was for the children. They had separate entrances and manned pill-boxes on the Springfield road side. The dorms house four soldiers each and each soldier had a bunk and small locker. The soldiers mostly slept in their clothes because of emergency callouts, usually during the early hours.

Joshua wore his crucifix as usual but didn't want to use its special powers because he was scared, and actually being there caused enough stress, anyway.

One night, dressed in combat gear, face painted black and rifle in hand he and his patrol were called out to do a road block at the south end of Springfield Road. Chance had it that a patrol from G Company would also be there which meant Joshua got to meet Sam again.

"Joshua. You're a sight for sore eyes," said Sam and smiled broadly.

"Miss me?" said Joshua.

"Like a hole in the head," They laughed and got a glare from the section leader. "Keep the noise down," he said. "And keep an eye open for smugglers."

Smugglers were people who transported guns from one area to another and usually hid them in the boot (trunk) of their cars, the gun parts separated and stored in a hollowed out section covered by carpet.

They stopped every car that came to them. Mostly, the driver and passenger were dressed as construction workers and explained to Joshua they'd just finished work and what a lovely day it was and wondered what the wife had cooked for dinner (tae) and the wife would be nagging them again tonight because they had to work overtime and she wanted them to watch the kids while they went off to play bingo. And they'd search the cars and find parts of guns and boxes of ammunition and detonators and the drivers' would deny having any knowledge of anything and it must have been someone who broke into their cars and deliberately planted the stuff and would come back later and break in again and take away their explosive booty.

Oh sure. And Joshua and Sam would roll their eyes skyward. So they'd arrest them and they got carted away swearing and cursing everyone to hell's damnation and hope their wives' tits fall off and their children die in terrible pain with cancer and on and so on and bullshit piled upon bullshit.

Joshua thought it a shame that a so-called civilized society could hate each other so much.

Sam and Joshua parted ways and Joshua, with the rest of his patrol headed back to the barracks to sleep (hopefully). His tour consisted of cold nights, sweaty and humid days, road blocks, running through housing estates (because it was far too dangerous to walk because of the snipers hiding in the roofs), dogs barking and kids throwing stones at army vehicles, profanity and insults that constantly bombarded Joshua from the very same people who, under different circumstances would be sharing a pint or two with him down the Irish club and probably enjoying playing some Irish music.

One sunny morning Joshua's patrol ran across Springfield road and went into an alleyway between a line of terraced houses. Snipers were out in force that day and Joshua didn't fancy being shot in the head today, thank you very much.

When they arrived in the alleyway, a couple of teenagers at the other end suddenly ceased their kissing and smooching.

"Lucky bastard," said Jock, a six-foot three Glaswegian. Far too tall to be fighting in Belfast; too easy a target for a sniper.

"Fuck off," came a reply from the male teen.

"Two's up," said Freddie, a short, balding cockney. (Two's up meant 'give me what's left).

"I'd take you all on and still have time to wash my hair," said the female, a short, red-haired girl with too much mascara around her eyes.

No one took any notice, as Joshua and the teens got to talking about the troubles and he mentioned that he was Irish and his parents were Irish and every generation going back to Noah's fecking Ark were Irish and also that his ancient ancestors were gypsies.

"Knackers," said the boy. (an Irish name for a Gypsy before the Political Correct name of 'Traveller' was introduced).

"I'm a knacker *and* a cracker," I said and smiled.

"You're a fucking nut job," said the girl.

"So what you doing fighting in the British Army," said the boy.

"I joined because I wanted to perform with the Scots Guards Pipe band."

"Not doing much piping here, are yer," said the girl.

"I guess not. But someday, maybe," he said. "Anyway, one day all this will be over and there'll be peace talks and the economy will prosper and our children won't have to endure this nonsense."

"You're definitely a knacker," said the boy. "Either you can tell the future, or you're full of shite."

"Let's go," said our patrol commander. "Talking won't win this war."

Joshua was last out of the alley, but before he followed the patrol back out onto Springfield road, he turned and said to the teens, "He's wrong. It's talking that *will* end this war."

He winked at them and ran outside.

*

The half brick struck Joshua's riot shield dead center and another hit the bottom of the shield. Without this tough plastic protection any soldier would have been cut to pieces by the bricks and stones and other projectiles being thrown at them by the mob. Always teenagers, or younger kids, soldier bashing for a day as if it were a national holiday and throwing bricks, including Molotov cocktails at the British Army was something you did after breakfast on a Saturday morning as part of the Northern Ireland daily routine. "Hey, Jimmy, after breakies – and don't forget to brush your teeth – do yer fancy nipping down to Springfield road for a wee bit of squaddie bashing?"

These kids, constrained in their own little cages, fearing to escape, to think for themselves, fearful of their peers or terrorist leaders or priests and religion and so they remained trapped in their little boxes surrounded by violence.

Brick after brick and stones and pieces of metal flew through the air like a stream of arrows and landed on the heads and shoulders of the line of soldiers.

The mob had congregated at the junction at the top of Springfield road near the betting and grocery shops. Hundreds of youths throwing projectiles; other youths arrived pushing wheelbarrows full of half bricks, the right size to grip in the hand and easier and further to throw than a full brick.

"These fuckers mean business," yelled Sam as a large stone smashed into the top of his shield. Behind them they heard the screech of tires as four Saracens pulled up and about thirty soldiers jumped out and formed two lines behind Joshua's patrol.

"The cavalry's here," said Joshua.

"About fucking time," said Sam. "Another few minutes of this and we'll be pulverized."

Joshua carried a rubber bullet gun and a supply of four rubber bullets. The gun barrel is wide and the bullets long and thick. The trick with these guns was to aim at the ground a little in front of the rioter and fire. The bullet would bounce on the ground and smash into the rioter's testicles.

But it was difficult loading, aiming and firing a gun while at the same time holding a plastic shield. "Sam. Hold this, will you."

Sam held the shield as Joshua quickly loaded the gun, aimed and fired at the crowd. A teenager screamed and fell to the ground holding his testicles.

"Bull's eye," said Sam.

"Hanley," yelled his patrol commander, Danny Carstairs. "Good shot."

The soldiers behind moved forward and lined up beside Sam and Joshua.

"Load one," shouted Danny. Each soldier on the right side of a plastic shield grabbed that shield with their left hands as the soldiers loaded their rubber bullets into their guns.

"Load two." This time the soldiers who had just loaded their weapons grabbed the shields on their right side so those soldiers could load their weapons while the stones and half bricks kept pounding and bouncing off the shields. The second line of soldiers had no shields but was protected by the front line.

"On three. Drop all shields and rapid fire!"

The crowd became more confident as they saw their projectiles hit their targets. They approached the soldiers.

"One."

"Fucking British Bastards," someone shouted from the front as they approached.

"Two."

"Long live the IRA. Go home you British cunts."

"Three. FIRE!"

Like a fusillade of cannon fire from a galley ship the bullets hit the ground then rebounded up and into the groins and upper legs of the mob. The front row of soldiers knelt and the second line fired over their heads.

The mob backed off, some ran down alleyways, others dispersed up into the housing estate. The patrols were ordered back into the Saracens and quickly drove back to base.

"I'd murder a pint of Guinness," said Joshua jumping out of the back of the personnel carrier.

"Drinks are on me," said Sam.

*

The air seemed to change just before the explosion. Joshua felt a pressure in his ears before he heard the 'boom' and then dived to the ground as a sudden gush of wind covered his body. Glass windows shattered in the line of terraced houses. Tarmac and parts of a car scattered and smashed into living rooms and outside walls.

Sam dived beside Joshua. They lowered their heads onto the pavement and tried to hide behind the base of a lamppost. A lone tire rolled past them and crashed through a fence at the end of the road. They heard nothing except a high-pitched whining noise. Then gradually their hearing returned and they heard screams and groaning, weeping and shouts for help. People staggered out of some terraced houses holding their wounds and looked like zombies in the thick smoke that surrounded them.

"And all I ever wanted to do was play bagpipes," said Joshua.

"Josh, Sam," shouted Danny Carstairs. "Are you alive?"

"What a stupid fucking question," said Sam. "If we were dead we wouldn't be able to fucking answer the twat," Sam said and shook his head.

"We're alive," Sam shouted back.

"Fucking barely," said Joshua.

"Stay put and cover us," yelled the commander. "We're going forward."

Danny Carstairs hailed from the Gorbals in Glasgow. Stabbings, gunfire and gang warfare were a daily occurrence in his neighborhood; he certainly knew how to handle himself. Compared to the Gorbals, Northern Ireland was a holiday resort. This was his third and last tour and was retiring soon with the aim of settling down with his family in the beautiful Lake District area of North West England.

Danny and the rest of the patrol ran along the street, jumping over dead and injured bodies, and surrounded the burning vehicle. In the distance sirens wailed.

A car bomb, the usual trick of the IRA. Gorilla warfare, hit and run.

"Josh, Sam," shouted Danny. "Get down to the alley and cover our backs."

"Yes, sir," they both shouted.

A shot rang out and pinged off the side of the burning car. Everyone dived to the ground. "Sniper, sniper," yelled Danny. "Two hundred yards, end house, roof. Tile displaced. Two 'O clock."

Four soldiers took aim and fired at the roof. Pieces of tiles flew in all directions, the top bedroom windows shattered.

"Cease fire," yelled Danny. "Josh, Sam, double round to the other side and cover the roof."

"Yes, sir," said Joshua.

"Wish he'd make his fucking mind up."

Just as two ambulances and a police car arrived Joshua and Sam hurried down an alley, turned right at the top and doubled down to the corner end house. They knelt down, rifles aimed at the roof, or what was left of it and tried to spot the sniper, if he was still alive. But Joshua had a feeling the sniper had escaped even before the other soldiers had returned fire.

He realized (as did all the soldiers) that as soon as the sniper fired his shot, he'd climb out of the attic down the center square in the ceiling and at the same time pass his rifle to someone standing by who in turn stripped the gun and handed the various parts to other people (usually teenagers) who in turn fled out different doors in the house and down alleys and into cars and sped away. The sniper, on his way out of the house usually donned a yellow construction jacket and safety helmet, jumped into a waiting car and drove away. And if the car was stopped at a checkpoint they'd spout the same old story: 'Well, we're on our way home. You know how it is. Gotta keep the wife happy, yer see, otherwise she'd be nagging me about being late and not able to look after the kids while she goes to bingo.' Blah blah fucking blah.

But today things didn't quite work out the way they should have done for the sniper or his cronies. Every angle *wasn't* covered on this day.

At the same time Joshua and Sam ran up the alley, Danny and the rest of the patrol skirted around the front of the terraced houses and rushed towards the sniper's nest.

Sam ran up and kicked the back gate open, followed by Joshua and they took up kneeling positions on the inside against the garden fence. A woman emerged carrying a baby and screaming." Save my child. He threatened to kill her." The woman ran past them and out the gate. Sam was about to follow her. "No, Sam. Wait," said Joshua trusting his gut instinct.

A few seconds later a man wearing a yellow construction jacket and white safety helmet rushed out the kitchen door holding a rifle. He stood for a split second and looked at Joshua and Sam, then raised his AK 47 and cocked it.

Joshua and Sam aimed their rifles at the man and both pulled their triggers simultaneously. Nothing happened. Misfire. The sniper aimed his rifle but before he pulled the trigger three shots rang out from behind him; the sniper smashed backward through the kitchen door.

Danny Carstairs stood in the gateway, his rifle aimed at the sniper. "You lucky bastards," he said.

*

Back at base camp their rifles were inspected, checked, fired, and nothing had been found wrong with them. And yet both rifles failed to fire first time in the heat of battle.

"I can't believe it," said Joshua. "It's a fucking miracle."

"A miracle we weren't fucking killed."

"But there's nothing wrong with our rifles. What the fuck happened?"

They remained quiet for a while as they sat on their bunks and cleaned and oiled their rifles.

"Danny shouldn't have been there," said Sam. He and the patrol were around the front of the house waiting for someone to come out. Why did he come around the back?"

"Intuition, maybe?" said Joshua. "Anyway, tonight, "I'm gonna shake the man's hand – and buy him a drink."

*

(Buckingham Palace)

Joshua blew into his bagpipes and marched with the rest of the band through the massive oak doors and into the banquet hall in Buckingham Palace. What an honor, he thought as he and the pipers marched in and circled the long dining table playing a selection of tunes. Queen Elizabeth was familiar with a lot of bagpipe tunes due to listening to her personal bagpiper play at Balmoral Castle in Scotland.

The ten pipers (minus drummers) stopped at the head of the table and performed for ten minutes, then marched back around the table and out through the entrance doors.

Pomp and circumstance began here with all the silver cutlery and candlestick holders and silver dishes and platters and plates and servants dressed in red and black and dishing out delicious food to heads of state and a president and his wife and many other members of government and heads of banks and wealthy people from around Great Britain and America. The Queen was at the top of the table with Prince Charles to her left and Prince Philip, her husband to her right. All magnificence and richness and excitement Joshua had never experienced before and never likely to do so again.

A man from a poor family with no future in education or profession, and here he was now performing around the Queen's dinner table. But all good things must end and so it was with Joshua. He decided to leave the army and seek Annie out wherever she may be. Sam decided to stay in the army for the full twenty-two years and would make a fine and brave soldier. He was a good man and a trusted friend. *And* he had saved his life.

The most important thing Joshua had learned in Northern Ireland was that life, every *single* life is precious. He and Sam's life had been saved by Commander Danny Carstairs from Glasgow. After their tour of Northern Ireland had ended, Danny left the army and settled with his wife and two children in the Lake District. Joshua and Sam could never, in a hundred lifetimes repay Danny for saving their lives.

*

Chapter 33

Joshua returned to Corby and stayed at his mother's house, did the wild party scene for a year or so, dating and bedding women like a kid craving candy; he moved into a small apartment and, after all the candy had been used up he decided it was time to call on Annie.

On the way to her flat he passed through the town center and the market stalls beside the bus station. He walked around the corner to catch the bus and bumped into Saffron.

"Oh, sorry," he said.

"Joshua?"

His stomach performed somersaults. "Saffron?"

"How *are* you," she said.

"Oh, you know, fettling."

"Oh, sorry, this is my husband, Michael."

They shook hands. Michael Sheridan, tall and broad-shouldered with mousy-colored hair, replied sarcastically. "And *you* are?"

"Joshua Hanley."

"I've heard a lot about you." Joined the army and did a tour in Belfast. Fought for your country, eh?"

Joshua didn't like his tone.

"More than *you* ever did," said Saffron.

Michael opened his mouth to say something but Saffron beat him to it. "I see your mother at Asda now and again," she said.

Standing behind Saffron and hiding her face, a little blonde-haired girl about five years old looked up at him. Joshua noticed she had blue-gray eyes and a little button nose, her teeth small but straight and milky white.

"Who is this?" He knelt down to get a closer look. "She's a little golden gem."

"Come on," interrupted her husband. "The bus is about to leave." He picked up the girl and walked towards the bus. "Come on, Saffron," he barked.

"I got well again," she said. "It took a few years to fully get my memory back."

"You'd better catch the bus," said Joshua, moving away.

"Saffron," said Michael angrily. "The bus is *leaving!*"

Joshua watched as the bus drove away with Saffron and her daughter looking back at him through the window.

He took a deep breath. He was strong, he was courageous; he was Joshua Hanley and had faced snipers' bullets and riots and gun battles. He was *not* going to cry. Not today. No *way*.

He cried anyway.

*

Annie lived in an apartment (flat) in Danesholme estate just up from the west end of Gainsborough road: A little red brick building with a small back yard and a gate leading inside with a flowering honeysuckle plant growing above the front door.

Joshua was about to walk around the side to the front door when he heard a man's groaning sounds coming from an open window. He quietly unlatched the gate and slid up to the side of the window, Carefully moved aside the lace curtains and slyly peeked inside. He noticed first the caricature drawings hanging around the room and an easel that held an unfinished work: a beach with high cliffs and a couple of cottages on top.

That's Annie's artwork, Josh, said his inner voice. *Guess she's taking time out for a bit of the old hanky-panky.* On the bed a woman had her legs spread wide and a man was thrusting into her. All he could see was the man's buttocks rising and falling. Was that Annie beneath him? It had to be, this was Annie's apartment. And she liked to draw and paint. They must be *her* sketches. He couldn't see her face. Her didn't recognize her legs simply because he had never seen them up close and naked. In fact he had never seen Annie naked; they had never made love.

Joshua's heart pounded in his chest. He felt dizzy and felt betrayed somehow. How could she write letters to him and keep in contact and then have a lover on the side? And then he realized what a hypocrite he was; hadn't he done more or less the same.

But still, he felt a pang of jealousy, of envy for the guy fucking his Annie. The bastard got there before him. Joshua wondered how many men Annie had made love to since he joined the army.

After leaving the army he had stopped sending postcards from places he had visited and told himself that, maybe one day he would write to her again. Yet he still loved her. Oh, the sex was great with the women he met in clubs and bars; they were not pretty like Annie but their bodies were beautiful and sexy and he needed, as most young men needed, physical contact. *Young, dumb and full of cum,* as Sam had once said. And that was life, Joshua supposed. He wondered if without testosterone the human race could even survive.

Joshua quietly shut the back gate behind him. He was about to walk away but his inner voice barked at him - *Knock on the door, Joshua. Find out who is screwing Annie. They're going at it like fucking rabbits.*

Joshua rang the doorbell. After a minute or so the door opened. A tall, half naked man wearing spectacles answered the door.

"Yes, can I help you?"

"Oh," said Joshua. "I was looking for Annie."

"She's not here," said a female voice from behind the man.

"Madge," said Joshua. "Thought you were in America?"

"Josh," Madge said excitedly. "Nice to see you again. Oh, I'm on holiday for a few weeks. Thought I'd come back and see what was what?"

"I was just passing and thought maybe Annie would be in."

"Annie won't shut up about you," said Madge.

"Do you know where she is?"

"Why don't you ask her yourself," said Madge looking over his shoulder.

Joshua turned around and there was Annie standing behind him with a wide smile on her face.

"About bloody time," she said, and hugged him.

*

Joshua stayed the night, and the next night, and the next week sleeping at Annie's apartment.

"Madge decided to stay at her mam's, " said Annie. "Don't know where her boyfriend got to."

There was a moment's silence and then Annie laughed. "So you thought that was me getting screwed?"

"I couldn't see your face."

"Peeping Tom, eh?"

"I thought, well …"

"You thought you'd catch me making love?"

"Well, no, erm, yes."

"You stopped writing to me."

"I know. Busy and all that. But I want to see you now."

"Oh, I don't know about that." There was a twinkle in her eye.

"You've got a boyfriend? You're married? You've got kids?"

"None of the above."

Joshua stood, picked her up and carried her into the bedroom and placed her on the bedroom floor; they kissed passionately, hungrily, and almost ripped off each other's clothes to get at each other's bodies. They collapsed into bed and made love.

And, for the first time since Saffron had broken his heart, he felt good with a woman; he felt contented and comfortable. He felt grand.

*

Piece by piece, little by little, each part of his existence started to fit in place like parts of a jigsaw. Maybe his life was a kind of puzzle where certain periods in his life cannot be completed until other areas were lived through and experienced.

Joshua had come to understand a little about the concept of being confined inside his hypothetical box. And having read up on and listened to Madge talk about what it was like to live in America, and what he knew about Great Britain, it seemed to him that these countries *and* the majority of the world's population were not only trapped inside their own imaginary created boxes but also allowed others to cause them stress on a daily basis.

Trapped, snared, caught in the box and living an existence created by others who wanted to keep you in that box, whether they be a government, Church Dogma, massive Oil Companies, or Banking Institutions, they all kept the common people trapped inside 'the box.' And Joshua's mission was to break free from the box, break free from being told what to do, what to eat, what to say, what to pray, what to buy; to break free from being sold advertising *so you too* can be better than your neighbor. To break free from consumerism, from hypocritical politicians, bosses, priests, reverends, pastors, bishops and popes, Kings, Queens and Princes.

To break free so a person cannot be persuaded by threats of poverty or thousands of trivial laws, or abused, degraded, even shot by the police and all this thrown at people and forced into the minds of the proletariat in the hope that they would be kept repressed and keep the line and buy and sell and make the wealthy richer, the government richer, the banks and corporations richer, while millions of poor and homeless people suffer the sins of greed.

Joshua had become a man, not because he had reached the voting age, no, but because he was learning how to think for himself, how to stand back from the crowd, how to *not* follow the latest technological fad, how to *not* be brainwashed and become part of a collective mindset; how to *not* fall prey to greed, selfishness, bitterness, thievery and the world's mindset of 'because I see something unattended it must belong to me, and I have a right to steal it. No. Joshua was slowly breaking free from 'the box' simply because he was starting to *think* as an individual and not part of a brainwashed society.

The American dream was a myth, like the British Dream, or any other countries' dream for that matter. The whole concept of the 'Dream' fantasy is simply a way for governments to ensure people find work, work hard – and pay taxes.

*

"And who was her mother?" Joshua's mother was full to the brim with questions for Annie.

"Maude," said Annie. "She's dead now."

"Oh, I'm sorry to hear that. And where did you live?"

"Mam," said Joshua. "This isn't twenty questions, you know."

"Just asking. No harm in that, is there?"

"It's alright, Joshua. We lived on Beanfield Avenue, near St Brendan's school."

"Joshua went there."

"I know, but I was three years ahead of him."

"Oh, I see. I'll get some tea and biscuits," said mother and made her way out of the living room, her slippers making squishy sounds as she slid along the floor.

"Don't take any notice of her," said Joshua. "She's not a full shilling." He bent over and kissed her fully on the lips.

"If your mother wasn't here, Joshua, "I'd …"

"Tea up," said mother as she slid back into the living room with a tray of tea and custard creams. This time it wasn't her slippers making a noise because with every step she passed wind.

Joshua and Annie looked at each other and burst out laughing.

"Find it funny, eh," said mother. "Wind from the stomach travels to the heart – ignorant people call it a fart."

They laughed again and, this time, the Wicklow Amusement Arcade Queen joined in and almost dropped everything onto Joshua's lap.

"Mrs. Hanley," said Annie. "I think we're going to get on like a house on fire."

Mother sank into the couch and laughed even louder.

*

"You're like a sunflower," said Annie as they walked casually around the town park. "You like to follow the sun."

"California has plenty of that," said Joshua. "Compared to this place."

"It'll be an adventure. And I know how you like adventures."

"Do you know," continued Annie, "that a sunflower will turn its head slowly and follow the sun from east to west. And at sunset the flower takes about eight hours to turn back to the east."

"You've been reading again."

"I read it in the paper last week. Some scientists studied them for a couple of years. They reckon that pollination works best when the flower is facing east, so that's why the flower turns during the night and nature benefits."

"Sounds amazing."

"What really is amazing is that the young and middle-aged flowers – to coin a phrase – only follow the sun, and when the plant gets old it remains facing east so the pollinators can get as much benefit out of the plant before it withers and dies."

"Sounds like grandparents to me," said Joshua.

"I never thought of that. Clever boy."

"Isn't nature wonderful, though. Everything is connected to everything else."

"Like we're connected?."

"Exactly. Like two sunflowers following the sun."

The sun hid behind some clouds as they passed the swings and slides and sat on a bench by the edge of a wood. Birds sang on trees behind them, a squirrel showed an appearance at the foot of a tree, stared over at the two young lovers and then swiftly climbed onto a branch.

They sat in silence and enjoyed the pleasantness of the day; a little tranquility amid a torrent of chaos. Outside the park the cars streamed past on the main road, people on their way to work or coming home from work, or out shopping and buses passing and trucks crunching their gears and children shouting and dogs yapping amid the general buzz of a busy town.

"Joshua?"

"Hmmmm."

"Do you like children?"

"I love babies, but I couldn't eat a full one."

"You're funny. No, I mean, would you like to have children some day?"

"You mean with you?"

"No! With the German Shepherd next door." Annie punched him playfully on the arm.

"Of course. A boy first and then a girl. That's it. None of this four, five, six or seven children nonsense."

"You don't like big families?"

"If you want to sacrifice half your life by buying things for a big family, spend your life without vacations and weekends at the beach because you can't afford any of it, and, when they leave the nest, you spend the remainder of your life giving *them* money and not being paid back, *and* babysitting for them when they suddenly decide to go somewhere, then, no, I don't like big families. Two is enough. Three is a crowd. Four is a mistake. Five is stupid. Six is fucking completely nuts, and seven means you should have booked yourself into a mental asylum and had your brain removed so you can suck the juice out of a lollipop all day and night. And never again be allowed out into society."

"You're serious?"

"Na. But two is enough for me. How about you?"

"I want nine children. Only joking. Two would be lovely."

"Anyway, why are we talking about kids."

"Oh, just curious," she said and snuggled up to him.

They walked through the botanical gardens, or twenty feet of a kind of garden inside a dilapidated greenhouse with equally decaying plants and withering flowers – a kind of poor man's garden - then bought a couple of '99 ice-creams at the corner booth beside the tennis courts. They decided to walk back to Joshua's house with the idea of sneaking upstairs to his bedroom and slipping under the bed sheets.

His mother usually did her shopping up town this time of day and his father was at work.

"Did you know," said Annie, "that Jesus chose Joshua to become the prophet after Moses died to lead the Israelites into the Promised Land."

"I do now."

"And that the name Annie means the prophetess from Jerusalem. It also means, 'graceful' and 'prayer' in Hebrew."

"Okay, Annie the prophetess, let's get you home. I want to peel your knickers off with my teeth."

"You're awful," she said and kissed him fully on the lips.

*

Joshua's father, Liam was not in Manchester today and was outside working in the back garden. Joshua's excitement at the prospect of peeling Annie's knickers off with his teeth was postponed until a more intimate setting could be arranged. 'The best-laid plans of mice and men go oft awry,' as that great Scottish poet Robbie Burns had once said.

The sun, this past week or so was not unlike a desert sun, the blistering heat wilting both humans and rose bushes alike.

"Hey-up," said Liam, sweat streaming down his forehead and cheeks.

"Hi da. Hot enough for you?"

"I don't need to go to hell when I die, son. I'm already there. Oh, hello, you must be Annie. Mary was talking about yer."

"Only bad things, I hope," Annie said and shook Liam's hand."

"She only says bad things about people she likes."

"He's only joking," said Joshua and squeezed his arm around Annie's waist.

"She likes you, Annie. And that's saying something."

Annie smiled her big, wide, beaming friendly smile showing her straight white teeth, a smile that Joshua thought could easily make a depressive person smile back.

"You've got lovely roses," said Annie and gently touched a pink petal.

"They've grown really well since, well, since Bonnie died and helped them along a bit."

"She's under that pile of earth over there," said Joshua. "And Clyde is next to her."

Liam busied himself clipping his roses, adding fertilizer and watering them. Annie and Joshua sat on a small bench beneath the dining room window and relaxed in the sunshine.

"No work, today, da?"

"Carpenters' are on another one day strike. Ejits. They get twice as much as I do so I don't know why they're complaining. They make wooden shutters and we fill 'em with concrete. Easy enough work for them, back-breaking work for us. Some people are just never satisfied."

In the distance a Jackhammer started up.

"Oh," said Liam, "they've finally decided to fill in the quarry."

"About time," said Joshua. "Imagine - we used to swim up there."

"What. In the quarry?" said Annie.

"John O'Malley drowned in one of those pools," said Liam.

Joshua explained the story to Annie; and then told her about Mrs. Feely's death.

"I remember reading about that bus crash in the newspaper," said Annie. "You never told me you and your mother was on that bus."

"Some things are … you know," said Joshua.

"Too painful to talk about," said Liam. "Your mother still stands over there by the fence and talks to herself."

"Maybe she's talking to Mrs. Feely," Joshua said.

Liam shrugged his shoulders and clipped another twig from his rosebush.

After a few moments silence, except for the repetitive pounding of the distant Jackhammer, Joshua cleared his throat and said, "We're thinking of living over in America, da."

"America?"

"California to be exact," said Annie. "That's where the sunshine is."

"Land of the brave, eh?" Liam said and clipped one of his roses too roughly and snapped the stem.

"We'll come back to England, da, just don't know when."

"The state of sunshine, high taxes and lots of homeless people."

"How do you know that, da?"

"Seen it on TV the other night."

"Well, we'll give it a try," said Annie. "Madge, a friend of mine already lives over there and we can stay with her 'till we can rent a flat."

"It's called an apartment, dear," said Joshua and smirked.

"Oh. I stand corrected, *dear*," replied Annie and smiled.

"You two seem to get on well," said Liam and, for the first time in many months, he smiled.

"Oh, you still have teeth," said Joshua.

"Feck off," said Liam.

*

Part Three
(Bakersfield, California)

Chapter 34

The heat is stifling. The air is dry; there are no clouds in the sky. I lie here naked on my bed. Annie is asleep beside me: an afternoon nap after our earlier lovemaking. Desert heat, don't really know if I'll ever get used to it. The sun burns my shoulders even when I take my shirt off for a few moments. It's like existing in a roasting oven. We hardly cook anything that requires the oven or hobs to be turned on. Salads, takeaways, iced-tea, that's our usual fare. In England tea has to be sipped hot to enhance the flavor, but here in Bakersfield, you *need* to drink cold tea to cool down.

I'm thirty now. Annie is three years older than me, though she looks a lot younger than her age. Father eventually left my mother. Came home on a Friday night, threw his cap in the side entrance and had it thrown back at him. Went down the Irish Club and got drunk, came home, straight to bed and up early before the larks. By the time my mother got out of bed (she told me a couple of weeks later when I phoned her) he had taken two suitcases and, with only the clothes on his back just upped and left. 'The shite also dug up and took a few rose bushes with him," she had said. Thirty-five years married. As you sow so shall you reap.

Still, I phone my father from time to time; he lives in a small flat in Kettering and told me he's as happy as a dog in a butcher's shop. I'm happy for him.

Annie gets up and goes to the kitchen and makes coffee. I turn the TV on and, for a few minutes watch the local news. I quickly turn it off because it's all about gang shootings in East Bakersfield and someone shot dead in the shopping Mall on Ming Avenue, and there's a video of two policemen holding down a black guy. No good news as usual.

We sit at the dining room table and sip our coffees. Annie bends down and looks in her suitcase and produces a small, wooden jewelry box. I watch as she opens it and takes out a crucifix and silver chain.

"That looks exactly like mine," I say.

She puts it around her neck and fastens the clasp.

"It's been in this box for ages," she says. "My grandfather gave it to me. He said it has to be passed down to the first female born in each generation."

"That's incredible," I say and take out my crucifix from under my tee-shirt. "My grandfather gave me this, too. My mother got it from him just before he died. 'That cross has been passed down through the years, and has to go to the first male born in each generation.' She also said there's a family secret attached to it, or at least my grandfather said so. If two of the same crucifixes come together then the magic begins to work."

"What does that mean?" she asks.

"I haven't got a clue, but there were times when past images came to me, or I found myself in a different place." I lean over and, with a little trepidation, press my cross against her crucifix. Instantaneously we find ourselves lying on a crowded beach and, before we have time to find out where we are, we suddenly appear inside a plane flying high above the clouds. We just sit there (I have the window seat); there are two whiskies on the table in front of us. The next instant we're back in the dining room.

"What just happened," I say.

"That was amazing."

"It's true. It's really true."

"This is crazy," says Annie.

"He's right about those magical powers."

"You're not kidding."

"No one believed him, Annie. But we were just on a beach, and then in a plane."

"Two whiskies on the table."

"I was sitting by the window."

"What's happening to us, Joshua?"

*

We sleep for what seems hours. I take a while to nod off thinking about where we had travelled – together – after our crosses had touched.

I quietly get out of bed and visit the restroom. I look at myself in the mirror. They have massive mirrors in America, whereas the UK (or the mirrors in my old house) were minute compared to these (My mother would just love these mirrors). Folks obviously enjoy looking at themselves over here, I guess. I take a closer look. *Dark hair, sideburns half way down my ears, equal on both sides, too. Shiny, brown eyes, high cheek bones, slight tan (that's good) narrow lips, a dimple on my chin, slightly elongated face, wide brow.*

I roll my tongue around inside my mouth and touch my teeth. *Two wisdom teeth missing and a big gap near the rear, right side.*

"What you doing in there, handsome," says Annie standing at the bathroom door.

"Oh, just admiring myself."

"Come back to bed."

Lying beside her she puts her leg over mine. "What you thinking about?"

"Let's travel somewhere," I say. "It's your turn. Try thinking of a place."

I lean over her and our crucifix's touch.

Annie and I are walking through grass and come to a parting in some rocks. On the other side is a small oasis surrounded by tall palm trees and in the center a magnificent swimming pool complete with diving boards and sun lounges. We are wearing swimming costumes; we dive in and fool around in the pool. And now we entwine and kiss.

And then things really turn crazy – Annie grips me around the waist as I begin to spin upwards. Together we rise ten, fifteen, twenty feet from the pool. We're now surrounded by mist so thick I can hardly see Annie's face. Slowly we descend through the mist and suddenly I feel solid ground beneath my feet.

"Where are we," Annie asks gripping me tightly.

"Maybe this is heaven," I say but with a sliver of sarcasm. The mist begins to clear and as it rises above our heads I see massive, snow-peaked mountains.

Green patches of grassland and clumps of dark trees cling to the mountain sides. The mist clears completely and I feel the sun's warmth on my face. Below and on either side of us are deep valleys covered with trees. Two hawks swoop down into the valley on our left and then soar skyward.

"This is beautiful," says Annie and removes her hands from around my waist. She inhales deeply. "But I was only thinking of the pool."

"I didn't imagine this," I say. "I wasn't thinking of anything in particular. Besides, I was enjoying the swimming pool."

"Where is this?"

"It looks a lot like Scotland," I say and gaze around at the gigantic mountains.

"How do you know?"

"I don't … just a feeling."

Annie looks behind her. I follow her gaze and spot a winding track which leads down into the valley. I take her hand and we walk down towards the valley basin. Bunches of thistle heather sway in the slight breeze. Birds chirp on the branches of fir trees. A gushing brook meanders down on one side of the track and under a small, wooden bridge while around and above us massive mountains, some tapering near the peaks like wizards' hats give me a feeling of peace, of being protected by nature herself.

We come to a clearing at the side of the track and in the center is a blazing campfire. Further back near where the woods begin is what looks like a gypsies' caravan, complete with horses and reins and harnesses.

We walk carefully pass the fire and stand outside the front door of the caravan. The top half of the red-colored door is open. The caravan is an old wooden, highly painted contraption with ornamental wood carvings around the eaves, gargoyles, ugly and snarling sit on the edge of each corner and small Virgin Mary statues are pinned around the edge of the door; a crucifix is nailed in the center of the lower half of the door.

Suddenly the door opens and out walks a long dark-haired woman of about fifty. "And what can I do for ye, young sir," she says in a broad Irish brogue. What teeth she has left in her mouth are crooked and there's half a halo of darkish hair on her top lip. She's dressed in a black, ankle length skirt with a big, scruffy and stained black coat slung over her broad shoulders.

"Sorry for disturbing you," I say and attempt a smile, "but who are you?"

"You don't remember?" The gypsy screams out a high-pitched laugh, more a cross between the cackle of a crow and a hyena. Annie jumps a little and grabs hold of my arm. I must admit this woman even scares me a little.

"Should I?"

"I read your palm. Your mother would remember me."

I look closely at her face. She is a lot older than I remember her as a child. "Rose?"

"And how's your mother?"

"Oh, I don't really know. I mean …"

"The universe works in mysterious ways," she says and walks down the three wooden steps slowly as if she's suffering from arthritis.

"But why are you here," I say.

"This is my world," she says intensely. "Go create your own."

"I think what Joshua is trying to say is …" Annie is cut off by Rose's sharp words and pointing finger.

"You don't belong here."

I'm about to reply to Rose when everything turns to blackness. I feel Annie's hand grip mine. Next instant we're standing in a kitchen. I take a few seconds to focus on where I am and suddenly realize this is my house. My mother is cooking something over the stove. She's wearing a scruffy flowery dress and a stained woolen dark brown cardigan with a food-splattered apron beneath, and on her feet is a pair of worn out pink slippers, one toe poking out the front. I suddenly feel guilty and want to buy her a new pair.

"That boy will be the death of me," mother says and bangs the frying pan down on the stove top. "As sure as there's a God in heaven."

She turns on the gas and opens a packet of sausages and proceeds to put them in the pan. They sizzle the way only my mother's sausages sizzle because she cooks them on high gas, that's why they have the distinctive look of dark leather and the flavor of burnt meat.

I walk up to her and squeeze her arm but she doesn't respond.

"Ma. Can you hear me? It's Joshua."

"Running away and leaving his poor mother to fret and cry and worry all night long. How could he do this to me?"

I glance at Annie and she shrugs her shoulders. "This is crazy," I say and stand back a little.

"Phoned that bastard up and he don't care. 'Leave it 'till I get home,' he says, 'I'll knock the shite out 'o the wee man, don't ye worry.' That's all the man knows. The belt across the ass. Aye. Just like he used to get from his father, and his father before him."

Annie and I exchange looks. They say you can see pain in a person's eyes. I wonder if she can see the pain in mine.

Mother turns the sausages over and pricks small holes in them with a fork. She breaks a couple of eggs and slides them into the pan. I can smell the meat and wish I could eat a sausage. She walks out of the kitchen, dragging her feet so her slippers make squeaky sounds across the linoleum and with each step she emits a tiny fart.

Maybe it's a gift she has, or maybe she's spent years developing her talent but I'm sure with a little more practice she will eventually be able to play 'God save the Queen' out of her ass, or even the 'Minstrel Boy.' But at least she's decent about it. After every 'botty burp' as she calls them, she says, "'Cuse me, 'cuse me." And if there is a longer and louder ass burp she emphasizes her words, "Ex..cuse …me."

I chuckle and Annie shakes her pretty head. "You could write a book about your mother," Annie says.

The kitchen is slowly filling with smoke. Nothing I can do but watch and hope she doesn't burn the place down. Mother returns with some mail in her hand. "Holy Mary Mother of God and all the saints in Heaven," she exclaims and grabs the frying pan, opens the back door and throws the flaming pan outside. It lands on da's best rose bush which bursts into flames; the fire spreads to all his rose bushes.

She stands there looking at the burning bushes and doesn't attempt to extinguish the flames. "Feck him and his roses," she snarls and lights a cigarette.

She goes to the wall mirror. I'm waiting for her to ask the mirror 'who is the fairest of them all,' but she just stands there and stares at herself. She inhales deeply on her cigarette and blows the smoke directly at the glass. "You could've done a lot better than marrying that one."

Something I can't understand is mother starts to reply to herself as if someone *else* is in that mirror and talking back to her. It seems like a two-way conversation and maybe inside her troubled and stressed mind it *is* a two-way conversation.

Annie squeezes my arm. I grip her hand.

"You're right there, missus," says mother to the 'missus' or whoever it is inside the mirror, "I could've married Sean Ennis from Blackrock. He wanted to take me out and dine me. A lovely wee man he was, too."

"Why didn't you take up his offer, Mary?" says the mirror, or my mother's mad inner voice speaking outwardly. The voice (from the mirror, although still my mother's voice) sounds slightly deeper.

"God rue the day I turned him down," says Mother. "I could've been living down south in a big house with beautiful furniture and nice clothes and he'd take me out to dinner and we'd dance and kiss and …."

"But it's too late for that, now, Mary. Far too late."

"You're telling me," mother replies, "far too late. What a waste. I took pity on him. Him and his poor family, half-starving to death and him the only breadwinner at twelve years old. Gypies they were. The lot of them. All gypsies. Fecking Knackers. I married him to get him away from poverty and look at me. Just *look* at me now. Out of the frying pan and into the fecking fire."

"But you *also wanted to escape the poverty, didn't you, Mary?"*

For a few moments my mother is silent, as if answering this question will maybe make her realize that taking pity on my father and marrying him wasn't the only reason she had for leaving the horrific poverty in Ireland at that time, and maybe she thought she could create a better life for herself in England.

I look at Annie, her mouth hangs open.

Mother lights another cigarette; she inhales the smoke deep into her lungs.

And then, my father, obviously drunk, barges through the kitchen door, his eyes wide, his mouth agape, his fists clenched and glaring at my mother. "You fecking bitch. You good-for-nothing fecking whore," he screams, drags her away from the mirror and slaps her viciously across the face.

"I didn't mean it!" mother screams.

"The one thing, the only pleasure I have in this life and you burn it to the ground!"

"It was an accident!"

Da then punches her on the side of the face and again slaps her on the other side of her face. He turns and slams the kitchen door behind him.

Ma sits, her cigarette now burning a hole in the lino on the floor; she weeps and her weeping is like the mournful, pitiful howl of an Irish Banshee.

Annie squeezes my hand; I glance at her with tears in my eyes. She points a finger at the bottom of the stairs just outside the kitchen. We see a little boy sitting on the stairs; tears trickle down his rosy cheeks.

It is me.

Memories flood my mind; I remember now sitting on those stairs and witnessing what had transpired. I felt suddenly ashamed because as my father had slapped my mother across the face I had *wanted* him to slap her again and again, in some weird, upside down emotional forlorn- crazy avenging feeling that I had at the time.

Now, as Annie and I look on, my mother's shoulders rise and fall and tears stream down her cheeks. "Out of the frying pan and into the fire," she says.

She takes a brown streak-stained handkerchief out of her cardigan pocket, wipes the wetness around her eyes and keeps repeating the words, "Out of the frying pan and into the fire. Out of the fecking frying pan and into the fire. Out of the frying …"

And then something even crazier happens, I'm now in my apartment and Annie and I are kissing, just like earlier, and then I'm suddenly on top of her in bed and I see her hair all tangled and sweaty and her eyes are closed and her mouth is slightly open and she moans something and I look down and I'm thrusting deep inside her and I see my hardness, and on the wall beside me is a mirror and I see my body thrusting and pushing inside her and her legs are spread in the air as I pound at her and I raise my head and look to the ceiling which is covered with mirrors and the four walls are covered with mirrors and I see our bodies writhing on the bed from every direction. And I look at Annie's face and it's Saffron's face that is on the pillow and in all the mirrors the smiling face of Susan Bletchley appears and then all the women I've fucked while in Pirbright and Germany and Corby appear in the mirrors and then they disappear and Annie's face is back on the pillow and inside my head I scream and scream, and in those screams I feel the frustration and pain of my father and the pity I feel for my mother and the loss of my friend and the decapitation of Mrs. Feely and the piping of Sean Flanagan and the arrogance of Michael Sheridan and the craziness of Sergeant Wilson and the bravery of Sam O'Neil and the intuition of Danny Carstairs and the fear of a little boy with rosy cheeks sitting on the stairs and my father hitting my mother and the tears streaming down her cheeks and her howling like a crazy Irish Banshee and the bullshit of the whole *fucking* world and the whole *fucking* world explodes in my head and simultaneously I explode inside Annie.

And it's the most beautiful, fulfilling, orgasmic feeling I've ever experienced, even better than Saffron. This is my paradise and the closest I'll ever get to heaven.

Annie softly kisses my neck and we both fall asleep.

*

Chapter 35

"Do you know we've been here a year," I say to Annie as she gets into her swimming costume. She is due in at work by noon. She's now a care-assistant at a Special Needs home in Bakersfield and her earlier training as a nurse helps her in this new line of work.

"That long?" Annie says.

"The true wild west. Folks keep shooting each other over here for some reason."

"At least it's sunny."

"Sure. At least they don't die in the rain, like in England."

"You're funny," she says and goes through to the kitchen.

"Hey, there's some strong Colombian coffee in the cupboard above the stove." I shout through to her.

I like this apartment. It's small and in a quiet area. Outside there's a medium-sized swimming pool in which I often dive into, especially when the temperature reaches over 100 degrees. I don't regret moving to California. I needed to escape the constant rain and cold weather of England. Always made me feel sad all those overcast clouds and never knowing if it was about to rain or even if the sun would make an appearance. I remember one day going out into my back garden and taking a photograph of the sun, so on gloomy days I'd take it out and gaze at it.

So here I am. Bakersfield, California, 100 miles or so north of Los Angeles. And lately I've become a time traveler for want of a better word. A time-traveling bagpiper. I play bagpipes at weddings and other social gigs but in Bakersfield, I mostly perform at funerals.

Annie sits with me and we sip our coffees. On TV the news is talking about the war in Afghanistan, and who has just been shot by police in Atlanta.

"Wouldn't it be wonderful to live in a world without wars," says Annie. "I mean, our world is sick."

"It's people who are sick, Annie, not the world. But wouldn't *that* be nice. But it'll never happen when there's so much greed around."

"Greed starts wars?"

"Greed and profit are the demons that drive men to start wars, Annie. Did you know that they shot Kennedy because he wanted disarmament and world peace?"

"How do you know all this," said Annie.

"Sometimes I grip my crucifix and the thoughts just come to me."

Annie turns off the TV. She walks into the kitchen.

"This kitchen is so old fashioned," she says in way of changing the subject.

"Well, I guess I'm just an old fashioned guy," I say.

"Fancy a swim," Annie says.

"Last one in is a twat!"

*

We swim like crazy porpoises up and down and under the pool then go indoors and drink some red merlot. Ninety-five degrees and rising in Bakersfield. I prefer to call it Baking-field because I feel like a pie that's being baked in an oven.

We make love in the bedroom, this time making sure we take off our crosses.

Annie and I gaze at the ceiling after our sweaty lovemaking. We shower together, washing each other in our private parts, then dry off and kiss in the hallway. We shuffle over to the bed, she holding me by my erect penis and then she lies on the bed beside me.

We explore each other, every nook and cranny, every piece of skin and then make love slowly, her sitting on me. We gaze into each other's eyes in what seems like hours. Our fingers touch and a spark ignites; I feel a gentle *love* flow inside me, around me, over me like a warm cascade of water, and feel not so much that I'm in paradise but that paradise is now in me.

She reminds me so much of Saffron. And then we slowly climax together. Such beauty, such lovemaking, such bliss.

After I catch my breath and my heartbeat returns to normal (poor old heart, it takes such a pounding) I lean over Annie and touch her cross with mine.

And instantly we are outside on a construction site. My father is shoveling concrete from a heap on the ground into a shuttered drain sewer. He stops shoveling, straightens up and stretches his back. He takes out a dirty handkerchief and wipes his sweaty brow.

Around me I hear jackhammers pounding stony ground and wood clattering to the ground and diesel generators buzzing and someone hammering nails into wood and someone whistling and someone else singing 'Oh Danny Boy' as my father bends down and begins to shovel the concrete into the drain.

A small twister spins toward us, swirling, growing, until it envelops us and my father. Thick dust and sand. I grip Annie's hand and hold her close to me as we begin to spin, slowly at first and then faster, faster.

Here we go again.

We twist speedily around in the sand storm; our bodies held together by the centrifugal force around us, pounding at us, sucking in our cheeks. Annie grips me tightly and her face digs deep into my neck. I open my eyes and now we're standing in the bedroom of my youth, and I see myself as a young man.

My young self is on the bed and naked, buttocks rising and falling. I'm screwing a girl about my own age. My arms stretch each side of her and her legs are wrapped around my waist.

"Call me by my name!" I hear the girl say.

"What's your name?"

"I told you already."

"I forgot."

"Sexy Susan."

"Can I call you Sue?"

"*Sexy Susan*, damnit."

"Okay okay. Sexy Susan."

"Fuck me harder and say it. *Mean it* for God sakes."

Annie and I become reluctant voyeurs in this sort of universal-magical tableau. And to be honest, looking at myself making love to someone kind of got my sexual juices stirring.

But there again it's *me* I'm watching. I look at Annie and she shakes her head, smiles and shrugs her shoulders. We didn't ask to be in this position, didn't ask or request to the universe to instantaneously (at the speed of light, no doubt) flip from one scene to another in this world – or any world for that matter.

A voice bellows up the stairs, "How's your homework coming along? Prehistoric, what was it?" It's my mother.

"Prehistoric animals!"

"Are yer done?"

"*Almost!*"

"I've a bit of tae for yourself and your friend. What's her name again?"

"Sex … *Susan!*"

"Tex Susan? What is she, a fecking cowgirl?"

"*Susan!*"

"Food's getting cold. Are you *coming*?"

"Yes, ma, almost … "

Annie and I are transported (only word I can think of using for now) through the spinning vapor and appear in the side entrance area of my house.

My younger self is holding Clyde under his left arm while struggling with Bonnie under the other. At the side door is my father trying to pull Bonnie away.

"Only one dog allowed in this house," says father and pulls again at the yelping dog. "I can't afford to feed two of the little shites."

"But da," tears run down my younger self's cheeks. "They're brother and sister."

"I don't care if they're Laurie and fecking Hardy," shouts father. "One stays one goes. Now choose."

"Sophie's choice," I say to Annie. She is silent.

Young Joshua lets go of Bonnie and father storms out through the side entrance door with the dog tucked under his arm.

My younger self strokes little Clyde and hugs him into his chest, swaying a little with him as you would a baby. "I'm sorry, little Clyde. I'm sorry. Bonnie will be fine. You'll see."

And then Annie and I are gone.

*

"Space, the final frontier." These words come to mind as I hold Annie's hand in the misty void, and then, instantaneously, I'm sitting in a seat and wearing a space suit. I quickly look around me at the dials and switches and blinking lights and out the narrow window and, oh God, I'm in space. Through the window I see a massive wing with darkened tile squares covering it. I'm in a space shuttle. There's no sign of Annie, maybe she doesn't like flying, or maybe this scenario has only me in it. Maybe she's outside repairing something at twenty thousand miles an hour? Maybe not?

Be careful what you wish for, now where did I hear that before?

Ever since watching Star Trek as a child I've always wanted to fly out into space and here I am. Joshua Hanley, thirty-five years old, space traveler (time traveler, in reality) out here in freezing cold space looking down on a giant blue orb. I wonder if I can see my house from here? Stupid. I laugh at myself, kind of a nervous, almost maddening laugh.

Maybe I'm slowly going mad and with each episode, each journey back and forth through time either makes me stronger or weaker. I don't feel weak in any way, not physically at least, so I must be getting stronger psychologically.

Maybe? Maybe not?

I stare out the window at planet earth below. What a beautiful, awe-inspiring sight. The blue planet. A man could quite easily die peacefully up here just looking down on earth. It looks so peaceful and innocent and new to me. The earth doesn't deserve populations to live on its surface. The earth to me is pure, a part of nature, of everything that's perfect except the people that load the world with strife and war and cruelty and murder and rape, and the people, intent on destroying our world either by blowing it to smithereens or over polluting it. Either way man will destroy both the world and himself – it's only a matter of time.

I close my eyes and scream as I soar like a speeding projectile toward planet earth. My space suit is now a jump suit complete with helmet and parachute. My face cheeks are sucked inward and my mouth puckers with the wind velocity. I'm flying!

Below I see massive holes filled with murky water and hills either side. Nearby is a housing estate and a school and in the distance a town hall clock and various sized buildings. I speed downward and at about one hundred feet from the ground I see a boy I recognize from somewhere – John, my best friend - he's running along the side of a main road with a little dog that only has three legs. That's Clyde.

John cuts to his left and runs across the road and reaches the other side but Clyde is lagging behind him, *the poor thing only has three legs, man,* I scream inside my head as a car speeds toward him and … oh God, Clyde's been hit and is now flying through the air and lands in the middle of the road and I'm falling toward the road, the car, the dog, and suddenly realize that I may need a parachute to stop my free-falling, but can't find a rip-cord anywhere and realize I'm going-to-be-fucking dead any second. I close my eyes and, when I open them, I'm lying on my stomach on my bed and being stroked across my shoulder blades.

"Is that you, Annie," I ask, still out of breath from my split second journey from free-falling to lying on my stomach.

"You know it is," she says soothingly, "I've been massaging you for twenty minutes."

"This is weird."

I wonder if what I'm experiencing is a series of interwoven dreams or thoughts. Visions turned into reality by mere thought. If so then they are uncontrollable, unless I can somehow keep my thoughts in check, try not to think of anything, which is impossible unless I become a Buddhist monk, or die.

Thousands of thoughts flash through my mind all day, but I don't experience all the visions in my thoughts, because otherwise I'd never stay in one place. I'd be appearing in so many places, one after the other that I'd probably go crazy. No. I'm beginning to realize that my visions or images or thoughts are connected to my younger self and my youth. Maybe Annie has similar experiences?

There's nothing I can really do except try not to fight my thoughts, let them happen and wait for the ultimate outcome.

I feel sorry for John and my three-legged dog.

*

*

Dropping to the ground like a stone and not being able to find my rip-cord is an experience I wouldn't wish on my worst enemy. Or even my best enemy for that matter. I thought my heart was going to burst out of my chest, especially hurtling so close to earth. And poor Clyde, too. 'It was God's will' as my mother would say.

"Your hands are so soft," I say to Annie as she massages my lower back.

"I'm glad you like it," she says.

"Just a little bit lower should do the trick."

She slaps my buttocks hard. "That's it for now."

"I fancy something juicy and fat," I say.

"A beefburger?"

"Good enough," I say.

We walk outside to bright, blinding sunshine and heat. It's like stepping into a blast furnace. We drive in my Toyota sedan down to a burger restaurant.

I look around at the wide streets that surround a shopping center and there is an Office Depot, and a Carl's Junior and Macdonald's at the junction of two main roads. On the corner of this junction is a guy wearing a black cowboy hat and swinging a sign in tempo with his dancing. Big trucks whizz past us with massive wheels; reminds me of toy cars. On the way to the fast food restaurant we pass a bus stop and a homeless guy sitting there smoking a cigarette. He's barefooted and wears dirty jeans and a filthy ripped tee-shirt. His arms and face are sun burnt.

"Can you spare a few dollars for the bus, sir," pleads the homeless guy.

"I'll buy you a meal."

"Oh, sure." says the guy and flicks his cigarette into the road.

We enter the burger place and I suddenly remember walking into many similar restaurants in England. There's an ATM machine in one corner.

I get thirty dollars out, give twenty to Annie and tell her to buy some food, what she wants, for both of us and something for the homeless guy, while I visit the restroom. She buys two burgers and fries and Annie settles for a strawberry milkshake.

Outside I walk over and give the homeless guy a couple of dollars and the food.

"Thank you, Sir. May God bless you."

I nod and rejoin Annie. We find a bench outside Office Depot and sit down and eat.

"I still can't believe how big these burgers are," I say.

"Look," says Annie and points with her milkshake. "There's another homeless person."

An old man ambles along this side of McDonald's dragging behind him a baby pushchair stuffed full of old magazines. We hear screaming to our right. A young man is waving his arms above his head. "God will save us all. God will destroy us all!"

"I wish he'd make his mind up," I say.

Annie almost chokes on her milkshake.

"Over there, look," points Annie. "That woman is pushing a trolley full of junk, it looks like."

"It's called a cart over here," I say. "Probably her world possessions. Look, there's another one at the bus stop."

"What's in all those black bags he's carrying?"

"Plastic bottles. They collect them and take 'em to the recycling center for cash. We don't have that problem in the UK 'cause we recycle for free."

"I feel sorry for them having no home to go to. No luxuries."

The screaming religious freak passes us on a skakeboard. "God will save you. God will destroy you!"

"A caring and loving society is judged by the way it treats its old, young and mentally ill."

"So what does it make this place?"

"Figure it out for yourself."

Annie takes a few moments to sip on her strawberry milkshake.

"Can you think of somewhere nice," says Annie, "some place where they don't have guns and kill each other every day, a place where's there's no homeless, no corruption, greed, selfishness and rape."

"I know somewhere that, compared to this place, is paradise."

"Where's that," says Annie excitedly.

"Hell."

Chapter 36

Annie enjoys her work in the care home on Chestnut street. A four bedroomed house with two men and two women with special needs. Sometimes she has to lift people out of their wheelchairs and onto beds which gives me the delightful job of having to massage her lower and upper back two or three times a week. Her past nursing experience is certainly helpful.

"You should go see a doctor about those pains," I tell her every time I massage her back, but she's a stubborn one and won't see any doctor. Back pain is all part of the job, she told me.

A 9 to 5 job at twelve dollars an hour, not bad, but for the care and love she gives, the woman should be on at least twenty dollars an hour. Still, with my wage of twelve dollars an hour we scrape by. I occasionally perform at funerals on the bagpipes say on average one funeral a month. Bakersfield, having a high percentage of Hispanics and African-Americans don't tend to hire a Scottish bagpiper for funerals or even weddings. Most of my gigs are for veterans who have Scots or Irish ancestors.

Still, we have a job, we have sunshine, we have a swimming pool outside our door, we have Pismo and Morro bay beaches about a two hour drive west, we both have reliable cars, and, most importantly, we have each other. And to add to all this luxury, myself and Annie are transported to various places in time (a different location every time, which is a pleasant surprise) without having to spend a penny.

Most evenings after work we dive in the pool, do step-ups (I also do some push-ups and weights) together while watching TV, cook and eat dinner, watch a movie, sip a couple of whiskies (Irish Jamison's), retire to bed, make love, and then press our crucifix's together. Some nights we just sleep. And that's our ritual.

So tonight, it being a Saturday we wiill enjoy a good lie in tomorrow, so we thought we'd try another adventure. Sometimes if we think of where we want to travel to, and then touch crosses, we arrive there. And at other times when we *don't* think of a place to travel to, we touch crosses and leave our destination to fate. It's weird, because when we don't think of where to go we travel back to my youth.

We touch crosses and, suddenly, we are flying through the clouds like eagles soaring; the wind flows over and under our imaginary wings. Then we're in the kitchen area of my youth. I look on as my younger self grasps a crucifix in his left hand. Mother is reading something from an old piece of paper, turned up at the corners and stained. I see a sketch drawing of the cross. I bend over to look closer and read the inscription beneath. 'Onyx cross. Property of Mr Paddy Doyle, husband of Iona Doyle, and father of Megan Doyle. To be passed on to the first male born of every generation. 1848.'

1848. What was it like existing in that time? So Megan Doyle is my great-grandmother, and Annie, my grandmother is her daughter.

I feel my stomach cramp a little every time something is about to happen, so I grip Annie's hand and we speed again through clouds and over green hills and pastures and look down on sheep and cows grazing and winding tracks and then we find ourselves sitting on a small couch in what must be my grandmother's cottage in Dublin. I know this because I lived here once as a child. We are, of course invisible to everyone though we can still see each other.

The cottage is small and quaint. The front door leads straight into the living-cum-dining room with square paneled windows along the front wall. The place smells a little of damp and dust motes float from ceiling to floor. There's a pair of tall ornamental glazed Persian cats atop an old French dresser against the far wall and a coal fire in the center. Two bedrooms lead off from the living room.

Two oil lamps, one on the mantelpiece above the fire and another near me in the corner. No electricity had yet reached my grandparents' area though I do know that parts of Dublin had lights on somewhere.

Vague memories stir around inside my head of sitting at the dining room table and staring curiously at those two Persian cats. The eyes, black pupils and white irises seemed to stare back at me and straight into my soul. I remember feeling scared looking at these cats as I munched on my porridge. My parents and I lived in this cottage for four years, according to my father, before packing up and making a new life in England, like so many other Irish people of that period.

Of course, I lived here from 1957 to 1960 and the year now is 1916, according to the *Irish Independent* newspaper lying on the table. My grandmother has had these cats all those *years*?

"My mother had Persian cats like those," said Annie. "Till my father smashed them."

In the distance I hear gunfire. *Gunfire?*

"What's that," says Annie suddenly sitting upright.

"It sounds like guns firing," I say and realize what's happening. "The Easter Uprising."

The far bedroom door opens and out walks my grandmother in an ankle length pink nightgown. I quickly figure out her age. I know my grandfather was born in 1884 and my grandmother is four years younger than him so he must be thirty-two and she is twenty-eight.

She lights the lamp over the fire then walks over to me and lights the one in the corner. I look at her. She is a beauty. Long mousy-colored hair that flows down over her shoulders, a high brow and pert nose. For a moment she glances in my direction as if she senses someone is sitting on the chair. Maybe she thinks there's a ghost watching her; in a way I am a kind of ghost, I suppose.

I look into her pale-blue eyes and see sadness, hardship, an endurance not known by my generation. She has a dimple in her chin and a slight olive tint to her skin. My mother has not been born as yet, neither has my father.

"How 'bout a little breakfast, me wee sweetness," a voice calls from the bedroom. And then my grandfather appears in the bedroom doorway.

Annie takes a quick intake of breath; my mouth drops open. I can't believe it. This man is the spitting image of me. The high brow, the dark hair, the aquiline nose, the thin upper lip, the brown eyes, a small dimple on his chin, too. Annie looks from me to my grandfather and back at me again.

"Incredible," she says. "You two could be twins."

"Annie. Are yer listening to me at all?" says grandfather.

"Of course I am, yer ejit," says grandmother. I'm sure I notice her left eyebrow rise for a moment.

"Flattery will get you everywhere," he says and hugs her around the waist.

"You're a beast, Martin Doyle," she says, turns to him and they kiss; a long lingering kiss.

Annie and I smile at each other. It's heartening to know that someone in our family actually connected emotionally with each other, and I'm sure sexually, too. I could never imagine my parents even looking at each other let alone getting close. I'm not used to this kind of connection between people, never having seen it or experienced it as a child. If only my parents were like my grandparents, I know for sure I'd act in a far better way regarding love and emotion. *Give me the boy for the first seven years and I'll give you the man.*

When my grandfather surfaces for air, he says "We should stay away from the Post Office today. There'll be a lot of shooting going on."

"I heard them already," she says. "Do yer think it'll make any difference?"

"We need to be free from the English. They've bullied us enough."

My grandmother goes over to the stove in the corner and lights the wood inside. "Soon have a nice cup of tae for yer," she says.

"You're the best, Annie, me girl. Best woman in the whole of Ireland." Grandfather sits at the table and reads the newspaper.

"Ah, this is not right at all. It says here that the boys at the Post Office are insane criminals and the leaders should be shot. Now that's loyalty for you."

"You don't have to read the papers to know they *will* be shot," says my grandmother." They're up against the British Army, Martin, not the Ballyfermot Boy Scouts."

"You're a clever woman, Annie. Far wiser than I'll ever be. I don't know how you put up with me."

"I'll keep putting up with you as long as you keep putting food on the table."

Annie brings a plate of eggs and a cup of tea over and plants them on the table in front of Martin. He grabs her around the waist and sits her on his knee. They giggle like children and kiss again.

"If we keep this up there'll be the patter of little feet around here soon," says Martin. "How many kids do you want, Annie. Pick a number?"

Annie rests her head on his shoulder. "Mrs. Flanagan down the street has seven."

Martin almost chokes on his tea. "*Seven*," he says.

More gunfire is heard outside.

"Keep the windows closed," says Martin, "Just in case a stray bullet comes this way."

Annie looks at him seriously and frowns. "Well, in that case wouldn't the bullet smash through the glass."

"Ah, you're the wise one."

"To be sure," she says. They both laugh and Martin blows a raspberry in her neck.

Easter Monday: 1916 Uprising. The rising lasted a week and 485 men, women and children died in Dublin. During the same week 570 Irish soldiers died in a single German gas attack on the western front. And a quarter of a million Irish soldiers fought in the First World War.

The Socialist Irish Citizen Army and the Militant Nationalist Irish Volunteers planned the rebellion and stormed Dublin's main Post Office. The British Army assembled a force that crushed the rebellion. Fifteen rebel leaders were executed in May 1916 (a sixteenth was hanged in London in August), and one of the rebels, James Connelly was executed by firing squad while tied to a chair (he was wounded and couldn't stand).

"Have you enjoyed your two days off," says Annie clearing up the plate and cup.

"Aye. Grand. Back to the old grind tonight." He walks over to Annie and hugs her again around the waist. He kisses her on the nape of her neck. She moans a little and turns towards him. They gaze into each other's eyes. Martin takes her by the hand and leads her back to the bedroom. The door closes. I hold Annie's hand and we smile at each other.

"Maybe this is the start of their family? I say and squeeze Annie's hand. "Just think, we may be present at the conception of my uncle Joe."

Time passes so quickly. My grandparents, born, lived, died in so short a time, it seems, yet they were in their eighties when they died together, in bed, holding hands, loving and adoring each other right to the very end.

Time flies like an eagle soaring.

*

Chapter 37

We like Bakersfield, (kind of) only two hours from the beach, shorter than that to Los Angeles, sunshine most of the summer months, gets colder than England sometimes in the winter months. Great supermarkets and a far greater range of goods than anywhere in Great Britain. Only bad thing about Bakersfield, well, America really, is guns. Seems weird to me that most folks want to own a gun, which is odd to me because my culture hasn't been brought up in a gun culture. Suppose it has to do with settlers fighting for their rights and land during the Wild West days.

Still, guns don't kill people, people kill people, and there's far too much gun violence and racism in America. I talk to and connect with all creeds and colors, but that's my nature. There's no bigotry or racism or malice in me or in Annie. I suppose we're among the minority, but, hopefully in the future things will change. They have to change otherwise there won't be many people left on earth to populate the planet.

A city of oil fields and agriculture. A place where Hispanics cut your grass and care for your plants (coming from Great Britain, I do my own gardening, thank you very much.) A city with its own gangs and gang warfare, of shootings, violence, robbery, burglaries. A city suffering from drought. A city where the police force reminds me of the German Gestapo, all dressed in black and shooting people in the back as they flee from a crime scene, just like the Nazis used to do to the Jews and many other cultures before and during World War II.

I found work as a security officer for a local company.

Most evenings when I arrive home I'm ready to dive in the pool. Usually Annie is already swimming, but tonight I find her sitting on the couch in tears.

"What's the matter?"

"Oh, it's nothing," says Annie, "Just feel a little sad."

"Well, tell me why you're feeling like this." I put my bag in the kitchen, sit beside her and hold her hand."

She holds her crucifix and touches it against mine and this time we remain in the room, or seem to remain here but the room begins to change and the next instant a scene of mayhem unfolds before us.

A man, seemingly drunk is picking up objects and throwing them through a smashed window. A woman cowers in a corner. She is shouting at him. In another corner a tiny girl cowers, her knees held up tightly against her chest – she is weeping.

"That's me," says Annie.

The man leaves the room and comes back with a frying pan in his hand and hits the woman over the head. The little girl runs to her mother and hugs her, and screams something at the man.

"My father, the drunk," says Annie, weeping.

"I'm sorry," I say. I hug her around the shoulders.

"So long ago," she says, "but it still haunts me."

And then we are in a bedroom and lying in a double bed is Annie and the woman from downstairs.

"That's my mother," says Annie. "She was a loving, caring woman. God knows why she married my father. I think she felt sorry for him."

"I know all about that, Annie," I say.

We watch as the child tries to wake up her mother. She shakes her again and again but her mother is still. And then the child moves in closer to her mother and hugs her. "So cold, mama. You feel so cold. I'll warm you up. So cold."

Tears stream down Annie's cheeks.

"My mother had taken a drug overdose when she went to bed. I don't think she meant to. Sometimes she'd forget when she had last taken her medication. I thought she was only cold, and didn't realize she was dead. I hugged her for hours before a neighbor came in and saw us."

I took Annie in my arms and hugged her. "It's okay, Annie. That's all in the past where it belongs. Everything will be fine. You'll see."

Suddenly the scene changes and we're standing outside in a back garden. There's long grass and bare patches of dried soil with a few withered plants here and there. A door opens and a young boy is literally thrown through the door and lands awkwardly on the grass.

"Yer little bastard," shouts a man and comes out the door, grabs the boy by the hair and punches him again and again with his right hand. The boy cries and wails and blood spurts from his nose. The man drops the boy to the ground and goes back into the house. The boy crawls along the grass and over to a wire fence.

I look at Annie and she is in shock, her bottom lip is quivering, she is about to cry. "That's my father," she says.

"The boy?"

She nods, kneels down beside the boy and reaches for him with a trembling hand; She strokes his head, though it looks like her hand is transparent, like a ghostly hand.

"How do you know it's your father," I say and kneel down beside her.

"He showed me a photograph one time."

She puts two fingers to her lips and kisses them. "I forgive you, father," then places her fingers softly on his lips.

*

Annie sleeps for a long time after witnessing the beating of her father. I look at her as her chest rises and falls with each breath. I love this girl and will do anything for her. She had a harsh and cruel upbringing.

I sit on the couch and watch TV for a while, or should I say I sit down to enjoy an evening of commercials (adverts) with a spattering of a TV program in-between. I hate American television. So trite and juvenile with so many adverts it's ridiculous. I turn the TV off and grasp my crucifix and simultaneously create an image in my mind of my Uncle Jack in a mental asylum, and not sure whether using the cross on its own would actually work. I was wrong ...

... I find myself in a long room and there are people with open mouths and tears streaming down their cheeks and arms reaching up to a doorknob. Nails scratch against the wooden door and the screeching sound grates on my nerves. Five people grouped together on the floor moan and groan and obviously want to escape from this room, this dormitory, this prison cell.

There must be at least twenty beds in this dorm lined up on each side. The walls are painted a dull gray but most of the paint is peeling off the walls. Beside each bed is a small wooden cabinet. None of the beds have any sheets or blankets.

I haven't lost my sense of smell in this mad world (unfortunately) and I pinch my nostrils as the smell of urine, feces and body sweat hit me. The stench is overwhelming.

People sit or lie on the beds, some kicking their feet in the air, some rocking back and forth on their beds. Two beds at the far end of the dorm have sheets stuck up like tents with the faces of two male occupants poking out the top.

If hell did exist then this must be it. How can the authorities allow fellow human beings to live like this, to be treated worse than animals? Those in charge I'm sure have pets which I bet they treat with more respect.

I wonder if my Uncle Jack is in this dormitory. Is he one of the patients lying in bed and kicking their feet in the air? Is he one of the rocking patients, or one of those beneath the tents?

I can't see him in this dorm and wonder how I can get out of here with these poor folks clinging to the door. I realize I don't have to physically move around so I close my eyes and think of the corridor outside – and here I am.

It's a long corridor painted the same as the dorm, the paint still peeling off the walls and at the end is a large, glazed window. Daylight streams in. I pass other dorms as I walk along the corridor and peek through the small wire-mesh square windows. People scratch on the windows in a vain attempt to escape.

Two male orderlies come around a corner and pass me. They are big, burly men with thick dark hair and wearing off-white coveralls. One of them is holding a strait jacket. I hope it's not for Uncle Jack.

At the end of the corridor I turn left and along another long corridor and at the end is a cafeteria area. It's empty except for a couple of cooks in white-aprons preparing food. I look in another two dorm windows and folks are lying on beds or scrambling on the floor, wallowing in their own dirt and feces. Is everyone locked up all day and night and only taken out of their respective dorms (cages) at meal and medication times? Maybe never taken out of their cells at all?

Further along the corridor I hear faint sounds, like muted screams. There are very few windows in this place, and the odd bare electric bulb emits a pittance of light. I turn another corner and then stop outside a door with no square window. I open the door and there is at least twenty naked patients standing in a shower room and being sprayed down with a high-powered hose by the two orderlies I passed earlier.

My Uncle Jack is not among them.

Suddenly from the far end of a corridor, a naked young woman, screaming and hollering skids around the corner and rushes toward me, with a doctor and two nurses in pursuit.

"Stop that mad bitch," the doctor shouts and, the nurses having caught up with the woman, throw her to the ground and wrap a thick blanket around her. The doctor catches up and sticks a syringe into the young woman's arm. She is quiet and still.

This place is evil. I can sense it in the air; it permeates every wall and dorm and corridor. It oozes from the pores of those nurses, doctor and orderlies.

I quickly remember reading Mrs. Feely's book about how some of these mental patients ended up in this loony bin. Committed for either masturbating, being a non-believer, idleness or some neighbor disliking someone and creating lies to have them committed. All this is the result of a Catholic religion that found it extremely easy to brainwash most, if not all, of the population of Ireland.

I walk on and turn another corner. There is another barred window; I press my nose up against the glass and look outside. Rolling green hills in the distance and a small wood near the hospital grounds. To one side of the main wing is a graveyard with many gravestones packed together.

I feel sorry for the dead occupants of those graves. Young, middle-aged, old, male and female patients, their lives cut short by being committed to this madhouse when there was nothing at all wrong with them. The simple things they did or were committed for would, by today's standards be laughed at all the way across the Irish Sea and back. If these stringent rules still applied today, ninety-nine percent of the population of Ireland would be incarcerated. I'm thankful I had not been born in the 1930's or '40's.

Walking further down the corridor I pass a room with its door ajar. The room looks like a prison cell minus bars and mesh windows and a single electric bulb hangs in the center. A young woman sits on a bed against the wall, no sheets nor blankets just a bare mattress, dirty and holes ripped in the center as if rats had dined there recently.

The woman, dressed in a long, dirt-smudged nightgown rocks back and forth with a mangy pillow in her arms. "Now now, me love," she mumbles to the pillow, "Mammy will feed you soon. Now, don't cry me wee one. Sssssshhh."

I notice she is developing a bald patch on the top of her head and the rest of her light-brown hair hangs in clumps over her shoulders.

"I will always love ye, me sweet," she says as I walk away. "No one is going to take ye away from me again."

I turn a corner and almost trip over someone lying on the floor. A balding man wearing a long, threadbare nightgown pulled up to his stomach is squeezing his testicles with his left hand and masturbating with his right.

A sight not normally witnessed by most folks and something I certainly didn't want to see, but here it is, alive and bare. Two nurses with black capes and shiny clicking shoes pass by. "He's always been a bit of a wanker, that one," says one nurse to the other. "He'll still be at it when we come on shift tonight," says the other. They giggle and continue on their merry way.

My Uncle Jack must see all this, day in day out.

And all these poor souls are trapped here with no chance of either escaping or being released back into society. Trapped, confined inside this horrific man-made box of torture. Stolen from life like apples plucked from a tree and incarcerated, to be forgotten, to deteriorate, to rot; to eventually die within these crazy walls of a man-made hell, created and sustained by the Catholic Church.

This corridor must go round the whole building. I come to a series of doors and peek inside. One is full of mops and cleaning material, all brand new by the looks of them and certainly not used in this place. Another room (the door is locked so I look through the glass) looks like a medical facility with gurneys and oxygen bottles and sinks. The floor is clean and highly polished. Must be for use by staff members.

I walk to the end of the corridor. Near the end is what looks like or is supposed to look like a recreational room – of sorts. Same dreary gray paint, same miserable peeling walls. I walk inside and see a ping-pong table, a small radio on a table near a window and a row of dirty, torn couches along one wall. No one is here except a man slouched over a hard chair beside a barred window.

I approach and notice the man is crying. It's Uncle Jack.

He's wearing the same type of hospital gown as the other patients. It's grimy and torn and covered with streaks of black. He has the same high forehead and thick, dark hair of my father. In photos I saw of my father and Uncle Jack when they were young, my father looked like the Hollywood actor, Victor Mature, and Jack had similar features.

Jack suddenly looks up, stares at me. Can he see me?

"Who is that?" he says, sits up and wriggles in his chair.

Okay. I don't think he can see me, but can he hear me? Up to now in this alternative world of travelling I've been in a kind of void where no one can see nor hear me, which is a good thing. But maybe Jack, because of his mental state, or maybe a higher level of communication due to his disability, can communicate with me somehow.

"I mean no harm," I say in a quiet voice.

Jack jumps up out of his chair and cowers down in a corner; his shaking hands grip his knees. I try to calm him.

"It's okay. No need to be afraid," I say and crouch down in front of him.

"Are you the angel of death," he says, his bottom lip quivering. "Have you come to take me away from this place?

"No. I'm not the angel of death."

"I want to leave. I want to go with you. I want to die."

I don't know what to say. But experiencing this hell I imagine other patients would rather take a walk with the angel of death rather than remain here in this tortured, horrendous kind of limbo.

"I'm in your mind, Jack. You are my uncle. I'm Liam's son and I've been able to come here and visit you, but I have travelled from a different world, from the future, that's why you can't see me, but at least you can hear me."

Jack goes over to the window and stares out over the green hills. After a few moments he cocks his head to one side like a curious mutt. He looks back in my general direction. "The boy with the bag of sweets," he finally says.

"Yes," I say. "You chased me around your mother's table, remember?"

The two burly orderlies stand in the door entrance and gape over at Uncle Jack in the corner. To them it must look as if he is talking to himself, a normal occurrence in this place, I imagine. They shrug their shoulders and leave.

"Little Josh," says Jack. "I only wanted one sweet, yer know."

"I didn't mind, Uncle Jack."

"I didn't mean to hurt her," Jack says and weeps. "It wasn't my fault. It was so hot and I couldn't hold it any longer. It wasn't my fault."

"What wasn't your fault?"

"She was screaming and I couldn't stand it any longer and they made me leave and I only had a little suitcase and the men in the car laughed and said I'd pay dearly for what I did. It wasn't my fault."

"What did you do, Uncle Jack?"

He gazes in my direction again but I sense as if he is looking me straight in the eye, not really knowing what my face looks like, but maybe creating my face in his subconscious and placing it in the front of his mind, like projecting an image onto a movie screen.

"I was trying to help mother. The pan was boiling over with hot water and I took it off the stove but the handle was so hot I let it fall and it burned mother on the legs. She screamed and it made me scream and the more she screamed the more I screamed."

"And they put you in here for that?"

Jack starts to rock back and forth in the corner. Maybe patients perform a rocking motion because of feeling stressful, or maybe it's a way of relieving their pent-up frustrations.

"I didn't mean to hurt mother. I told her I was sorry. So sorry, so so sorry"

I don't know what to do or what to say. What *do* you say to someone who has gone through so much pain and has been incarcerated for the best part of their life? I lowered my head; I couldn't look at him because I knew if I did I would weep and weep far worse than any deserted Irish banshee could ever do. So all I could say was, "I love you, Uncle Jack."

His mouth drops open; he raises his arm toward me maybe trying to touch an invisible spot in front of him, maybe attempting to touch me, hold me?

And then he is gone.

*

And I am back on my couch. How lucky I am. How fortunate am I that I can live a full and free life. The madhouse is actually that – a house full of mad people, or so the Irish authorities maintain. The stench and cruelty is unbelievable and something to be ashamed of in this, the twentieth century.

This kind of horror should have been wiped out after the Victorian era with their poor houses, horrific asylums, debtor prisons and the like. The smell of Grangegorman hospital asylum lingers still in my nostrils, and the way the patients were treated, including my Uncle Jack is totally unacceptable to me.

I count myself a very lucky man. I wonder why some people have to experience hell on earth while others have a relatively easy life? Is it, somehow the nature of the universe to show us how lucky some of us are by creating opposites as in poverty, cruelty, selfishness, greed, pigheadedness, egotism?

Annie alights from the shower and stands in the bedroom doorway. She is naked and is beautiful. She winks at me and walks into the bedroom. I follow her. Well, at least *this* existence does have its good perks.

*

Our lovemaking is out of this world, literally. The instant I reach my orgasm is at the exact moment our crucifix's touch and instantaneously the room is filled with a swirling mist and we are now twisting in the air. We cling to each other as flashes of light shoot around us, through us, everywhere there are beams of light. Suddenly we are standing on the lower slope of the clay-hole quarry and directly in front of us is my younger self making love to someone. Why is it that every time Annie and I are transported to another time, I'm almost always making love? What's up with that kid, I think, but then realize that the 'kid' will grow up to be *me*.

This is the quarry. The clay-hole or pool must be on the other side of this hill.

"That's Saffron," says Annie.

I don't say anything. I mean what can I say? We watch as the kid raises himself from the young girl beneath. They straighten out their clothes and then run together down the main road.

We climb the small hillock. At the top we gaze down on a boy swimming in the pool.

"That's John," I say.

A swirling wind surrounds us. Annie grips my hand tightly.

And then there is silence.

*

The silence is broken by the sounds of pigs snorting and cows mooing. We are in a small farmyard. The stench of pig-shit is overpowering. A sty is to my left and Annie is on my right and pinching her nostrils together. Slimy mud covers the cobble-stoned yard and there's a tiny gray-stoned cottage off to the side.

A small child runs up a lane and into the cottage. "Annie," shouts a woman from inside the cottage, "Stop running, ye'll fall over and hurt yerself."

We stroll over to the kitchen door and walk into the tiny kitchen. Laced curtains cover small square panes of glass. The walls are whitewashed but covered with big patches of soot. The woman is washing dishes at a deep old-fashioned enamel sink beneath the window sill. She is facing the window so I can't make out her features. A wood fire is burning and smoke bellows out occasionally. Various pieces of clothing hang on a wooden frame above the ancient Aga stove. There's a round bench-like dining table in the center of the kitchen and a few pots and pans piled up in a corner.

The girl appears in the doorway which I assume leads to the living room.

"Where's me pink dress, ma," says the girl.

"Having I already told yer. In yer drawer in yer room."

The girl takes a few steps backward and runs upstairs.

"And don't be out too late, young woman," the woman shouts after her daughter. And to herself, "I don't know. Kids of today, out gallivanting 'till all hours. Jesus, I wasn't allowed out after four in the afternoon and I was fecking eighteen years of age."

Annie, beside me, nudges my elbow. I hear her giggling.

There's a soft knock on the kitchen door.

"Is that you, Martin," asks the woman.

"It is so," says the little boy of about seven.

"She'll be down shortly. Just gone up to put on her pink dress. Come in and sit yerself down."

Martin walks in and sits at the table. The woman turns from the sink, a dishcloth in her hands and looks at Martin. She wipes away a few stray hairs that cover her face. I suddenly realize that this must be my great-grandmother because she looks so much like my mother.

Annie runs down the stairs two at a time, spots Martin sitting at the table, runs up and kisses him. on the cheek. Martin stands and looks over at Annie's mother as if pleading and asking permission by way of eye contact.

The woman smiles and nods at the boy. Martin takes Annie's hand and together they walk out through the kitchen door like two young lovers.

"Oh to be young again," sighs my great-grandmother, "and treat each day as an adventure."

I close my eyes and Annie and I are whisked away on another sojourn.

*

I hear voices. "Morning to yer, Mrs. Grafton. Sure isn't it a grand day." Irish voices. I open my eyes. It's raining and humid. This must be Dublin. We are standing at the end of a narrow road which seems to be covered with a dark layer of some liquid, water and mud mixed, maybe.

I can *smell* the poverty surrounding us. Feces, mold, rising damp.

The dirty-colored brick buildings are tall which makes the road passage seem even narrower. They look like tenement buildings and probably house large families in tiny apartments. Some of the windows are smashed and others are covered with stained newspapers, most likely to keep the cold out and the warmth in, or to cover open squares where the panes of glass were once housed. Some bricks are split and others missing completely. An eerie mist hovers around the top three stories. Through the mist I can just about make out the hazy face of an old woman wearing a black shawl over her head; she is leaning on the windowsill and looking down onto the street.

In front of us is a wooden buggy that looks decrepit and worn with slats of wood missing. Standing beside the buggy is a woman of about thirty with short bobbed hair and a soot-covered dress that starts at her neck and ends just above her ankles. She looks pregnant and is clasping her stomach. She looks at me as if posing for a photograph, although she can't see me or Annie, or I hope she can't see us. She's wearing a muddy pair of old wellington boots.

Two young boys and a girl are playing a game of tag further down the road. We walk towards them. The girl is wearing a dirty, smudged flowery knee-length dress and a brown-colored cardigan. The boys have on some type of knee-length dungarees tied with straps over their shoulders. There's not a clean face among them.

The air is thick and muggy, suffocating, though the rain has now stopped. Asthma, bronchitis and pneumonia must be a big problem here as well as a lack of food and heating.

Annie is silent. She holds my hand as we walk toward the tenement building on our left. I don't know why we are heading toward this building - I'm following my instincts.

We stop outside the ground floor flat. The number 7 is scribbled in chalk on the center top of the paint-peeled door. The door opens and a big, broad-shouldered man with thick black hair walks out. Annie and I give a little gasp as the man literally walks through us and out onto the street.

From inside we hear a woman's voice, "Come straight back here after work, Paddy. No going down the pub with yer pals to drink the days' wages!"

"Feck off," comes the reply as the big man paces down the narrow street with long, striding steps.

"This must be Paddy Doyle, my great-great-grandfather and his wife, Iona."

"How do you know for sure?" Annie whispers to me.

"I just know," I reply in a whisper. "And why are we whispering? They can't hear us."

I think when the Irish say 'Feck off' it's not really derogatory, more like 'get lost' but in a comical sense of the word. And it also depends on *how* the word is said, rather than the meaning of the word itself.

I grip Annie's hand and we walk into the flat. Inside it's a small, darkened slum of a room with a kitchen sink in one corner, scruffy rugs on the wooden floor and a low bed against the far wall. The bed is nothing more than a line of wooden slats held up by four blocks of wood with a few threadbare blankets strewn across the top.

My great-great grandmother, Iona is cleaning clothes in the sink using one of those scrubbing boards with the raised wooden slats across the wood. She probably has to scrub something every day, then wring them with her hands and hang them out on the clothes line. People of modern times just don't realize how lucky and fortunate they are to own washing machines and driers. Even the poorest family in America can find some way to wash and dry, even using a launderette facility. A crib of sorts stands in another corner. A baby cries.

"Ah, now," says Iona, "don't after be starting yer whinging." She dries her hands and picks up the baby. "There there, are yer hungry. Let's see what we have over here for yer."

She opens a cupboard next to the sink and takes out a glass Guinness bottle with a rubber teat jammed on the end, sucks on the teat a few times, and puts it in his mouth. "There ye are now, Phil," she says and rocks him in her arms while feeding him. "Soon be full and back to sleep, eh, me little marvel."

I look at Annie. "Isn't this weird. I'm watching my great-grandfather being bottle-fed. You couldn't write about this stuff."

"No one would believe you, anyway," says Annie. "They'd lock you up in a mental ward."

"Don't talk to me about mental wards. I've had enough of them for one lifetime."

I close my eyes and the next instant Annie and I are on a quayside down the docks and surrounded by barges with men walking up planks laden with heavy sacks.

Men shout to each other as foremen give orders to the winch operators and those wheeling cart loads of sacks along the quay to waiting horse-drawn wagons.

I notice Paddy carrying two medium sized crates along the plank and onto the quayside. Just as he reaches the side he trips and falls. One of the crates smashes to the ground. "Yer fecking ejit," yells a man, probably his foreman. "Get up outta there or ye'll not be getting paid tonight."

We stand beside my great-great-grandfather and watch as he picks up metal shafts and cog wheels and other items that had fallen out of the crate and notice him picking up a crucifix, complete with silver chain. An onyx cross, *the* cross that I now wear around my neck.

The side of the crate reads, 'Romania.' So that cross has travelled hundreds of miles across land and sea to land in Dublin to be taken (stolen) by Paddy and henceforth become a legacy to be passed down the family line.

Paddy slips the crucifix into his pocket and loads the parts back into the crate.

So that's how he got it. I am just about to talk to Annie about Paddy and the cross when instantaneously a gust of swirling wind seems to come out of nowhere and Annie and I are swept up in it, twisting, twirling, spinning and as quick as it starts it ends.

We are now standing in a wood or forest and see a group of people sitting around a camp fire. Near the group are four caravans, the type gypsies live and travel in. Horseshoe shaped sides painted in red and blue with big wooden wheels beneath, the rims painted yellow.

Someone in the group starts to play a penny whistle. I approach him and notice he has thick black hair and long eyebrows, also a high forehead. We look very similar. He closes his eyes and plays a slow, lament-type tune, bending and sliding some notes to make the music sound as if it is weeping for the souls of the dead and forgotten.

"A gypsy camp," I say to Annie.

"Didn't your mother say you come from gypsy stock?"

"A lot of Irish people have gypsy blood," I say. We move a little closer to the fire.

"Look, there's a set of pipes."

The penny whistle player straps a set of pipes around his waist. They look like a set of Uilleann pipes but only have two small drones and no wrist regulators that, in later years, are added and attached to the top of the drones.

He begins to play and the music is sweet, heart-wrenching, yet beautiful. The whole group sway from side to side as the tune reaches the second octave and back down to the first and then the piper hits high notes and then the lower ones before finishing with a long vibrato note.

His audience erupts into applause and someone passes a bottle of something to the piper who takes a long swig, puts the bottle down, burps and then lets out a long fart. The group burst into spontaneous laughter. Annie and I smile at each other.

"You're definitely a gypsy," says Annie.

"I'll let you know that that fart is in the key of G. And besides my musical butt, I've also got itchy feet. Don't seem to be able to stay in one place for too long."

"Runs in the family."

An old lady, dressed all in black and with long colored beads around her neck, alights from the caravan and carefully treads on the wooden steps and reaches the ground. She makes her way over to the piper, kisses him on the forehead and hugs him. The gypsies stop talking and look on.

The old lady takes something from around her neck and puts it over the piper's head and down around his neck. The crucifix. Is that *my* crucifix?

She speaks in some foreign tongue, most probably Romanian because my mother mentioned my father was descended from Romanian gypsies (not realizing she too was descended from gypsies, though she would never admit it if she knew the truth). The old woman makes the sign of the cross and saunters back into her caravan.

The piper grasps the cross in his left hand and kisses it. A young woman walks over and sits beside the piper. He kisses her softly on the lips and says. "Annie. This one is for you." He begins to play a lament on his pipes.

"Annie," I say. "She looks like you."

*

The troupe of caravans travel along a well-worn track between fields of tall grass and fern and surrounded by high, snowy-capped mountains. Annie and I sit on the roof of the piper's caravan as we trundle along. The morning sun is hot and the air humid. Even though no one can see us, we can still experience the environment and climate around us.

Someone in the second caravan (ours is at the end of the line) is playing a guitar and quietly singing a folk song.

I look down on the driver's area and the young woman that looks very much like Annie has her head resting on the piper's shoulder. His head is resting against hers. They make a beautiful couple, so much in love, so connected. And connection is the key to all happy relationships. Something no one can force or create; the connection between two lovers is either present or not there at all.

I look at Annie sleeping now in a groove on the side of the roof where suitcases or other baggage is usually stored. Her chest rises and falls with each breath. I admire her. She is strong. She is, like me, a little confused about it all. When *will* it end? What will the ending entail? Questions, questions, always questions.

The yellow and red flowery summer dress she is wearing is smudged here and there with dirt. There's a tiny spot of dirt on her cheek. I want to go to her and softly wipe it clean with my finger. Her hair, the color of marigold, streams down each side of her face and cascades over her shoulders.

I smile, thinking how lucky I am to be able to love this woman.

Suddenly shots ring out. Annie sits up quickly. The guitar playing and singing ceases. I hear more shots and bullets hitting the sides of the caravan. Annie and I lie flat on the roof. Who is doing this?

I see a line of heads in the tall grass and rifle barrels pointing out near the track. A barrage of gunfire strikes the caravans again but this time the drivers whip their horses and pick up speed, riding away from the shots.

I look behind as we speed away and see at least five men with guns standing in the center of the track. Who are they? Villagers frustrated with the mess that gypsies tend to make wherever they set up site? I don't know but these guys mean business. The caravans roll as quickly as they can along the lane and into a wooded area. They make a circle and stop. Men jump out of the first two caravans and grab rifles from the boxes on the sides, some dive beneath the caravans, others hide in nearby bushes and two men climb trees.

We climb down from the roof and watch as the piper, with his sweetheart in his arms places her on the ground. She's been shot.

The old woman kneels beside her and says the rosary, her frail fingers counting off the beads as she mumbles a prayer. The old woman takes a crucifix from around the girl's neck and puts it in her pocket. The piper grips his crucifix, kisses his girl and then sobs into her neck.

The piper is weeping still as we spin into the twirling mist and leave the gypsies to their sorrow.

*

Chapter 38

I open my eyes; we are back on the bank of the clay-hole. Annie grips my hand as we watch my young self trying desperately to save my best friends life.

If only I can dive into the water and untangle his trapped leg, wind my arms around the John's waist and heave him to the surface to breathe precious air. If only I had the power, but, no, I'm helpless in this endeavor, helpless to save my friend's life. We watch as young Joshua surfaces and screams again and again and again.

We watch like invisible angels but neither Annie nor I can do anything to change John's destiny.

We now watch John's funeral and the piper playing a lament. As the coffin is lowered into the earth his mother almost topples in after him.

We watch.

And at the wake we look on as relatives wail and the mother and father hug and weep.

We watch.

We look on as young Joshua and Saffron sit stone-faced at a table and sip their drinks and gaze at nothing but thin air.

And later still when Joshua gives Saffron a goodnight kiss and holds her hand and weeps again for their friend, John O'Malley. We watch.

We watch – but this time we too, weep.

*

Chapter 39

The sun's light shimmers off the swimming pool as Annie and I dive in and swim to the far side. It's a pleasant enough pool surrounded by six one-storey apartments with shrubs and small trees arranged in the borders. It's another crazy hot day.

"I'm still confused why all this is happening to us, Joshua," says Annie.

"Seeing things differently, I suppose," I say. "It's made me understand it better. Come to terms with it, maybe?"

"What about those gypsies? Were they us? I mean, are we, well, or have we been reincarnated or something?"

"Questions, questions, and not any answers. You know, the more we travel and find out about the past, the more confused I get."

"Maybe it's a healing process or something. A psychological thing, kind of, if you know what I mean."

I take a hold of Annie's wet hair and gently push it to the side of her head.

"What's the matter," she says. She can tell something is upsetting me. I think she can see it in my eyes. Maybe a hint of sorrow is in my voice?

"You had a tough upbringing, Annie. Mine is nothing compared to what you had to go through."

Annie kind of half-smiles; she turns and swims to the other side.

I watch as she climbs out of the pool and goes indoors. Did I say something wrong? I didn't mean to hurt her. I go into the apartment and she is sitting on the couch, her head in her hands.

"I'm sorry," I say, "I didn't   "

"It's not you, Joshua," she says weeping. "People say to get over it. Put it at the back of your mind. Own the pain. Move on. Live your life. Be happy. So easy to say those words. But the pain never goes away. It's always niggling at me. Those memories surface and become alive somehow. They seem to want to make sure I feel guilty all the time, that I never forget."

I sit beside her and put my arms around her shoulders.

"I know now my father was abused as a child and that's what made him abuse his children, his wife. Turned him into a drunk. I understand that. I've forgiven him and that has made me a little happier. But instead of hugging my mother thinking she was cold I could have called a neighbor. They'd have called the doctor and an ambulance. She'd have still been alive today if only I did the right thing."

"You don't know that, Annie. If she died in her sleep then you or anyone else for that matter couldn't have done anything about it."

"How do you know, eh?" Annie shrugged my arms off her shoulders. "How would you *know*. You weren't there. You weren't the one that felt how cold she was. You didn't try to warm her up."

Annie weeps and I feel inadequate. What do I say? What can I do to make it better? Can I make it better or is it up to her and her alone to fix this?

I grip my crucifix and, without informing Annie of my intention, quickly press both crosses together.

We are now back in the living room of Annie's youth. There is a large piece of plywood covering the front window. Annie's mother is sitting on a couch, and on a low table in front of her there are bottles of pills. A glass of water is on the table. Sitting on a chair opposite is little Annie.

She is dressed in a pink and white spotted summer dress and wears ankle socks and brown sandals. Her hair is tied up into a bun at the back of her head.

Annie grips my hand; her hand is trembling.

Her mother picks up a bottle of pills and draws them close to her face. She squints as she tries to read the label. "I can't even pronounce the name," she says.

"Are they sweeties, mam," says little Annie and swings her legs back and forth under the chair.

"Not the kind you like, luv."

She separates a few bottles and places them on her right side. "These two are my sleeping pills. This one is for my depression, though I should be happy now that bastard's gone back to sea." She takes the pills, sips out of the glass and bangs it down on the table.

"This one must be, let me see ..." her mother squints again and holds the container so close to her face it touches her nose. "... Propoxyphene. Now that's a mouthful." She places the container on the right side.

"She used that drug for pain relief," says Annie. "My neighbor told me that later. It's not as strong as morphine or codeine. I remember watching my father hitting her in the ribs and jaw. He broke three of her ribs and her jaw."

I wait for Annie to cry, but she is holding up well at the moment.

Her mother picks up another pill container, attempts to read it, gives up and places it on her right. She takes a swig of water and reaches over for the bottle she had just put down. "Which one is it, now? No. It wasn't that one, that's my depression pills. Must be this one." She picks up the bottle and squints at it. "No. That's not it. My memory gets worse by the day. Oh, never mind. They'll all end up in the same place, anyway. "

"I remember father ripping the glasses off her face and standing on them," says Annie.

Her mother opens the containers and takes a pill from each one – and washes them down with a swig of water.

Suddenly the scene changes and we are in a bedroom; the curtains are closed and a small bedside light is on. We watch as her mother takes her pills, washes them down with water, and then leaves the room. We hear the toilet flush and then she returns and goes to bed, pulls the blankets over her head. About ten seconds later, she sits up in bed, reaches over for her pills and takes another dose.

"She doesn't remember already taking her pills," Annie says. "My aunt and neighbors insisted she killed herself due to the abuse of my father. I never believed them. My mother would never purposely kill herself and leave her child to suffer. She was a good mother."

The door opens and little Annie runs in and snuggles up to her mother in bed. "I had a nightmare, mam."

Her mother sits up, kisses her on the forehead and tucks little Annie in bed beside her. She lies back and turns on her side. Annie hugs her from behind.

Now, the sun is rising outside the window and rays of the new day stream through the curtains. We watch as little Annie wakes and hugs her mother and pulls the blanket up and wraps it around her shoulders.

"You're so cold, mam. So cold."

Little Annie rubs her mother's shoulders with her tiny hands, and then rubs her hands and arms and neck. She reaches down to the end of the bed and pulls up a spare blanket and covers her mother. "This'll warm you up, mam."

Annie goes to the window and opens a curtain. I stand behind her and hug her around the waist. "I'm so sorry, Annie. No child should have to endure that."

She turns and rests her head on my shoulder. "It was accidental. I always had this feeling it was an accident. I just *knew*."

Annie weeps and I'm glad she is now letting it all out.

"I want to leave this place, Joshua. "

And with that we touch crucifixes and leave little Annie and her dead mother and find ourselves standing beside a big oak tree in a thick wood. Shots are fired, someone screams. People scamper past us and we instinctively take a couple of steps backward. They are all carrying firearms. A troop of soldiers pursue the first group deeper into the woods.

"They're German soldiers for Christ sakes," I say.

"This is *Germany*?" says Annie.

"I'm not too sure, but it's definitely during the second world war."

The soldiers continue to fire at the fleeing people that had just passed us. We follow the soldiers up a deep incline and stand at the top of the hill and look down into a small ravine. Around the top of the incline the German soldiers stand pointing their guns at the people now trapped in the ravine below.

"Partisans," I say. "They're the French resistance."

"So why are we here?"

The next instant Annie and I are standing in the center of the partisans. They have long beards and muddy faces and torn jackets and trousers and filthy shoes and wear cloth caps and thick woolen sweaters. Some of them are on their knees praying. Others kneel and start to shoot at the Germans. The Germans return fire and, one by one, the resistance slump to the ground with gaping, bloodshot wounds. All around us they fall until only one man is left standing.

The Germans cease firing and run down to him.

The resistance fighter is small and wears a full hood over his head. An officer strides up to the man and slaps him across the face with his hand. "Where is the rest of your group," says the officer.

The man takes out a crucifix, holds it against his lips and kisses it. The officer punches the man and this time he falls to the ground.

The officer spits on the man, "Gypsy scum," he says in English and pulls out his luger and shoots him. He turns and, with the rest of his troop marches out of the ravine and disappears over the hill.

"Bastards," I say.

Annie kneels down beside the resistant fighter. "Look," she says and points to the crucifix around his neck. She looks closer and sees that on the bottom edge there is a tiny chip of stone missing. She takes her own crucifix from around her neck and compares the two. "See, Joshua. They both have tiny pieces missing on the lower edge. I'm wearing his crucifix."

Joshua kneels beside Annie. "He's a gypsy?

Annie opens his jacket to maybe find some kind of id and quickly pulls her hand back. "Oh God. He's a *she*."

"What?" And sure enough, under the jacket and bulging out a little are two breasts, covered by her shirt, of course. "She's definitely a woman."

"She couldn't be more than twenty," says Annie and, before I can see where she had been shot we suddenly appear inside a farmhouse.

British soldiers are aiming their rifles through the windows. There's about a dozen soldiers cramped into a small kitchen area.

In a corner is the gypsy woman we had just seen shot by that German officer.

"Fire," someone shouts and a barrage of gunshots ring out, deafening. The smell of cordite hits my nostrils. I grab Annie's hand and we go over to the young gypsy woman; there is a young man leaning over her. The gypsy appears to be whispering something to the young man. We watch as the man takes the crucifix from around her neck and places it around his own.

"O'Connell!" a sergeant shouts from one of the windows. "Get some more ammo over here, now."

"That's your name," "I say and look at Annie.

"He's my grandfather," says Annie. "He told me he once fought in France."

"I played at his funeral."

O"Connell grabs a few belts of ammunition and starts to hand them out to the soldiers at the windows.

A soldier is shot in the head and falls onto the kitchen floor. O'Connell goes to him but the soldier is obviously dead.

"Who is it!" shouts the sergeant above the cacophony of whizzing bullets.

"Brendan Feely," O'Connell shouts back. "The Irish guy!"

Another soldier falls to the floor.

We don't see the outcome of the battle because the next instant we find ourselves standing in a tiny cottage-type kitchen. A woman is bending over an old enamel sink and in her hand is a piece of paper. She is weeping. She straightens up and turns towards us. It's a young Mrs. Feely, for sure. Tears have created long streaky marks down her cheeks. She drops the paper onto the floor. I notice it's a military telegram. Blackness surrounds me.

I open my eyes; I'm lying in bed. Annie is asleep beside me. We're back in our apartment, safe. What does it all mean? Is everything and everyone connected in some mysterious way?

I only wish I knew.

*

I receive a letter from my mother. All the usual so and so said this and what's-his-name did that and oh, by the way, your old bagpipe teacher Sean Flanagan died. One of the pipers from the band played 'Flowers of the Forest' at his funeral. His wife said a few words at the church, "Old musicians don't die,' she said, "They only decompose." I wish it had been me who had performed at his funeral.

*

Chapter 40

I've almost come to the conclusion that my earlier experiences, like many other people, have helped me to comprehend what this life is all about. My childhood upbringing, my schooling, my friends, the death of my friends and relatives, the funerals, the meanings of not only my life but others whom I have had the good fortune to peek into from time to time. All these experiences, all the knowledge learned along the way has helped me to almost climb out of the box that has confined, trapped my thoughts and actions like so many millions of people.

'Thinking out of the box,' is a brilliant and true saying. I am the living embodiment of thinking out of the box and realizing that we can all change our lives for the better if only we severed those traditional views of religion and creed and become what we know we can become – loving and caring human beings.

And, over many years I now know that is what I have become simply by trying, *attempting* to break free from the box, with the help of course, of the crucifix's ability to show Annie and I the pain, the emotions, the connections between all families in whatever lineage they may be genetically and destined to be born into.

I've learned that there's only one race and that's the human race. There's no room in my mind for racism, bigotry, foolishness, greed, selfishness, pig-headedness, being self-centered. When you really think about it and realize that we've only got a certain amount of years to live on this planet, what *is* the point of making our lives a misery, upsetting ourselves and others each glorious and beautiful day. I've learned this lesson, the most valuable lesson any man, woman or child could ever learn. Many people think like me, but a whole lot more need to find a way out of their own individual boxes, to 'think outside the box' before this world can become a paradise for everyone. If an intelligent and wise person needs a religious crutch to break out of their box, then it won't work, because it's that very dogma that imprisons that person in the first place.

*

Chapter 41

Annie sits me down on the couch, takes my hand and gazes into my eyes.
"What's up," I say.
"I'm pregnant," she says.

*

Chapter 42

The decision to move back to England is easy. As soon as Annie broke the news of her pregnancy we knew without even talking about it that we had to get out of Dodge City and find a decent place to bring up our child.

Growing up in a City with so many different cultures did have its advantages, but with so many guns and shootings and killings, and a military-style trigger-happy panicky police force, we decided it's not a place to live for us and certainly no place to raise a child. I suppose not being born here, we're lucky to have the choice to live in a different country. A country that doesn't have gun laws and guns and all the trouble that brings with it. Britain does have its own problems, but at least we don't exist in a culture that relies on weapons to survive.

Annie and I give notice to our employers. In England I can always find work in security. We have discussed moving to the county of Cornwall, south west England and, though the properties are more expensive than central or northern England, we can always rent a little flat and, when the baby is born, hope to be as happy as three peas in a pod.

At this particular time I imagine all our flipping from one century to the next, of visiting ancestors and past family conflicts, is all over. We can settle down like normal people, both go to work (until the baby is born), live, shop and holiday in Cornwall with its beautiful beaches, quaint villages and friendly people. But, as usual in my life nothing is quite that straightforward.

I have nearly broken out of the box, but my gut instinct tells me that very soon a far bigger and more dangerous box may await me in England.

*

Part Four
(England)

Chapter 43

We drink red merlot. We're exhausted after our twelve hour flight from Los Angeles and the four hour drive in a hired car to finally reach the village of Port Isaac - our new home.

We arrived here in August and have been here five months now. Annie is six months pregnant and her face blooms like a healthy flower. We are safe. We are secure. We are happy – so far.

Bakersfield wasn't too bad, but it's so hot over there. No respite from the constant high temperatures. When we landed at Heathrow airport it was raining heavily and very humid. It's good to be home.

Port Isaac is a fishing village on the Atlantic coast of north Cornwall. The nearest towns are Wadebridge (where I work on security) and Camelford, both ten miles away. Port Isaac is Cornish for *Porthsek* which means 'corn port' from the days of trade in corn from inland. Population, 700-800.

We intend to visit the beautiful beaches of Portreath with its mountains as green as Irish meadows; Millock: a sandy beach with a backdrop of massive cliffs and the historic St Ives and its beach which is usually packed with tourists during the summer months.

We clean, paint and decorate our little paradise. The flat is small but homely. Small windows with wide sills on the inside (you can sit on them) and uneven thick stone walls and wooden beams across the low ceiling. The stable-type doors are cut in the middle so we can open either top or bottom separately which is good to let air into the flat and keep stray cats or dogs outside.

The flat is more of a cottage, well, it is a cottage but on a smaller scale and not isolated but packed in snugly among other properties. The name 'Rainbow' is stenciled on a wooden plague beside the front door. Rainbow cottage; I love the name.

We love it here, it's quiet. We have the occasional sunny day, mixed in with a few days of rain; overcast some days, then windy and cold the next. But I suppose we will get used to it. No more painting walls in my shorts (sometimes painting naked) in Bakersfield and its oven-like heat. The only problem with English weather is that when it does get hot, it becomes extremely humid. And I'd forgotten what it was like to walk a few paces and feel the sweat trickle down my brow and stick to my torso.

'Two out of three ain't bad' as Meatloaf once said. You can't expect everything to be perfect.

I've no qualms about the security job I have in Wadebridge. Easy work. Sit in a cabin with a heater (no cooler) record people and vehicles coming and going into the business premises (An Energy Company), nod and smile at folks, nod in agreement at managers, complete daily reports, and in-between listen to a local music station on a small radio. There's also the excitement of drinking coffee and tea, eating my sandwiches, reading the newspapers, practicing new and old tunes on my practice chanter, and, for a few hours, write short stories on my laptop (I'm getting quite good at this story-writing now, don't know if it'll get me anywhere but it certainly keeps my mind stimulated).

Of course, I never had the opportunity or the money or the inclination, certainly not the inspiration from family to work hard and go through university and earn a degree. Not in this life, maybe (hopefully) the next (if there is a next). Maybe I'm destined to do exactly what I'm doing and what I've done and achieved. Maybe it is all about a person's destiny or fate whether they are born into well-to-do families and are pushed in the educational direction, or born into poor families with no chance of succeeding though some poor people do struggle and eventually go through university, but that's quite rare and maybe that's also *their* destiny.

Annie is painting the kitchen walls and I'm painting the living room walls. The choice of colors is easy – everything is painted white, simply because there's not a straight wall or edge in the place and it's far easier just to cover the whole place in one color. Painting straight lines on wall corners, edges and ceilings with different colors is a nightmare. It's good, though, because on overcast days the white walls (inside and out) make the place look a little cheerier, or at least cheer us up a little on a wet and dreary day.

But today the sun is out and it's relatively warm, not warm enough to go out in a tee-shirt and shorts but because of the brisk sea breeze we wear jeans and sweaters.

We stand at the top of the village (not far from our cottage) and look down on the white and gray cottages speckled across the 'U' shape of the land and the small port below. I'd read that stone, ore, limestone, salt, as well as corn were shipped in and trans-shipped to other places from Port Isaac. There is a fishing community here but tourism is also important. This whole area is hilly with streams running down to the sea. The village itself is built on a hill and has narrow alleys winding down steep hillsides.

"This is paradise," says Annie.

"This is *our* paradise," I reply.

*

Annie brings me a cup of green tea over to the couch. I take the cup and enjoy a quick sip.

"Thank you, Annie," I say. "This is good."

"Oh my god," she says.

"It's not that good."

"I think I'm having the baby."

"I know you're having a baby and I'm looking forward to seeing the mite."

"No. I think I'm having the baby, now!"

I look down at the pool of water at her feet and take a few seconds to realize what has happened.

Oh shit," I say and jump up and fall flat on my face sending the cup and green tea sliding along the stone tiles. "I'll get the car," I say. "No I won't. I'll phone for the ambulance. Sit down here. Relax."

"How can I relax." Annie doubles over in pain.

"Are you alright," I ask stupidly, not really knowing what to ask or what to do.

"I had a few pangs earlier, but nothing like this." She stands then sits down again.

I pick up the landline and phone for an ambulance. Ten minutes tops, says the woman on the other end. There's an ambulance in the area. I'll have to help with the delivery if need be.

"Ambulance is on the way," I say and kneel beside Annie. I take her hand and squeeze it hoping, foolishly, that this will slow down the contractions. It seems to speed them up. "Don't worry. The ambulance'll be here soon."

"I can't wait that long," Annie says and screams. "I think the baby's coming."

I start to panic. I rush into the kitchen and put the kettle on. "I've just put kettle on, luv."

"This is no time for tea!"

"Hot water for the delivery."

"Oh my God!"

"I've never delivered a baby before," I say and help her lie down on the couch.

"I've never given birth before, you idiot."

I'm about to reply but suddenly realize that women can go a little crazy during childbirth, so I keep my mouth shut.

"Take short breaths. That's it. Read that somewhere."

"Joshua," says Annie, panting and puffing, her face now reddened and her face cheeks bloated. "It's coming."

"Let me have a look," I say and poke my head between her legs. Sure enough, I see a head wedged halfway out of Annie's vagina. Before I can even think of what the hell do I do, the head pops out, followed by one shoulder (I put a finger inside and nudge over the other shoulder and it slips out) and then the rest of the body slides out.

The baby kicks and spits and screams.

"My baby," says Annie and cries.

I carefully lift the baby and umbilical cord and place it on Annie's chest.

I haven't even looked to see if it's a boy or a girl. There's a knock on the door.

"Come in," I say, "It's open."

A male and female paramedic rush in and get to work on Annie and the baby.

"What is it?" I ask.

"Don't you know," says the male paramedic.

"I've been kind of busy delivering it, you know."

"It's a boy, Joshua," says Annie. "We have a beautiful baby boy."

*

We name him Samuel.

*

Keeping Annie in bed to rest is like asking the Pope to canonize me after I'm dead. She insists on cooking for me and washing up afterwards.

"You need to rest," I say. "I can look after myself."

I persuade her to lie on the couch and watch TV as little Sam suckles on her breast. I sit nearby and watch as the baby, his eyes closed tightens his lips around Annie's nipple, sucks and breathes, opens his eyes, sucks and breathes and closes his eyes.

"My turn next," I say and Annie laughs and grimaces at the same time.

"Stop making me laugh, Josh, it's painful. Men couldn't handle it."
"Men wouldn't *want* to handle it. Anyway, I blame Eve."
"Is she one of your ex's?"
"Eve, you know, Adam's other half. It was Eve who tempted Adam with the apple from the tree of life, according to the bible, and when Adam took a bite, God showed up and told Eve that from that day onwards, women were going to suffer the pain of childbirth, or words to that effect."
"Really?"
"Cross me heart and hope to die."
"What a bummer. So what if Adam tempted Eve and she took a bite of the apple, then what?
"I guess men would be having babies."
"I like that version better."
"You would."
"Joshua?"
"Yes, dear?"
"Why are we talking about this?"
"I don't know. Is Sam finished sucking your tit?"
"Suckling, Joshua. And he's suckling my *teat*."
"They ain't half grown lately. Never seen 'em that big before."
"And you won't see them this big again, unless we have another child."
"I want a girl next time."
"Oh, you do, do you. Well, you'll have to wait."
"How long?"
"Can you pass me a tissue. Over there on the dresser."

Annie wipes her nipple and the baby's mouth. Sam is almost asleep. I take him and place him in a small crib beside the couch; he gazes at me and yawns. I snuggle up to Annie.

"You did a beautiful thing, Annie, giving birth. Now that's what I call a miracle."

"I'm happy you're happy."

"I love you, Annie."

"I love you, too."

I rest my head on her shoulder and gaze across and through the lounge window and see skies of blue and little puffy clouds floating by. It's quiet outside except for the sweet song of chirping birds sitting on the telegraph wires and garden walls.

"Annie?"

"Hmmm?"

"You make me want to be a better man."

She snuggles into me and we soon fall asleep. Three birds together in a nest built of love.

*

We are awoken by Sam screaming.

"What's up with the guy," I say in frustration.

"He's got colic," says Annie hugging him in her arms.

"How do you know; it could be something more serious."

"Not according to the health nurse. She says lots of babies suffer from colic."

"And what is colic?"

"According to her, no one really knows what causes colic. It could be a growing digestive system, wind, a developing nervous system …"

"It's giving me a deteriorating nervous system already … Hey, I know. My mother used to give us gripe water."

"Mine, too. And that's what the health visitor recommended. So I need you to go to the shops and buy some."

"Your wish is my command," I say, kiss Sam on the cheek and Annie on the lips. "I won't be long."

"You'll have to drive to Wadebridge to find a chemist. Be careful."

"What'd you want for tea? My treat."

"How about a nice salad."

"Rabbit food. How about a nice Indian Curry, made by yours truly? I won't make it too hot."

"Last time you cooked curry I had to put the toilet paper in the freezer overnight."

"You're *so* funny."

"Sarcasm is the lowest form of wit," says Annie; she turns on the TV.

"And the highest form of humor," I say, wink at her and grab the car keys.

Our car is a small diesel Citroen. Manual drive (not like the American atomatics which I found easy to drive). We call it (her) 'Little Tea' (pronounced Te-a).

I may as well get some groceries while I'm in Wadebridge and find a Boots chemist (Pharmacy) that sells good old gripe water.

Driving through this village is both exciting and frightening, due to the very narrow streets and lanes. Each side of the lanes is two-storied white-washed cottages, shop fronts with black-painted facia boards around four-squared paned windows. Folks cling to the sides of the walls as I drive pass. I see a red telephone box, unique to Britain; I haven't seen one of them for a long time.

I pass a white cottage with a white picket gate and a small garden full of a variety of colorful flowers. Port Isaac School comes into view with children playing and running about. A beautiful village, no wonder TV and Film companies come here during the year to make their programs. It's an English Garden of Eden.

I whistle to myself as I drive, happy to be a father, happy to know and love Annie, and happy to have returned home.

*

Chapter 44

We sunbathe on Millock beach. Fine sand with massive cliffs behind us. A rare sunny day. We have a picnic basket filled with tuna and tomato sandwiches, packets of Walker's cheese and onion crisps, cheese sticks, cans of soda and food for Samuel.

Sam, as we now call him is almost ten months old. Time does fly like an eagle soaring. Anyway, to take a visit to the beach in England, even with the sun burning our skins, we take an umbrella, coats, gloves and hats because at any moment storm clouds could cover the sun and we'd be cold and drenched.

It's a habit hard to get rid of, even in Bakersfield when we took a trip to Pismo beach, we'd take all the paraphernalia needed for winter, while other folks drove to the beach in shorts, tee-shirts and flip-flops.

"A man could get a tan lying here," I say.

"A man certainly could," says Annie, "but I don't see any men around here, do you?"

I grip her around the waist and tickle her, which always sends her crazy. Sam crawls over and throws tiny handfuls of sand at us.

We eat our little picnic as the gulls fly overhead hoping for leftovers, though English gulls are notorious for swooping down and stealing food out of your hand just before you take a bite. We should have used Herring gulls during the Second World War to pinpoint more precisely enemy positions. We call them 'Shite-hawks' because they're always dropping their shit on folks.

Further up the beach there's another family but otherwise we have the beach to ourselves. Mind you it is the middle of the week and my day off work.

Sam decides to go on a crawling journey – towards the sea.

"I think he's really a fish," I say and follow him. I pick him up and place him with us. He crawls back towards the sea. I pick him up again and bring him back. He again crawls towards the incoming waves.

"This guy definitely thinks he's a fish," I shout over at Annie.

I pick him up and decide to take him on a tour of the beach, though there's not much to investigate, but nevertheless I find little craps lying among tiny pebbles, and the skeleton of a fish (this is one of your relatives, I tell him), and then stand by the water's edge, the waves licking my toes. I kneel and stand him in the water.

He gasps as the cold water tickles his toes.

"Water," I say. "The sea. This is the Atlantic Ocean." I point westward. "Over there is Ireland, further up is the Isle of Man, and straight up there all along the coast is Wales and Liverpool and the north of England. And look," I point westward again and Sam follows my finger. "Way over there is America where your mum and I used to live." I don't know if he understands me but maybe my words sink into his subconscious. Still, I like talking to Sam and holding him and showing him plants and flowers and anything really that we happen upon while in town or in the countryside. Something I never had as a child and aim to make up for those lost years and experiences by being close to my son.

Sam rests his head on my shoulder, then snuggles his face into my neck. Annie comes up behind me and hugs me around the waist. I reckon she's proud that I take the time to communicate with my son. She kisses me then looks deeply into my eyes. It turns me on.

The other day we stopped outside a shop in the village and she just stood in the lane and gazed into my eyes. I got an erection. It's all in the eyes. No need for words; there's no words good enough to describe that look. "I think we need to go home and sort that out," she had said.

I quickly covered that area with my sweater, but later at home when Sam was having his afternoon nap we played grown-ups and gave our next door neighbor something to gossip about.

I carry Sam in one arm and hold Annie around the waist with the other as we walk through the sand and back to our picnic.

*

Mrs. Formby, our neighbor is a pleasant and calm kind of woman. She's in her late sixties and widowed. "Oh, I had a good marriage. Time to take it easy now," she says. "You two remind me of when Bert and I were young. They were great times. We had all the neighbors talking back then, I can tell you."

Annie and I decide to keep the sexual noises down a little. Every time we bump into Mrs. Formby, she has a little smile on her face and giggles to herself. But she is a superb babysitter for Sam. Heaven sent I say.

We decide to have dinner at the local pub and ask Mrs. Formby to babysit for us.

"I really appreciate you doing this," I say.

"Oh, I don't mind. As long as I can find time to go swimming down the pool, I'm happy."

"You like to swim," says Annie.

"Always have done. Ten laps of the pool every day. My daughter and I used to love to go swimming together."

"Wow," I say, "you must be as fit as a butcher's dog."

She laughs. "Haven't heard that saying for years," says Mrs. Formby. "My father had so many of them. Dying out these days."

"Not with Joshua," says Annie. "He keeps all the old sayings alive and well."

"I used to love swimming in our local quarry when I was knee high to a grasshopper."

"There he goes again," says Annie.

"I read about kids drowning in those quarries," says Mrs. Formby. "They called them 'clayholes,' I think."

"Well, yer," I say, not wanting to go into any detail. "They closed them all down eventually."

"Anyway, enjoy your meal," says Mrs. Formby. You should try the Cornish pasties."

We walk casually through the narrow, winding lanes to the 18th century Golden Lion pub and dine upstairs with a view of the beach and harbor. The bar staff are very friendly. We order drinks from the 'Bloody Bones Bar' which has a secret smuggling tunnel which leads down onto a causeway on the beach. I order Annie her usual dry white wine and a red wine for myself and we climb the stairs to the dining area. The food is great. We took Mrs. Formby's culinary advice and ordered a traditional Cornish pasty and baked potato with garnish. It was very filling.

"That pasty was huge," says Annie, not able to finish her meal. "I couldn't eat another thing for days."

Cornish pasties are made out of beef, potatoes, turnip, a white onion, butter or clotted cream, an egg and a little milk.

"You're not wearing your crucifix anymore," I say.

"We've not, done anything lately, you know. So why wear it?"

"Maybe we've seen all we need to see. I mean we know where the crosses came from, why we have them and how they work. Yer, I suppose we should put them away somewhere safe 'till Sam is old enough."

"No more adventures," says Annie. "They were scary but also exciting."

"Back to normal old boring day to day living like the rest of the human race. Still it was fun while it lasted."

"Anyway, we've got each other, we love each other ..."

"We *live* each other."

"We love and *live* each other and have a beautiful boy."

"Do you mind if I ask you something, Annie?"

"Fire away."

"What would you say if I told you I wanted another baby."

"I'd say you were nuts."

"Well, it's been almost a year since Sam was born. I want another baby. A girl this time."

She sits there and gazes into my eyes for what seems an eternity.

"You're turning me on," I say.

"Okay. A girl it is."

"How do you know it'll be a girl?"

"There's one sure way to find out," she says and grips my hand.

*

*

No need for a babysitter while surfing through time because no matter how long we are in another place, when we return to our original time, maybe only a few seconds has passed.

That night after we dined, we took a stroll down to the harbor and sat on the wall. "Should we do this, Joshua," says Annie. "I mean, we haven't done it for so long and maybe things have changed."

"Nothing will go wrong," I say and hate myself for saying it. Usually when a person says nothing will go wrong then something bad happens. I suddenly remember what my grandfather had said to my mother, 'Always be careful what you wish for.'

We walk home and thank Mrs. Formby for babysitting. We offer her some money but she flatly refuses it. "Good neighbors help each other out for free," she says before closing the front door.

"She's a good woman," I say. "Not many of them to the pound."

"You're not funny."

We go to the bedroom and check on Sam who is sleeping soundly in his cot. Annie takes her crucifix out of the top drawer of the bedside cabinet and places it around her neck.

"Let's do this."

We sit on the edge of the bed; I hold my crucifix in front of Annie. She takes her cross and holds it for a moment. She leans over and kisses me on the lips. "Just in case something happens, you know." I smile – nervously.

Our crosses touch and instantly we find ourselves inside a massive glass dome. I see sun and blue sky outside. The floor is a white marble. On one side is a long line of train terminals. People get on and off the trains but are not carrying any type of luggage, not even handbags or backpacks.

A voice booms over the tannoy, "The direct service from Heathrow Airport to Edinburgh Waverly Station will depart at 16:30 and arrive in Edinburgh at 16:45."

I look at Annie. "That's usually an eight hour drive if you're lucky."

"Look," says Annie and points to an orange machine of some kind swirling around, sweeping, mopping and drying the floor all at once. On the side opposite the terminals there are shops with no windows. Inside the walls are blank and painted white. I watch as a man walks into one of the shops, talks to an assistant who in turn types something into a keyboard and suddenly a black suit appears on the wall. The suit seems to just dangle in mid-air and the customer walks over to the suit and the suit slips over him. He walks out of the shop wearing the suit.

All the males are wearing black suits and the females, white. At the lower end of the dome is a clock, or rather a square contraption with digital numbers in the center. We walk over to the clock. "It says 01-08-3016."

"One thousand and sixteen years ahead of our time."

"Jesus, Mary …" says Annie, shocked, amazed.

"And Joseph," I say and sigh.

Next we find ourselves in a cubicle on a train. The compartment is lit up very well, probably because there are no windows. Maybe because this train travels so fast it would make folks dizzy looking at the countryside whizzing past. At this speed (whatever speed we are travelling) everything would just be a blur. The seats are comfortable and there's plenty of leg room.

Sitting opposite is a young couple, him in black, her in white, but they are giggling and whispering things to each other, holding hands, kissing. They have similar facial features to us. Sitting in the seats beside them is a young boy and girl.

I'm about to say something to Annie when the young couple open their palms and reveal two crucifixes. They kiss their crosses then place them together.

    They all vanish.
    As do we …

*

We find ourselves back in our bedroom. There's an extra bed in the corner and Sam is asleep, but he looks older than before. On Annie's side of the bed is a cot and a young girl is standing up in the cot and holding onto the side. She looks about one year old and has curly blond hair. She is looking at someone or something in the corner. We turn around and see the young couple and the two youngsters standing and waving at the girl, but the girl doesn't respond. Maybe she can't see them, in the same way other people can't see us. Maybe she just senses them?

The young couple touches crosses and they and their children disappear again followed by Annie and myself. Next instant we are back on the train with the young couple in front of us; this time they are holding hands and sleeping, her head rests on his shoulder. The two children are also asleep.

"Can you see what I'm seeing, Annie."

"The boy looks like our Sam."

"And the girl?"

"Like the one in the cot. Our cot."

"We have a girl," says I, "or *will* have a girl. You don't seem very excited, Annie."

"*You* don't have to give birth."

"If I could I would, but I can't so I won't," I say and grip her hands.

She frowns and smiles awkwardly at me.

"So our future selves can travel back and visit us," I say, "and we can travel back and visit our ancestors *and* travel to the future."

"I'm getting a headache thinking about it," says Annie and rubs her forehead.

"Our genes definitely live on in the year 3022. The bible says we will live forever, which really means, that through genetics we will live forever. There is your eternity."

The next instant we are back sitting on the edge of our bed, little Sam is asleep in his cot. We quickly take our crosses off and place them in the bedside drawer.

"What now?"

"You need to ask?" I say.

*

Chapter 45

Baby Annie was born on Christmas Day 2000. She almost popped out in the ambulance on the way to the maternity ward. Annie senior was fine.

It rained most of that day. Gone are the days of my childhood when every year it always snowed before, on, and after Christmas Day. We used to make snowmen in the front garden (and passing kids used to knock them down – but we'd rebuild them just as quick), and father and I would throw snowballs at each other. The snow in Britain is different from most countries in that it's colder and more icier; my hands got so cold they were numb.

Anyway, summer has not arrived (for what it's worth) and we are again down on Millook beach enjoying a picnic. There is a slight breeze and it is a bit chilly. Still, we sit on some rocks under the winter sun.

I look over and spot little Annie crawling towards the sea (another one who wants to be a fish) and I run over and pick her up. Sam yelps at me and I also pick him up and together we do our usual discovery journey across the beach looking for dead craps and seashells.

I notice Annie looking over at us and smiling. I smile back. I have a great wife and two beautiful children in my arms. We live in a picturesque village in an impressive county. I feel content and excited to be alive. I have a job. We have an apartment (rented), we have good neighbors, good friends. I've had great friends during my childhood, oh, a few hiccups along the way, but life is grand. The army was amazing; the soldiers doing their duty and looking out for each other, saving each other's lives. I learned to play bagpipes, Uilleann pipes, penny whistles, even a little keyboard and have performed at many funerals and weddings and other social gigs. When I was in the Scots Guards Pipes and Drums I had the honor of performing for the Queen of England, marching with the band around her massive dining table in Buckingham Palace. Performed for the 70's band, the Bay City Rollers on TV, travelled around the world to Expo's and many other gigs, and experienced many different cultures.

Yes, I've lived my life fully up to now and, with each experience learned, little by little how to become a better man. And having the unique fortune to be able to connect with my crucifix and travel back and forward in time is a fantastic addition to my life so far. What else could a man ask for? I'm happy. I feel content and excited to be alive. I'm grand.

*

I receive the telephone call from my father at 2:00am on the 17th of October, 2001. My great, Irish, cantankerous, humorous, stubborn, defiant, strong, soft-hearted, loving and caring mother is dead.

*

It seems weird, a bit creepy maybe, sitting here in the front pew of St Partick's Church. It's become a kind of second home to me over the years especially concerning death: Father O'Brien. John O'Malley. Mrs. Feeley. Sean Flanagan (died while playing 'Flowers of the Forest' at a friend's funeral), Father Luke and now my mother all expired and, depending on peoples' beliefs, have either gone to that great paradise in the sky or that great nothingness in the ground.

Father is sitting beside me and has my children perched on his lap. He'd already visited us down in Cornwall a few months back and the kids love him. He's a different person around my children; he makes a better grandparent than a parent. I think maybe as a young parent, or at least in my generation, parents had to concentrate on putting food on the table, keep the house warm, pay the bills, and that was their contribution to the loving and caring nurturing of their children.

I look at the kids hugging him and snuggling into his neck and almost weep with a kind of sad joy. I feel so good for him and sense that he has now, at last found a way to express the love that is in every man and woman, having had to suppress such emotions because of his own upbringing.

Annie is sitting the other side of me and I nudge her to take a look at my father. She takes a quick peek and squeezes my hand. I notice a tear trickle down her cheek. Her own childhood hadn't been the proverbial bed of roses, and I think she wished her father was alive to either witness this, or be sitting on the other side of my father and sharing the children.

Father Luke is long dead and gone. They reckon he tripped over in the vestry and banged his head on the edge of a table (They – whoever *they* are - also reckoned the priest had been imbibing red wine at the time).

So Father Doyle (this church seems to be having services for as many priests as there is congregation), is at the altar mumbling a prayer to himself (or maybe his God) and he looks up at his congregation and we all stand.

Father Doyle is a young priest (they seem to be getting younger every year) and a handsome guy, even if I say so myself. He should be out there living his life instead of standing over a coffin and waving incense around and wearing long robes. Still, each to their own, I guess.

Father Doyle nods in my direction which is my cue to stand before the congregation, say a few words and play my low D whistle.

"My mother was a character, to which I think you will all agree. A great woman and with a heart of gold. She'd help anyone and everyone. I remember when I first started to learn the pipes she'd come out into the back yard to hang out her washing, and do a wee jig in front of the neighbors. I think she was proud to have someone musical in the family. She was a good singer, though I think she was more renowned for her laughter. As my father would often say, 'that woman would laugh at a bucket of shite.'"

The packed congregation, made up mainly of Irish folks, fill the church with laughter.

"I remember one day mother asked me to play 'Danny Boy.' I knew the tune; I was brought up on that song. And, having listened to it for years, didn't really want to learn it or play it, I was more into learning new and exciting tunes from Sean Flanagan, bless his soul."

The congregation mumble 'bless his soul' together and bless themselves.

"So, ironically, a few weeks before my mother died I suddenly had the urge to learn how to play the song on the low whistle. And, to my amazement it sounded more emotional on the instrument. So, I'm going to perform 'Danny Boy' and hope my mother forgives me for waiting so long to learn it. To mother. I love and will always love you."

I adjust the microphone in front of me and begin to play the song. Not a whisper anywhere. Utter silence. The notes echo around the church and as I hit the high notes the sun makes an appearance and beams through the stain-glassed windows as if God Himself has been moved by the tune and has sent streams of light down to show his approval. There is complete and utter silence for a few seconds after I finish playing, then the congregation erupts into applause and give a standing ovation.

"And thank you for applauding my mother," I say and walk over and touch the top of her coffin. "I love you, mum," I say quietly and then return to my seat.

Annie squeezes my hand and, to my shock, my father reaches over and grips my other hand and squeezes it tightly.

This time a tear forms in my right eye, it settles for a short time on my eyelid and then streams down my cheek.

*

The return journey home to Cornwall was pleasant. The kids behaved themselves and slept most of the way in the back seat of the car. The drive was long but well worth it to get back to our quaint little village.

That night I took out our crucifixes.

"I need to see my mother before she died."

"We can do *that*?" Annie is puzzled.

"I don't know, but we can try, can't we? Concentrate on my mother."

After a minute or so of thinking of mother's face, I place my cross over Annie's cross (she still has her eyes closed) and the next instant we're in a doctor's surgery. My mother is sitting opposite an Indian doctor.

"Your angina seems to be getting worse," says the doctor. "Do you still smoke, Mrs. Hanley?"

"Like a chimney, doctor," she replies.

"I've increased your medication but you will have to take it easy and not get so stressed out."

"Easy for you to say, doctor," mother says and slips a hankie out from her sleeve, wipes her nose and sniffles. "But I blame my husband."

"For your angina?"

"For fecking leaving me. He's the cause of all my stress, doctor," says mother and starts to weep.

"I'm sorry to hear that, Mrs. Hanley. "I must stress, however, that you cut down on your smoking."

"That'll kill me too, I suppose."

"It's not helping your angina, Mrs. Hanley."

"Well," says mother and stands, "At least we only die once."

*

If only she knew.

*

And then we find ourselves standing outside our cottage in Port Isaac and gushing up the narrow alley in front of us is a massive wave. The skies are black and lightning strikes the chimney pots and roofs of nearby cottages. The wind is howling. We are drenched with rain.

The next moment we are lying back in bed, breathless but dry and cling on to each other for a long time.

*

Chapter 46

Marriage is where a person gives up their single individually to gain a kind of duo individually. One becomes two. Conflict arises when either one or both partners cling onto their own individually, which is understandable, since growing up we've always wanted things done *our* way.

Still, Annie and I decide to tie the knot because we love each other and we have two children. The system is mainly built around marriage so it makes it easier for administrative and tax purposes.

Today we are in the registry office in Truro standing before the registrar who is going to perform the ceremony and we'll be married in the name of the law. Our witnesses are Mrs. Formby, our next door neighbor and Dougie Marsh, the landlord of the pub in Port Isaac.

Sam is the ring bearer, and Annie holds a small bunch of flowers.

That done, we drive back to the village for a reception in Dougie's pub. The kids hang around for a few hours then Mrs. Formby takes them home.

"Another wine, Mrs. Hanley," I say and kiss my bride on the lips.

"Yes, please, Mr. Hanley," Annie says and blushes.

It's a quiet wedding reception in the sense that there'll be no speeches, no wedding cake, just a small buffet and a boat load of alcohol. And we're happy with that. The whole point of our marriage is that this is *our* day and that *we* are happy.

There is a small dance floor in the center of the pub and we dance to the song, 'You are the wind beneath my wings,' chosen by Annie as her wedding song. I also chose the same song so we danced twice. We plan to honeymoon in London sometime in the future.

We drink the night away, leave the pub about two in the morning, stagger home holding each other up, thank Mrs. Formby for looking after the kids (sound asleep in bed), get undressed, fall on the bed and are both asleep within seconds.

Such a grand life.

*

Mrs. Formby is a good neighbor. Whenever we need a babysitter she volunteers enthusiastically. Since her husband Bert had died a few years back she has mostly kept to herself, nipping out only to visit the grocery shop down in the village square.

According to Dougie the landlord, or so he had told me at the wedding reception, Mrs. Formby had a daughter. 'Died of leukemia when she was about young Annie's age. She never quite got over it. Bert suffered too, and most folks think that was what accelerated his cancer, all the worry and stress. He wasn't as strong as his wife. Still, she seemed to walk around in a daze for years afterward, though we did spot her swimming out in the bay every morning.'

I feel sorry for Mrs. Formby; still, the kids love her.

Mrs. Formby's family can be traced back to the early days of piracy and smuggling along the Cornish coast, or so she told me. She gave me a small book on Cornish history. European Celts arrived in Cornwall about 1000 BC. They lived in tiny villages, mined for iron, copper and tin. They are the ancestors of modern Cornwall. Then the Romans invaded Britain, though they never took much notice of Cornwall.

Cornish folklore is unique. There were giants (Celts) and Piskies (Bronze-age folks); there was the mermaid of Padstow. The 'Spriggans' were ugly folks with large heads and small bodies – they stole babies. The 'Knockers' were elves who lived in the mines – the miners used to leave food out for them so they'd leave the miners alone.

Cornwall is also famous for its saints: St Neot, St Piran and St Petroc, who slew the last dragon in Cornwall. It's believed King Arthur was a Cornishman who had defeated the invading Saxons (early Germanic tribes).

Port Isaac's long sandy beach which is protected by high, rocky promontories on either side provided an easy entry for men and horses to smuggle and transfer contraband inland.

"There's a storm on the way, for sure," says Mrs. Formby. "I can feel it in my bones."

A brisk, chilly breeze sweeps up from the ocean and swirls around Mrs. Formby and I as we chat over the low, garden picket fence.

"That book you gave me has some amazing facts about Cornwall and smugglers and the like," I say.

"They were my ancestors," she says. "Smuggling is in my blood."

"I'm a bit of a gypsy myself," I say. "We go way back."

"I suppose we were all a bit of a gypsy at one time. People have travelled to different countries since man first learned how to walk."

I gaze towards the cliffs and the vast ocean beyond. "It's so beautiful. I've travelled a lot myself and must admit this area is awesome."

"It's a tourists' paradise. Not much work down these parts. We rely on tourism."

"Well, there's plenty of security work," I say.

"You've also got your music," says Mrs. Formby. "*And* your writing."

"Don't know about the writing. I'm still a novice."

"It's who you know not what you know that nearly always makes you famous," she says. "Oh, now and again a writer breaks through with their first novel, but that's rare. The majority of writers end up shelving their work and do something else to put food on the table. But every well known writer I've talked to over the years had known someone. A friend who knows an agent; A cousin who works in a publishing house; A father or mother who are already writers; A brother or sister who works in the media, or in TV or films. There are some amazingly talented writers out there still not discovered."

"I guess. Ah, well. I'm not going to get famous today.

Annie and the two children step outside.

"Hello, Mrs. Formby," says Annie; she is dressed in a black, knee-length white polka dot skirt. It looks as if someone had sprinkled the dots haphazardly over the material.

"Shopping, is it?" says Mrs. Formby.

"We're nipping over to Truro," I say.

"A day out for the kids," says Annie and takes the children and picnic basket down to the car.

"Thanks for the book," I say."

"This is a magical and fascinating place," says Mrs. Formby. "I hope you like it so much that you'll stay."

"A hidden paradise," I say. She steps inside her front door, gives a little smile, then slowly and quietly closes the door.

*

I crunch and grind the gears as we climb the hill out of the village and onto the main road. "Sorry, little tea," I say to the dashboard.

"Mummy," says Sam. "Why is daddy talking to the car?"

"I don't know, Sam," says Annie. "You'll have to ask him."

"Daddy?"

"A car, son, is like part of a man," I say and try to explain, though I don't really know what I'm talking about. "See, if you talk nicely to her, then she will respond back in a pleasant manner by not bursting a radiator and not breaking down in the middle of Bodwin Moor."

"Joshua," says Annie. "He's too young to …"

"*And*, if you talk sweetly to her and tenderly and smoothly slip your gear stick into the correct position, without scraping the sides of the box and hurting her, then she'll love you even more."

Annie looks out the side window but I know she is trying not to giggle.

"Oh," says Sam and seems satisfied with my answer.

"Daddy?" says little Annie.

"Yes, me wee beauty."

"Why is there white smoke coming out of the back of the car?"

"Oh shit," I say.

"Language," says Annie.

Sure enough, there's a white plume of smoke behind the car, so thick I can't see the road behind. "Main gasket's gone," I say and pull over to the side of the road. "Not to worry. It's a great day for a picnic.

"Yay," the kids say simultaneously.

So we get out of little Tea (Te-a), our most reliable, loving and caring car that will never break down because its owner talks sweetly and tenderly to her and shifts gears so smoothly. Maybe the car does hear what I'm saying and doesn't like my tone.

We sit on a small embankment near the car and nibble away on tuna sandwiches and crisps and biscuits. The kids have an orangeade each and myself and Annie sip good old English tea (not Te-a).

"At least the sun is shining and the scenery is great."

From our vantage point we can see the Atlantic Ocean and further up the coast the white tidal waves gush against the beach. It's so beautiful words cannot do it justice. And here we are, Annie and I, our two gorgeous children, a broken down car, sitting on a hill having a picnic. Such great and momentous moments such as these, to me, is better than living in a luxurious mansion in Beverly Hills and being enormously wealthy. Such moments as these are so precious and fleeting; it's what life is really all about – being content and happy with your lot in life in the present.

A farm tractor appears at the top of the hill near the main road, and is about to turn into a field, but stops and drives down the hill towards us. The farmer turns off his engine and steps down from his tractor.

"Morning," he says and lifts his cap. He speaks with a Cornish dialect so morning sounds like 'Maw-or-ning.' "Bit 'o trouble, I see."

The farmer is tall and thin. He has a long chin and pointed nose. Patches of gray hair poke out from beneath his gray cap.

"Little tea, I mean the car has blown a gasket," I say.

"Thick white smoke?"

"Very thick," I say.

"Head gasket, I be a-reckoning. Could see the smoke up the hill. 'Appened to Big Bessie one time over there on yonder field."

"Big Bessie," says Annie.

"Ah, Big Bessie," says the farmer and points to his tractor. "What do you say, Big Bessie?"

There is a few moments silence in which I imagine Big Bessie will reply to the farmer. I'm even waiting for an answer. Stupid me.

"Mummy," says Sam. "That man is talking to his tractor."

"Just like your dad, son, I know," says Annie. She shakes her head and rolls her eyes skyward. "Men and their bloody cars."

"Would you like to join us for a picnic?" I say.

"Reckon I will," he says and sits besides us, leaving Big Bessie blocking the road.

"Live round these parts, do ye?" says the farmer and takes a big bite out of a tuna sandwich. "Hmmm. These be good sarnies, I reckon."

"Annie made them. Delicious, eh?"

"Reckon best sarnies I've 'ad for years."

Annie blushes.

"She's the best sandwich maker this side of the sun."

"I reckon you be right."

"We live in Port Isaac," I say. "That line of cottages overlooking the beach.

"Ah, up there by Mrs. Formby's place?"

"We're right next door."

"Her daughter drowned in the bay. She swam out to her but couldn't save her. Sad affair it was."

I didn't know how to respond, so I remain silent.

After a few moments, I say, "She's a good babysitter."

"Reckon she must be perking up a bit."

"I'm Joshua," I say and offer my hand.

"They call me Stringy," says the farmer and shakes my hand.

"This is Annie, my wife, and Sam and little Annie."

"Pleased to meet you all. Reckon we should get you over to Timmy's in Wadebridge. He'll fix her up for you."

"How will we get there," I say.

"I'll hook her up to the back of Big Bessie and there ye have it."

"Oh. Will we all fit in the tractor?"

"You stay in yon car. I tow."

"I want to ride in Big Bessie," says Sam.

"Me, too," says little Annie.

"No," says Annie. "We'll all sit in the car."

We get in the car, kids in the back, while Stringy, who is munching on our last tuna sandwich, turns Big Bessie around and hooks up a rope around her rear and under the lower front hook on my car.

I poke my head out the side window. "Are you sure it's safe," I say.

"As safe as a bull in a China shop," says Stringy and readjusts the cap on his head.

"What'd he say?"

"Something about a bull," says Annie.

"Huh?"

"Steer her steady; don't brake unless you have to. Keep her in neutral and she'll be fine."

He jumps into his cab and starts the engine. After a few moments he moves off slowly and we follow. The kids are all excited and gape out the side windows. We reach the main road and turn left towards Wadebridge, which is about nine miles or so away.

"If this was in America we'd get jailed," I say.

"You'd probably get 250 years and another double life sentence with no parole and put in solitary confinement for 249 of those years," says Annie.

"You're funny. Anyway, you have to be towed by a tow truck. Here, it doesn't matter. They treat you like men over here, not children. A big old rope does the trick. Saves a lot of money, too."

"You done this before?"

"A few times. There's an art to it. You have to keep the rope taut while getting towed otherwise if there's slack there's gonna be a whiplash when the pulling car speeds up and the rope tightens." Anyway, just pretend this is an electric car with no engine and everything is quiet."

"Won't work," says Annie. "You'd need a very long power cable."

"Huh?"

"Joking," says Annie and slaps me playfully across the head.

The journey is safe enough and we pull into Timmy's garage on the outskirts of Wadebridge. Stringy unhooks us and chews the cud with whom I assume is Timmy. I go over and offer Stringy some money. He flatly refuses and tips his cap at us all, gets back in his cab and drives Big Bessie back onto the main road.

"That was very nice of Stringy to help us," says Annie.

"Reckon so," says Timmy.

"He seems a good man," I say.

"Wasn't always that way," says Timmy. He takes his cap off and scratches his balding pate. Timmy is a little too wide around the middle and has a chubby and reddened face, as if he suffers from high blood pressure. "When he lost his wife to cancer a while back, he went off the rails for a time. Drunk every night. Farm started to fail. But we helped him a little and he pulled through."

"His wife died of cancer?" says Annie. "That's so sad."

"Ah," says Timmy, "see he's tall and skinny and his wife, in her hay-day was, shall we say, a little overweight. She called him Stringy and he called her Big Bessie."

*

Little tea, now fitted with a new head gasket is ready to hit the road again. The repair only took two hours and we found a café in Wadebridge and then took the kids to a park to play on the swings and roundabout.

Now, back inside the comforts of our car (the back seat is torn and Sam keeps making the hole bigger), we make our way onto the main road and head toward Truro, our initial destination. The sun is still smiling down on us, though there is now a brisker wind than earlier. In the far distance I see darkened clouds.

"Maybe Mrs. Formby is right, Annie. We might be in for a bit of a storm."

We drive into the Market City of Truro which is also the center of administration for Cornwall. There are some great shopping areas here. The Cathedral dominates the City's skyline with its 250 foot high towers. It has a green spire and gothic features. Also there are pleasure cruises along the tributaries of the River Fal. Today we are only doing the weekly shopping but hope to come back to tour around the City.

We do our shopping and head back towards Port Isaac just in case a storm does arrive and we're caught in the middle of it on those winding lanes that lead back to the village.

*

Tonight it rains and rains and rains, but no great storm materializes. No flashing bolts of lightning or rumbling thunder, but the gardens and plants, I'm sure appreciate the downpour. I meet Mrs. Formby in the morning and she says there is a bigger and greater and more dangerous storm coming soon. She can feel it in her bones.

I wish she'd make up her mind.

*

Chapter 47

"You've a fine family, so you have," says my dad sitting on the couch with Sam and little Annie either side of him.

"Are you *really* our granddad" says Sam.

"What've you been telling these kids about me, Joshua," says my dad jokingly, or I hope he is joking.

"Oh, the usual. Beat the hell out of me. Took my dog away from me."

"You didn't," he says, a look of sadness in his eyes.

"Of course he didn't," says Annie. "He's only joking, kids."

I notice little Annie snuggling up to him; she is smiling. I do reckon grandparents make far better parents, or some do at least.

I had picked him up this afternoon at Truro railway station. On the drive home he seemed a little quiet. Depressed, maybe? There was some awkward silent moments that I wanted to fill in with all kinds of trivial and insubstantial nonsense, but when I started talking about Annie and the two kids, he had opened up a little.

"It's a shame your mother isn't alive to see her grandchildren."

"Maybe she can see them, dad. You never know."

"You never know," he had repeated. We were quiet for a few miles and then he said, "Your Uncle Jack has died."

I was silent, but felt a lump forming in my throat.

"He died in the mental hospital. Poor Jack."

"I hope he finds peace," I said and refrained from condemning the system that had locked him up most of his life. My words would not have changed anything.

Now, Annie is cooking a Dublin Coddle stew, my dad's favorite. But she adds other ingredients like turnips and lentils, even a few spoons of tomato sauce, a spoon full of sugar (helps the medicine go down) and parsley. Even the kids love the stew.

We sit at the dining room table and eat in silence, something unknown or heard of in our house, usually Sam is teasing little Annie and she cries and then throws a spoonful of stew at Sam who looks at me as if I should rebuke little Annie. But tonight the kids are quiet and very well behaved.

Maybe every family should invite grandparents around for dinner (tea) to help stop the kids from misbehaving.

"There's a storm on the way," says dad.

"Don't tell me," I say, "you can feel it in your bones."

Annie laughs and almost chokes on a piece of potato.

"How do you know?"

"Mrs. Formby from next door, Liam," says Annie. "You don't mind me calling you, Liam, do you?"

"It sounds a lot better than what Joshua's mother used to call me."

"Liam," says Annie. "Can you pass the salt?"

"Now don't be wearing me name out," says dad and passes over the salt.

"How can you wear a name out," says Sam.

"Well," says dad, "If you say a name too much then it loses its … can't think of the word."

"Value," I say.

"No. That's to do with money."

"Potency," I say.

"No," says Annie, "that's to do with power or something."

"Same thing, isn't it?"

"Freshness," says dad. "That's it. It loses its freshness."

"Does that mean your name is as fresh as a flower, granddad," says little Annie.

"Don't be silly," says Sam and giggles.

"Anyway," I say, "A rose by any other name would smell just as sweet."

"You should be a writer," says dad.

We all laugh and I feel good that my father is here and the past is not in this dining room and all is good with the world. I mention to dad that there is a music session on tonight down the Golden Lion pub and would he like to come with us. Mrs. Formby will be babysitting.

"It'll be fun, dad. A few pints of Guinness, fiddles and Uilleann pipes and guitars and whatever. Fancy it?"

"I just fancy an early night."

"You're turning down a drinking session," I say, amazed and shocked.

"I've had enough drink to last me the rest of my life."

"Suit yourself. But you'll miss a great session."

"You haven't heard him play lately, have you," says Annie. "He's really good."

"Ah, you're only saying that, Annie," I say.

"I know," she says.

"What do you *mean*, you know."

"Only joking," she says and picks up the plates. Dad and the kids sit on the couch and turn on the TV.

Annie passes me on the way to the kitchen, bends down and whispers in my ear, "I get the best of two worlds. I get to *hear* your chanter, and in bed I get to *feel* it."

*

The pub is packed. It looks like the whole village is here sipping pints and glasses of wine and whiskies. Annie and I sit in a corner (last two seats) and I get the Uilleann pipes out and tune them as best I can, considering all the background noise. Stringy is standing at the bar supping a pint. He looks in our direction and nods.

There's a fiddler, a banjo player, a guitar player, a Bodhran player, a melodeon player and a few other people sitting in the circle that are obviously there to listen, applaud and drink. British people certainly like to drink and that includes the Irish. They certainly know how to let their hair down as my mother used to say.

They have no limits to the amount they imbibe, no thought of kidney failure or liver disease or cancer, not while drinking, anyway. They just get in the mood and enjoy themselves. I wonder if it's the lack of worrying about the effects of alcohol that keeps them alive.

The fiddler plays a tune I know called, 'The Bride's Favorite,' an upbeat jig about a young bride dancing the night away at her wedding. I close my eyes and imagine the woman dancing and merrymaking and it brings a smile to my face. I join in and soon everyone is playing the tune. Usually a tune is played twice or thrice and then someone leads the group into another tune and off we go again.

Irish music is exciting with jigs, hornpipes, reels, slip jigs, marches, and the slow, heart-wrenching airs. The laments or airs were mostly written during periods of war or subversion by the English invaders who stole Irish farms and only allowed the Irish to grow one source of food – the potato. And when the potato famine struck (most folks believe the potato disease originated in England and was carried across the sea to Ireland by the English invaders), everyone starved because there was nothing else to eat, hence the mass migration of Irish people to America and to the rest of the world.

After the fast tunes are played I perform a lament called, 'The Mass at the Rock,' a tune composed soon after the English raided a secret gathering of Catholics who were having mass near a big rock on a hillside. The English, hundreds of years ago banned the rite of mass in Ireland, in the same way they banned the wearing of the kilt in Scotland. One day, while the priests were praying at the mass the English army arrived and hung and quartered the priest before killing him as an example to the congregation. The air, with its bending notes and overall sadness cannot but bring a tear to the listener, English or Irish.

Uilleann pipes (Gaelic for elbow) are in concert pitch which means there are two octaves (sometimes three with a squeeze) and use a bag and bellows to pump air into the drones, regulars and pipe chanter reeds. The Highland bagpipes (Scots) have only one octave and are limited when trying to play tunes with a mixture of low and high octaves. I graduated (just like Sean Flanagan had predicted) from the bagpipes to the penny whistle and on to the Uilleann pipes. And I'm so happy that I could achieve this transition because at a session, I can choose between three different instruments.

After playing the slow and emotional lament we gallop like a herd of wild horses into a bunch of reels and folks begin dancing in the center of the pub, some knocking over drinks and tables. Annie even gets up to dance with Stringy who swings his cap in the air and slaps his thighs and hollers like a wild coyote. The British and Irish have a great way to relieve stress, and it works.

The barman rings the bell twice for last orders, which is laughable but has to be done because of the law, but last orders never come until folks are so drunk they can't drink anymore and have to return home to sleep. This is a Saturday night so folks can stay in bed most of Sunday morning and recover from their hangovers. Sunday breakfasts and lunches, either in the pubs or at home is the food needed to soak up all that alcohol and put a person back on track in readiness for another week at work on Monday morning.

I don't consume much alcohol because I'm playing the pipes. As I'm performing I think of Sean Flanagan and silently thank him for teaching me so much about the Scots bagpipes and the Uilleann pipes.

"I thwink tis 'twime to go," says Annie, as drunk as a Duchess.

I carry my pipe box under one arm and Annie almost under the other as we stagger our way through the dark alleyways in an effort to get home.

"I live ya, ya kna," says Annie.

"I love you, too," I say.

"Na, I means ah *live* ya," she says.

"Oh. I *live* you, too."

To live someone, Annie had told me a while back, is to love someone very deeply and unconditionally and then some. Live, love, love, live.

We twist and turn through the alleyways.

"Why hiss sit so di-ark," Annie says.

"'Cause it's night-time," I say.

"Oh. Then five seconds later. "Clever sh-dick."

I laugh and she giggles as we pass an empty barn-type house.

There is a recessed doorway in the center. "Jos-hu-ha," says Annie.

"Yes, Annie, the sweet love of my life."

"You 'hould be a wri ... a writ-or," she says.

"I should, eh. Maybe one day my boat'll come in."

"Jos ... Jos-hu-ha?"

"Hmmmm?"

"Fancy a fuck?"

"You said that without stammering," I say.

"Eh?"
"It'd have to be a knee-trembler."
"Wha's one 'o them?"
"I hold you up against the wall and, you know ..."
"And fluck me?"
"Fluck you, yes."
"Can I 'ave one 'o them, peeese?"

I put my pipe box down and step into the recessed doorway with Annie. I lift her up against the wall and hold her buttocks with one hand and manage to pull my pants down a little, then take out my penis with the other hand, slip her panties to one side and, while kissing her neck and then her lips, enter her and thrust into her as she groans and digs her nails into my buttocks.

"Jos-hu-ha?"
"Yes, Annie?"
"Can you fluck me."
"What'd you think I'm doing?"
"Oh."
"Jos-hu-ha?"
"*Yes*, Annie?"

She doesn't answer. "Annie, what the ..."

She starts to snore, which I guess is my cue to take her home. I help her along the lane until finally, after a few more twists and turns, we make it back to the cottage.

"What a night," I say, opening the front door.

"What a fluck," says Annie and stumbles upstairs to bed.

Mrs. Formby is pleased to see us home and safe.

"Good night had by all," says Mrs. Formby.

"A great night had by all," I say. "There'll be a few sore heads in the morning."

"The kids are sound asleep. They're like two little angels."

"Thanks for watching them. How much do I owe you?"

"Oh, I'd never dream of taking any money from you. It was a pleasure just holding and loving on them."

"Are you sure?"

"Of course. Good night," Mrs. Formby says and goes home.

"She's a good woman," I say to myself. I go upstairs and into our bedroom. Annie is sprawled on the bed fully clothed. I undress her and tuck her into bed, kiss her softly on the lips. "Goodnight my sweet angel. Sleep well."

I undress, put on my pyjamas and turn the bedroom light off. I sleep almost immediately but wake during the night. The clock on the bedside table says 2:00am. I visit the toilet and, on the way back to my room I notice my dad's door slightly ajar, so I take a peek inside to see if he is okay. His bedside light is on but his bed is empty. Has he packed his bags and left us already? I search his room but he isn't there, so I search the other rooms, including the bathroom but he isn't there, either.

Where the fuck is he? Maybe he nipped down the pub after all.

I walk outside to see if I can see him either walking up the alley or maybe lying in a heap in one of the garden bushes. It makes me think of how William Shakespeare, that brilliant playwright had died. On a winter's night, he got drunk at a tavern and, on his way home, fell under a bush and froze to death. My father isn't a great playwright but he could still fall under a bush and freeze to death.

I notice a light on in the hallway of Mrs. Formby's house, and through the translucent glass I notice a frosted image of someone standing with his or her back to me. Curiosity kills cats, they reckon, in which case I should have died long ago, because I climb over the dividing hedge, get down on my knees, lift the letterbox flap and peer down the hallway.

And there's my dad, buck-naked, his hands resting on his head and Mrs. Formby on her knees giving him a blow job.

For the love of God!

*

I'm up, shaved and showered and now cooking breakfast just before 10:00am. Annie is asleep still and I'll take her up some eggs, tomatoes, bacon and sausages with a good serving of Heinz baked beans and some toast and, of course, a good strong cup of Tetley's tea. A necessity after a great night's boozing.

Dad is sitting with the kids at the dining room table. I don't mention, nor will ever mention spying on him with Mrs. Formby. What grown-ups do in their spare time is up to them and not up to me to judge. *Judge not lest you be judged, as Father Luke used to say.*

I serve him and the kids a plate each.

"Enjoy yourself last night, son" he says, a sly smile on his face, as if he had just stolen a cookie from the biscuit tin and the crumbs were stuck to the side of his mouth.

"Great night, dad. Had a few pints of Guinness."

"Do yer the world of good, son," he says.

I remember Sam and I as kids sneaked into the rear of the 'Pluto' the local pub and stole a crate full of Guinness. We sneaked into the shed in my back garden and started to drink them. My father walked in, stood there and just shook his head. "Ah, well, you'll be drinking some day. Get it down you - it'll do you the world of good."

Later, when most of the bottles were empty and Sam and I were drunk and didn't feel very well at all, we staggered out into the garden and vomited. My father came out of the house and said, "Get it up, son - it'll do you the world of good."

When you take beer bottles back to a pub you get money for them, so the next day Sam and I put the bottles in plastic bags and returned them to the same pub. We got ten bob (ten shillings) for the lot of them.

I take Annie her breakfast. It takes me forever to wake her. She sits up and looks at me. "Who are you, then?"

"I'm your new cook and cleaner, also your lover when Joshua is working in Wadebridge. I know you like plenty of sex and well, you can have it as many times in a day as you wish."

"Does the cook have a big ladle," says Annie, a gleam in her eye.

"It can stir many a pot and is just the right size to satisfy my lady."

"There's a *lady* in here?"

I place the breakfast tray on the floor, take my pyjamas off and climb into bed. "Like a good cook, I'm here to serve."

After we make love (always wary of the kids bursting in on us) or should I say, connect our lustful bodies together for two whole minutes, we sit up in bed and eat breakfast.

"Will the cook be calling in again next Sunday," says Annie.

"I reckon so, why?"

"'Cause I'd like to play with his ladle again."

*

I tell Annie about my father getting a blow job from Mrs. Formby and she doesn't believe me. "You can tell a tall tale, Joshua."

"I'm serious, Annie. She was down on her knees sucking the shit out of him."

Annie shakes her head then starts to laugh. "Ah, well, suppose you can't blame him – or her."

"Poor guy. I bet he only had sex the once in forty years of marriage and that was to sire me. Could be his first blow job, too."

That night in bed Annie and I are woken by loud banging noises against the bedroom wall from next door. We look at each other and shake our heads. "He's insatiable," says Annie.

This goes on for a week. Dad looking after and taking the kids down the beach with Annie during the day, and, at night sneaking next door to Mrs. Formby. He tells us he likes to stroll around the village at night and we smile and nod and turn a blind eye, so to speak.

Saturday morning and it's time for dad to leave and travel back to his own apartment up north. He enjoys a morning stroll this time, then gets his suitcase and I drive him to the railway station.

"Thanks for being with the kids, dad, "I say. "They really love you."

"They're precious, son. Don't ever forget that."

"I won't. Oh, Mrs. Formby's a good woman, don't you think?"

"A fine lady," says father. "Might have to drop down for another wee holiday."

"You're always welcome, dad."

"A woman needs a bit of company now and again."

"As does a man, dad. As does a man."

*

Chapter 48

After I drop my father off and we awkwardly hug each other like Irish men do, I drive home in the pouring rain. Annie and the kids are asleep already so I undress and slide in beside Annie, hug her and spoon her for most of the night.

Until the storm hits.

I wake and listen to the wind howling and screaming outside and the panes of glass vibrating. Lightning flashes strike across the sky. The thunder roars and the kids run in and jump on me, scared out of their wits.

Annie wakes and hugs them.

"This storm is big," I say.

I peer out the bedroom window. "Christ, the waves are halfway up the cliffs. Can't see the beach at all."

Lightning streaks across the cliffs and strikes a telegraph pole which bursts into flames and falls sideways onto another pole that topples onto a cottage roof on the other side of the lane. The kids scream.

Another massive roar of thunder claps through the air. And the waves rise from the sea and shoot up and over the high cliffs, each wave like crazy possessed white-capped demons having just found a port-hole in which to crawl through and escape from the bowels of hell itself.

I see lights being turned on in the cottages and then the lights suddenly vanish as currents of rushing water sweep through the lanes and alleyways and small roads and avenues and crooks and crannies and crash into gates and fences and bikes and benches and drag them away down the lanes and alleyways. And then a second wave of what can only be described as a tsunami swirls and twirls its way over the cliff and around it and along roads and pathways and speeds up the center of the village and smashes into cottage after cottage and windows and doors and chimneys and tables and chairs and beds and vases and gnomes and clothes and cars and bikes and trash and bins gush past beneath my window.

"We need to get out of here, Annie."

"Where'll we go."

"Find higher ground."

We dress as quickly as we can and rush downstairs. I start the car and Annie and the kids jump in. The rain is so heavy it's almost impossible to see a few inches in front of me. But there's no other choice. Our cottage could be demolished next. Mrs. Formby opens her front door.

"Mrs. Formby. Come with us!"

She holds her raincoat over her head and fights her way against the wind and rain and gets in the car.

I drive. Don't really know where I'm driving to, but know I have to save my family. The windshield wipers are on full but I can barely see out of the window. I open the side window and look out that way, which is almost as bad but at least I can see the edge of the road and, as the car climbs higher, I navigate by keeping an eye on the hedges by the side of the road. Annie tries her best to placate the kids, screaming and hollering in the back. Mrs. Formby sits stiff-backed in the passenger seat with her eyes tightly closed.

More lightning, clapping thunder, even heavier rain and howling, high-speed winds buffet the car from side to side and, as the car slides from one side of the narrow road to the other, the kids scream again and again. I close the side window.

Suddenly we reach the top of the hill and the rain stops, the wind stops, the thunder and lightning stops. At the junction of the road I turn the car side on and look down the lane I had just driven up. Most of the cottages in the village are damaged and some roofs missing. It looks like a wide river is flowing through the center of the village.

Annie screams. The kids scream. Even Mrs. Formby screams. I want to scream too but, for a few seconds my brain can't fathom what is coming towards us at a tremendous speed. It's like a reservoir wall had collapsed and the whole lake is now gushing down toward us. The storm is everywhere, it seems; it's like the storm had divided in two and the village side took a battering, and the split portion had come ashore further upland and crashed over the lowland areas and is now returning to the main body of the storm back down in the village – and we are in its path.

Now *I* scream ...

*

(The Train)

"Is there no end to this rain? And the wind, it howls at me as if seeking vengeance from my soul for the things I haven't done in my life. It scares me. I can't ... move this metal ... off my legs. It's so cold. The water is rising. Joshua is happy and has a family. I'm glad. He deserves the best. More than I could ever give him but it is what it is, I suppose ... I'm sorry, Mary. Maybe in another life we can do better? Well, I guess this is it, Liam Hanley. The last time you will ride a train, smoke a cigarette, drink a pint of Guinness; get a blow job. The water is now at chest level. I feel at peace. I'm ready.

I close my eyes and welcome oblivion.

Chapter 49

… And I scream again as the tsunami gushes over the car and spins us round and round and up and down and we swirl and scream and are lifted out of the water and ride the tip of a massive wave like being thrown around like a piece of driftwood. Thunder and lightning bombard us as we speed down the hill towards the village, the car now riding the massive waves. I can't believe what I'm seeing: complete devastation, whole cottages, trucks, cars, telegraph poles, tents, bicycles, motorbikes, small boats, bigger fishing boats, lampposts, red telephone boxes, tables, chairs, all swishing about in the current. Dead people float face up, face down.

Suddenly the car submerges. Mrs. Formby struggles to release her seatbelt. I climb into the back of the car and undo the kids' seat belts. Annie is holding Sam and Annie, a look of terror on her face.

"Take a deep breath," I yell. "Annie, when I open this door, grab the back of my belt." I kick the back door open. Water rushes in. I grab Sam and Annie in both arms; Annie holds onto my belt and together we slide through the open door and struggle towards the surface.

The current has calmed down some over the past few minutes so I reach out for a passing boat and heave the kids inside. I grip Annie under the arms and almost throw her into the boat. God only knows where I find the strength, but it's a strength much needed. I dive down again toward the car and yank open Mrs. Formby's door, struggle a little with the belt but get her free of it and lift her out and up towards the surface.

We both gasp for air as soon as we surface. Annie has tied the small boat to a shop door sign at the side of the lane. I swim with Mrs. Formby towards the boat. A freak wave gushes over the boat and picks up little Annie and throws her over my head and into the water near Mrs. Formby. I turn and try to swim back that way, but another wave lifts me up and pushes me onto the other side of the boat.

Annie is about to dive in to save her daughter.

"Stay where you are, Annie," shouts Mrs. Formby. "I've got her."

Mrs. Formby holds little Annie by the arms and tries to swim with her back to the boat. Waves envelop them both and Mrs. Formby raises little Annie's head above water. She swims with little Annie towards the boat but is constantly pushed back by the strong current and swishing waves.

I swim to the boat, climb in and pick up an oar lying on the bottom..

"Mrs. Formby. Tell Annie to reach for the oar."

Little Annie's arms reach out and, with the help of Mrs. Formby grabs hold of the oar. I slowly pull her back to the boat.

Mrs. Formby is still afloat. I shout to her again and again to swim towards me. Not far. Only ten feet or so. "You can do it, Mrs. Formby," but she just floats there, a look of serenity on her face, as if she knows she is about to drown and has given up all hope of surviving.

I am just about to dive back in again when I notice another small boat speeding down the top of the lane buffeted by wild waves; the boat hits off the sides of the shops as it descends closer to Mrs. Formby.

"Swim. For God sakes, swim towards me," I yell at her.

The boat shoots out of the lane and across the open area and crashes directly into Mrs. Formby. She is dragged away by the boat and the strong current.

She had lost a young child of her own, but had saved another.

*

Chapter 50

The hospital stay is short. There are worse injuries to be treated other than small scratches on Annie's arm and a few bruises on the kids' legs. I have a big bruise on my upper arm from banging into the door while escaping from the car. We all had the usual examination including chest X-rays which is a normal procedure. My X-ray was clear but Annie's had a dark shadow at the top right of her right lung.

I tried to persuade her to check with her doctor; to find out what that shadow was, but she refused, thinking it was nothing and that it would go away by itself. I nagged her for months to at least get another X-ray but she ignored me. I think she knew she had cancer but was in denial. Later I found out that if she had gone to see her doctor earlier he would have admitted her to hospital for an operation to remove the tumor.

*

It will take a long time before Port Isaac is anywhere near back to normal. Most of the villagers are living with friends and relatives in other villages and towns.

We are extremely fortunate that our cottage is on the top of a hill. It's still standing as is poor Mrs. Formby's cottage, though both our gardens, fences and plants are destroyed and some of the windows smashed.

I am about to visit Wadebridge to buy some glass when I get a phone call on my cell from Corby.

My father is dead. The train he was on had been swept away and destroyed by the flooding waters.

One of my father's brothers had travelled over from Dublin and was helping to sort out his affairs, since they couldn't get in touch with me with the storm from hell going on in Cornwall.

His funeral was to be on Saturday at none other than St Partick's Church.

I sit on the couch and put my head in my hands.

*

I've been to so many funerals over the years I'm seriously thinking of opening a funeral home, or that's what I tell Annie on the drive up to Corby.

The service is a quiet one and I say a few words about my father, then perform "Oh Danny Boy,' for him on the low D whistle, a dedication to both my mother and father hoping, that if there is a heaven, then they are up there now swearing and cursing at each other.

At the cemetery, Annie and I place a white and red rose on his coffin. The sun breaks through darkened clouds and a hint of rain is in the air as my father is lowered into the ground.

*

Chapter 51

"And this x-ray, as you can see shows a shadow on the top right side of your lung," Mrs. Hanley.

I grip Annie's hand.

"Have you suffered from any back pain over the past few years?"

I look at Annie. She lowers her head.

"She was a nurse and care assistant," I say, "and had to lift people in and out of beds and wheelchairs."

"But that was muscular," says Annie.

"And also referred pain from the tumor," says the consultant.

Annie grips my hand tighter.

"We can try to treat the tumor with chemotherapy."

But now is the moment of truth and there is no denying that truth. Annie has lung carcinoma. And it has already begun spreading to her brain, which means she will also need radiotherapy treatment.

We drive home from the hospital in silence. What can I say? What can I do? How can I comfort her? Why is this happening to us? I try to concentrate on the road. Annie looks out the side window. I reach across and grip her hand. She squeezes my hand.

I glance over at her and notice a single tear trickling down her cheek.

*

I give Annie a couple of spoonfuls of oxycodone. This is a semi-synthetic narcotic with similar actions to morphine. She is allergic to morphine. "There you go," I say," get that down yer, it'll do you the world of good."

She can't help but smile, but then grimaces in pain. "How does it feel today," I say and sit beside her on the couch.

"Not so bad," she says. "It could be worse."

I talked to our local doctor who calls in from time to time and asked him to give me a straight and honest answer to how long Annie had left to live. "About seven to eight months," he had said.

So I suppose it could be worse, for instance if she only had three to seven months left on this earth. I don't tell Annie what the doctor had said. I couldn't tell her. Christ, she'd die even sooner. I have to be strong, not only for Annie, but also for Sam and little Annie.

And I sense that Annie wants me to be strong, to be courageous in caring for her and the kids, because I think it may give her the strength to survive the anguish of dying.

We don't talk about the details of a funeral, or what money is where and who gets what and when and all the other hundreds of things to be done when someone passes on. And, in a way, most people can't talk about such things. It's as if by planning the whole thing out then they're speeding up the process of dying, of giving up hope, of surrendering to the inevitable.

"We need to go on honeymoon," she says.
"That sounds nice. Take the kids, too?"
"I've never visited Buckingham Palace, or the Tower of London."
"We could stay at a nice hotel. Take a walk in Hyde Park."
"That'll be nice," says Annie.

She coughs and clears her throat. She holds my hand. "I know you are strong, but at the end, I need you to be extra strong for Sam and little Annie."

"I will," I say. "I promise."

"You're the best person I have ever had the privilege of knowing and marrying," she says.

"I love you."

"I *live* you," she says.

What more *can* I say?

*

(The Honeymoon)

We drive down to Bedford Town railway station and park the car there for a small fee. Bedford to Euston station, London is a short but comfortable journey. There's no way I'm driving into London with so many cars and crazy drivers on the road. I know London pretty well having experienced the city while serving in the army. There are lots of places to visit: great restaurants and plenty of traffic pollution - a tourists' paradise.

I push Annie in her wheelchair (on loan from the National Health Service) from the train to the taxi stand and soon we arrive at the West End hotel just up from Piccadilly. Annie is exhausted but the children are excited. We all go to bed early in the hope of getting a good night's sleep and seeing the sights tomorrow. Easier said than done, especially when the majority of restaurants, museums, and other tourist places have very few wheelchair ramps, something that I'm sure will be rectified in the future.

Honeymoon. I read that back in the sixteenth century and during the first moon cycle, couples drank mead (a honey-based alcohol believed to have aphrodisiac qualities) at the ceremony and for a period afterward until the moon waned. As Samuel Johnson, the English writer and moralist once said, "The first month after marriage when there is nothing but tenderness and pleasure is related to the changing moon which is no sooner full that it begins to wane."

This morning, I make coffee, give Annie her medication, wash and dress the children, help dress Annie, then it's down to the hotel restaurant for a good old English breakfast. I, and Annie, love nothing more than a plate of sausages, eggs, bacon, beans, hash browns, toast, jam and tea. The breakfast alone, in my eyes is well worth the trip, let alone all the other exciting things we have planned.

The hotel is near Piccadilly so I can easily wheel Annie around and the children hold on each side of the wheelchair. We visit Shepherd's Bush market, Madame Tussauds on Marylebone Road (the life-size wax replicas of celebrities and famous historical figures is both fun to see and, as Annie stated afterward, 'A little scary.' We stroll down the Royal Mall towards Buckingham Palace, stand outside the gates and take a few photos.

"Your dad used to play bagpipes in there," says Annie to the kids.

"Did you have tea with the Queen?" says Sam.

"And custard creams and ice-cream," says Annie.

"No such luck," I say. "The band only played for the family and presidents' or kings and queens visiting from other countries. Massive dining room table, though,"

We stroll through Hyde Park and take a trip over to the Tower of London.

We're having fun, and that is the general idea, to get away from village life for a while and have Annie enjoy her last months (maybe weeks on this earth). We don't talk about her impending death, but try to remain happy, for everyone's sake.

We have dinner in the hotel restaurant and retire early to our room. I put the children to bed and sit with Annie watching TV. She still smokes ('I'm not going to get cancer twice, now am I?'). True enough, what's wrong with her enjoying her pleasure for what time she has remaining.

I'm watching TV and don't realize that Annie has fallen asleep on the couch and has dropped her lighted cigarette onto her blanket.

I smell smoke and look over at her – the blanket is on fire. I pull the blanket off and roll it up on the floor, extinguish the flames and open the windows. Annie remains asleep. I place the blanket in the bath tub and turn the water on, wring it out and put the blanket in the trash.

I kneel in front of Annie. "Annie. Wake up.' She slowly opens her eyes and yawns. "You almost set yourself on fire, Annie."

"Don't be silly. I was asleep."

"You fell asleep while smoking a cigarette. The blanket caught fire."

"Oh my God, I'm so sorry," she says and begins to cry.

"It's fine. I put the fire out."

"What would I ever do without you, Joshua?"

I hug her close to me and we rock slowly back and forth.

"We've had a great time, Annie. And the kids loved it, too."

"Thank you for doing this for me," she says. "It really means a lot."

We hug again.

Our honeymoon is over. The first moon cycle has reached its peak and now our moon is waning. Tomorrow we travel to Bedford to pick up the car and then it's a four hour drive back to Rainbow Cottage, our earthly paradise.

*

Chapter 52

Routine rules my day. Lift Annie out of bed, take her downstairs and place her on the couch, cover her with a blanket, fix her pillows, make her comfortable, turn on the television, give her medication; feed, wash and dress the kids, take Sam down to the village nursery, amuse little Annie with dolls and word books.

Sometimes I'll place little Annie on her mother's lap and she'd read a story to her. I'd get myself showered and shaved during this time. I'm allowed to keep all the painkiller drugs at home, so I learn how to become a home pharmacist. She is on a series of drugs, mostly to do with the actual cancer, but Oxycodone is the main painkiller and that stuff is strong. At one time I had to phone the on-call doctor because Annie was in great pain and I ended up giving her six spoonfuls of oxycodone, which took the edge off her pain. Her joints would drive her crazy with pain, usually during the night or first thing in the morning. Her face is thinner now, her eyes sunken and her teeth gradually becoming discolored due to the effects of the drugs.

Yesterday I helped wash her in the bath and, as I held her arms to aide her into the tub I noticed the back of her thighs – large flabby pieces of skin just hung from her thighs - the cancer striking hard. It's so sad to watch your lover, your best friend, your wife deteriorate and suffer so much.

The cancer is digging deep into her brain; sometimes she says whole sentences with all the words mixed up, but she *thinks* she is saying them correctly.

"To want the store go you I with," she says. Although it's a terrible situation to be in, nevertheless it is humorous, and I just can't help but laugh. And as I laugh then Annie, bless her soul, laughs along with me thinking she has just said something funny, which makes her say something else which is even funnier.

"Around grip hands I'd like to your chanter long thick and."

"I'd like to grip your long and thick chanter," I'll repeat in the correct order and laugh and she'll laugh along with me. It is so sad yet so exhilarating. Sad that the disease has entered her brain and exhilarating because she can still laugh, and laughing being the best medicine, gives me hope (and most probably Annie in a different way) that maybe she will be miraculously cured of cancer.

Hope springs eternal.

*

We set out for the store in the village, still under reconstruction. It's a busy time now with the construction of new homes and stores and rebuilding older cottages and structures. Funerals have been taking place. We attended Mrs. Formby's service. We owe her a great gratitude for saving little Annie's life. It'll take a long time to get this village back to normal, but the British people are strong and very resilient. We know how to endure calamities, disasters, wars, high stress.

I push Annie in her wheelchair with Sam and little Annie holding on each side. I worry about my children. Last night, before it got dark, they went out to the garden and picked a bunch of daisies for their mum.

"I hope you get over the flu, mum," said Sam and handed her the flowers.

"Me, too," said little Annie. I had to turn away until the children went upstairs.

It's a beautiful, sunny day and birds chirp in the trees as we pass. Today we will stop to smell the roses, as they say. Everyone we meet is very friendly and smiles and pats the children on their heads. No one stops to have a chat. I mean, what *do* you say to someone who is dying of cancer?

But being noticed is good enough, I think. Annie waves and tries to put on a brace face, she smiles even though I know she is in pain. I gave her some oxycodone before we left so she should be fine for a few hours, though her eyes look a little glazed over.

The narrow lanes are clear of water and debris and we make our way down pass the fishery toward the harbor. I buy some ice-creams from the small shop nearby; the kids sit on a bench. We all look out across the small bay.

Sam and little Annie then sit either side of their mother and lick their ice-creams. I stand behind her, holding the wheelchair with one hand and stroking her soft, blonde hair with the other.

I wish I could freeze this moment, this image and lock it deep inside my heart. I feel sad, sad enough to weep, but I can't. I have to be strong for the children, and strong for my sweet Annie.

*

This morning she is sitting on the couch in the lounge. She is more lucid than the day before and is able to talk normally. The kids are playing upstairs.

"I want to give you something," she says, and picks up a scissors from the table and snips off some of her hair. "I want you to have this, Joshua."

I take the hair and softly rub it against my cheek. She hands me a little plastic sandwich bag. I carefully place the hair inside.

"I want you to do something for me, Joshua?"

"Yes," I manage to say. "Anything you wish."

Outside a wood pigeon coos seven times.

"I'll miss that little fella," says Annie. Every day at this time he sits over there on that tree and coos his little heart out. Seven times he coos and then rests for twenty seconds."

"You count them?"

"I often wonder what they are saying."

"They?"

"There's another one somewhere. Coos back at him."

"Maybe they're lovers. Having a good old conversation."

Annie smiles; she reaches over to me and finds the crucifix around my neck; she holds hers close to mine. I know what she wants to do.

"Are you sure about this, Annie," I say.

"What harm can it do? I mean, will it *kill* me?"

I hold her crucifix and touch it with my cross.

And then …

*

… We are standing on a beach on a warm, sunny day. Donkeys walk down by the edge of the sea. We are both barefoot. The sky is a light blue and, although the sun is shining, it doesn't hurt my eyes when I gaze at it.

I look at Annie. She looks healthy, her cheeks are rose-tinted and her eyes sparkle like gems. She stands upright, proud, her full lively self again.

In the distance two hazy, shimmering figures approach.

"Here's the reception committee," I say. We walk down to the water's edge. There's no sign of the donkeys.

"Guess I'm not riding any donkeys today," she says as the small waves cover her feet. The two figures come nearer and become clearer.

They approach Annie and stop about two feet from her. I take a few paces backward and watch as Annie gapes at them. They look as if they're in their early thirties. I don't know who this man and woman are, but I think Annie knows - there is a shocked and surprised expression on her face.

And then they turn, walk away and slowly fade into the shimmering light of day. I go to Annie and she lowers her face into my neck.

"They are waiting for me," she says.

"Who are they?"

"My mother and father."

I stroke the back of her head. "They didn't say much."

"They didn't say anything, Joshua. But I heard them all the same. I feel so good inside. I'm not frightened anymore. I feel pure joy. Love, Joshua. It's all about love."

"They looked kinda young," I say.

"That's the way you look when there's no more stress or strife. They told me that, 'Death is just the beginning not the end. We can create our own heaven or hell either here or on earth. We can slow down and smell the beautiful fragrance of a rose, or rip it from the earth as we pass by. Our choice."

I close my eyes and hold Annie's head in my hands; I kiss her tenderly on the lips. I open my eyes and take my lips from hers; we're back in the lounge. Outside I hear the wood pigeon and it coos seven times.

*

Why is this happening to you, Josh, me boy, eh? But you have to know, you have to understand that this kind of thing happens to millions of people around the world, always has, always will. So stop feeling so sorry for yourself, Joshua. That poor woman lying downstairs on the couch is dying, and she hasn't got long for this earth and you're up here in the bedroom weeping and moaning and groaning and feeling sorry for yourself. Buckle up, boy. Get a life. Face what's happening like a man. Haven't you understood that concept yet, Josh, me boy. Father tough on you. Mother tough on you. And all because they *didn't want a boy to grow up too soft in a world filled with evil people. And the church feeding you all that bullshit and cramming it down your throat breakfast dinner and supper time and only confusing you and making you feel bitter towards the church with their restricted, brainwashing false dogma that doesn't mean shit to you or any other intelligent or wise man. And the box, Joshua. Don't forget the box. It took a long time, Joshua, but you have finally broken free from being the* boy in the box, *and now are almost breaking free from being the* man in the box *by finding contentment and happiness and real love and finally become a free man, a free thinker, a free spirit that can slow down and smell the beautiful fragrance of a rose and the coolness of the wind on your cheeks and connect with a woman and sire two children and then -* then *lose your wife to cancer.*

When Annie dies what do you think is going to happen? You're going to go straight back to living in that box! Do you hear me? You're going to slide backwards. And do you know why, Joshua? Because you cannot completely escape from the box; you cannot remain outside the box for too long because everyone remains inside the box, a confined space of their own making. Fear is what keeps us inside the box. Fear of asking questions, fear of taking the next step, fear of making decisions, fear of being an individual, fear of fleeing from the flock of religious sheep, fear of insecurity, fear of poverty, fear of losing possessions, fear of an non-existent God, fear of a true God, fear of losing our friends, our loved ones. The second we are born we begin to create the barriers that confine us day in and day out. We are born *into a box. The second we* breathe *we begin to fear life itself, and the only real escape from the box is death.*

I take a few deep breaths, gather my wits together and go downstairs with that nagging subconscious voice ringing in my ears. *The second we* breathe *we begin to fear life itself, and the only real escape from the box is death.*

Annie is lying on the couch and the kids sit beside her; they are holding her hands.

*

Chapter 53

Doctor Matthews calls in as he has done from time to time and I offer him a cup of tea. He smiles and nods. I make the tea as he goes in to check on Annie. The kids are sitting in front of the TV watching a children's program called 'Jackanory.'

I take in his cup of tea and a small plate of custard creams and place them on the small table beside the couch.

"And how is young Sam and little Annie today," says the doctor.

"Very well, thank you," says Sam.

"I'm very well, too," squeaks in little Annie.

"Very well mannered kids, Joshua. Good job."

"Oh, you'd have to thank Annie for that, doctor."

He smiles and turns towards Annie. She is semi-conscious and I watch as the doctor takes her temperature and blood pressure. He takes out a syringe and fills it with a liquid from a small bottle, then injects it into Annie's left arm. He nods at me to follow him into the kitchen. I take the tea and biscuits with me.

"She's very ill," he says and takes a sip of his tea. "I've given her a shot of diamorphine. How are you and the kids coping?" Doctor Matthews is about forty, going a little bald on top but has ample dark brown hair on the sides. He has a rugged kind of face and I bet he's played a few games of rugby in his time. Smaller than me, but he has very broad shoulders which overstretch his gray suit a little.

"It's all happening so quickly. I mean it's seven months since she was diagnosed, but it seems like yesterday. I think I'm okay, but I'm not sure about the kids."

"They should be with her at the end," says the doctor. "It'll make the grieving a little less painful and give them some sense of closure."

"Thanks, doctor. I'll work something out."

"You need to find a small bed or something similar for Annie to lie down in. Now, this is important, Joshua. When she passes, do *not* call the ambulance service. They'll defibulate her and bring her back, only for her to experience more suffering. As soon as she stops breathing, phone me and I'll come round to confirm her death and write you out a death certificate. After that she can remain where she is until such times as you wish to make contact with the undertakers. They will arrive and take her to the funeral home and prepare her for visitations. Is there anything else you might want to know?"

"I don't think so, doctor Matthews. "I'm just kind of well …"

"Scared? It's hard, Joshua. And I'm so sorry we couldn't have done more, but she had a very aggressive tumor in her lung."

"She hardly smoked," I say. "Only the occasional social cigarette."

"I've known athletes who didn't smoke or drink and ate all the right foods and did everything right and still got lung cancer and other cancers, and died young. Some people are born with mutations in their genes and there is nothing anyone can do. It's just the luck of the draw."

He takes another sip of his tea, takes a couple of custard creams from the plate and shakes my hand. "The Health Visitor will call in later tonight to give Annie another shot. She'll also help you with putting her in the bed."

"What's the shots you're giving her?"

"Heroin. The generic name is Diamorphine. It's for severe pain and is also sometimes used as a cough suppressant. He pats me on the shoulder. "If there's anything you need, Joshua. Anything at all, please phone me."

"I will, doctor. Thank you."

I stand at the front door and watch as he gets into his car and drives down the narrow lane. I wouldn't fancy his job. I think about what he had just said: 'When she passes, do *not* call the ambulance service. They'll defibulate her and bring her back, only for her to experience more suffering.'

I walk into the living room and stand for a moment looking over at Annie, lying on the couch, dying. I look over at my two children and feel for them. They are about to lose their mother and they don't yet know this. How can I tell them? How *do* I tell them? What do I say?

I gaze at the back of my children's heads and feel completely useless. I feel lost, as if trapped again in my thick-walled box, caged up again and restricted, not by religion or narrow-mindedness but, ironically by life itself.

"Dad?" Little Annie turns round and looks at me. "Is mum going to get better?"

*

The health visitor nurse calls in about 7pm. She is short and blonde and has a wide smile. She must be in her late twenties or early thirties. Her teeth are straight and very white. She has the same bluish-gray eyes as Annie.

"Cup of tea?"

"Oh, I'd love one, luv. Been busy today. Fourth call in a row."

"Sugar and milk," I say.

"Yes, please," she says, "I'll just check on Annie, shall I, luv?"

I half smile to myself. This woman is certainly the cheery type, full of energy. Pretty, too. She has a northern accent, maybe from Yorkshire, or somewhere near there.

I open a packet of oven chips and put them in the oven for the kids' dinner. I take the nurse her tea and a plate of custard creams (some leftover from Doctor Matthew's earlier visit) into the living room and place them on the table beside the couch.

I offer my hand. "I'm Joshua."

"Oh, sorry, I didn't introduce myself. "I'm Beryl Saunders. Pleased to meet you. Oh, and *who* are these sweet little angels?"

"Sam and little Annie. We call her little Annie because her mum's name is Annie."

"Hi-ya," says Beryl. "Yer alright?"

"Huh?" Sam says.

"Pardon," says little Annie.

"Oh, it's me accent. We talk all funny up there in Doncaster."

I smile.

"Annie'll probably wake up soon. We need to get her on a bed."

"I have a fold-up bed upstairs," I say.

"Perfect. We can put it up down here so the kids can be here, too. Oh, can you find a fresh pair of pyjamas."

I climb the stairs into our room and find a pair of Annie's pyjamas in her dresser drawer, then grab the fold up bed which is in the kids' room against the wall where it's been since my father had last visited. I get it downstairs and into the living room and set it down by the end of the couch, and hand the pyjamas to Beryl.

"Right. If you guys can go into the kitchen for ten minutes I'll sort out Annie."

We stand in the kitchen and I pour some tea out for the kids. I must be an expert on tea-making by now. I take some chicken I had cooked earlier out of the fridge, slice it up and put some on two plates, then share out the oven chips. The kids' get stuck in, poor guys, must be starving. And then I think they won't have a mum to feed them. I'd better learn how to cook and quick.

My manager at the security company is good with the situation allowing me time off to care for Annie and the kids.

Just as the two hungry-horses (anyone who eats a lot) finish their chicken and chips, Beryl pipes up, "You can come in now."

We walk into the living room and Annie is lying in the fold-up bed, dressed in her fresh pyjamas, her hair combed back and tied into a bun at the back of her head. She looks comfortable. Thank God Beryl is here. I sit beside Annie and hold her hand. Sam and little Annie sit opposite and both hold her right hand. I suddenly think of standing on that beach with Annie and her talking to her parents and wonder if that really happened? Or did we both dream it? Or did only I dream it as Annie sat on the couch and didn't travel anywhere? I'm finding it difficult to comprehend such a dream, or reality, or of touching crucifixes and becoming part of the magic of the universe?

But if it was a dream that both of us shared during this stressful time, then maybe it was meant to ease Annie's mind, to make her feel better about herself, to alleviate some of the emotional pain of knowing that very soon she will pass on. Maybe the cancerous cells in her brain are playing tricks on her, and somehow I can see her fantasies? Or her subconscious is compensating for the lack of cognitive thinking and replacing her thoughts with visions, but, even then, I experienced her visions too, which would be weird, maybe even impossible. But, as they say, impossible is only something not yet discovered.

"I love you, mummy," says little Annie.

"I love you," says Annie and opens her eyes. Her voice is croaky and hardly recognizable.

"And I love you, too, mummy," says Sam.

"I love you both, too," she says and cringes in pain."

Annie tries to sit up and Beryl comes over and gently holds her down

"I've put a pillow under your head, luv," she says. "That'll make you more comfortable. Beryl beckons me to her and whispers into my ear. "She's going to get very agitated for a while and panicky. She's almost ready for her diamorphine shot."

Annie's eyes are glazed over. She looks at Sam and little Annie, strokes their heads and tries to smile at them. They start to whimper, then weep.

I kneel beside her and kiss her on the lips. Annie looks at me; our eyes connect, our souls are already weeping. She lifts her left arm and hugs me around the neck, then grips my crucifix and says in a hushed and croaky voice, "Believe, Joshua. Believe."

"I love you," I say.

Beryl kneels beside me, pulls up Annie's pajama sleeve and injects her with diamorphine. She looks at me; I see tears forming in her eyes. She stands quickly and guides the children out to the kitchen.

"Goodbye, mummy," says Sam. And in a quiet voice little Annie says, "Goodbye, mummy. I love you."

Annie is fighting to keep her eyes open. She opens and shuts her mouth in an attempt to speak to me, but I think she is now too weak, and the diamorphine is now taking affect and making her drowsy.

I place my ear next to her mouth and she says in a croaky, husky voice, "I live you."

"I live and love you, Annie." And I hear myself saying something that goes against almost everything I have made myself believe in, "They are waiting for you, Annie. They wait inside the light. Go to them."

Annie gasps; she makes a guttural sound that comes from deep in her throat. She stops breathing. Her mouth drops open, then, after a few seconds her eyes open wide and she looks over my head and toward the center of the living room wall as if staring at the spirits who have come to greet her.

Death is just the beginning not the end.

*

I take the crucifix from around Annie's neck and place it in a little cardboard box along with my cross, the cutting of her blonde hair, her wedding ring and my wedding ring. I wrap an elastic band around it and place the box in my bedside cabinet. Ironic, I think, that most of my life I've questioned everything and kept an open mind in order to escape the restricted confines of existing in a metaphorical box, and almost everyone I know has either been buried or cremated in a real one.

*

Chapter 54

I open the door to the funeral director. The usual tall solemn looking person dressed all in black. I have a quick mental image in my head of undertakers turning up dressed in white, just to be different. Why not? But then I'd be accused of disrespecting the dead. Old habits die hard.

"Mr Hanley," says the man. "I'm John Foster from the Co-operative Funeral Service.

"Come in," I say, still not quite believing all this is happening. Annie lying dead in the *living* room; the kids upstairs and being cared for by Beryl. She had volunteered to call around to watch the kids during the removal of Annie.

"Please. Come in. She's in here."

"Leave this to us, Mr. Hanley," says the undertaker who is followed by his assistant. "We're going to be carrying Annie out through this door and I advise you to turn away during that time."

I don't really understand what the man means, but I remain in the kitchen as they do their work. A few minutes later the men come out of the living room and through the kitchen to the front door. Against my better judgment I turn and see Annie, wrapped in a black body bag being carried out through the door. I suddenly understand John Foster's words. The image of Annie leaving our home, wrapped in a body bag and never able to return back through that door, is now etched deeply into my brain.

I walk into the lounge, sit down on Annie's deathbed and weep.

*

The image of Annie being carried through the front door plays over and over in my mind for days, during the funeral home visitations, through the funeral, at the scattering of the ashes into the Atlantic Ocean.

Most of the villagers attend the funeral. Doctor Matthews and Beryl sit in the row behind me. I sit in the pew with little Annie on one side and Sam on the other and hug them. Annie's Aunt and Uncle attend, the only two representatives of what is left of her family. But Sam and little Annie live on in honor of her, their genes will live eternally.

'You are the wind beneath my wings,' is played over the stereo system. I think it more fitting to play Annie's favorite song rather than playing the bagpipes or low D whistle.

I sit the children on my knee and we quietly weep as the coffin moves backward on roller tracks and the curtains slowly close.

*

We stand by the sea on Annie's favorite beach and scatter her ashes into the water. A crowd of villagers stand behind us, their heads bowed. Beryl hugs me; she looks into my eyes, maybe into my soul. The sun shines still; the breeze flows around us, the gulls fly overhead.

We live then we die.

*

Cready's coffee cafe is half full. Sam and little Annie sit each side of me sipping their chocolate milkshakes. I take tiny sips of my expresso and gaze out of the window at the folks passing by, some locals and lots of tourists.

Beryl walks in, spots us and waves. She comes over beaming her wide, accepting and friendly smile.

Sit down, Beryl" I say. "Join us. Would you like a coffee?"

"Oh, yes please. I'm gagging."

I order a coffee from a passing waitress.

"Hello, kids, how's it going?"

"I miss my mummy," says little Annie and starts to cry. Folks in the café look over at us. I kind of half smile back at them. They must be feeling sorry for the kids. Most of the villagers had lost a loved one or two during the big storm. We all share something in common - connected in grief and love.

The waitress delivers the coffee and Beryl takes a big sip.

"That's better," she says. "Hit the right spot."

I wonder where she gets her energy from. I also wonder how amazing it is that she has a bubbly personality. I suppose under these circumstances it'll be quite some time before I can get back to finding happiness again.

"How you feeling today, Joshua?"

I raise my eyebrows, take a deep breath and exhale slowly.

"Depressed, lost, oh, and not getting any younger."

"I know what you mean. Well, not the depressed part but getting older. It's a bummer. How old *are* you, Joshua, if you don't mind me asking?"

"Forty-four. Forty-five in December."

"You're still a young man," says Beryl and gives me a big smile.

"And you?"

"Oh. Thirty. Let me see ... fourteen years younger than you."

"Not much difference."

"Age is only a word," she says and takes another sip of her coffee.

Beryl reaches over and pats the kids' hands. "Fancy a picnic down the beach on Sunday?" She pats my hand and winks at me. "And daddy can come, too."

"Can we have a milkshake," says Sam.

"Of course you can. And what do you want, little Annie?"

"My mum," she says and weeps.

*

Chapter 55

Sam, little Annie and I sit on the beach and gaze at the ebbing tide. Gulls soar overhead. The sun is shining; there is a slight coastal breeze.

I am thankful for these precious moments with my children. And sitting on the beach brings some peace to my mind and soul. The cottage seems to have trapped Annie's sad energy inside and surround me with feelings of grief and sadness. Even the walls seem to be weeping and wailing for Annie.

"Where's mummy gone," says little Annie.

"We threw her in the sea, silly" says Sam.

"Has she gone to heaven, dad?" says little Annie.

"Yes, Annie. I think she's gone to heaven?"

"She'll be waiting there for me. I know she will."

I stroke her hair.

"Is there room for one more, guys," says Beryl as she approaches and sits down beside us. "As promised. One picnic. What do you say to that?"

"Yay," say the kids and run over and hug her.

"Well, I'm privileged to have so much attention."

"Here you go," says Beryl and hands out two chocolate milkshakes.

"One for you. And one for you."

"Manners, kids."

"Thank you," the kids say simultaneously.

We eat ham, cheese and tomato sandwiches and custard creams and jam tart cakes washed down with sprite. A great picnic feast.

Sam and Annie go dip their feet into the sea as Beryl and I just sit back against a sand dune and watch them play.

"Have you any children, Beryl?" I ask. "If you don't mind me asking, that is."

"No," she says, "but I was married for a few years. Never worked out."

"Oh, I'm sorry."

"Well, he preferred Mr. Scots Whisky to me. Glad to be rid of him."

We are silent for a few moments. Maybe she wants me to keep asking questions, but I don't want to pry.

"Should never have married him in the first place. I was told marriage would never change his drinking habits. Live and learn, eh?"

"Divorced?"

"Oh, yes. A long time ago."

"Family is everything, I say."

"I love kids," she says.

"I couldn't eat a full one," I say.

"Couldn't eat a …" she laughs. "You're funny."

"I've been told I'm a bit funny in the head."

"Well, we're all a bit insane. I mean look at the things people do."

"The definition of insanity is doing the same thing over and over again and expecting different results."

"Albert Einstein."

"Clever girl."

"Well, thank you."

I close my eyes and breathe in the fresh air. I open them and see Sam and Annie splash each other down at the water's edge.

Gray clouds blot out the sun. It begins to rain. "Come on kids," I yell down at them. "Let's go."

We pack up our picnic basket and walk the hundred feet or so back to the cottage. Imagine having the Atlantic Ocean right on your doorstep. I feel so lucky, though I haven't got Annie to share it with anymore.

"Thank you for the picnic," I say. "The kids loved it."

"You're welcome," says Beryl.

"Can Beryl stay for tea?" says Sam.

"We're having chicken and chips," says little Annie.

"Only thing I can cook without burning it," I say.

"And lemonade," says Sam.

"I've got some red wine, too," I say.

"Sounds delicious."

Chapter 56

After dinner we watch TV for a while. The kids ask Beryl if she can put them to bed and read a bedtime story to them like their mum used to do.

I wash the dishes and clean up; pour out two glasses of merlot.

"Those kids are so cute," says Beryl and sits on the couch beside me.

"Oh, you don't mind me sitting here, do you?"

I hand her a glass of wine. "Of course not."

"Cheers," she says and we clink glasses.

We sip our wine and gaze at the local news on TV. After a few moments our knees touch momentarily and I instantly feel a tingling sensation in my stomach. I quickly cross my legs.

I rest my left hand on the sofa not realizing that Beryl's hand is there, too. Our fingers touch. She squeezes my little finger.

"I need to use the bathroom," I say and rush out.

I gaze into the bathroom mirror. *What are you doing, Joshua? Are you insane? How can you be so disrespectful to Annie?*

A tear trickles down my cheek. What *am* I doing? What am I *supposed* to do?

I return to the living room. "I'm sorry, Beryl. I didn't mean to be rude, but, well, I …"

"I understand."

She picks up her handbag and puts on her coat. "You need time. I understand."

I look at her and slowly nod as she exits and closes the front door quietly behind her.

I go into the kitchen and find a bottle of Jamieson's in the top cupboard.

Tonight I will get drunk.

*

*

It takes time to heal and *time flies like an eagle soaring*. I had to return to work two weeks after the funeral, which was good for my sanity – and my liver. And what a godsend Beryl turned out to be. I met her in the village café about three months after Annie had passed and had asked her if she'd mind dropping the kids off at pre-school in the mornings (I'd drive them to her cottage on my way to work) and then pick them up in the afternoons. Five days a week she now cares for them, takes them down the beach some days, sometimes around the village and does some shopping for me. I pick them up on my way home from work. Beryl's shifts are from 6pm to midnight so she gets plenty of sleep. I receive half of Annie's work pension and most of that money goes towards paying Beryl.

*

Four months to the day after Annie had passed we spend a full day on her favorite beach. The kids chase each other on the sand.
"How are you feeling?" asks Beryl.
"A lot better," I say, "Time heals, they say."
"When my mother died I was devastated. She had ovarian cancer."
"I'm so sorry," I say and squeeze her hand.
"And then my dad died a year later of stomach cancer, two weeks after his diagnosis."
"God almighty," I say, "And there's me rambling on about Annie."
"It's like a flesh wound, it takes a long time to heal and then you're left with a permanent scar."
"Is that why you chose the nursing profession to give people some care and comfort up to the end."
"Oh, I don't know. Maybe."
"Give credit where credit is due, Beryl. You're a wonderful person and what makes you stand out is that you care about people."

I reach into my pocket and take out Annie's crucifix. "I'd like you to have this, Beryl. Annie, I think would want you to wear it. As a big thank you, maybe." I place it around her neck.

"It's beautiful,"

We stroll back to the cottage; the kids run on ahead. I have a strong urge to hold Beryl's hand; I squeeze it tightly. I look at her and smile. She smiles back.

Then we kiss.

*

Beryl comes downstairs after reading a bedtime story to the children. She is smiling and looks happy. I'm happy that she is settling in nicely and that we connect. She sits on my lap.

"There's something weird and wonderful about that cross," I say and hold it in my hand.

"What do you mean?"

"It's difficult to explain because when I do you'll think I should be committed to the funny farm."

"You're scaring me, Joshua," she says and sits beside me.

"Hell, I scare myself sometimes. So, my mother goes to Dublin to visit my dying grandfather and, before he died he gave her a crucifix and told her …"

*

... Beryl doesn't believe a word I tell her about the crucifix and Annie's crucifix and the time shifts we encountered and the places we travelled to and the ancestors we had met. But I suppose anyone sane wouldn't believe it either.

"Seeing is believing," she says.

"Then we'll see," I reply.

"You *are* funny," she says and sits back on my lap.

I close my eyes and feel her long hair touch my forehead and tickle my face and then I quiver as I feel her tongue lightly touch my lips; I feel her lips fully on mine and a tiny electric shock shoots up my spine; I feel her tongue in my mouth; I touch her tongue with mine.

"Look into my eyes," she says.

I look into her eyes but can only maintain eye contact for a few moments.

"Keep looking into my eyes, Joshua. I feel connected to you."

So we gaze at each other for a long time until I push her back onto the couch and pull her panties down, then lift her dress as she rips away at my clothes and soon we are naked and making love slowly, tenderly, gazing still into each other's eyes. Soon, we begin to kiss hungrily as if we'd been starved of food for a week, gnawing at each other, our teeth gnashing, our tongues squirming, swirling, dancing. And then we make fast, furious love. It's amazing. I am in paradise.

And as I orgasm I feel the bliss enveloping me as if the sun had suddenly found a way into the darkness surrounding my heart and brilliant bursts of sunlight penetrate my body, my mind, my soul.

Thoughts of Nature, the universe, the beauty of everything and all things, of Annie, of Saffron, of Beryl, of beasts and men, all governed by the power of nature rush through my mind. Everything *is* connected. Everything *is* wonderful. We can *all* break *free* of our imagined boxes because we are *all* connected. We *are* the universe.

I lie on her for a few moments to catch my breath. My heart beats so fast I think it's going to burst out of my chest and the blood spurt all over Beryl's face.

She gently and softly strokes my neck and back.

I lower my head onto her chest – and quietly weep.

*

We lie in bed propped up by pillows, both naked, both unashamed of our nakedness, of our lovemaking.

"You were amazing," I say.

"You weren't so bad yourself," she says and cuddles up to me.

"Was that the first time or the third time?"

"I wasn't counting," she says.

"There's something to say about that tantric sex. Boy oh boy," I say. "Is it something new?"

"Been around for thousands of years," she says. "It's an ancient Hindu way of lovemaking."

"It's not so easy looking into someone's eyes for so long."

"It'll come with practice. Tantric sex also increases intimacy and gives you powerful orgasms."

"You're not kidding! Best orgasm I've had since the last one."

"You're funny," she says and leans over and kisses me. Her lips are tender and soft.

"I think I'm falling in love with you," she says. "I know it's so soon after Annie's death but a woman can't help the way she feels."

I don't know what to say or how to answer her. Annie's not that long passed and here I am in bed with another woman, the very woman who nursed her near the end of her life. And it's ironic that when Saffron was in a coma in hospital it was Annie who helped nurse *her*. Crazy how a lot of things are connected and we don't really notice.

But still I feel dreadful. I feel as if I'm deceiving Annie, being disloyal to her. What can I say?

"I'm sorry, I shouldn't have said that." She kisses my cheek. "Take your time."

I stare at the cracked white ceiling. I still love Annie, but I think I'm falling in love with Beryl. I try to change the subject and brighten things up a little.

"Did you like Doncaster?"

"Oh, not so bad. Bit better than that other place I lived in."

"Let me guess. Leeds?"

"No."

"Burnley?"

"Erm, no way."

"Liverpool?"
"No."
"Manchester? Lancaster? Preston? Barrow-in-Furness? I give up."
"Corby," she says.
"Corby, the steel town?"
"Yes."
"I lived there, too," I say.
"That's weird, both of us lived in Corby and then we meet in Port Isaac."
"The world is a weird and wonderful place," I say and kiss her fully on the lips.

*

Chapter 57

We sit by a sand dune; the kids play in the sand nearby. I look skyward and see a Herring gull swoop and soar beneath the clouds. I think of myself as a bird, a free spirit, spreading its wings. I think of my soul: always looking and searching, seeking a better way to live, to love, seeking happiness, searching for love, looking for a connection. Yes, it's been staring me in the face all along? Connection. To hell with my inner thoughts, I'm in love with Beryl. These immense, beautiful feelings I have for her is the key that will unlock the constraints of my thinking, of my confinement. It's not death that will release me, but love - the only true way to escape from the box.

"Joshua?" Beryl says and takes a sip of her tea.
"Hmmmm," I say.
"I'm pregnant."

Chapter 58

A week later we decide to take a trip up to Corby to celebrate St Patrick's Day and what better place to do so than Corby. The folks are fine people, English, Irish, Scots, Welsh, all trying to get by, work hard, play hard.

We arrive at Kettering railway station, jump on the bus to Corby, (the same 292 bus that myself and John used to ride when we hitched it from school) and gaze out the top deck windows at the scenery.

"Nothing seems to have changed," I say. "Look. That old tractor over there in that farmyard, I'm sure it was in that same position when I was a kid."

"Might be a different tractor but parked in the same spot," Beryl says and hands Sam an orange drink. Little Annie was asleep, her head resting against the window.

"Poor thing is exhausted," says Beryl, "She'll sleep well tonight."

"I hope so," I say and squeeze Beryl's hand.

Beryl's mother was the first to die, succumbing to ovarian cancer. And then her dad died of stomach cancer after only two weeks of his diagnosis. Maybe that's why she chose the nursing profession, to give people some care and comfort up to the end.

We arrive at a nice little hotel not far from Sean Flanagan's old place. His wife and grown up kids had left Corby and had returned to Wicklow County, just below Dublin, from where their clan hailed.

We all snuggle up in the double bed and, within ten minutes everyone is asleep except me. Soon, my eyes begin to droop and, before I nod off to sleep I whisper into the darkness, "Thank you, Universe, for my amazing life. May I live long and love long."

*

Chapter 59

The church bells sound for St Patrick's Day as we approach the church. People both young and old stroll inside. The car park is full. I look to the sky and see jet contrails overlapping each other; they resemble a cross. Is this a sign for me to connect our crosses? To show Beryl, to prove to her that I am not insane and living in some dream world

Beryl and I and the kids sit near the rear of the church.

Folks mumble between themselves. I notice some of them wear a clipped Shamrock piece in their lapels. Then it is silent as the priest walks up to the altar.

"Good morning," says the priest. "My name, for those who don't already know, is Father Boyle. And this is my second mass since arriving here so I'm still, as they say, a bit wet behind the ears."

The congregation laughs and nod and smile at each other.

I gaze around the church and notice the Stations of the Cross (the same pictures from my youth) hanging on the walls. The more things change, it seems, the more things remain the same.

Father Boyle, a new priest aged about twenty-five, gives a sermon about caring and loving each other, which, to me is what the church should be mostly teaching.

"Do you trust me?" I whisper into Beryl's ear.

"With my life," she says and grips my hand.

And then I lean over to her and touch her cross with mine.

*

Chapter 60

Instantaneously, we fly high in the air and swoop through the jet contrails. Below are high-peaked mountains, some covered with snow and wide green valleys and meandering rivers. I grip Beryl's hand and quickly glance at her face. She has her eyes closed. This has never happened before, usually Annie and I just appear somewhere in time, but we've never flown like this.

Now, mist all around us. Distant shapes emerge from the mist and approach us. A few at first, then more and more and hundreds, maybe even thousands of shapes surround us. These ghostly figures have faces but they are blurred. They form a tunnel for us and we speed up and shoot through the gap, my face cheeks suck in and I grip Beryl's hand tightly. The next instant the mist vanishes and we find ourselves in a massive garden with colorful flowers spread over and between tall and small trees and twisting vines: A wild expanse of beauty.

Some plants and flowers I recognize and others are new to me. The sun is low in the west, like a low October sun about to reach sunset. Maybe, I think, this is our time, our sunset; the end of our day?

"This is amazing," says Beryl and touches a honeysuckle. Suddenly hummingbirds appear and encircle the fragrant trumpet-shaped flowers then hover in front of us, their tiny wings flapping at a tremendous speed.

"Is this heaven?" Beryl asks with a broad smile on her face.

Before I can answer the hummingbirds disappear, I mean they just vanish into thin air.

"Joshua?" the voice is calm; there is an innocence and beauty-like tone to the voice.

We turn and there, standing not six feet from us is a tall, thin man dressed in an immaculately tailored navy-blue suit, white shirt and red tie. "Welcome."

"What is this place?" asks Beryl.

"And," I add. "Are you … God?"

The man laughs, a deep, guttural sound that echoes around the garden. "Far from it, Joshua. Do you like my garden?"

"Is this the garden of Eden?" asks Beryl.

"It's the garden of whatever you want it to be," he says.

"Really," I say and closed my eyes. I concentrate for a few moments and when I open my eyes the garden has changed into a valley with a thunderous waterfall gushing down over a cliff in front of me. The sun is high in the sky. "Did I do that?"

"What do you see, Joshua?" asks Beryl.

"Can't you see the waterfall?"

"I see a beautiful garden. Oh, look. The hummingbirds have returned."

"We see what we *want* to see," says the suited man. "We *create* what we see through our thoughts, whether we realize it or not. That's how your world was created and is constantly being created."

"What do you mean *our* world?" I say, a little confused. "Don't you belong on Earth?"

Maybe I asked the wrong question at the wrong time because Beryl and I suddenly find ourselves in my grandfather's cottage in Dublin. He and my grandmother are sitting on a small couch holding hands. The two ornamental Persian Cats stand proudly behind them on the old dresser. They scare me still after all these years.

"Granddad," I say, "can you see us?"

"As clear as day," he says and smiles.

"We've been waiting for you," says my Grandmother.

"Hello," says Beryl. "My name is …."

"Oh, we all know who you are, luv," says Grandfather.

The front door opens, as if by itself and one by one people begin to walk in and stand behind my grandparents. I recognize, from my travelling back in time everyone I had seen on my journeys back through time. And then the suited man walks in at the end. He stands behind my grandmother and squeezes her shoulders.

"Family is everything," the man in the suit says. You, Annie and Beryl in different ways have had the privilege of seeing for yourselves how, through the various stages of each generation how they lived, survived, suffered, worked together to make ends meet, and how by staying together as a family led the way to teach other generations in the future."

"This must be heaven," says Beryl excitedly.

"Call it what you will," says my Grandfather. "But as Shakespeare once said, 'What's in a name? That which we call a rose by any other name …'"

"… would smell as sweet," I add.

"Romeo and Juliet," adds my Grandmother, a smug look on her face. "Act 2, scene 2."

"Clever clogs," says Grandfather and gives her a kiss on the cheek. My Grandmother blushes.

"There are millions of people out there with secrets like ours, like yours, Joshua," says the suited man. "You and Annie's family line has the onyx cross to travel back in time and meet your respective families; other families have other means of doing the same thing. And yet others dream about the past, about meeting their ancestors. It is all meant to show you that you are and will always be loved by your family past and present."

"But is there a heaven and angels and demons and Satan and God and all that religious stuff?" Beryl asks.

"We see what we want to see. We believe what we think makes us feel secure, for ourselves, for our families. We build churches and create statues to kneel and pray to. We feel secure, especially with all the mayhem and war and terrible things that people do to each other and we create a refuge to escape to, a religion to believe in with a God and its opposite, Satan. The greatest work of fiction ever created was the Holy Bible."

Beryl's mouth drops open. All the other folks in the room look at each other and slowly nod in agreement.

"What's the truth about Angels?" I ask.

"Angel derives from the Greek word *angelos* which is a translation of a Hebrew word meaning 'messenger.' In essence we are all angels, at least those who care and assist others less fortunate than ourselves, and those who are lost either in mind or soul."

"Does God exist?" I ask, already knowing the answer.

The man in the suit raised his left eyebrow. "God is a state of mind. God is a savior to those who remain confined to the box they create for themselves from an early age, from the teachings of their parents and their parents before them, from school, from the Church. All is energy. The universe, the vastness of endless space, all the other universes, you, me and everything you know, see, feel and experience is pure energy. And that energy no one will ever truly understand. It was, it is, it will always be. This energy has always existed and always will exist."

"So there is no beginning or end?" says Beryl.

"Everything everywhere has always existed and will always exist. This is very difficult for people to understand because they tend to think in beginnings and endings. This energy, call it love or whatever, works in our lives every second we breathe. Take cause and effect, for example. You do good, good comes back to you. You do bad, bad comes back to you. And, as Christ said in the Bible (some of his sayings were amazing) 'Give and it will be given to you: good measure, pressed down, shaken together, and running over will be put into your bosom.'"

"Was Christ the son of God? I ask.

"Christ was and still is a great sage. On earth he was an ordinary man but with an advanced wisdom. Back then, remember, not so many people could read nor write and, in the spirit of those times, craved for security and a God to follow. The early Christians, determined to expand their new religion used Christ as their martyr and created the story of him being the Son of God. In reality, we are *all* Sons of God, Sons of the all powerful universal energy. Christ said that the 'truth shall set you free.'

He wasn't talking about Christianity or religion of any kind, he was relating to the immense power of universal energy. This energy which is everything, permeates everything from an atom to a grain of sand to animals, humans, air, sky, space, *everything* you see, feel and breathe, is what he called Father, or God.

"What confuses me sometimes," I say, "is people keep talking about Satan as if He is a real entity. Is there such an Angel?"

"You often hear murderers and rapists and other criminals (including mentally disturbed people) blame Satan for their particular acts. Sometimes they actually believe this to be true depending on their religious convictions, and sometimes it is used to try to receive a lesser sentence.

"But, believe me, no such entity exists nor ever did exist. It is all fantasy, like religion is fantasy. Evil is in the mind. People are evil or they are good. It's as simple as that. The true and only way to live and enjoy your life is through doing, giving, caring and loving. That in itself is the great reward, not some fictional place you create in your mind."

"But where is this place?" Beryl asks.

"We exist," says the man in the suit, "wherever we wish to exist because even *we* don't know where here actually is. But we learn how to use the universal energy to visit your dimension, from this, shall we say, our dimension."

My grandfather nods in agreement and grandmother smiles. My other ancestors mumble among themselves, nodding and smiling and then they all hug each other.

Everyone is suddenly silent and they make an opening in the middle of the group for two people to walk through. My mouth drops open. Standing in the center, just in front of me is my father and mother. My father winks at me and mother smiles. They are holding hands.

A tear streams down my cheek and Beryl squeezes my hand.

And then slowly the man in the suit begins to fade and is surrounded by a thick mist and out of that mist appears a small, blond-haired woman and she is smiling.

"Annie," I say and almost faint."

"Joshua. My one and only true love," says Annie and comes to me. Holding my face in her tiny, warm hands she smiles, a brilliant white smile of glee and contentment.

"It's amazing, Joshua. The feeling of pure love."

"But how …"

"Sshhhhhh, Joshua. 'Sometimes less is more.' I am always with you and the children. We shall be together again. You, Beryl, our children, everyone we know. Everything is family and family is love."

And then we suddenly find ourselves back in St Patrick's church.

"And, being a bit wet behind the ears," continues Father Boyle, "makes me humble and willing to learn as much as I can about my congregation. This family of the universal God."

I bend down and pick up my children, one in each arm; Beryl hugs me around the waist. I hug my children close to me and whisper into their ears, "And the truth shall set us free …"

*

… And the truth set me free from the box …

The End

Made in the USA
Middletown, DE
08 March 2022